Inspired Urges

D1825823

A scintillating saga of rags to riches set on both sides of the Atlantic. Filled with deep sexual prowess and a dangerous ambition.

About the Author.

Wendy Anne Lake, was born and raised in Lancashire and now lives in a pretty little country village in Kent.

Apart from loving to write, Wendy is also an avid reader. She loves quiz games, crosswords, ballroom dancing and watching sport, especially cricket.

Having worked with the C.I.D., her secretarial studies led her into research and development. She has worked mainly with men and has obviously been the butt of many a leg pull, but normally gives as good as she gets.

Her family and close friends are important to her, but all recognise her need to write and hopefully express her inner most thoughts.

Also by Wendy Anne Lake

Cinder Path
Labyrinth Of Desire
Sensual Rhythm Of Perfect Melody
You've Been Wonderful To Your Father

All five are also published by AuthorsOnLine in both paperback and electronic format, details of which may be obtained at:
www.authorsonline.co.uk

An AuthorsOnLine Book

Published by Authors OnLine Ltd 2001

Copyright © Authors OnLine Ltd

Text Copyright © Wendy Anne Lake

The front cover design of this book is produced by AuthorsOnLine ©

ISBN 0 7552 0019 5

Authors OnLine Ltd
15-17 Maidenhead Street
Hertford SG14 1DW
England

Visit us online at www.authorsonline.co.uk

authors
OnLine

Inspired Urges

By

Wendy Anne Lake

CHAPTER ONE

Debbie tried desperately to unwind her grief stricken body. Great cramps of cruel pain kept her doubled. The spine chilling screams continued to mingle with the sounds of the angry sea, which now lashed the rocks below, leaving a white lather of foam filled bubbles. "Oh, dear God, tell me I'm dreaming," ripped from her in choking sobs. "No, no, I won't, I can't believe this!"

Gradually, her shaking hands parted the curtain of her dark hair, revealing her misery laden eyes. Today she was totally alone, her mind addled with confusion, shock, fright and utter dismay.

It had been four years since she had been here, yet something had compelled her to come today. Sighing heavily, she allowed her tear filled eyes to take in the panoramic view. She was shocked beyond belief, to find herself sitting high on the Lakeland Hill, overlooking Morecambe Bay.

This had once been her favourite spot. She and Paul had discovered the perfect privacy on one of their many walks together. Sitting on the rich green headland, her eyes drifted to the fishing boats that still bobbed about, the way she remembered. The ever friendly light almost blinded her as it flashed comfortingly from the lighthouse on the pretty Isle of Walney.

She shivered, it was always fresh up here, but now, in the early spring, it felt bitterly cold as did her heart. Another tirade of sheer misery washed over her. Paul had declared his love for her here, teaching her heart to sing. She recalled how painfully ignorant of life she had been then, but she could never have begun to guess that her very naivety was a magnet in itself.

Somewhat reluctantly, she allowed her mind to roll back over the last several years. Her body shuddered as the memories came tumbling back, engulfing her in goose bumps.

Rubbing her forearms in an act of soothing, she felt herself drawn to the end of her schooldays. Although poverty had been a close companion, she had been so happy then. Her life was steeped with love and her parents adored her as she loved them dearly.

**

Debbie remembered with great fondness, the way her friends had admired her father, Jim Hudson. He had just reached forty and was perhaps the kindest man she would ever know. His six foot body was slim and youthful, but his dark brown hair was already lightly peppered with grey, giving him a real look of distinguished sophistication. His dark, penetrating eyes had a rich tenderness in them, expressing a deep sincerity. He literally lived for his little family and his work.

There was no doubting the brilliant brain that ticked away constantly. Jim had qualified as an accountant and during his studies, had also enrolled in the classes for master bakers. Much to his surprise, he had qualified in that particular field with honours.

1

Standing at the crossroads of his life, he had apparently been very undecided as to which route to travel. That was before he had met and fallen madly in love with Debbie's mother. Ellen had just completed her course in advanced confectionary, able to ice beautiful cakes for all occasions. She was trying to find an opening to put her skills into operation and it was a natural conclusion for her and Jim to work side by side.

Not only would they become partners for life, but would lease a small bakery and combine their skills. Ellen was just over five feet tall, with a dainty, yet curvaceous figure. Her fair auburn hair was reminiscent of burnished copper. She had tiny freckles across her button nose, over which were huge, brown velvet and direct eyes. They showed her every emotion and had been inherited by Debbie. Everything about Ellen was neat and trim. Her small, deft fingers could handle the most intricate of designs.

They had taken a small shop and flat in Preston. Together they had baked scrumptious fresh bread and mouth watering cakes. There was always a long queue outside and after the initial struggle, the little shop had begun to show a profit.

Apparently, Jim and Ellen had been delighted when their daughter was born. All too quickly though, she had grown up and begun her schooling. By the time Debbie was fifteen, they had managed to take on two assistants to serve in the shop.

Money had always been tight, but Debbie never remembered anything other than deep love from and between them. They had worked hard to give her a good education and she had worked equally hard as she wanted to make her way through college and study in the field of fashion and design. It therefore, was a huge boost to her own finances when she was able to help in the shop on Saturdays

They had all been filled with horror as they learned that one of the major bakeries was to take them over. The move had left them homeless and jobless, with just a mere smattering of compensation. Immediately, Debbie realised that at sixteen, she may well have to place her own future on 'hold'.

The pain hung from Jim's haunted eyes as he tried to explain, "Debs, Mum and I would like to invest the little capital we have. In fact, dear, we have heard of a small tea and bakery shop on Old Heysham. It will be a tremendous upheaval for us all, unfortunately the affect on <u>you</u>, does worry us. I mean, how would you feel about such a move?"

A sick knot had replaced her stomach, she didn't want to move. Yet they had no home and she knew that her help would be not only needed, but a true necessity. Her voice trembled, "Dad, obviously I never gave a thought to moving, but then, neither did you or Mum. I feel certain that I can settle elsewhere!"

Seeing the look of sheer relief pass between her parents, she could feel the dreadful pressure they faced. Ellen's eyes filled, "Debbie, perhaps you could enrol in night school and complete your course. By then, who knows? Dad and I may well find ourselves able to manage without you!"

"We'll be fine, Mum," she smiled.

Debbie knew her parents loved Morecambe and she had instantly fallen in love with it herself. To her delight, she had been able to enrol into the local night school and with swift ease, she settled into the new way of life.

**

Old Heysham was a very picturesque little town, with quaint little cobbled streets. Gift shops were scattered about like confetti, encouraging many holiday makers to wander around. That in itself was good for trade. Many trippers were only too happy to call into the shop for welcome cups of tea or coffee. Most of them also loved to sink their teeth into freshly baked pastries.

Debbie found the work to be challenging as well as rewarding, in fact she loved to wonder where the trippers had come from, where they would return to and work. The customers quite obviously fell in love with her spontaneous personality, her care and attention to serve them, her eager ear to listen. The smile that lit her face as she whipped from table to table with unobtrusive ease, made her special and this often showed in the generous tips that were handed to her.

At the end of the day, she felt tired, happy and knew that the takings, plus tips were keeping the shop from its knees. They had clawed their way back and happiness once again filled their hearts.

It seemed that everyone worked hard during the summer season, as trade slackened during the winter months. Nevertheless, the bread orders were building and orders for special cakes were literally pouring in. Their latest coup, had been a daily contract from a couple of large hotels.

The welcome rush of trade had helped them all to settle quickly. They now lived in the more than spacious flat over the shop, only too grateful they didn't have to travel.

Equally well, they knew it would take a couple of good seasons before any profits could actually be seen to be made. This was the spade work, the initial preparation for the future and the hours were long and tiring. The great reward would be upon them soon enough, when once again, they could employ extra help, for the time being however, life was full and happy.

It was obvious that Jim and Ellen were deeply in love with each other, but the long hours were taking their toll. At times they both looked worn out as was Debbie and her heart went out to them. Her Pop had developed a slight stoop from constantly bending into the huge ovens. He made light of it, yet Ellen worried for him.

Within a couple of months, their world had toppled once again.

Debbie sensed something was drastically wrong when she returned from evening class. Her parents were distraught and Ellen beckoned her to a chair.

Terrified, Debbie sat down as Ellen turned to her, "Debs, I've just learned that I'm pregnant again!"

"I thought you couldn't have more children," gasped Debbie.

"We were told we never would, but whilst this is a dreadful shock, I am pregnant and Dad or myself will not hear of an abortion!"

3

There was a distinct defiance in the statement. Jim turned to her, "I know we can't afford this at the moment, but Mum's health will have to be watched carefully!"

Looking into their troubled faces, Debbie knew then, that her plans for the immediate future would have to stay on 'hold'. Without compunction, she responded, "You can rely on me. I'll be here to help, you both know that!"

Suddenly the defiance crumbled, Ellen broke down completely and sobbed, "Debbie, what about your studies? Oh, Jim, if only we had known!"

"Well, we didn't know, Ellie," said Jim as his arms enclosed his wife. Smoothing her hair, he looked at his daughter, "Thank's Debs, who knows, if we go on as we are, we may well be able to afford some help?"

Bitter stabs of disappointment rushed through Debbie. If her father was right, she could rejoin her classes, but a dreadful sense of deep foreboding had settled and although she had brought relief to her parents, she was filled with frustration.

The ensuing six months had found Ellen to be dreadfully ill. Jim and Debbie had coped with everything between them. At times they wondered how they could maintain the pace, but at least it was a temporary measure, Debbie would assure herself and found she got on so well with the customers as they frequently poured out their own problems. She also became more than eager to learn how they had solved them, if indeed they had done so.

Many friends of her own age came into chat with her. And although she was often asked to local parties, she was too jolly tired. Her apologies therefore, held that extra note of sincerity, of course she would have loved to go, but when the parties began to 'hot up', it was time for her to get up.

Almost with a jolt, she realised she had never been out on a date and began to wonder if she ever would. Jim would stack the ovens in the morning and Debbie would wait for the first load to come out. She would then take it through to the shop, or indeed prepare the hotel orders.

Even in the mornings, Jim was always cheerful and they would often sing along with the various songs on the radio, their eyes meeting and worry seemed to turn to hope.

Once the first batch was out and the second under way, Debbie would make a brew for her and Jim, he would then take a cup up to Ellen. Taking his cup one morning, he placed it onto the side and pulled her into his arms. "I wish you didn't have to work so damned hard, Debbie. At times I feel riddled with guilt, yet a man couldn't wish for more in a daughter. Hell, though, you should be able to enjoy a party or two!"

She noticed his voice was thick with emotion and felt the need to reassure, "Don't worry about me, Dad. I'm young enough to catch up," she chuckled and returned his hug.

At times it felt strangely odd to be nearly seventeen and realise that she would soon have a brother or sister. In the evenings, she would sit for the odd hour with Ellen. Together they would knit tiny garments for the new babe. At

4

least it seemed to relax Ellen, but with Debbie, something seriously strange was happening.　.

She would pick up the yarns and fondle the textures, truly fondle them and her brain would spring into action as ideas flowed at a speed that she could scarcely manage to control. Her fingers were ready, ready to pick up the ideas and before all of their eyes, the most beautiful garments would fly from the needles. It was as though she was charged into action with a magic that must have always been buried there. The textures, the ideas, the sizes, the colours, it was like dropping them into a mixing pot and pulling out perfection.

Jim and Ellen were spellbound by the skills of their beloved daughter. They also knew she was wasting her precious talent, and if it hadn't been for the kindly shopkeeper in the wool shop, who didn't mind laying yarns aside, Debbie would never have afforded the small amounts she collected.

Ellen turned her clumsy body to Jim, her voice worried, "Jim, if Debbie can do so much with so little, just imagine what she could do with a completely free hand. We are wrecking her future and she has so much talent. Once baby arrives and I'm better, she must return to college!"

"She will, Ellie, but believe me, this is how she want it to be. I don't think she has a selfish bone in her body. At times I wish she did, somehow I wouldn't feel so bloody guilty. She is growing into a lovely young lady," he added with pride.

Debbie found her love of Morecambe had become a full blown affair. Every second she could spare was spent drinking in the beauty of the bay. She could allow her mind to think of what might have been, whilst at the same time, feel the breeze whip through her hair, giving her a taste of sheer unadulterated freedom. She adored the tranquil sea as it lapped softly onto the pure, pale sands. Conversely, she loved the roar of the angry sea as it raced in and lashed the sea wall. Leaning on the strong rail above, her dreams would run riot, but that she reminded herself, was a luxury and savoured the moments as such.

One morning as Debbie prepared to follow Jim down into the kitchens, her bedside clock seemed to smile mockingly as it informed her it was four thirty. This particular morning, she had been more than surprised to hear Ellen calling, "Debbie, come here, luv!"

Smiling with fondness, she left her room, calling a cheery, "O.K Mum!" She had inherited a good old Lancashire accent and at times, especially under pressure or excitement, she heard her parents lapse into the warmth of the northern charm.

Arriving by the side of Ellen's bed, it was obvious she was in great pain. Her face creased as she gasped, "The babe's on its way, would you come with me, Debbie? Dad can't afford to leave the shop till the bread's baked!"

"Alright, Mum, I'll ring the ambulance, tell Dad and be back!"

She tried to cover her impending fear with a light hearted chuckle and after ringing for the ambulance, went and found her father. His face was ravaged with worry as Ellen had made her way downstairs, "Let Debs take me, Jim. I will see you later and don't worry, darling!"

Debbie smiled to herself as she realised Ellen might just as well told him not to breathe. As they arrived into the labour ward, Ellen gripped her hand, "I'm so relieved you came, Debs. I would have worried myself silly if Dad had closed for the day," she broke off as another pain racked her body.

Apparently, it was just becoming popular to involve the father in the birth. The sister turned to Debbie and almost smiled, "You can help your Mum, can't you?"

Terror enveloped her, she had expected to be on her way back to the shop. She knew little of this, but found herself agreeing anyway.

Turning back to her mother, she noticed the beads of perspiration forming on her forehead. Taking the proffered sponge from the nurse, she began to bathe Ellen's pain etched face. She looked dreadfully ill, her face turning puce as she pushed with every ounce of strength she possessed.

A very serious sister buzzed for the doctor. He arrived to examine Ellen and then spoke quietly to the sister as they both looked serious. There was no seeming respite from the pain and Debbie had never seen anyone suffer like this.

Somehow, she felt this would have made her father feel worse. Perhaps it was better that she should have accompanied her mother after all. To her astonishment, she realised that she had grown up fully during the last few hours.

Again she felt nails digging into her hand. With a huge struggle, her little brother was finally born. Debbie looked swiftly at the doctor's face, he was shaking his head, the sister rushed to bring in the paediatrician.

Shaking from head to toe, Debbie cradled Ellen's head and whispered, "Mum, you're alright now. You have a little boy!"

Ellen was not placated, tears ran down her face and her whole being seemed desperately uneasy. "I want to hold him," she cried, but was given an injection instead.

Waves of sickness rushed over Debbie as she turned to the paediatrician and asked, "Is my mother alright? Is the baby alright? Please tell me what is happening?"

His eyes were soft and gentle, his voice kind, yet firm. Inhaling deeply, he explained, "Your mother will be alright, she will sleep for a while. Can you ask your father to come in to see me?"

Debbie knew then, there was something drastically wrong with the little one. Her voice was barely audible, fear had taken over completely, but looking at her mother, she saw her lovely face was now at peace, courtesy of the injection. "I will ask my father to come directly!"

Once outside the hospital, she took a deep breath and began to run. Resisting the urge to run and talk to the sea, to scream out her outrage and fear, she knew she must get home. Arriving breathlessly, she found there was a queue already forming outside the shop.

Biting her lip until it hurt, she unlocked the door and held it open, "Please, everyone take a seat, give me a couple of secs and I will be with you," she gasped.

"Ows yer ma, chuck?"

The concerned enquiries almost choked her as she called over her shoulder, "Give me half a mo., and I'll be back!"

To her relief, she noticed the urn was already on, rolls and bread were placed neatly behind the counter, ready to serve as she scampered into the kitchen and practically collided with Jim. For one dreadful moment, she thought she would break down as her arms went around him. He held her as a child, "I know, dear. The hospital have told me they wish to see me. I will be as quick as poss., but if you feel under too much pressure, close up. The orders are completed!"

Her eyes misted as he physically squared his shoulders and left to face whatever he must. She followed his example, it was down to her and she wouldn't let her family down, her shoulders thrown back, her smile back on her face, she set about her work.

The rest of the day passed in a flurry of activity. And although she basically worked on 'automatic' her sunny disposition was clouded with severe worry for her parents. Her nerves seemed to jar during the odd quiet moment. Part of her prayed for her father's return, whilst at the same time, she dreaded it. When he finally dragged himself wearily up to the flat, she could see his naked pain.

Suddenly, he looked old, his face was ashen, his eyes haunted as he sat down. "Debs, although Mum is very ill, she will be alright, but little Tony is chronically handicapped!"

He seemed to notice the fear spring to her eyes, his shoulders slumped in bitter dejection, "Hell, you have had to place your career on hold and Mum and I are desperately worried about the future. I feel I have let you all down badly, perhaps I did choose the wrong blasted profession, I'm so bloody sorry!"

"Don't ever say that again, Dad. I wanted to be here with you and Mum and we must just do our best!"

Momentarily, his eyes lit up. "You're right, dear. We must do our best for Mum and Tony. I never stopped thanking God for you, we love you dearly," he muttered affectionately.

CHAPTER TWO

It had taken almost a year for Ellen to recover. Everything that could go wrong had done so. Debbie had to help with her care, feed Tony and help in the shop. It was exhausting and she thanked God for her gift of health, sadly realising she had probably inherited Tony's share.

Poor little chap, he had been in and out of hospital and the fares to and fro, just drained their meagre resources. Yet Tony was a happy little boy and so very easy to love. Debbie vowed, he would want for nothing, not as long as she had breath in her body.

He was always ready to impart beaming smiles and Debbie would chat to him for ages. Tending to him was a joy to her, she would hold the supple little body close, her lips would travel over his gorgeous face, "One day, Tony, if I ever do get married, I want to have lots and lots of babies!"

She would confide her secrets to him and he would gurgle as though he understood. They had all had to accept the fact that he would never walk. Yet by the time his second birthday arrived, he had graduated to a wheel chair. Debbie often pushed him along the beautiful bay. He was so like her, he loved the sound of the sea lashing against the sea wall.

Debbie adored the way he squealed with delight as he watched the seagulls. The whole vista was picturesque, almost postcard like as the blue sky met the sea far away over the horizon. Rich salty aromas wafted by and carried headily in the swirling breeze, whipping colour into both of their cheeks.

Tony had an insatiable appetite for knowledge and could now hold quite healthy conversations. It took so little to please him, his only real need was their love, which was the one thing they could all afford.

Day after day, he contented himself sitting behind the counter, watching Debbie serve and hoping she would have time to take him out. He loved to chat to the customers and had managed to captivate them with his fiercely frank, direct replies. He too had picked up a broad Lancashire accent, which seemed to make him even more endearing. He was sitting there when Paul Howarth walked in.

**

When Debbie lifted her eyes to him, her mouth dried and her stomach flipped over. Her hands shook uncontrollably and as the words formed on her lips, they stubbornly remained there.

Paul was man personified. Tall and slim, his blond curly hair was cut to perfection. His eyes, with the longest lashes turning upwards, were the colour of the Caribbean Sea and set into a rugged complexion. The firmest of jaws encompassed a mouth that just screamed to be kissed and revealed gorgeous white teeth, when he smiled. His smile began in those delicious eyes and spread over the whole of his face.

Debbie felt a flush rise from deep in her belly as his gaze lingered on her. Fortunately, the shop was reasonably quiet, allowing her time to struggle with the confusion in her mind. Suddenly, the cause of her falling apart, was up and on his feet as he almost seemed to saunter to the counter to pay his bill. He leaned over to Tony, "Hi there, young man. My name is Paul Howarth, what do they call you?"

"Tony Hudson," came the grown up reply.

Smiling fondly at Tony, she hadn't realised that the blue eyes had returned to her. Paul's voice was cultured and low as he asked, "Do you live near here? I have just moved into a flat in Morecambe and don't know many people yet!"

Trembling like a fool, she heard her voice raise about a couple of octaves, "I .. I live here, with my parents .. and Tony is … my little brother," she stammered.

"His name is Paul, Debbie," chuckled Tony, having taken a real shine to the man before her.

"That takes care of the introductions then," smiled Paul. "How would you like to join me for a meal this evening, Debbie Hudson? Perhaps you could show me some of the breath taking sights that Morecambe is famed for. I must admit, I love to walk, especially away from the crowds."

Whatever was the matter with her stupid heart? It was now fluttering into her throat, restricting her airways. Painfully, she gulped, "Well, I would certainly like to go walking, but I must help Mum with the meal!"

Paul Howarth watched her flush, she had a beautiful air of simplicity about her that he found refreshing. Although her uniform was somewhat unflattering, he felt there was a real woman stacked inside. She was like a flower waiting to bloom and although he had only just met her, he began to think that he would like to be around when that did happen.

Her eyes were frank and direct, her mouth trembled sensually as she tried to hide her obvious discomfort. He knew he wanted to get to know her better and smiled warmly, "Fair enough, I will pick you up around eight, is that convenient?"

For some reason he held his breath, her reply was almost one of imperative urgency that shocked him. He saw the words choke from her, "Yes, that would be fine!"

He went swiftly over to Tony, "See you soon young man," he promised and was gone.

Tingles ran the length of her spine as she realised she had never had a real date before and knew little of man, but yes, this was a definite date. Floating upstairs in a trance, her mother's words made her jump, "Debbie, you look flushed, dear, are you feeling alright?"

"Oh, Mum, I've just met a man. He's out of this world." She positively drooled and did a little twirl. "He is calling for me at eight. Apparently he wants me to show him some of the pretty walks around here!"

Trying hard to control her shaking body, she could still see Paul. He had been smartly dressed, in a lightweight grey suit, with trousers holding the sharpest of creases. His silk tie had been neatly clipped with a beautiful pin, matching his cuff links and everything about him screamed 'elegance'.

Ellen watched her daughter's flushed face with a mixture of joy, mingled heavily with guilt. Debbie had given them so much and had never moaned once. She was eighteen and should be out dating. Yet, sadly, Jim and herself had barely noticed the woman that had sprung from the child. "Debbie, its about time you went out and enjoyed yourself, after all you're eighteen now!" She sighed heavily and added, "What does this young man do for a living? What will you wear?"

The question certainly brought Debbie back down to earth with a bump. She could either wear her blue or yellow sundress, both of which she had made herself, together with matching boleros. She smiled wryly as she looked at the sorry state of her wardrobe and turned to hug Ellen, "I think I'll wear my sundress. I don't know what Paul does, he has only just moved to Morecambe!"

Her mother's eyes misted over as she stood beside her. "This isn't fair, Debs. We really must get you some more clothes, hell, you work hard enough. Everything will soon improve now that I'm back on my feet though!"

"Soon we will, Mum. My dress is fine for now and I've scarcely worn my court shoes!"

Debbie was far too excited to eat. After she had helped with the meal, she chose to have a nice, lazy bath. Having washed her long, dark hair, she brushed it till it shone like rich, polished mahogany. Fortunately it had a natural curl and hung seductively around her shoulders.

Her skin was a rich olive and she only needed the merest hint of make up. Her stomach churned, her hands shook as she virtually had to scrape the lipstick from the near empty tube, onto her lips. Yet she couldn't begin to conceal the sparkle in her dancing eyes.

A strange shyness had suddenly washed over her as she wondered if Paul would kiss her goodnight, or even want to. Silently she prayed he would as once more she felt that strange feeling deep in her groins, a feeling she could not ignore. With somewhat of a shock, she realised, at least from what she had discussed with friends, that her body was crying out for sexual pleasure. She understood it now and fear that Paul would be able to read her mind, made her shake from head to toe.

Stunned to her primal roots, she selected the lemon dress. It was strapless and clung to her rather generous, firm bust. She did have a good figure and mentally thanked God, she needed no bra, which was another huge saving. Slowly, she buttoned the dress from bust to hem. The pretty skirt swished as she moved to pop her feet into the leg flattering, court shoes.

Standing back from the mirror, she suspected she looked as good as she felt. Nature had been kind to her, her waist was tiny and her hips curvaceous. She felt intoxicated with eager anticipation. After popping on her bolero, she kissed Tony and hugged her parents. She was all ready to leave when the doorbell chimed.

Debbie found herself running to the door and stopped dead in her tracks. She paused to inhale deeply, she must at least try to appear a little dignified as a deep excitement had taken her over. Opening the door, she couldn't contain the gasp that left her lips.

Paul was before her, looking even more handsome than he had earlier. He had changed into a blue shirt, emphasising the gorgeous blue of his eyes. His jacket was slung casually over his shoulder, held by placing his finger through the loop in a most nonchalant manner.

His smile was one of obvious approval, unbalancing her further. "Hi, Debbie, you look good enough to eat. I doubt if I would have recognised you from this afternoon. Shall we go?"

There was a total, almost enviable ease about him. He spoke softly, "Shall we walk along the promenade and then go for a drink? Is there something special that you would like, Debbie? How about we wander where he will takes us?"

Although she was hardly a woman of great wit, or indeed brilliant conversation, she did manage to chat comfortably with others, but right now, her mouth had dried as her body continued to shake. After a few deep breaths, she managed to stammer, "Yes .. that .. would be … fine!"

Having reached the sea front, they found themselves leaning over the rail and watching the sea. The evening was perfect as the moon began to rise slowly in the pewter coloured sky. Inhaling the rich ozone air, Paul said, "Isn't it absolutely wonderful here, so relaxing and yet so vibrant!"

"Mmm, it is. I often bring Tony down here, he loves to watch the seagulls and listen to the sea. It takes so little to please him," she said wistfully.

Paul turned to took at her, loving the way the breeze lifted her hair. Feeling she was being watched, her eyes lifted to him. His smile was filled with warmth, "You really do love that little fellow, don't you, Debbie? He is so friendly, what *did* happen to him?"

His eyes were filled with sincerity and she felt herself flush under his gaze. Her stupid heart pounded painfully against her ribs. The roar of the sea was almost deafening as she replied, "Sadly, he was born like that. He has been in and out of hospital, but he is so cheerful, he puts us to shame!"

To her everlasting relief, she found herself begin to relax. Paul was easy to talk to and obviously took an interest in general conversation. His eyes still held hers, "Will you always have to work with your parents? I can see you are needed, but do you want to follow them into the trade?"

"Not really. I wanted to work in some kind of design. They have always worked hard to give me a good education, I s'pose it was only natural to stand by them," she sighed.

Taking her hand into his, he suggested, "Let's go over to the pub, we can have a drink and sit in the fresh air. I want to know all about you, Debbie Hudson. In spite of your uniform, I couldn't take my eyes off of you this afternoon. And to think of that funny little hat, hiding all that beautiful hair!"

They both laughed contentedly as they found a nice secluded table. The sky had changed again as twilight fell. Paul ordered the drinks with complete ease, drawing her like a magnet into his world. With equal ease, she asked, "What about you, Paul? What do you do for a living? Was it your job that brought you to Morecambe?"

Debbie had never had a drink before, but had sought refuge in the odd cigarette. Paul lit two, his long lashes resting onto his cheeks as he looked down. Her body shook when they lifted to reveal the wonderful blue of his bright eyes.

Handing one over to her, he cleared his throat and added, "I work in advertising, my boss owns the 'Ventura' fashion magazine in Preston!"

Ironically, she knew where the building was. She found it to be painted in loud colours, giving a look of ostentation. Golly, she thought, he must be very clever. She watched him as he puffed on his cigarette, somehow managing to make that look distinctly sexy.

Tapping the ash into the glass ashtray, he continued, "I have been sent here to open a new branch, down there," he gestured to another huge building and carried on, "I have been preparing the offices and staff for the grand opening next month. I don't want it to look anything like the Preston branch, it certainly is hard work, but the money is good!"

Gasping at the enormity of his work, she realised that he could only have been in his mid twenties and already he was in charge of the expansion from Preston. He looked clever and well informed and Debbie asked, "What's your boss like?"

Imparting a mischievous smile, he replied, "Well, Eric is a decent enough chap, that's if he happens to like you. Yet he always demands everything to be done yesterday. His first love is money, followed closely by his daughter. She is a mean and spoiled brat, but he idolises her."

He paused and took a drag of his cigarette, "Honestly, Debbie, she holds quite a senior position badly and treats everyone with a kind of contempt. I'm lucky, I manage to steer clear of her!"

There was no disguising his dislike, but Debbie said nothing. The sky was now a rich navy blue. The full moon bathed everywhere with beauty as the stars twinkled around it. She knew she could have stayed there all night as the strains of music drifted from the many arcades and added to the magic of the evening.

With great reluctance, she cast a long and direct look towards him and stated, "I really ought to get home. I must be up early, but I have truly enjoyed myself, thank you, Paul!"

Walking slowly, he had taken her hand into his, making her heart thump with wildness. By now she was just praying that her jelly like knees didn't collapse beneath her. For the first time in her life, she did not want to go home, did not want this evening to end.

Arriving at her door, Paul whispered, "I would like to see you again, Debbie Hudson. Your company has been deliciously refreshing. In my job, I meet so many people with airs and graces, sometimes very artificial. You are down to earth and simplistic, can we do this again tomorrow?"

Suffocation swamped her, his eyes locked hers. He was even more devastating in the moonlight, she thought as her voice trembled, "Yes, I would like that very much. See you tomorrow then!"

Turning to unlock the door, she felt him pull her gently back into his arms. Those sensual lips brushed hers, sending fire through her. Holding her tenderly, he gulped, "You're lovely, your mouth is so inviting and innocent. Those beautiful huge eyes speak for you. Hell, I s'pose I shouldn't have done that!"

Total joy was hers as he managed to do it again. Headily she felt his lips brushing hers apart as his kiss deepened. His body shook slightly as he folded his arms around her. Crazily, she felt herself responding and sensed that he was enjoying their embrace. With a tender brush of her cheek, he released her, "Till tomorrow then!"

**

Paul stood motionless outside her door. He had never enjoyed an evening as much as he had tonight. Time seemed to have sprouted wings and flown by. She was a charming companion and his eyes had been constantly drawn to her lovely breasts as they rose and fell to the unpredictable pattern of her breathing. He had longed to take her into his arms all evening, but knew not to try and rush her.

Her sweet kisses were filled with innocence and he had felt her hardened nipples dig into the hard wall of his chest. He would never know how he had kept his hands from her, yet he did not want to frighten her. There was no doubt about it, he wanted her in the fullest sense of the word. His manhood had given him a few sharp reminders throughout the evening. She was inexperienced and he vowed he would never hurt her.

**

Debbie's mind reeled as she went inside. She could feel his kisses burning her lips. Not having been kissed properly before, she could never have dreamed it would be like this. She hoped that she hadn't behaved as she felt, totally ignorant of love and man. Could Paul have realised that she was a complete novice in this particular field?

Her hands were still shaking as she lit a cigarette and relived those heady moments. Constantly, she pinched herself to make sure she wasn't dreaming, yet knowing if she was, she wanted to stay locked in that dream.

**

For the next couple of months Debbie and Paul went out every evening. They found themselves walking from one end of the bay to the other. This lovely old seaside town enchanted them. They even discovered places that Debbie had not known existed, never tiring of the beauty, no matter what the weather was like.

Debbie was certain that she was falling in love with Paul. He had never tried to take advantage of her obvious innocence. At times he would stop walking and take her into his arm. His breathing would become laboured, as did hers.

She loved the feel of his strong arms around her. He made her feel incredibly safe. One night he gripped her tightly to him, his hands ran gently over her back. A groan escaped him, "Debbie, you're so lovely, its bloody hard to keep my hands to myself. I haven't felt like this about anyone before!"

Instinctively, she had looped her arms around his neck as his body shook with hers. With a strangled gulp, his lips brushed hers apart and for the first time, she felt the smoothness of his tongue. As it invaded her, she felt the world had simply burst into flames.

Paul was not prepared for the inexorable pleasure as his tongue sunk into the silken sheath of her mouth. She was such a desirable woman, her slender body gelled in his arms, pressing into him, not dreaming of what she was doing to him. He had become painfully hard and was now in danger of losing all control. His lips flew to the pulse that beat fast in her beautiful neck.

He could hear her heart thumping with his own. He was blinded with love for her. Scarcely able to breathe, his hand covered her voluptuous breast and felt the taut nipple beneath the cotton material. Moaning his need, his hand entered her dress and at long last, closed over her bare flesh. With a gentleness he could never have believed, he began to fondle her, extracting soft little yelps of delight from her.

Filled with inexplicable desire, she did not know what to do next and confusion entered her. Lost in a wonderland of love, she pulled Paul's mouth back to hers. Rubbing his thumb nail over her bead like nipple, he recognised her innocence. His cock was on fire, burning and straining against his fly. With a tortured groan, he wrenched himself from her.

A thousand million pangs of bitter disappointment rained over Debbie. Paul leaned heavily onto the tree trunk and she watched as he bent his head to light two cigarettes. His composure seemed to have vanished. One arm stuck rigidly to the tree and with the other hand, he passed her a cigarette.

Tenderness filled the eyes that locked hers. "Hell, Debbie, I shouldn't have done that to you. I can't apologise, pet, 'cos I enjoyed holding you. Unless I'm sadly mistaken, I felt a need in you and I desperately want us to make love. Does that shock you?"

"No, Paul. Why did you stop?"

"*How* did I stop, would be nearer the point. Christ knows I want you. I feel sure you're not on the pill and I haven't any sort of contraception with me. We must behave responsibly, darling." His eyes smouldered as he had spoken.

"I thought men always carried something," she gulped.

"I s'pose they do, if they know they'll get it!"

"Do you usually get it ... I mean, do you, Paul?"

Her words faltered as they left her trembling lips. His arms crushed her to him, "Come on, I'm going to take you home, before I get carried away again!"

Choking with confusion and blinded with love for him, she invited him in to meet her parents. From the moment they all met, a bond seemed to form between them. When he finally left that evening, Ellen called, "In future, Paul, you must have dinner with us before you take Debbie out!"

After that night though, Paul still met Debbie with his usual eagerness, but she felt a difference in their relationship. Somehow he had managed to put his feelings to one side, obviously respecting her too much to take advantage. With a stunned shock, she realised that she missed his deep kisses and longed for him to make love with her.

She knew she must do something about the situation. Paul had gelled into the family as though he had always been with them. Tony was totally besotted with him, which made him all the more endearing.

CHAPTER THREE

The shop was enjoying a rare quiet moment. Jim carried a tray of fresh rolls in from the kitchen and smiled, "I can watch the shop for a spell, Debs. Is there anything you want to sort out dear?"

"Not really, Dad, you have a sit down and relax for a minute. You can help Tony with his puzzle when he comes down," she chuckled, knowing full well that Jim detested puzzles.

Keeping his eyes on his daughter, he took a fresh roll and spread a pat of butter onto it. Before taking a bite, he asked, "Are you serious about Paul? Mum and I are very fond of him and both feel you deserve someone like him!"

She sighed a little ruefully, "I'm certain that I love him, Dad, but he hasn't mentioned it to me. To be truthful, I sometimes wonder if I'm too immature for him. He tends to wrap me in cotton wool!"

Jim chuckled as he hugged her, "You go up and have a chat with Mum. She'll put you right, you'd better believe it!"

Debbie found Ellen up to her elbows in icing. The sideboard was already filled with beautifully iced cakes, all ready to be encased into boxes.

"I'm nearly finished, Debs. Is something bothering you, dear. Do you want to talk?" Ellen asked as she looked up from her work.

Ellen was pretty certain where the problem lay. Paul was a man of the world and thanks to her own illness, Debbie had no idea of the finer things in life. Reflected in her daughter's eyes, was the confusion of a young lady in love. The time had come to try and point Debbie into the right direction. She smiled reassuringly, "Would I be wrong in thinking you are worried about sex, Debs?"

Debbie rolled her eyes heavenwards and gulped, "What d'ya mean, Mum?"

"Oh, I think you *know* what I mean, Debbie. I don't wish to pry, but I still remember my first time. Love is a beautiful act to share, but both parties must want the same thing. I think Paul is more than ready and you are frightened. Am I right?"

Her voice was soft, warm and comforting and to her astonishment, Debbie felt tears prick the back of her eyes. "Mum, I do want the same as Paul. In fact I want him very much, but he seems to have gone off the idea. I think he is scared of taking advantage!"

Suddenly floods of relief filled her. It was so good to talk to someone who understood how she felt. Somehow, she had never thought of her parents as therapists, yet Ellen knew exactly how she felt. Her heart beat lighter as she watched with admiration, the way her mother worked on the cake, which sprung into a cricket pitch, complete with stumps, bat and ball, beneath the talented fingers.

16

Ellen completed the work with a swift flourish. She could see the relief begin to fill her daughter's lovely face and a sigh escaped her, "Debbie, it is good that we can talk to each other. God knows, I couldn't have coped with Tony's birth without you. How about you popping down to the family planning clinic? Go now and they will put you on the pill. I don't advise lightly, dear, but your happiness is more important to us than anything else!"

Barely an hour later, Debbie found herself having a thorough examination. After many searching questions, she came home with the increasingly popular pill. To her embarrassment, she felt her body flushing, almost as though she was on fire. How could she tell Paul that everything was safe? Hell, he would think she was some sort of sex maniac, perhaps she was, but she did want his love and suspected this was what was needed to fulfil their deep relationship.

The next few days followed in much the same vein, with a slight tension between them and Debbie found herself growing restless. Her heart pounded with longing for Paul, she missed feeling his arms tightly locked around her, missed his deep kisses and knew it was time for her to act.

Lost in companionable silence the following night, they had climbed the hill. Moments later, they had discovered this idyllic spot, high on the hill. They had almost missed it, there was a huge oak tree blocking the tiny path. Easing around the tree, they had followed the little turning that led them here.

Standing high on the headland, they felt majestic as their eyes roamed the vista before them. Even then, Debbie sensed that this place was going to play a major role in their lives. Her niggle now, would Paul tire of her? Did he intend to carry on seeing her? Was he bored with her comparative, or rather total ignorance?"

The full moon was like a ball of gold as it bathed them. The grass was soft beneath their feet and a small thicket of green shrubbery, formed an almost exclusive room around them. Yet there was no way in which she could ask Paul the very questions for which she sought desperately for answers. They were little clouds on her own horizon, she thought worriedly.

Almost as though he had read her thoughts, Paul asked, "Debbie, I know its way ahead, but I would like you to accompany me to our firm's Christmas party. It is a rather lavish dinner dance at the Guild Hall in Preston. Will you come with me, darling?"

She couldn't disguise the sigh that left her lips, at least he intended them to be together then. Her fear of losing him overwhelmed her. She couldn't envisage life without him and swiftly replied, "Oh, Paul, I would love to come with you, but won't it be a little posh?"

His arms engulfed her as they fell to the grass. His voice grew deep and deliciously throaty, "Debbie, to me, you are gorgeous and posh all at the same time!"

He turned her chin towards him, the moon exposed the intense blue of his eyes, making her whole body weaken. "Dearest, Debbie, I do believe that I have fallen in love with you!"

Feeling his arms tighten around her and then, at long last the depth of his kiss, she could never conceal her devotion to him. She knew she would give him her body with complete abandonment, indeed she wanted to. Suddenly he broke away and groaned huskily, "Hell, babe, we can't go on like this. Come, I'll take you home!"

"No, Paul, its still early," she gulped.

Without further thought, she knelt up and opened the buttons and allowed her dress to drop to her waist. In her heart, she knew this was what they both wanted and gloried in the complete shock of Paul's face.

Paul gasped at the sight of her breasts. He had often tried to imagine them, yet had missed by a mile. They were so utterly young and heavy, yet so firm that they rode high on her chest, tilting upwards with their rose nipples hardened and pointed.

Debbie felt an exquisite brazen yearning as she noticed her nipples so hard, they could almost lift from her skin. Right then, embarrassment was like a foreign word, her heart hammered without mercy as she watched Paul's eyes drinking in her nakedness. She instinctively knew he would treat her with great care as slowly and deliberately, his hands closed over those opulent breasts.

The joy in his intimate touch was like a throb of beauty. Her hands reached to his chest and he could feel them shake as she began to unfasten his shirt. Debbie placed her hand flat over his heart and delight at the frantic pumping sent her spiralling with glory. He brought one hand to help her to remove his shirt, allowing her to gaze on his thick rug like chest.

Gently, he breathed over her eyes and into her mouth. He brushed her lips apart and pressed his tongue into her. Paul was no stranger to the sensuality of women, but no woman had made him stop and think, stop and truly care.

This beautiful woman he loved, he was certain she was still a virgin. She was only too eager to give herself to him, yet could he trust himself to treat her with the tenderness and care of a first love? Could he control himself long enough to bring her to the brink of delicious fulfilment? Could he control his ever demanding cock that was already seriously engorged?

With a strangled gulp, he gripped the sides of her head and rested her head onto his chest. "Debbie, darling, are you absolutely sure about this?" He panted helplessly and feared she may just change her mind.

"Yes, Paul, I got the pill," she replied simplistically.

Her voice was silky soft as her eyes met his with frankness. Under the golden moon, her body was pale, her eyes glistened like a rich ebony and her sensual lips seemed to tremor prettily.

He slid down and pulled her over the top of him so that her breasts were above his face. She leaned onto her elbows as she gazed down at him, with a look of intense curiosity.

He groaned and again his hands closed over her breasts, pushing them together so that he could take both of her nipples into his mouth at the same time. With all the pulling and sucking force of his lips and tongue, he feasted on the hot buds as if he could make them open and flower inside his mouth.

For many moments, his whole being was concentrated on the nipples he held so firmly. He suckled her without mercy, teasing her with the tiniest little bites, causing her a pleasure so wonderful that she bit her own lips Frantically she tried to force even more of her breasts into his mouth.

She pressed down on him with her hips, without realising what she was doing, pushing so urgently, with such insistence, that finally he knew it was time to tear himself away from her sensual buds. He prayed for self control as never before.

Carefully, caressingly, Paul took her by the shoulders, turned her over onto her back and without hesitation, opened the rest of her buttons and slipped her panties from her.

Debbie lay spellbound, suddenly stilled with only her hair to cover her shoulders. As she watched Paul, a question again glowed in her eyes. He stood beside her and stripped himself, trying desperately hard not to rush.

She stared at him, her eyes widening at the sight of his tanned body as it shone in the moonlight. He was slim as she'd thought, but she hadn't imagined that his arms and legs would be so filled with muscles, or his chest so broad. Nor had she envisaged the powerful, heavy, masterful penis, longer and thicker than she could have believed, that now stood out and up from the fair hair between his legs. She gasped, stunned, incredulous, unable to look away, shocked into a glorious immobility.

Paul knelt down, his knees holding her thighs gently apart, while he kissed her open mouth over and over, making sounds that sent erotic sensations flowing through her. She threw her arms around his neck as she tried with all of her strength and with an element of awkwardness, to pull him down on top of her, desperate to be crushed under him, to feel his skin all over her own. She needed this act to happen, almost as though it had to happen before she could get on with the rest of her life.

Finally, he sat back on his heals, consumed with a need so savage that it frightened him. She was adorable, her adolescent shyness, her clumsiness, her distinct awkwardness, sent him dizzy with desire.

He paused to take a deep breath, Christ, he mustn't hurt her. If the first time wasn't so utterly special, it could ruin her for the rest of her life. Her hand reached up to touch his face, he grabbed it, kissed it and placed his throbbing penis into it, gulping as he felt her grip it tightly.

His hand moved over her body again, touching, caressing the soft swell of her abdomen, revelling as her body writhed sensually. With a masterful hand, he moved towards her dark triangle of pubic hair and pushed forward with a questing finger. She was like a ripe juicy peach and he knew she was ready for him.

Slowly, he held the weighty heft of his penis and steadily, relentlessly pushed it deeper and deeper into her inflamed body. He paused with every inch of progress, never had he found so much difficulty. Holding back from this eager, sensual lover of his, was almost an impossible, inhuman ask. At last he was in to the hilt and a sigh escaped his body. His arms gathered her to him and then he eased himself completely out of her and guided the underside of his penis carefully back and forth across the fiery axis of most flesh between her legs.

Only when he felt the first unmistakable tightening and lunging of her buttocks, only when he heard her begin to cry out, did he allow himself to quickly re-enter her warmth and give himself up to the rhythm that would bring them both to the fullness of their beautiful passion.

They lay on their sides, clasped in each others' arms, his penis still inside of her. "At last, it happened," he said in a voice that seemed to belong to a stranger.

Paul raised his head and allowed his eyes to search her body again. Her complete and flawless body now belonged to him, she had given it to him without condition. The gift had been without question, without doubt, but with love. Hell, he was humbled by such a gift, he was also exceedingly honoured.

His mouth brushed her face as she clung to him. Her voice still trembled, "Did I do it properly, Paul?"

Tears almost blinded him, he had been her first, yet her prime concern had been for his own pleasure. Running his fingers over the damp tendrils that sat around her face, he smiled, "Debbie, you wouldn't know how to do anything *but* properly. Dearest, I have wanted you for so long. It was a wonderful experience, certainly worth waiting for. What about you then? You didn't tell me about the pill," he gave a low chuckle and kissed her.

"I didn't know how to. Paul I'm such a greenhorn, aren't I?"

"Your innocence draws me like a magnet. When two people are in love, they must learn to love together, probe and touch, give pleasure. I love you, Debbie Hudson. I love you with all of my heart!"

Debbie was intrigued by the shaking that still remained in Paul's voice. For in a cloud of wonder, she realised that he did love her. Above all, he respected her and her heart fluttered wildly as she turned to him, "Paul, I love you. I'm so relieved I got the pill. Have all your women been on the pill?"

"I don't know, Debbie!"

"You don't check?" Her brow rose.

"I don't trust, Debbie. You are the first woman that I have ever made love with, without protecting myself. I should say had sex with. I trust you implicitly, darling."

With a little stretch, she pulled herself up. Sitting there she couldn't believe that at long last she had made love. Her body tingled from the aftermath and she knew, it was something she would look forward to and then flushed with the wonder of what had happened.

She began to wonder if she should dress, should she at least cover herself? Should she feel embarrassed? The simple answer was, she felt fabulous.

Feeling Paul's breath on the back of her neck, she turned to him, "Paul, what a blessing this place is so private, I mean, what if someone had seen us?"

Kissing her tenderly, his voice shook, "They would only have been jealous, darling. My flat is almost finished now. Next time we will go there. I'm being a little presumptuous, there will be a next time, won't there?"

He smiled and cupped her face and as she threw her arms around his neck, she chuckled, "I do hope so. Paul, you made me feel so safe and so much in love. I can't believe that you love me!"

"Believe it, babe, bloody well believe it!"

Instantly she felt the shock charge between them. His hands covered her breasts and to her everlasting joy, she saw him become erect. With a happy sigh, she parted her lips for him and as he kissed her she knew, she wanted him inside of her all over again. Her heart sang, he did love her. Yet he could have his pick of sophisticated beauties and he had chosen her.

This place was deliciously special and somehow, she knew, that day had marked a precious milestone in their love.

CHAPTER FOUR

At long last, there seemed to be a new found happiness in Ellen. Not only had she made a full recovery, but could play a full roll in the shop. Her heart was happy in the knowledge that Debbie had found someone to cosset her, just as she had found Jim.

There was something about Debbie that simply defied definition, her eagerness to help, her thoughtful nature, her adoration of Tony and now she had fallen headlong into love with Paul. She had listened carefully as her daughter had explained about the dinner dance and silently vowed she would have a beautiful dress for the occasion.

She was desperately worried about Jim's back. They had all prayed for trade to pick up and now Jim was having real problems and Ellen smiled to herself as once again, Debbie seemed to come up with some kind of solution.

Debbie realised this was perhaps the only cloud left on her horizon, her father could not carry on without assistance. Granted Ellen's return to the shop had shifted a lot of pressure, but as the trade built, the real pressure went back into the kitchens.

Running her tongue along her lower lip, she spoke thoughtfully, "Mum, I think we should advertise for an apprentice baker. He could do the heavy work, like humping flour and bending down into the ovens etc."

"But, Debbie, we couldn't afford to pay much. I just don't know what the answer is," came the tormented reply.

Debbie's mind raced, helped on by the worry of the situation. Looking around their home, it was spotlessly clean, yet blatantly epitomised the severe shortage of money. An idea was forming, it was becoming a picture and she allowed it to develop. "Mum, we could afford it!"

Her eyes danced with excitement, "I mean if they lived in. We could bring Tony in with me, make his room into a bed sit and provide full board. That way we wouldn't have to find too much for his wages!"

Not only had she surprised her mother, but herself also. Ellen was deadly serious, "Do you think that would work? Are you sure about having Tony in with you, Debbie?"

"Of course I'm sure, he's no trouble at all. It would solve the problem. Let's place the ad., and see what happens!"

Turning to impart of hasty hug to her mother, she left to do just that. This way, she wouldn't have chance to think too much about it. After all, perhaps nobody would apply, but it was the only solution Debbie could think of.

When Paul arrived that evening, she told him what they were trying to achieve. He was serious as he turned to Ellen and Jim, "I think that is a wonderful idea. I will help to move Tony in with Debbie!"

Debbie's heart felt lighter as they finally left for their walk, knowing they would be heading to their favourite spot. His arms drew her to him, his lips found hers and once again the fire flared between them.

Lifting her chin, his eyes locked hers, "I know you won't be nineteen until November. If my memory serves me correctly that is Scorpio and you certainly fit the bill!"

"Really, Paul, what bill is that?" She chuckled happily.

Her chuckle captivated him, he knew he would always love her and smiled, "Your loyalty is rich, you are so sincere and very sexy indeed. Hard work doesn't bother you at all. Yet I have never seen the famous scorpion sting, perhaps it only comes out when you are angry. Enough fooling, Debbie, I want to ask you a very serious question, would you mind?"

She looked directly into his eyes and saw mirrored there, her own happiness. Subconsciously, she had held her breath, "Debbie, I love you dearly. Will you marry me? Or do you think I'm too old at twenty five?"

Exhaling the breath in short bursts, the lump in her throat became inflamed. She knew he was teasing about his age, but now wondered if she had heard him properly. Taking her silence as a put down, he groaned, "Debbie, it can be next year, longer if you need time. Will you at least think about it?"

Her eyes grew like huge saucers, "Paul, I don't need time to think, I would be honoured to marry you, but it would have to be a small wedding. Darling, I love you body and soul!"

Relief flooded him as he held her in a manner indicating he never wanted to let her go. His voice hoarse in acknowledgment of her worry about expenses. "Dearest, there is no way in which your parents would be asked to pay for the wedding. You can have any sort of wedding you like, just as long as you end up being my wife!"

Never could Paul have dreamed how much depended on her reply. Her frank sincerity ate into his heart, choking him. He who had vowed never to marry and this gorgeous young woman captivated every ounce of him. She was adorable and she was his. Tenderly he ran his fingers through her beautifully clean hair and crushed her to him, "Do you want to choose your ring, darling? Can we make our engagement official on Saturday? Debbie Hudson, you have made me so darned happy, I can hardly think straight!"

"I would like you to choose the ring, Paul. I would be happy to make it all official on Saturday and I pray that I can always make you happy," she gulped and brought his lips to hers.

Holding her to him, he wished, and not for the first time that he could disassociate himself from his rampaging manhood. He battled night after night with it and no matter how many cold showers he took, nothing worked.

Taking her hand into his, he gulped, "Debbie, at long last the flat is finished. I had bought it and arranged to have it done up to my liking, that was before I met you. I just pray it meets with your approval. Darling, let's pop and see it?"

Wordlessly, they meandered around the bay, Paul stopped short, "It looks as though the McHughes are selling up. I have an interview to cover there.

Apparently the son is marrying a New Zealander and moving out there. It is rather sad to see such a splendid old home go onto the market!"

They were looking up onto a hill, almost opposite to the one they called their own. A huge castle type building stood well back and looked very inviting indeed. A large 'for sale' sign, swung precariously in the bracing breeze. Debbie snuggled closer to Paul, "I would love to look around the place. It looks like something in a fairytale, doesn't it?"

Paul found his grip tighten on her. It took so little to please her, reminding him sharply of little Tony. His mind flew into overtime, "Debbie, once its empty, I will see if I can borrow the key and take you to see it. I wouldn't mind a good old nose myself. Sadly, they will probably have to sell cheaply, it isn't the everyday type of home, is it?"

The excitement that danced in her eyes was almost as though he had given her a precious jewel, not just an offer of a look around an old building. He was the luckiest man alive to be marrying her, he had never known the feeling of such a deep and undemanding love. Suddenly, he felt insecure, it was now vital to him that she liked his flat.

He should have known better than to have doubts. She had a charisma about her, one that fitted into any situation. She was delightful and it saddened him to see how hard she worked. Yet he wouldn't change a thing about her. He also loved her parents, they had brought her up to care for others and she loved them unconditionally.

All of his life, he had missed the feeling of being part of a family. He had convinced himself that he never wanted a tight bond in his life. How far off beam could he have been? He was never happier, than when he was sitting in the bosom of her family, unless, of course, when they were alone.

Never had he dreamed of anyone stealing his heart. He enjoyed women's company and his sex life had always been totally uncomplicated. The women he bedded, were like himself, enjoy a meal, followed by a mutual desire to screw, with no strings attached.

From the moment he had met Debbie, he had not known how to keep his hands from her and never given another woman a thought. She had certainly been worth the wait, although he would never forget the torment of his yearning for her body.

Her eager hand tugging his, brought him back down to earth as they had arrived outside of his door.

Debbie had never given a thought to the fact that she might not like Paul's home. It was as she expected, immaculate and detailed. Excitement entered her as she began her so called inspection.

The beautifully fitted kitchen had work tops that gleamed, concealing a washing machine, fridge and even a dishwasher. At the far end was a breakfast bar with four stools around it, and standing on a gorgeous polished parquet floor. "Oh, Paul, its beautiful," had fallen from her lips.

Her hand gripped his as they walked into the bathroom. "This is sumptuous," she gulped, taking in the rich green suite and mirrored walls.

Entering the lounge had almost taken her breath away. It was large and spacious, overlooking the sea. The rich pile carpet was almost like walking through a field of wheat and coloured just the same. Matching velvet drapes dressed the huge windows to perfection.

One wall housed two very big mahogany book units, filled with beautifully bound books and a cocktail cabinet, cleverly concealed, made up a third unit. An exquisite soft leather, tan three piece suite was placed strategically in the room. Great attention had been paid to lighting, giving a warm and relaxing sensation.

In spite of the central heating, a fireplace had been built with various coloured pieces of stone. A gold marble effect ran through it, in fact it was truly masonry personified. The imitation log fire gave a rosy glow, completing the magical scene.

Paul's eyes never left her as he watched with delight, the various expressions that crossed her eager face. Gulping heavily, he asked, "Do you like it, darling? Is there anything you want to change?"

"It is absolutely gorgeous, Paul. There is nothing I would change, but what made you buy it?"

She had walked over to one of the huge windows, her eyes watching the sea. Joining her, he smiled, "I thought it would be a jolly good investment. I've still got a couple of years before its entirely paid for, but it's a damned sight better than paying endless rent!"

Debbie gave a little chuckle and rolled her eyes heavenwards,

"But you're hardly ever in it, Paul!"

"Not at the moment, darling. Its only just been completed and we couldn't have come here with so much mess. When winter comes along, we can't live on our hill, can we? Anyway, once we're married, we'll both be in it!"

Smiling happily, she allowed herself to lean into him and sighed, "Than sounds perfect, Paul. What about your parents?

Do you see them often? Will they come to the wedding?"

A frown furrowed his brow and his tone grew flat as he told her, "We're not very close, Debbie. I doubt they would come to the wedding. They are retired in Cornwall now. You see, they were both high flyers in the advertising world and I was born late in life for them!"

He stopped, his eyes now looking out to sea. She could feel his hurt, almost wishing she had never mentioned his parents, "Sorry, Paul, I shouldn't have pried!"

Dropping his arm onto her shoulder, he gripped her, "Debbie, you have every right to know about my background. You see, they never wanted children. Apparently, I was a total accident and was constantly reminded of the fact. At times I felt like an intruder and was literally brought up with a string of nannies!"

Her eyes filled as they lifted to his. She could see the naked pain in them. "Paul, when we have our babies, they will always feel loved and will be tended by us. How many little ones do you want, darling?"

He swallowed heavily, "I never wanted any at all, but with you for their mother, I would like a couple, I think. Mind you, you are speaking to a man who was never going to marry either," he laughed lightly, "Honestly, Debbie, I know that I would love them, no matter how many came along!"

Feeling the tension in his body, she could envisage just how badly he had been hurt. Granted he had never known hardship, but had missed out seriously in the love department. Shrugging his shoulders and dismissing the subject, he whispered, "You haven't given the bedroom your seal of approval yet!"

She allowed herself to be drawn to the door they had not yet entered. The bedroom was fitted throughout with a giant sized bed almost begging to be climbed onto. The whole flat was what could only be described as a lavish penthouse. Beneath it were the two floors that housed the 'Ventura' offices. She could almost imagine herself living here, working in the gorgeous kitchen and keeping it spotlessly clean for Paul.

Her love for him overwhelmed her. Slowly, deliberately, she walked over to the window. Instantly, he was behind her, his arms slipping naturally about her waist. His breath was hot, his voice soft and smooth, like honey, "Debbie, night after night, I have imagined us making love in that bed. Shall we?"

The question was beautifully simplistic and Debbie had become addicted to her new life. Nothing gave her more pleasure than when Paul's careful caresses roamed her body. For some reason, she felt absolutely free from any form of embarrassment and totally comfortable when Paul gazed upon her naked body.

She climbed onto the bed and slowly removed every last vestige of clothing. Her hands reached behind her head and clasped tightly, the look on her face was one of supreme fascination as Paul climbed naked beside her.

His mouth moved over her face, her neck, whilst his hands fondled her breasts, bringing the tormenting buds into his mouth. She loved the feel of his silken tongue as it ravished her nipples, sending delightful erotic movements through her body and sent Paul's pulses racing. This was the first time they had truly had the privacy to explore fully and he didn't want to miss one tiny crevice of the body before him.

Debbie lay enveloped in wonder. She felt his fingers travelling delicately over all of her body, touching, probing, sliding into every shadowed crevice, until his hand finally moved towards the division of her thighs. Entering her triangle of dark hair, his finger located the little bump of her swelling clitoris and gently, rhythmically, he began to rub it.

Her body surrendered to the pleasure of Paul's touch. Panting with ecstasy, she opened her eyes. He had moved down between her legs, parting her, he began to examine her as he would a precious, hothouse plant. Just when she thought she could stand no more of his utter pleasure, he gripped her buttocks and raised her lower lips to his mouth, kissing and licking her until she writhed and screamed out. He had taken her into a sensational orgasm without using his penis and when her body began to settle from the aftermath, he held her shuddering in his arms.

When he brought his mouth to hers, she could taste herself on his lips. "Oh, Paul, darling, there is so much to learn. You know so much more than I could ever learn," she gasped into his panting mouth.

"We learn to please each other, darling. Do whatever you would like to me, I think I can promise to enjoy it," he groaned.

To his utter amazement, she sat up. Then she turned to him and placed her hands onto his shoulders, denoting he stay put. Her mouth moved over his face, eyes, ears and back to his mouth. Although he could still detect her beautiful innocence, there was no doubting she was enjoying her trip over his features. Hell, he wanted to push her mouth downwards until she took his penis into her mouth. He moaned his pleasure when her mouth covered his hard nipples, her fingers tripping through his chest hair with love if not expertise.

Suddenly, her mouth moved over his abdomen and his breath halted within his chest. Her breathing was laboured, excited, her concentration deep. He mustn't ask her to do anything to him, it must come from her. Helplessly, he allowed his legs to part. Debbie noticed his body muscles flexing and continued her search, his heavy pulsating penis lay hard against his stomach and she wanted him inside of her. The soft moans leaving him only served to excite her more. Her body shot down the bed, eager to please him. His testicles hung loose in the middle of his fair pubic hair, his inner thigh muscles were shaking out of control.

Paul raised his head slightly needing to watch her. She was turning him inside out, without any help from him. He saw the fascination grow as her hands lifted his balls and squeezed them softly. Gently, she planted a kiss and nuzzled deeply into them. Christ, he could take no more, he would come all over her and much as he wanted to, she wasn't ready, not yet.

An anguished groan left him as his arms reached out and gathered her to him. He turned her almost roughly onto her back and her melt down began. Her swirling hips confirmed she was more than ready for him.

His penis was so hard, he had to wrench it from his stomach and ease it into her warmth. He gave himself entirely to the burning, imperative flood, that forced itself upward, growing, hardening and tightening, until he burst inside of her in long, excruciatingly good spasms of fire that brought a scream of ravening triumph to his lips.

Much, much later, their eyes locked. "What shall we do to celebrate our engagement?" Paul asked.

"It would be nice to spend the evening with my family. I think they could do with something to cheer them up. Then we can come back here for a while!"

"To make love," he whispered.

"Mmmm," she flushed and snuggled closer to him.

Crushing her savagely, his love for her almost constricted his breathing. She hadn't asked for expensive meals, just a simple evening with the family. He also knew beyond doubt, his future wife loved the sexual side of their love. Tenderly he chewed her ear, "Mmm, I would like that very much. Do you think they'll be surprised. I s'pose I should have asked them!"

Finally, Paul put the kettle on, "Do you want coffee here? Or should we …?

"Go back and tell Mum and Dad? Yes, darling, I want to tell them!"

Without thought she had cut his sentence off, choking him. He knew now that his lovely rosebud was blossoming and looked even more beautiful than he could ever have dreamed.

CHAPTER FIVE

Jim and Ellen had been watching television in their usual companionable silence. Ellen was first to speak, "Jim, I feel that Debbie and Paul are serious, but how the hell can we afford to give her the wedding she deserves?"

Looking at is beloved wife, he smiled, "I agree, they make a mighty handsome couple. If she does want a big wedding, perhaps we could ask the bank for a loan. As you say, darling, she richly deserves a day to remember. I just hope she can still work with us, the customers love her welcoming smile!"

Ellen noticed the dreadful strain in her husband. How much her pregnancy and subsequent ill health had hurt him. Perhaps the only good thing that had come out of the tragedy that had beset them, was the fact that their daughter had met someone like Paul.

Granted, they loved Tony dearly, but had everything not happened as it had, the shop would have been showing a healthy profit by now. But things *had* happened as they did and she knew that Debbie had not resented one moment of her time to help her family.

At the time Debbie had been born, she and Jim were devastated that they couldn't have had at least one more child. As time went by, they understood why they had only been sent one child. Debbie had all of the beautiful attributes rolled into one. She sighed and realised that Jim was still waiting for a reply.

Taking his hand to her lips, she said simply, "Let's see what Debbie wants, dear. I can't see her wanting anything too lavish. And I truly think that Paul would do just about anything to make her happy. Hopefully, he will agree to allow her to work for a while, just until …!"

Her words trailed off as pain entered her eyes. Jim pulled his wife into his arms, "Don't think about all of that now, dear. As you say, Debbie has a wise head on her young shoulders. We'll be guided by her!"

An intimate smile then passed between them as they heard the front door close. They could almost feel the excitement of the hurried footsteps running towards them, good news was definitely on the way.

**

Debbie's face was flushed as she entered the room, "You knew, didn't you?" She threw out the challenge happily as her parents reached out to hug the life from her. Jim smiled, "Of course we did, well, we hoped we were right. Welcome to the family, Paul!"

Paul had never felt so much warmth, his eyes danced with happiness. "Thank you both, I give you my word that I will make Debbie happy. I also understand that she wanted to continue to work in the shop, for a while at least. That will certainly be with my blessing!"

Debbie didn't think it possible to love him more, not more than she did at that moment. He had confirmed that she would continue to work with them, without putting them into a position of having to ask.

The odd tear of joy fell from them all. Jim suggested, "We will have a couple of drinks on Saturday evening. In fact, I might even run to a bottle of champagne, unless of course, you two have other plans!"

Paul's arms went around Debbie, his smile unflinching, "To tell the truth, Debbie wants to do just that. Only her version was for me to bring the champagne and that will be my pleasure!"

Although they had literally rushed up the stairs, they now walked down slowly. Her body melted into him as she kissed him a very ardent goodnight. His hand raised her chin to him, his lips brushed her forehead, "Goodnight, Debbie Hudson, soon to be Debbie Howarth!"

She had to admit she did rather like the sound of that. But whatever she was called, she couldn't have been happier than she was at that moment. Lady luck had surely smiled on her the day she had guided Paul into their shop.

**

Matthew Ross ringed the advertisement and put the paper down. It was high time he moved on, yet he had enjoyed his life working with the fairground group. Lighting a cigarette, he allowed his eyes to roam around the small caravan that he had used as a dwelling for the past three months. It *was* small, but when all the windows and indeed the door, were wide open, a comforting breeze managed to circulate, bringing with it the salt of the sea air.

He opened the wardrobe door, noticing it was still hanging by one hinge. With a wry smile, he took out his navy, two piece suit and realised it needed a good pressing. He remembered the last time he had worn it, for a moment a frown puckered his brow. He had been so proud when he had graduated in law at Liverpool University. That had been over a year ago now. And to all intents and purposes, he had bummed around Morecambe, as an odd job bod.

Everyone was friendly and homely, totally enjoying their way of life and allowing him to share the things they held sacred, Yes, they were a great bunch of people and although his own native home was rich with friendship, it didn't beat the hospitality here. He had been a bloody fool allowing life to smack him into the ground, but thanks to these folks, he was back on the up.

The thought of leaving Morecambe, filled him with a deep sadness. Almost the same sadness he had felt leaving his native Ireland, but he couldn't return there. The advert in the paper, although he didn't know why, somehow intrigued him. He also fancied the idea of being with a family again, when the little gang he had worked with moved on.

Swinging his suit over his arm, he set off with a new purpose in mind, to the laundry huts. He didn't relish the idea of wearing a suit again, he had become used to jumping into jeans and working naked from the waist up. The work was damned hard, yet thoroughly enjoyable and when he tumbled into bed at night, there was no need for him to count sheep, he was usually bushed.

Matthew had become used to the music filtering around the fairground and the happy laughter of the holiday makers, yes, he would miss the friends he had made. They had invited him to go along with them, but Morecambe clamped its full atmosphere around his heart, holding him a willing captive.

As he walked alone, he noticed that Gypsy Rossita, was sitting at a small table by the entrance to her palmistry tent. Normally there would be a long queue outside, but as she waited, Matthew noticed the gnarled old hands were busy peeling and slicing a peach.

Smiling broadly at him, she called, "You got the day off then?"

"First time I see ya not working. Can't ye get one of them lasses to press yer suit for ye laddie?" She spoke some sort of gaelic and mixture of northern accents, no doubt picked up by her various and numerous clients.

Matthew chuckled, "I'm going for an interview, Rossita. Look into your crystal and tell me how I'll get on?"

"Tha never believes me lad. I told ye that ye would meet a raven haired beauty, but ye laughed. Mark my words, that was very clear!"

His eyes met the tired old grey eyes. He had never believed in any of this, yet the gypsy woman had been right about so many of the folk in the fairground. She was a true gypsy, dressed in long skirts and always wore a red bandanna over her hair. Matthew had managed to build a good rapport with her and persisted, "Will I get the job?"

Wiping her hand on her apron, Rossita took his hand and turned his palm towards her. "Let's see now. Ye, I can see a job. I can still see that dame ye don't want!"

"Tis not that I don't want, Rossita, rather the fact that blonds are my weakness. A redhead bust me something rotten. Anyway in this new ere o' women's libbers, I'm not so sure at all, at all," he grinned, mocking her with a touch of his Irish accent.

Whistling light heartedly, he passed the stand where a row of scantily clad girls were dancing, enticing holiday makers in to see the main show. They smiled as he went by all of them saddened by the fact that he wouldn't tour with them. Part of him regretted the fact, after all, they had provided mental and physical needs for each other.

Early in his life, Matthew Ross had learned that he had an astonishingly healthy sexual drive. But with the advent of the permissive society, he was able to make himself understood. Yes he needed to screw and be screwed, but was by no means ready for any sort of commitment. And the women were now of the same mind.

He smiled as he pressed his suit and remembered the first time he had been propositioned. Suzy, a voluptuous blond had followed him into his van, "Gorra drink for a tired old gal?"

She had smiled seductively and feeling exceedingly horny, he said eagerly, "Sure, come on in!"

31

Handing a drink to her, she had taken a slow sip, pressed her breasts into his chest and drooled, "I see you have a real hard-on, Matt. Is it me or just the need of a quick screw?"

"Both I s'pose, since when did women make he first move?"

His mind still dwelt on that evening as he carefully hung his trousers over the hanger. After regaining his equilibrium that particular night, he also thought it a great idea for a woman to chase what she wanted. Suzy's pale green eyes had rounded, "I didn't have you down as a country bumpkin, Matt. A gal can get as horny as a fella and right now, I feel like a good, long delicious fuck!"

He detested being called Matt, but in this life everyone's name was either abbreviated or substituted for a nickname. Suzy had come to him directly after her last performance, the scant gold briefs and matching bra, scarcely covered her and in one swift movement, she stood naked before him, naked that was, apart from her very high, four inch heeled shoes.

Slowly and deliberately, she began to move to the music. Her hands fondled her breasts till her nipples stood firm and then continued to the cluster of blond pubic hair. Matthew was amused and fired, never had he been treated to a solo performance before, fair enough, women gave into him, but no one had moved on him like this one.

With a sensual move, she turned her back on him, bent forward and gripped her calves. He could see right into her hungry passage and his cock engorged as it pulsated against his fly. In a flash, he was on his feet, his trousers down to his ankles, his left arm flung around her waist, his right hand guiding his red hot penis into that delectable passage.

"Mmm," he gasped as he rammed into her. He saw her grip the side of the table to stop herself falling as he plunged without mercy. Hell, this hadn't happened to him before and he realised he had missed out. Suzy was groaning with ecstasy as she felt the firm, hard dick filling her.

His legs were growing weak with standing, yet he was being drawn tightly into her, she let out a long, low squeal and he felt her come. He carried on pumping till he felt his own release burst from him. When he withdrew from her, she had knelt down and sucked him completely dry.

Breathing a sigh of overwhelming delight, his first conscious thought was that he had trapped himself and gulped, "I'm not in the market for anything heavy, kid. Christ knows that was bloody great, but that's all it was!"

"Of that you can be sure, Matt. That's why we are on the pill, I mean everyone needs to get it off and neither of us wants more. Call me next time ye feel horny, 'cos, I promise I'll call on you!"

She had done just that, he reflected as he finished pressing his jacket and made his way back to the van. Passing Suzy, he had imparted a fond wave. They had been close through the season, but both knew that was all it was. Matthew would never trust a woman again, not after he had played his bat straight down the middle, been faithful, only to find that he had been cruelly cheated.

Pushing everything else from his mind, he fastened his tie neatly and left his temporary home. It was only a short walk and he would enjoy the good clean fresh air and hope he could manage to stay in Morecambe, the town he had come to love.

**

Debbie's feet had scarcely touched the ground that day. Apart from floating with love, the shop was exceedingly busy, almost like an omen that things were definitely on the up.

She noticed Matthew Ross come in and took his order for coffee and scones. Somehow, she guessed he was not a holiday maker. His suit was well pressed and his pale blue shirt was spotless, the navy tie matched the suit.

As he ordered, Debbie had recognised a hint of a very cultured Irish brogue in his voice. He must have been about the same age as Paul, in fact he could almost have been a client of his and recommended to the shop.

Seeing him approach to pay his bill, she was drawn to him. He was fairly tall with almost black hair, huge blue eyes that seemed to hold a lot of pain, yet a smile that would have charmed the Devil himself. His swarthy complexion indicated some sort of outdoor living.

The lovely Irish lilt was exceedingly cultured as he stated, "I'm interested in the job here, is there still a vacancy?"

His question stunned her. It was obvious that he had noticed her amazement as he continued, "Don't worry, I'm not afraid of hard work. I know the wages are low, but I feel I would enjoy the challenge!"

Confusion joined the flush that covered her. She had not meant to be rude and stammered, "Pl ... please forgive me. .. I was .. I was just surprised that you would want a job here. You look like a typical business man!"

If only her stupid mouth would stay shut, she was now up to her neck in turmoil, jumping in deeper every time she spoke. His face had grown serious, "I was. I graduated in law at Liverpool University. I had intended to return to Ireland and set up a law practice. I had also intended to marry, but she left with someone else and emigrated. I wasted a year fretting and after losing my beloved mother, I decided to travel. My father had died just a couple of years prior. There is nothing back home anymore!"

Shocked and saddened by his mini life saga, Debbie noticed him gasp for breath. "I am sorry, but you don't owe me an explanation. I didn't mean to be so darned rude!"

Suddenly, his eyes lit up and she could see that beneath his pain, lurked a probably fun person. His smile was warm as it reached his sensual mouth. He seemed to realise that she had been expecting a youth and had taken her by surprise.

Imparting a wicked grin, he chuckled, "Look, if I am to be considered for this position, you will have to know my background. Truth to tell, I've never told anyone my business, not the way I opened up to you. My name is Matthew Ross and for the last three months, I have been working casually on

33

the fairground. Having fallen in love with Morecambe, something seemed to draw me here. I take it you're the daughter?"

He then pretended to be out of breath after his revelations, truth was, he had never expected to say so much in such a short time. There was something rather delicious about the body behind the counter and the thought of working around her gave him a distinct buzz.

Debbie was flabbergasted by his seemingly quick perception. She then realised that the advert had quoted 'family baker and tea shop'. If she had gradated in anything at all, it must certainly have been stupidity with a capital S.

Desperately trying to pull herself together, she gasped, "I am, my name is Debbie Hudson. You had better come and meet the family, before I put you off entirely. My father went to university, so you'll have plenty in common with him!"

"I've embarrassed you, Debbie, please forgive me? Hello, young man, what's your name?"

Tony beamed as Matthew paused to shake his hand and Debbie rushed ahead to warn her father. He was almost as surprised as she was. By the time Matthew reached them, she had managed to calm herself. "Dad, this is Matthew Ross, Matthew, this is Jim Hudson."

She then scurried away leaving them to chat over the details. Ellen had just come down to relieve Debbie, her eyes now held the old sparkle and Debbie knew that her engagement had brought delight to both of her parents. Mentally she prayed that Tony would keep well for a while, for everyone's sake.

Having filled her mother in briefly, Matthew and Jim were by her side. Matthew was chuckling with Jim as he announced, "I've been accepted to commence work on Monday. I could move my belongings in later today, if that's convenient. You must be Ellen," he smiled as they shook hands.

Instinctively, she knew that her parents had taken to him and he to them. She was then volunteered to show Matthew his room. She could see immediately that he was more than well pleased with it and hope began to flow into her. He looked very reliable and she was sure he would work hard to relieve Jim.

Chatting like old friends, she explained the problem fully. She knew only too well that her father would not have bothered to allow anyone to know how bad his back was. Matthew smiled, "I think they are very lucky to have a daughter like you. Jim told me, you gave up your career for them!"

"I didn't give it up. It hadn't actually started. I do hope you'll be happy here. Do you have any hobbies, Matthew?"

His totally laid back manner began to infect her. She loved the Irish lilt as he replied, "Yep, I'm a photograph nut. Only working to feed my habit. I've a few quid for a rainy day and it can stay where it is. Jim tells me you've just become engaged. Why do I always seem to miss the boat?"

They laughed and Debbie felt that they would become firm friends. Somehow it felt like having an older brother around. And although the idea of a bed sitter had been to give the family and the applicant some privacy, she had a strong feeling that Matthew wouldn't spend too much time on his own. He seemed to need to belong in a family.

CHAPTER SIX

Debbie found herself shaking with excitement as she waited for Paul to arrive. Tony had been allowed to stay up for a while, his little hands clapped with delight, "Debbie's going to marry Paul," he chanted without understanding the true meaning of the words.

Jim had explained to him that it meant Paul would become a member of their family. He had also explained that Matthew was about to join them. Ellen had secretly iced one of her special cakes and invited Matthew to join the party. The table looked gorgeous as the finishing touches were added.

Paul arrived and rubbed his hands as he joined in with Tony's chanting. Then he took Debbie's hand, his other hand delved into his pocket and produced a small box. Tenderly, he removed the ring and placed it onto her engagement finger. "Debbie, please accept this ring as a token of my love. Right now, darling, I can't wait for you to wear the gold band that makes you my wife!"

Her body trembled with emotion. It was a truly exquisite ring. A beautiful half moon of diamonds, alternating with sapphires, glittered as the light caught it. "Paul, it is absolutely beautiful," she gasped, "I too look forward to wearing the gold band!"

After receiving his deep kiss, she found herself enveloped in her parents' arms. Ellen's eyes spilled over as she turned to Paul and hugged him. "Paul, Jim and I have longed to see such happiness on our daughter's face. And we couldn't think of a kinder, more thoughtful person, for her to share her life with!"

Jim carefully placed the champagne onto the table and turned to face the happy couple. "Debbie, you must tell Paul about Matthew. I hope you don't mind, Paul, but we invited him to join the party!"

Debbie felt Paul's arm around her waist. "What's all this? There's another man in your life, Debbie?" He had feigned mock surprise. Happiness almost choked her, then she told him briefly, the story of Matthew and his tragic losses.

Paul's eyes had grown tender, "I think I can understand why he changed direction. He must have been really gutted, I mean, losing so much in one fell swoop. Well, at least his luck has changed now and I'm sure it will work out for you all."

Almost as if he had been cued in, Matthew arrived. He and Paul hit it off from the start. Paul helped him in with his belongings and Debbie heard them chatting and laughing with each other.

Seconds later, they returned. Matthew was quick to observe the table and gasped, "I feel like an intruder. I could have easily moved in tomorrow. This is obviously a very private family occasion!"

Tony broke the ice, "You *are* family Maffew. Daddy says you are going to live with us!" The wide eyed, childlike simplicity, had enchanted them all.

36

Matthew ruffled his hair, "Thank you, Tony, how about I get my camera and take some photographs? We must record this special occasion!"

Jim turned on the rather dilapidated record player. Tony's favourite records were of Elvis Presley and they all joined in to sing along. The champagne was opened and drunk, the evening one of magic. Debbie felt completely intoxicated with love, champagne, but most of all, with a deep inner gratitude for the arrival of Matthew.

Once everyone retired for the night, Paul swept her into his arms and kissed her. It was then she confided her worries about her dress for the dinner dance. He chuckled softly, "Why don't you hire one, darling. I know that's what Eric's wife does. I understand that women don't like to wear the same dress twice!"

Relief flooded her as her arms looped around his neck. She knew that if Paul had realised just how tight things were, he would certainly have helped. But that seemed to be a betrayal of her parents. Fair enough, he knew they were short of money, yet without actually checking the books, no one could have guessed just how pushed they were.

There was a hire shop in Morecambe and she knew that her mother would help her to choose something appropriate. Apart from her gorgeous ring, she did have a pair of drop, gold earrings she could wear. And although Paul loved her hair loose, she would definitely have it set into a sophisticates style.

A happy sigh left her, "If only I had spoken to you before, Paul. You make everything so simple. It has worried me dreadfully, but I feel much better now!"

His voice held a tremor as he whispered, "Darling, promise you'll come round tomorrow. I want to make love with you. So stop worrying!"

**

Eric Morgan, proprietor of 'Ventura', paced his Manchester based office. His aim one day, to own a magazine in every large City in the world

Right now he was in the process, after a lot of pressure from his daughter, Amanda, to open the London branch. She was clever, beautiful, domineering and handled staff with swift directives that brooked no arguments.

He stopped and stared impassively at the chap before him. "Right then, Bill, you want to take over the London branch, is that it?"

"Yop, that's about it. I can't stay in Preston with Amanda. And I do have as much experience as her, however, Eric, it is up to you, I don't wish to cause strife!"

Bill Peters had worked with the magazine over the past six years, almost as long as Amanda. He was sick to the back teeth of her tantrums, her total disregard for any ideas that weren't her own and felt sure it had been she, that had driven Paul Howarth to Morecambe.

Eric leaned forward, concealing his smile of satisfaction. His daughter was like him, knew exactly what she wanted and bloody well took it. She had not however, managed to get Paul Howarth to toe the line. Equally, Eric didn't want to lose Paul, he was a brilliant editor and his nose led him anywhere to find a good story.

There was no way he could blame his daughter, he had brought her up to be tough and ruthless, much to his wife's distress. At the moment though, Amanda was compromising him badly. They had fought bitterly when Paul had insisted on the move to Morecambe, and she was now insistent that Eric finally open up in New York, with herself and Paul to head the venture.

Eric allowed the shudder to run down his spine, "Right, Bill, once Amanda signs your contract, the London job is yours, old chap. She will probably insist that Howarth or she herself, tags along for the first few weeks, there will be long and hard interviews for the staff in the smoke!"

"Thanks, Eric," replied Bill with stiff lips.

Driving back to Preston, Bill gripped the wheel with a strong anxiety filling him. He dreaded the thought of facing Amanda. She was the horniest little cow he had ever had the misfortune to come up against. So far, he had evaded her, not so subtle, come ons, but could he keep it up? would she allow him to?

Rumours were wild about Paul succumbing, but Bill knew better. Paul would screw around without a qualm, but not mix business with pleasure. Suddenly, he felt a surge of comfort, he would pop and see Paul as soon as possible and simply ask him for some advice.

**

Amanda replaced the 'phone into its cradle and smiled malevolently. Bill was on his way to her and the rest of the staff had already left. She had insisted he come to her for the contract he longed for. Although still determined to hook Paul, right then, Bill would more than suffice.

Nothing pleased her more than an inordinately heated screw, especially when the poor bastards puffed and panted with unadulterated lust, dropping to their knees when she preferred to be pulled off with their greedy mouths.

Many times she had managed to arouse the charismatic, Mr Peters, her heart would pound with satisfaction when she saw the bulge in his trousers. But, always someone had disturbed them. She knew he was happily married, yet she loved nothing more than something seemingly out of reach.

She opened her desk drawer and took out her gold compact. Her skin and make up were flawless as always. Taking the comb, she flicked it casually through her very pretty, ash blond hair. It was short, closely cropped to her perfectly shaped head, her green eyes glinted with lust. Slowly, with deliberate meaning, she removed the odd item of clothing.

Leaning back on her luxurious white, leather, swivel chair, she lit a cigarette, inhaled deeply and exhaled in short, jerky movements. Oh, yes, Mr Peters would be at her mercy, and she possessed none whatsoever.

Bill knew, the moment he entered the building, what was in store. Had he had his way, he would have gone straight home, but if he wanted the contract, he had to stop and collect it. He opened Amanda's door and couldn't contain the gasp that left his lips. She was a really beautiful woman, she was also a real bitch. As she raised her arm to touch her immaculate hair, he noticed she was not wearing a bra under the soft chiffon of her blouse. He could see the small, almost perfect breast with its hard nipple. Christ, he defied any man not to harden under such conditions.

With tantalising outer calm, she beckoned, "Come and sit down, Bill. I understand that congratulations are in order. I mean Daddy did agree the London appointment, subject to my signing the contract, didn't he?"

"Sure did and thanks, Amanda. I must get off home, unless there is anything special," he gulped stupidly, of course there was something special – the bloody contract.

Amanda swung her chair round to face him and held her hand towards his. Leaning forward naively to shake the outstretched hand, she gripped his and placed it onto her breast. The fine layer of material seemed to make the firm breast more erotic than ever and he couldn't help himself. She looked so fucking seductive and his cock reminded him that he was only a mere mortal after all.

Her eyes remained fixed on his as she pushed herself forward to the end of her seat and leaned back heavily. Allowing a sigh to escape her sensual mouth, she raised both hands and placed them firmly onto his shoulders and without a qualm, he sunk to his knees.

Abruptly, he reached into her open blouse, grabbed her breast and with a satisfied glint of spite he tweaked the rigid nipple. Bill's head was level with her knees and with tormenting deliberation, she parted them. She was a true blond alright, because she was bare beneath her skirt, revealing an almost silvery fair bush.

Removing her hands from his shoulders, she placed them between her legs, excitement surging as she saw his eyes stand out. Nothing was more pleasing to Amanda, than to have a man ogle her and with complete abandon, she allowed her hands to part her pubic hair.

Moving her hips slowly, she ran her finger across and through her bush and having located her clitoris, she rubbed it with competent relish. "My God you're a bitch," he grunted as his cock forced against his zip.

Crazed with lust, he gripped her legs and placed her thighs over each shoulder. She was wide open to him and he could see into her passage, as it winked with wet invitation. He was sure he had hurt her as he wrenched her in a position to suit himself, she bloody well deserved hurting. His hands ripped savagely at her blouse and he gripped both breasts and twisted her nipples

Hearing her moan, he brought his hands down to release his engorged cock. He would screw her alright, fuck her hard and long, but at his pace, in his own time. She would get it, oh, yeseree, she would get it.

Amanda tried to move her legs, but they were locked over Bill's shoulders. "For chrissakes, Bill, fuck me. D'ye hear me, I said I want it?"

"Oh, I will, dear. I will give you one you'll never forget," he sneered.

How he hated this spite filled woman, who loved power more than life. His hand held the weight of his penis and he half rose and pressed it into her as hard as he could. Hearing her gasp of anticipated fulfilment, he pulled it out again.

"No, put it back," she shouted.

Pushing it back in, he eyeballed her, "You have signed my contract for London, haven't you?"

"Yes, Bill, but later for pity sake," she panted helplessly.

Pulling out again, he saw the strain on her face, the sheer desperation in her cruel eyes, "Where's the signed contract?"

"Can't it wait?"

"No," was his final word and she knew it.

"Under the blotter. Its ready," she practically cried

Again he plunged into her, feeling the urge to come, but not till he had checked. He would never believe how filled with guile he had become, but that was Amanda's gift to anyone who wanted help in their career. Yes, Paul had warned him, he was dealing with a woman newly liberated. He knew he couldn't keep up for long, yet couldn't reach the wretched blotter, "Show me then, bitch?"

His legs were aching as he gave her the inch she needed to reach it herself. With a moan of pain, she waved it under his nose, "See, you bastard, it is signed, sealed and fuckin' well delivered!"

"Good girl!"

Bill knew she would be fuming at his condescension, but he hadn't enjoyed himself like this for a long, long time. To think he had run around scared of her advances, when this was all he had to do. Seeing her grimace of pain only served to make him harder, and now he pumped at his pace, faster and faster. Suddenly, he knew she was about to climax and whilst he knew he would oblige, he would make her plead for it.

Her head thrashed about and he swiftly withdrew from her. An anguished scream left her, "Don't stop, Bill, for fuck sake don't stop!"

Briefly, he felt his own power and revelled in her desperation. His eyes focussed on her face, her mouth was almost a thin line of anger, "Beg for it? Go on, bitch, beg," he panted as he ran his rigid weapon over her burning slit, just allowing the tip to roam over the opening.

"Please," she shouted.

It was his turn to call the tune. He sunk himself back into her and felt her orgasm immediately. Her body writhed and then he burst, burst in floods as he poured his juices into her. His legs were filled with excruciating pain, but he had fucked the evil bitch once and for all. Totally mindless of her feelings, he pulled himself free and pushed it unceremoniously back into his trousers. Picking up the contract, he grinned, "Thank you very much, Miss Morgan!" The gob smacked expression on her face and her indignity would satisfy him for a long time.

.

CHAPTER SEVEN

Matthew had settled in so quickly, it seemed as though he had always been with the Hudson family. Jim looked much better and Matthew was as good as his word, throwing himself completely into the job.

His free time was spent outside with his camera. He had breezed in one day with the photographs of the engagement party. Paul had gasped, "These are professional, Matthew. You should think about entering competitions!"

Matthew grinned, "What do you think, Debbie? I love taking photographs in Morecambe. The views from one end of the Bay to the other are breathtaking, I love it here!"

Debbie looked at them carefully, "They are brilliant, Matthew. Honestly, you should listen to Paul, it seems almost funny, he spends his time organising layouts and you take the pictures. I have no doubts about your entering!"

They were all engrossed around the dining table. A place that always seemed popular for discussions. Tony also loved the pictures, especially as Matthew often took him along to watch them being taken. And Debbie certainly hadn't realised the true extent of the beautiful scenery, not until Matthew had brought it all to life.

His voice was eager, "Honestly, I was surprised to find it is possible to capture the old world charm of Heysham, right across to Barrow. I managed to get some good shots of that lovely old building at the far end of the bay. Its up for sale, yet if it were mine, I would never want to sell it!"

Paul leaned his elbows onto he table, "That just reminded me, Debbie wants to look over it one day. I suppose if I can arrange to view, would you like to join us, Matthew?"

"I certainly would, Paul. That's if I'm not intruding!"

His rich Irish lilt became more pronounced, as it always did when he was explaining something he found to be exciting or even sad.

The end of the busy season now loomed. To everyone's delight, Paul had managed to put a couple of further large contracts their way. Tony would soon be three and had managed to keep well for almost a year and Debbie had not seen her parents so relaxed since they moved here, nearly four years ago.

In spite of the lack of holiday makers, the shop remained very busy. Many shoppers would call for their fresh bread and cakes, bur fortunately had begun to linger over tea or coffee. At times it was similar to a social club, but nevertheless a healthy one.

Debbie had been rushed off her feet that day, when the 'phone rang. Hastily grabbing the receiver, she heard Paul's dulcet tones, "Darling, I'm going to be working late tonight. I wonder, would you mind coming to the flat on your own? If I stop to come and collect you, it will curtail our time together!"

41

Consternation registered, "Is everything alright, Paul? If you're really busy, perhaps you would rather leave tonight. Granted I will be disappointed, but when I agreed to marry you, I knew there would be times like this!"

"Bless you, darling. Nothing's wrong. I'm under quite a bit of pressure, yet not enough to abandon our evening entirely!"

Her heart fluttered uncontrollably at the sound of his voice. She gave a contented little chuckle, "I will make us a meal while you finish off, darling. If I come round about seven, it will give me time to prepare something. Don't worry about anything my, love!"

"Debbie, you'll be tired, although I must admit that I do like the sound of that idea. I could nip up and take a couple of steaks from the freezer and after we have eaten ... Debbie, hang up, before my mind wanders too far away from work. Tonight, I will show you no mercy!"

"Promise," she added seductively.

Paul replaced his receiver and allowed his thoughts to drift momentarily. He was deeply aroused by the conversation he had just had with his beloved Debbie. How he loved the woman who had promised to become his wife. How he sensed fear as they waited to tie the knot, he would know no peace until he placed the gold band onto her finger.

He rubbed is forehead and allowed his anger to return. He was infuriated by the call he had received from Eric. He was sickened by the call from Bill Peters and knew he would rather respond to Bill's cry for help, than leave him in the clutches of one conniving, twenty six year old, sex crazed wench.

**

Flushed with eagerness, Debbie arrived at Paul's flat. Her wildest dreams were coming true, she would work in his gorgeous kitchen, just as she had imagined herself. Her feet danced across the polished floor as she prepared the evening meal.

Her heart raced as she heard Paul mounting the stairs. This was how it would be after their marriage, she thought as love engulfed her. Headily, she rushed into his waiting arms, his body telling her everything she could possibly want to know.

After eating hungrily, he lit two cigarettes. His gorgeous eyelashes rested on his cheeks before they revealed the depth of his eyes. "That, my dearest, was fit for a king!"

"To me, Paul, it *was* for a king. I love you!"

His love that evening was richer than ever. Each time he loved her there seemed to be a new delight for them to enjoy. She felt completely uninhibited with him and now understood the exact meaning of turning to him.

As they finally shuddered their way back from their own private paradise, he rolled onto his back, taking her with him. His hand caressed her cheek, "Darling, I'll have to be away for the next month or so. Eric is to open another branch in London. He wants me to go down and sort it out and I will be helping an old mate. I'm dreadfully unhappy about leaving you, but there is no way around it!"

A gasp, "Oh, no, Paul," had left her lips. His hands gripped the sides of her head, pulling her mouth to his. The stab of disappointment was so sharp, it knocked the breath from her. Tears stung her eyes, "Paul, I can't imagine my life without you, in fact it feels as though we have always been together!"

Running his hands over her body, he groaned, "Once Christmas is over, we will have our wedding to look forward to. Debbie, let's set a definite date for February, or sooner. Hell, I want so much for us to be married. I'll ring you daily!"

His voice was almost pleading for her to understand. For the first time she saw uncertainty in her fiancés' eyes. He was desperate to name the day and overwhelmed by the depth of his insecurity, she nuzzled his neck. "Paul, book the wedding, book it as near to Valentine's Day as possible. We have no reason to wait!"

Ignoring the sick knot that had replaced her stomach, she watched Paul dress. His body was so masculine, she wondered how she could live without him. His eyes raised, "Oh, I meant to tell you, there's a very large competition at the Guild Hall. I think it's the first week in December. Anyway, knit something and enter!"

"Just like that," she quipped.

His mind was so quick, he was used to thinking on his head and coming back with quick gimmicks. That was a large part of his job. He chuckled as he acknowledged the banter. "Truly, darling, I think you should try. Ellen told me how you designed patterns for Tony. The first prize is about five hundred quid, plus a contract with a major wool company, to design for two years or something. I have the details for you anyway, and it will certainly keep you out of mischief while I'm away!"

Suddenly, the moon shafted across her body, casting a delicious shadow over it. She looked tantalising as she lay there watching him. Her hair was gloriously tussled, her arms folded behind her head. How easily she had learned to be comfortable with him, he thought to himself.

Her eyes locked his as she rubbed her arms seductively, her voice mocking, "I haven't much time for a master piece, its barely six weeks. Let me think about it, sir, thanks anyway!"

Debbie knew she would miss Paul desperately. She would miss his love and the more she thought about it, the more the urge to knit became an attractive solution. She would have every long, long evening, plus a couple of afternoons when the shop was reasonably quiet.

Hopes were running high in the shop, they all realised if they could just get through the winter, they would run into profit. Nevertheless, when Paul left, she felt inexorable pain embed itself into her heart.

Ironically, Debbie knew better than to give way to the desolation and when her break came, she sat down and studied the rules and regulations for the competition. As she looked through the seemingly unending list of suggestions, her hands began to shake with a strange quiver that she vaguely remembered from three years ago.

43

Her eyes constantly returned to the two piece suit. Yes, it would lend itself to many varied ideas. She took a very delighted Tony with her to buy the yarn, he loved the sea front even when it was deserted. Debbie reasoned that the lashing of the sea, had the same soothing effect on him as it did on her.

He had developed into a real little chatterbox and Debbie loved him dearly. In fact everyone that knew him, loved him. He had the knack of eating his way into everyone's hearts. Debbie busily selected to use a range of blues, from navy to baby blue and make the outfit in her own size. At least it wouldn't be wasted, she thought as she once again asked the friendly shopkeeper to reserve part of her requirements.

Pleated skirts had just come back into fashion, with the new mini style. She decided to use a mock type pleat and realised that if she used the various colours, tapering into the different shades, it would give a rainbow effect. Profound excitement began to stir within her.

Once again, the strange and wonderful ideas poured from her brain, into her hands, almost burning her fingers. At times she was lost in a world far removed, so deep was her concentration. Even as her fingers flew across the needles, she had managed the art of swiftly jotting down each stitch with methodical accuracy, until, finally the skirt was finished and she couldn't have been more delighted. Not only was it very feminine, but exceedingly neat and smart.

With an almost religious regularity, Paul kept his word and 'phoned her each day. Time was passing quicker than she had dared to hope, her longing for him and his love created a yearning inside of her. His voice seemed to sound weary, his need real, "Darling, Debbie, you will meet me at the flat when I return, won't you? I mist you so much, how's the knitting coming along?"

"I'll be waiting for you, my darling, Paul," she assured him, but said nothing of the knitting.

**

Paul felt guilt as he hung up on his beloved Debbie. He knew she missed him as much as he longed for her, but Bill Peters had needed him more right then. Bill was still devastated by his experience with Amanda Morgan.

Although Bill had enjoyed leaving her in the office that day, he was still running scared of her next move. Both men had guffawed when Bill had given Paul the low down, yet both men knew the scorned woman syndrome. Paul wanted to be with Debbie, he also craved being back in his own branch, despite the knowledge that his number one assistant, Vanessa Fairclough, was more than capable of keeping the work flowing.

After supper one evening, Bill had turned to Paul, "How did you manage to skate past the Morgan bitch, Paul? Although I gave her what she was begging for, in no uncertain terms, I don't think I have heard the last of her!"

Anger at Bill's discomfort choked him. Tapping his ash from his cigarette, he stated, "You'd better believe it, Bill. I was lucky to get out. Its bloody ironic that a woman like her can literally terrorise men. Mind you, she is a persistent cow. I even took her by the shoulders and told her, I would never fuck her if she was the only woman left on earth. And I never kid myself that she will always be on the lookout for revenge!"

Paul ran out of breath after speaking with so much emotion. He could feel Bill's misery. Inhaling deeply, he added, "Bill, have you sat down and told your wife what happened?"

"Christ, no," she'd go spare.

Paul spoke with vehemence, "I hate to be a wet blanket, Bill, but until you tell Judy, you are vulnerable. Hell man, you don't need me to tell you that. You've supplied Amanda with a perfect lever to play her ace, she will make sure Judy finds out!"

"I know, Paul. I only came here to please Judy. She will most likely leave me if she finds out. For Gods sake, would you tell Debbie?"

Paul rubbed his chin and spoke wryly, "It would be soddin' hard. But, yes, I'm sure I would. She couldn't take it from someone else, not that she'd take it very well from me. I'm sure she'd be angrier if I didn't tell her. You see, Bill, if a bloke hides something for the best reason on the world, I think women take it as a sign of guilt!"

He breathed a sigh of relief as he thanked the Lord he didn't have to tell her anything like that. Bill was entering a very important time in his life and it was marred by sexual harassment. His worried eyes raised to Paul, "You're right, Paul. If Judy does check with you, I mean, oh, hell, will you confirm about Amanda?"

"Sure, old chap. Just get her told!"

**

Debbie worked as though possessed and watched with an eager pride as the top developed. She had chosen a pretty lace type of stitch, again with a wavy line effect, to introduce the many shades. She had then dressed the neck with a little stand up collar, giving a chic, polished finish.

Excitement surged as she ran to try on the entire ensemble. With utmost care she stepped into the skirt and popped the top over her head. Slipping into her court shoes to emphasise the outfit, she stepped back from the mirror and gasped. The suit not only looked stunning, but felt luxurious and she knew that she would thoroughly enjoy wearing it. Paul would love it, competition or not, she thought happily.

Rushing out of her room, to show her parents, she literally collided with Matthew. "Debbie, that is truly beautiful. I just know you'll win, so ye will," he gulped and hugging her, he escorted her into the living room, his eyes dancing as he paraded her to her family.

She couldn't help noticing the look of pride that passed between them. Matthew ran to get his camera and for the next hour, even Tony joined in the fun, as Matthew put Debbie through a series of model poses. She twisted and turned as he instructed, his camera snapping every angle.

Ellen had radiated happiness as she helped Debbie to put her hair up and then down. Stand up and sit down, until they were all gloriously exhausted.

But they had truly enjoyed the little session and it had come as a welcome respite.

A couple of days later, she re-read the rules, just to reassure herself that all the necessary details were enclosed. She noticed that there was to be an award for the best photographer. And when Matthew presented her with the photographs, her eyes had misted.

They were absolutely beautiful, every stitch had been picked up with precision. The model looked like a true professional, not like her at all. To her further astonishment, she realised that Matthew could earn a rich living from his so called 'hobby'. Turning to him, she gasped, "Matthew, you know that I know, don't you?"

"Know what, Debbie?"

"That you could earn a small fortune with photographs such as these. You have a rare quality that oozes from your work … Would you make me a promise?"

"If I can, me darling," he teased.

"Seriously, Matthew. If you are offered a position, you mustn't allow your loyalty to our family to stand in the way!"

He looked at her, she was so young in years, yet seemed to have the perception of a woman twice her age. His photographs had only shown exactly what he had seen. A beautiful and innocently provocative woman, with a sensually gorgeous body. He could move away, but he had fallen in love with her family. And sadly, he had fallen in love with her. He only had to think of her and become hard, yet as it was she he longed for, no one could solve his problem.

Night after blessed night, he tried to cope with his horny overtures. It wasn't a question of a hurried screw anymore, he had fallen head over heals in love and doubted that anyone could relieve the constant throbbing of his demanding, wayward member.

Seeing the direct look in her rich, brown eyes, he knew she was deeply in love with Paul and he with her. Never would he even try to come between them, even if there were a smattering of a chance.

He realised he couldn't stay, yet knew he couldn't leave. Somehow, he felt right here, basically he couldn't have been happier. From now on though, he would have to be extra careful, she must never know of his feelings for her.

Covering his dreadful confusion with a smile, he choked, "Debbie, no one is going to offer me a job. Honestly, me darlin', I love working here with you all. Fair enough, *you* like my work, but I'm sure they wouldn't pass any sort of professional milestone. However, I do promise, I won't put my loyalty before the fabulous offers that will undoubtedly pour in!"

Chuckling happily, she knew they all had to wait for the dreaded day of judgement to arrive. She folded her entry carefully into tissue, together with the photographs and added, "I didn't say huge and fabulous offers, you damned well know what I meant, Mr. Matthew Ross!"

CHAPTER EIGHT

After completing her mini marathon, Debbie felt intensely restless. There was no doubt in her mind, she would miss that particular part of her life. It had been very hard work, but had allowed her to express her inventive self to the full.

Paul was already a week late in arriving home and it was now nearing the end of November as she realised he felt as miserable as she did. The infernal delay niggled into her heart, she had heard the longing in Paul's voice and had been unable to conceal her disappointment. He was due to ring her later in the day, when she hoped he would be able to announce his arrival the following day.

Although it was bitterly cold, Debbie decided to stroll to their special hill. She felt near to Paul there and even as she sat down with the cold, warmth surged through her. With a sharp shock, she realised that her body needed an urgent fix. Her loins ached with a need that until now, she hadn't been able to account for. A flush covered her as it hit her, she not only wanted Paul, she wanted his naked body next to hers. She needed to feel his hands caressing her, his mouth tormenting hers before moving down to take her hard nipples, to feel his hardness moving within her.

Varying shades of grey made up the vista before her. The dark beauty gave her an air of tranquillity. Just listening to the angry waves lashing the cliffs, seemed to bring peace to the spot she and Paul had made their own. Drawing her knees under her chin, she hugged them, remembering that this was where they had first consummated their love.

It had taken such a short time to fall in love with him. He had proposed to her here and although they wouldn't celebrate their first meeting until next March, it was almost impossible to remember her life without him. Totally lost in thought, she realised that they both saw this spot as their own personal place. A smile crossed her face as she remembered how they had practically missed it. Having found it, they intended to share it with no one and ironically, they had never seen anyone near and no evidence of someone having been there.

A slight movement beside her, made her look up with a start and she was staring into Paul's eyes. Pinching herself to make sure she wasn't dreaming, he was definitely beside her, his arms swiftly encircling her. His breath was hot on her face, "I thought you might be here. I went round to the shop and Ellen said you had gone walking. Oh, my darling, I missed you desperately!"

His hungry lips found hers until she managed to gasp, "Paul, why didn't you tell me you were arriving today?"

For a moment they sat quietly, just savouring being together once again. Taking a box from his pocket, Paul handed it to Debbie, watching eagerly as she opened it. She gasped when she saw the gorgeous heart shaped locket, complete with fine chain. Crushing her to him, he moaned, "A present from London, for my special girl, especially as I missed your birthday!"

Taking his hand to her lips, she kissed the palm. "Darling, Paul, its beautiful. Golly I've missed you," her voice shook with sheer emotion. Their eyes locked and without a word, they jumped up and virtually ran to the flat.

They arrived flushed, hot and breathless from the run. Paul switched on the shower and without further thought, they stripped and stepped under the cascading water. Their torrid bodies clung together in a new found wonder.

Headily, they ran the soap over each other, until shuddering with desire, they ascended to a paradise of sublime love. "I hated us being apart, Debbie. I can't wait for our marriage!"

"Neither can I, Paul. We barely have three months to wait, I'm sure it will fly!"

The following day, Paul had insisted on her trying on her competition outfit. He gave a long, low whistle, "It looks absolutely perfect on you, darling. You know, you could write some knitting tips for the magazine, it would pay fairly well, think about it!"

With a shudder of excitement, she realised she certainly would think about such a proposition. They could all use the money she may be able to earn. Paul also agreed with her about Matthew's work. Taking the photographs over to the light, he smiled, "He is a damned good photographer. From a purely selfish point of view, I'm glad he took them. I'll keep one for myself after the big day."

**

A couple of days later, Debbie and Ellen had gone along to the dress hire shop. It was difficult to know which one of them was the most excited. The young assistant came forward and gave them a courteous smile, "May I help you?"

With total confidence, Ellen explained the situation and type of function. She wanted her daughter to have the latest fashion for the occasion. After sorting through the many pretty materials, they finally found just what they were looking for.

Debbie was helped into a black, chiffon, slim line dress. It was strapless and hugged her generous bust, nipping tightly into her tiny waist and gently flowing over her slender hips. The front of the skirt opened to her knee with a soft, ruffle effect, starting from the opening and going along the bottom and back up to the opening again.

Not only did it look and feel perfect, she felt very sophisticated, in fact her figure had never looked so good. She knew Paul would love it and the locket he had bought for her would be all she would need for the neck. Her gold drop earrings would dangle as her head moved, especially if she had her hair up. And her exquisite engagement ring would complete the whole heady impact.

Her mind finally was at peace. She felt relatively confident about the big occasion, which was just a week after the competition, but her nerves fluttered wildly as she thought about her entry.

The competition was fortunately on the Sunday afternoon. Matthew had offered to stay at home with Tony, but Paul had been so insistent, "Matthew, there is plenty of room in the car, the wheelchair will fit in the back. After all, they are your photo's. We'll all go, won't we Tony?"

Tony was so precious, he would have agreed to whatever was suggested. After a very early lunch, Paul and Matthew loaded the car and they were off.

Although deep in her heart, Debbie didn't think she had a chance of winning, her mind was ticking wildly. Maybe, and it was a big maybe, she could meet someone with the hope of knitting up a few 'exclusive designs'. That would at least help to swell the coffers and her fingers were certainly itchy once more.

Seeing the crowds milling around the Guild Hall, almost made her turn and run back to the safety of the car. There were so many beautiful designs, she felt somehow inadequate, but her entry was already on display and that was that.

There were about a dozen judges, together with a top designer from Hayward's Knitting Company. She was an elegant lady, a little short perhaps, but lovely and slim. She wore a delicious knitted navy suit, with smart suede court shoes. Her make up looked superb under the lights and Debbie felt she would be a rather nice person to meet.

Perhaps she would find time to have a quick chat with her, even ask her for a job. Someone must knit up the patterns for them, why not herself? Yet deep down, she knew she would prefer to design, but beggars can't be choosers, she thought.

The hall was hot and Debbie had taken Tony to the back of the room. He was not used to large crowds and she didn't want anyone falling over his wheelchair. At long last, the time for the announcements were ready to be made. As the organiser made his way over to the microphone, the silence had become almost deafening. There was tension in the air as he spoke, "I have the results in reverse order!"

Huge cheers rang out as the first and second runners up were called. They both received cheques for two hundred and fifty pounds. A restless buzz had begun, everyone now a little impatient for the winner to be acclaimed. Tony was still clapping his little hands, till once again, silence reigned. "The judges were unanimous in their decision for the first prize. The five hundred pounds, plus a contract for two years with Haywood, goes to …!"

Tension was almost claustrophobic, people were shuffling uneasily. A drum roll sounded, the gentleman spoke, "For a tasteful outfit, with an almost simplistic design, the award goes to Miss Debbie Hudson, from Morecambe. Com on up, Debbie!"

She was rooted to the spot. Her whole body broke out in goose bumps as tears blinded her. Paul was guiding her towards the front, her knees turned to jelly and for one dreadful moment, she thought she was going to be sick. Her parents had taken Tony, both had tears in their eyes. Matthew hugged her, "See, Debbie, I told ye, so I did!"

During the tumultuous applause, the organiser had introduced Haywood's representative as Alma Jennings. She had come forward to present the cheque as Debbie finally arrived onto the stage. Alma's hand held hers, as she quickly explained, "Keep hold of the cheque with your other hand, Debbie. The press will need the pictures. Very well done!"

Debbie smiled her gratitude as photographers' flashes almost blinded them. Standing close to Alma, Debbie could see that she was a very attractive middle aged lady. Her hair shone like copper and her hazel eyes were warm and gentle. Her smile was soothing as she said, "Now then, Debbie, would you like to tell us how you will spend the money?"

Blinded by tears and shocked beyond words, Debbie felt the dryness in her mouth. Any traces indicating she possessed a brain seemed to have vanished. The sea of faces before her, resembled a blur of colour. Fighting for control, she stammered, "Thank you. I'm .. not sure .. about the money at the moment. I'm to be .. married in February and part can go towards that. Most of all, I would .. like my parents to have a break, they work so hard. Thank you once again!"

'Great', she thought. Perhaps she should have mentioned buying some yarns. Hearing the crowd clapping and cheering for her, had almost been too much to bear. The whole of her body shook with sheer nerves as Alma whispered, "Come on, Debbie, let's go out back and sign the contract. Your family will be brought through to you!"

Following Alma, somewhat zombie fashion, she heard another blast of applause from inside the hall. Alma was looking at the photographs, "These are excellent, would you like to keep your own photographer?"

Several pinches later, she came to with a jolt. The family had been escorted to the room at the back as they all hugged her and tears streamed down Ellen's face. Tony just carried on clapping, thinking it was the order of the day. He chanted happily, "Debbie won and Matthew won!"

Debbie realised that must have been the reason for the second burst of applause. In spite of her shock, she felt a glow of happiness, to think that Matthew had also won. Suddenly Paul appeared, his arms closing around her. She felt safe again, his smile disarmed her, "Debbie Hudson, I knew you could do it. And you promised in front of all those people to marry me. Hell, it felt so good!"

Alma was at her side, "Is your photographer here, Debbie?" He was and what was more, he was looking through the contract. Obviously the lawyer in him had never died. She ran over to him, his arms gathered her, both of them excited and offering congratulations to each other. He then kissed her with a warmth, slightly unlike a brother. But then, she thought, they were all happy.

After Matthew had signed the contract, he and Debbie had to pose for more photographs and then with a couple of shots of the family.

With a contented sigh, Debbie realised she had come here, with the express purpose of finding some work. Not only had she done so, but also found herself with a very lucrative job, which would enable her to help her parents and pay for her own wedding. She was determined that Jim and Ellen would have a long weekend in Jersey. They had honeymooned there and often spoke of returning one day. That day had finally arrived.

Paul was back at her side, "Let me book the holiday, I can sort out a discount with one of the holiday firms who advertise with us!"

"That's wonderful, Paul, make sure it's a really nice hotel!"

Guilt then flooded her, it had never occurred to her to ask Matthew first. Turning to him, she gasped, "Matthew, please forgive me. I should have asked you first, I never expected to win and the words just fell from my mouth!"

Even as she spoke, she knew he would more than cope. He was elated to be her own personal photographer. Debbie knew then, that Matthew more than belonged in the family. She also knew that she would have her hands more than full with Tony, but she was determined that her parents should go away. Almost as if Paul had read her mind, he said, "I'll come round in the evenings and help with Tony. He'll go to bed for me, won't you, son?"

Tony imparted a wide grin, "Will you read my story, like Debbie does?" His little face was filled with happiness, yet he didn't really understand the reason for all the celebrations. Whatever the reason though, he certainly enjoyed it.

Jim and Ellen had put forward many reasons for not leaving, but Matthew turned and stated, "You may just as well go, so you might, otherwise we'll lock you out!"

With a loving smile, Jim turned to his wife, "Ellen, dear, I think we should give in gracefully. They want to do this for us. I never dreamed of finding someone to help, let alone take over. We really can have a second honeymoon, come on now, dear, say yes!"

Hearing her father talk about a second honeymoon, made Debbie realise yet again, that they were still very much in love. And somehow everything seemed much brighter.

The newspapers carried stories of her success and much to her surprise, the local radio station had asked her to join in with a couple of chat shows. They were to be squeezed in during the week following the dinner dance and before her parents' departure, the weekend after.

Various magazines had contacted her with a view to running the story. Some of them asked for simple designs to run in their later copies. Haywood would be thrilled with the free publicity for their yarns.

Debbie knew only too well that she was going to be under some pressure, but sheer determination would drive her on. The only cloud on her horizon was the dreaded function, she felt a strange foreboding about it. Yet she had to acknowledge, it was a huge step in Paul's career.

CHAPTER NINE

Maralyn Morgan had showered in hr sumptuous bathroom and wrapped a huge white Terry bath towel around her over developed body. She sat down at her dressing table with a view to applying her make up, after all, tonight was her husband's big night.

Gazing into the mirror, she recalled how she had rushed into marriage with Eric, at the age of eighteen and by the time she was nineteen, she had given birth to Amanda. Now at the age of forty five, her skin was still firm and supple, her hair still a pretty blond. Her figure however, had seen fit to go a little astray. Her breasts had always been large, but now they were huge, yet fortunately, had not really begun to droop. Her hips were larger than she preferred, although Eric seemed to like her as she was.

Eric had been a darned good provider and had always been insistent that his wife stay beside him. Never had she been smug enough to think that he had always been faithful, because she knew he had screwed just about every woman he had come into regular contact with.

Sadly though, their daughter had taken after him and Maralyn knew that Amanda would seduce anything in trousers to get what she wanted. Unfortunately, she wanted Paul Howarth and Maralyn knew he didn't want anything to do with her.

Repeatedly, she had argued with Amanda, advising her, "You have beauty, brains and a lovely figure, Amanda. In fact you have everything you want, don't try and ruin Paul's life!"

"I'll get him, Mother, and he won't know what's hit him," promised her wayward daughter, before adding, "He's got himself engaged to some tart in Morecambe, but he sure ain't married yet. He'll see reason," she had giggled.

Dragging herself out of the short reverie, she watched Eric come into the room, still rubbing his hair dry. He was a funny shaped man, somewhat akin to a pear drop on legs, yet he held a vivid attraction towards the opposite sex. Almost instantly, she felt the familiar damp spring between her legs. Eric had always managed to satisfy her needs, that was until .. Never mind that now, she thought, she was prepared to beg him not to embarrass Paul's young lady tonight, in fact not even to discuss business at all.

Feeling his gaze on her, she allowed the towel to fall from her. She knew exactly what she was doing and a tingle of joy shot through her as Eric became instantly erect. He had a funny shaped penis, a little on the short side, but very, very thick and he knew exactly how to use it. When he pumped on top of her, he somehow managed to rub the base of himself along her clitoris, sending her into wild erotic passion and she would come with the speed of light.

Nothing pleased Eric more than a voluptuous woman and his wife was all of that. He locked the door and lay on the satin covered bed, his arms outstretched to receive her body. She was always more than generous to him and it still gave him deep satisfaction to know she enjoyed his body.

His cock jerked in tortured agony as she folded those huge knockers, with the blood red nipples, around it. His hands closed over them and she allowed him to rub himself up and down, not too much though, she wanted to come herself.

Leaning up, she straddled him and ran her breasts, with slow deliberation, over his panting mouth. He responded immediately, sending arrows of fire through her. Her nipples strained into buds so hard, she paused as he suckled unmercifully. Scarcely able to breathe, she gulped, "Eric, promise me something!"

"What?"

"Not to discuss business with Paul tonight!"

His eyes held curiosity as well as lust, "Why the fuck not? Anyway this isn't the time or place," he groaned as she slipped down the bed. He writhed as he found all of his concentration had now landed into the sensations in his hardness. She took it into her mouth, her tongue swirling meaningfully over the angry tip. Before she lost herself entirely, she gasped, "Promise, Eric?"

"Okay, Maz, I promise!"

She raised herself again and quick as a flash, Eric held a breast in one hand and placed the other hand into her red hot furnace. She was deliciously wet and ready and to his joy, she straddled him again and impaled herself firmly onto his cock.

It never ceased to amaze him, this woman of his always knew how to turn him on. Yet he loved to screw about with younger women, especially when they sought promotion. They came to him and offered their greedy little quims and he loved nothing more than virgin territory.

Once they had fully satisfied each other, Eric poured drinks. "That was a wonderful start to the evening Mazza. I can't agree with you about Paul though, we love to live in the lap of luxury and therefore, must keep opening branches," he argued, not unreasonably.

Maralyn shrugged her impatience, "Suit yourself, Eric, but I'll not support any nonsense from you or Amanda, Paul is obviously very much in love with his girl and we must face it, Eric, he doesn't want our daughter!"

As she had spoken, she had kissed the top of his head. He idolised their daughter, they both did, but Eric could see no faults in her. He stood up, "Alright, Maz, but she and Paul do look good together. I mean if she did marry, we could have at least one grandchild. When you and me couldn't have more, I sort of longed for grandchildren, hopefully to carry on the business!"

His voice had shaken with an almost sad surge of emotional longing. An overwhelming lump of guilt landed in her throat. Poor Eric, ever since Amanda turned eighteen, he had longed for her to fall in love and marry. He was almost obsessed with the ideas that he could share with his grandchildren.

For a brief moment, she was tempted to spill her heart and mind, once and for all, but instead, she turned back to the mirror and grimaced at her reflection.

**

Every nerve in Debbie's body tensed as she prepared herself for her evening with Paul. The only bright spot, was the fact that she would stay the night at Paul's flat and return the following morning, dropping her dress off en route.

Her hands shook as she applied her make up. Ellen's eyes danced as she watched her daughter's transformation take place. Debbie's hair had been set into the most sophisticated of styles, with small curls framing her pretty face. The gold earrings really added a touch of true class.

Debbie's heart raced with anticipation, mingled with a large helping of fear. Matthew had come to vet her, drawing his breath in slowly, "You look beautiful, Debbie. Paul is a lucky chap. Have a super time, me darling," he added with swiftness, before he dashed once more to his room.

Paul looked dashing in his evening suit and as they entered the Guild Hall, they felt almost regal, especially after the happy memories of the previous week. The vestibule had now taken on a majestic décor. Rich red carpeting and gold braided drapes led into a lavish ballroom.

Their names were announced and they were inside. Debbie just stared at the beautifully dressed tables, the white damask seemed to sparkle under the lights. There was a long 'top' table, where she learned with horror, that was where they would be sitting.

Palpitations fluttered nervously into her throat. Already, she wished they could turn and run. Paul had taken a couple of glasses from the many trays that the waitresses carried. His eyes met hers and fleetingly, she felt safe again.

As if from nowhere, a dapper little man stopped before them. "Oh, there you are, Paul. And you must be Miss um," he gushed, scarcely looking at Debbie. Paul's blue eyes narrowed, "Eric, I would like to present my fiancé, Debbie Hudson, Debbie, this is Eric Morgan!"

Eric had taken her hand and bent down to kiss it as he said, "You are every bit as lovely as Paul tells us. It is a real pleasure to meet you!"

Why had she picked up the feeling that he meant nothing of that sentence? He was obviously a born sycophant, short and portly. His dark hair was greased well back from his forehead. His smile began and ended around his over generous mouth.

Lighting a huge Havana cigar, he began to speak to Paul as though Debbie was absent. "Paul, we're hoping to open a branch in New York next year. I might well need you to set it up, Amanda would like to run the branch, what d'you think?"

"Eric, that's entirely up to you. Personally, I don't think Amanda could handle the situation. She would have to change her attitude to members of staff. And if she gets fed up, it would cost you the earth!"

Paul's voice sounded harsh, even cold. It was obvious he felt extremely uncomfortable as he tried desperately to include Debbie into the conversation.

Eric's wife then joined them. She wore a low cut expensive dress, leaving quite a lot of her hanging out. Her cigarette was placed into the end of a long, beautifully decorated holder.

Her smile was warm as she greeted Debbie, yet sadness seemed to lurk in her direct eyes. Glowering at her husband, she spoke with sarcasm, "I thought we weren't discussing business tonight!"

"But, darling, we must put Paul in the picture. You know how much this means to Amanda," he gushed in her direction, without actually looking at her. Paul shifted about with unaccustomed embarrassment, which in turn unsettled Debbie.

Amanda now walked towards them, making sure that everyone saw her. She looked delightful with her blond hair closely cropped and gleaming. Her flawless skin was expertly made up, her sultry mouth had a definite pout, making her look even more seductive. Her figure was model like and she knew it.

The gold of her perfect, tunic style, almost transparent dress, just about matched her hair. Her dainty feet were covered with shoes, that must have cost a fortune. The mass of jewellery she wore, tinkled attractively as she moved.

Debbie found her confidence rapidly deserting her. Amanda drooled, "Hi, Paul darling, how are you? What do you think of the New York idea?" She had cleverly wound her body around Paul and slipped her arm around Eric. Paul's voice was curt and clipped, "I would like you to me my fiancé, Debbie Hudson!"

Stepping forward with her hand outstretched, Debbie found Amanda totally ignored it. Instead, she shot a somewhat sympathetic look in her direction and nodded, "Hi!"

Nausea swept Debbie as she noticed that Amanda was still draped around Paul. Women seemed to look at her with envy, men looked at her with lust. Paul looked at her with utter distaste. The pout deepened as she whined, "Daddy, darling, tell me I can run the New York branch, pleeeese!"

Eric grinned, "You must try and persuade Paul," he soothed. Placing both arms around Paul, she whimpered, "Pretty please, Paul. Can we do this together?"

Never had Debbie seen such a blatant display of sexual flaunting. She knew that Amanda wanted Paul and having looked Debbie over, felt she was in with a definite chance.

Paul was flushed with embarrassment as he tried to untangle himself and pull Debbie towards him. Amanda then turned to her, "You won that knitting thing, didn't you? I couldn't be bothered messing with anything so petty!"

Her words were delivered with deliberate spite. Paul's anger was rising as he stated, "Yes, Debbie did win, Amanda. She is a very talented young lady!"

His fists had clenched and for a dreadful moment, Debbie thought he would smack the smug grin from Amanda's face. To her intense displeasure, Debbie found Eric by her side, "I think the world of Paul. He's a bloody hard worker. I think he would go down well in New York. Although I don't suppose that you would want him to go, would you, Debbie?"

Confusion accompanied the angry flush that crept over her, she swiftly realised what Eric was up to and desperately wanted to leave and go home. But the dinner gong had sounded, cutting off further thoughts of retreat. Amanda still clutched Paul's arm as they walked to the table. Much to her dismay, she had to admit, they looked an attractive couple.

Paul turned to take her arm and Debbie realised that he knew full well that Amanda was his for the asking. He was finding it hard to conceal his total dislike and utter shame of such a display.

To her further horror, Debbie found that Amanda sat to the right of Eric, next to Paul and then herself. She could feel Paul's humiliation and knew full well, that the New York trip had come as a shock to him.

Another shock loomed, she knew that Paul couldn't afford to leave the magazine, not for a while anyway. Eric was not only affluent, but very influential and in a position to make or break anyone that even thought of crossing him. She felt a sudden stab of fear, Amanda wanted Paul, Eric wanted her to have Paul as he also totally excluded Debbie from the conversation.

Bill Peters was seated beside Debbie, with his attractive wife beside him. He took in the scene with loathing. He owed Paul so much, he had listened to his advice, taken it and although Judy had justifiably fumed, they were now ecstatically happy.

He turned to Debbie and said, "Sickening, isn't it? She's a real bitch. Sorry, my name's Bill Peters. I run the London branch, Paul helped me to get off to a flying start. He hated being away from you, but do watch your back with precious Amanda. She let's nothing and no one stand in her way!"

Flashing him a grateful smile and moved beyond words, by his bitterness, her reply was cut off. Eric stood up to make a speech, or rather, deliver an epistle. He went on and on about New York and Maralyn's chest rose and fell with annoyance. Paul took Debbie's hand, squeezing it reassuringly.

Amanda had drunk far more than was necessary and giggled stupidly. Seeing Paul's hand gripping Debbie, she pretended to pout and pulled his other arm around her. Anger finally sparked in Debbie, she wanted to leave and go home, before she really did lash out. Yet she was determined not to let Paul down.

After what felt like an eternity, she found herself on the dance floor. Paul's arms held her tightly, his breath hot on her forehead, sent a heady excitement through her. "Darling, Debbie, I am deeply sorry. I had no idea of any of this taking place. We will make some excuse to get away shortly, is that alright with you, pet?"

His gorgeous blue eyes smouldered with passion and anger as they locked hers. Her heart raced with love for him, yet she could feel the knife in her back. Amanda was watching them, her face riddled with spite.

Paul's mouth brushed hers as her eyes lifted lovingly to him. "Yes, Paul, we will leave as soon as you feel the time is right. Golly, darling, I'm glad I'm not in this line of work!"

They didn't have to look far to find Eric. He was waiting for them with Amanda draped around him. He guffawed, "Paul, old chap, I need you to come over to our place for the weekend, yes a weekend in February, let's see now!"

He had taken his diary out and begun shuffling through the pages. Placing his arm tighter around Debbie's waist, Paul scowled, "Well, I'm getting married in February, Eric, as you well know. Providing it doesn't clash with that, I can come over, but not to stay!"

"It would take the whole weekend, Paul. Let me see now!"

Almost as though Paul hadn't spoken, he carried on looking through his diary. Amanda sulked, "You can't get married yet, Paul, it'll ruin your career!"

Her look of contempt landed squarely onto Debbie's shoulders as Eric had found a clear weekend. An angry Paul now responded, "If I stay over, I would bring Debbie along and that is my final word on the subject!"

It was more than obvious that he was becoming irate, but Eric still added, "It will be boring for Debbie. We will be discussing business and she would be better off at home!"

Seeing the objection spring to Paul's lips, like a fool, she gasped, "Don't worry, Paul. I'll have plenty to keep me busy!"

"Oh, yes, your little bakery, how quaint," the steel was naked and cutting from Amanda.

For another dreadful moment, Debbie thought Paul would smack her face, his dreamy eyes now smouldered with anger. After bidding them a frosty goodnight, he took her arm and led her towards the exit.

Amanda's eyes narrowed with fury as she vowed to take Paul from little Miss Innocent. Once he felt her own body naked next to his, he would jolly well melt.

On their way out, they found many people only too willing to shake hands with Paul and show Debbie some sincerity. Paul introduced her to Vanessa, who was virtually his right arm at the Morecambe branch.

Vanessa was a young widow and devoted to her work. Her smile was rich with warmth as she said, "Don't take any notice of Amanda, a darned good spanking would do wonders for her. It is lovely to meet you, Debbie, although we feel we already know you. Paul has told us so much about you. Congratulations on winning the competition!"

"Thank you, Vanessa, I have also heard how very valuable you are to Paul. At least I feel I have one friend inside of 'Ventura'.

Watching Debbie and Paul leave, Vanessa's heart went out to Debbie. Yet only she, Vanessa knew, the despair that must be choking Maralyn. Unobtrusively, she made her way into the cloakroom, to suggest that she and Maralyn met for tea the following afternoon.

CHAPTER TEN

Paul's humiliation spilled over as they arrived into the car park. Drawing in his breath, he fumed, "When we have our children, they will not be spoiled. I would be ashamed to admit that I had fathered a bitch like Amanda!"

The whites of his knuckles gleamed on the steering wheel, giving him away. He was so downright angry, Debbie felt herself giggle at his total indignation. Snuggling closely to him, she whispered, "I like the sound of that, darling!"

"The sound of what?"

"When we have our children. Honestly, Paul, I give you my word they won't be spoiled!"

Paul found himself driving with a new eagerness. How very simplistic she was. Most women would have given Amanda the mouthful she deserved, and although he knew Debbie had been at boiling point, she had remained cool for his sake. Just feeling her young body pressed into him sent his manhood raging. He had noticed with pride, the way heads had turned in her direction. She was beautiful indeed and totally poised.

He had found a knot in his own stomach. The things he had suspected and dreaded had come true. Amanda wanted him, Eric wanted her to have him. Never did he kid himself it was for love, just a case of what Amanda wants, Amanda gets.

Glancing down at Debbie, he marvelled as he knew only too well, that without a word being uttered, she also knew. And bless her beloved heart, she had not sought answers to the questions that must be bobbing around in her mind.

With crystal clarity, he realised they must talk. First of all though, he needed to hold her in his arms and kiss that sensual mouth. Leading her into the flat he did just that, feeling his blood turn to fire as it coursed through his veins. He wanted her desperately, but first they must talk.

Fighting to control his passion, he eased her away from him. With slow deliberation, he poured them both a drink and lit two cigarettes. Walking over to the window, with her beside him, they both seemed to be soothed by the lashing of the angry sea.

Inhaling deeply, he gulped, "Hell, Debbie, I can't tell you how bloody sorry I am about this evening. We do need to talk!"

"About Amanda's desire for you? Paul, we don't need to talk my love. I know you love me and indeed, I feel sympathy for Amanda, loving you and not being able to have you!"

She had broken into his sentence, amazing him with her quick perception. Her closeness intoxicated him, her understanding of the situation rocked him. Would she ever know the sheer magnetism she possessed?

His voice was flat as he swallowed his drink with haste, "Debbie, Amanda has made several attempts to seduce me. Tonight though, I did sense real danger. Its not a question of her loving me, she is just obsessed with wanting to own me. After all, its more or less a condition for promotion. You know the sort of thing, men have to swallow their pride, principles, you name it as she sets out to screw them. She nearly destroyed Bill's life. He was worried sick when I was in London with him!"

He thumped his palm with his fist as her tormented question fell from her lips, "Oh, no, Paul. Does his wife know?"

Taking a deep drag of his cigarette, he looked moodily over at the sea. "Bill and Judy are fine now, darling. But, I mean, can't you see, Debbie, it would be wrong for me to stay over a weekend with them. Amanda is quite capable of making something out of nothing. Before you ask, I never gave in to her. As Eric's blue eyed boy, he didn't want to lose me at the time and promoted me over her head. That very fact will make her more dangerous!"

The sea was angry. Paul was angry and Debbie was certainly angry as she gasped, "Stop worrying, darling. It must be hell for you having all this on your shoulders. Sadly, Eric also wants you for his daughter and I can't blame him for that. But we will practically be married when you go!"

"Do you think that will bother Amanda? Christ, Debbie, Bill was married and still had to screw the bitch!"

Debbie was shocked by the frustration in him, she could feel his body shake as worry etched his face. Her heart held his worry, "Paul, I wonder .. Could we start our own magazine? You have the know how, Vanessa may agree to work with you and with Matthew's photography, perhaps there is a way!"

Fighting the urge to crush her to him, he lit a further cigarette and paced restlessly, "We could do all of that, darling, but Eric would block it before it even lifted from the ground. We just haven't enough capital to fight him, not yet anyway. I feel like resigning instantly. It would be a struggle for a while, but I will not go to New York with Amanda!"

"Let's not think of them for a while, darling. I love and trust you and we will find a way!"

As she had reassured him, she had slipped carefully from her dress and eased his jacket from him. Never before had she been instigator, always the eager recipient. This was something he had never anticipated. Her misty eyes met his as he gathered her to him. With a heavy gulp, he placed her onto the bed and allowed his eyes and hands to roam her body, removing the last vestige of clothing from her. He felt himself slipping, sliding and spiralling as she dropped him just this side of paradise.

**

Ellen and Jim had left for Jersey. Debbie had received her first assignment and. realised that she was going to be under some pressure. Mercifully, determination was her inspired companion as she absorbed the task. Haywood had just developed a new cotton yarn and her job was to produce a booklet for the whole family, using the new yarns. She would have to knit each garment and be very careful to record the details of the patterns.

Once everything was completed, Matthew would be able to photograph the various designs. The whole lot would then be presented to the printers and it would all have to be ready by the end of January, in time for Easter.

Fortunately Debbie had not had much time to think about the dreadful evening at the Guild Hall. She had truly had so many things on her mind and been called into the radio station.

At first she had been horrified when placed into a chair and proffered a set of head 'phones. Her mind boggled as she watched the presenter popping switches up and down. Having introduced Debbie, she found herself answering questions from the general public. Her nerves seemed to vanish as she became quite relaxed with the many eager questions. Time had just seemed to zip along.

Sometimes it felt almost unreal as there had been so much coverage of her success, that all of a sudden, everyone wanted to offer money. Even the shop trade had increased, as not only did the regular customers come in to congratulate her, but many people called in just to meet her. At long last, it seemed that life was well and truly on the up for them all.

**

Debbie had not realised just how busy they would be and already missed her parents. She was literally rushed off of her feet, what with the shop, Tony and trying to sort out her assignments. The evenings were great though, Paul came round to put Tony to bed and she would smile to herself, he would make a wonderful father.

Matthew was truly hooked with her work, sometimes he would sit and write down the details for her, which saved her having to keep stopping. He never ceased to be drawn to her long, nimble fingers as they deftly handled the needles. He could almost see her brain racing as she turned threads of yarn into items of beauty.

Debbie worried about him as he seemed never to want to go out and one evening, as they waited for Paul, she turned to him,

"Matthew, do you think you will ever find a nice girl to marry? You never seem to go out and it worries me!"

Giving her a direct look, his Irish brogue was rich, "I wouldn't go through that pain again. I can't trust women, unless of course it just happened to be yourself!"

Picking up a cushion, he threw it in her direction, both of them chuckling. They were still laughing when she warned, "You should learn to trust again. As you said, you trust me and there are plenty of women like me around!"

"That's where you're totally wrong, me darling!"

With a touch of sadness, she added, "You should just wait and see, you'll find someone worthy of you. Anyway, you have always said that you wanted a large family. Even you can't do that alone!"

A wistful look had crossed his face, "I would love lots of children, but it would have to be a special sort of woman to want that. No, Debbie, I'm happy as I am!"

Matthew absolutely loved being around her. She would never know what she was doing to his heart. Everyday he felt his love for her deepen and wished he could hate Paul, but he knew that Paul adored her and *was* worthy of her love. He was besotted to the point of desperation with her and would swing for anyone who managed to hurt her.

For some unknown reason that evening, the three of them had all moved to sit at the table. Matthew offered his cigarettes round as he spoke, "I think we should try and think of a way to relieve some of the pressure from the business. Debbie is going to be kept busy with her work and Jim and Ellen have to work far too hard. Any bright ideas?"

Debbie knew he was right. Although Tony was a dear little fellow, he was also a real handful and her parents did need to take more of a back seat. Knowing they would never give up the shop entirely, she had visions of them finding a little bungalow. They could live there and cut their hours down.

Paul was deep in thought and added, "They are far too young to think about retiring, but they do need some help. Matthew, are you intending to stay put? If you are, perhaps you could buy into the partnership. They could then take on a trainee baker and manageress for the shop!"

After pausing to pour them all further coffee, he continued, "If we did that, it would leave them free to come in a little later, just to oversee and sort out anything special. It they could find somewhere to live, Ellen could even bake cakes at home!"

His mood still pensive, he went on, "Mind you, we would have to put it to them carefully. They might suspect that we all think they can't manage!"

Debbie's eyes had widened like saucers. She knew this made so much sense, also she found that she had begun to dread Matthew moving on. Even if he did have a contract to photograph her work, he could still just pop in and do that. She realised, with somewhat of a shock that life wouldn't be the same without Matthew.

He rose to *his* feet, pacing up and down, deep in thought. His honest eyes were troubled, "Honestly, Paul, that's almost what I was thinkin', yet felt it wasn't my place to mention it. I have no plans to move on and I could afford to buy in. I think we should talk to them, what do you think, Debbie?"

She was still breathing sighs of relief, knowing that Matthew wouldn't be moving on. Her voice trembled, "I do agree with you both, but Mum and Dad would have to live here for a while. They could cut their hours down, if my work continues to be lucrative, I might be able to think of helping them with a deposit for a home!"

Shudders of excitement attacked her spine. Life could be so much easier, provided of course, that she could continue to work successfully. In spite of herself, she had to state, "Matthew, you do realise that if we don't take off properly, you might lose some of your investment. Although we do have the shop to fall back on!"

With complete confidence, he grinned, "You will be *very* successful. And if you are, I will be too. I have no qualms whatsoever. And as you say,

Debbie, should it all go wrong, we will be the same as we are now, so stop worrying!"

CHAPTER ELEVEN

Monday teatime Paul had drive to the airport to collect Debbie's parents. They looked radiant, relaxed and almost indecently youthful as she ran out to greet them. They had thoroughly enjoyed every moment of their second honeymoon.

Debbie had prepared a hotpot for supper and Tony's eyes danced with the presents from his parents. Jim smiled, "Well, it appears we haven't been missed, Ellen!"

His eyes beamed with mischief as they gazed on his wife. Debbie shivered, it seemed light years ago since she had seen that look of contentment. Once everything was washed up and Tony had been settled for the night, two very bewildered people were seated at the table.

Before anyone could ask questions, Paul interjected, "Nothing's wrong at all. In fact the three of us have been chewing ideas over!"

Debbie watched the various expressions cross her parents' faces. Paul and Matthew had worked out details to present before them. Even to herself, the idea sounded heaven sent and Jim leaned forward, "I think the extra capital would enable us to do just that and this is a good time of year to train someone, before the holiday rush!"

Debbie could see that her father was choked to think how much had been discussed. After all, they had an inbuilt, although not practising solicitor in Matthew, not to mention an accountant in Jim.

An ambiance rich with love filled the room. The room that resembled a board room, with a very important meeting taking place. Suddenly Paul spoke, "I'll be able to run a feature on the shop in our January issue. It can run alongside the article I've done on Debbie and Matthew!"

Giving him a playful kick, she chuckled, "You never told us that you were running a feature on us!"

He also chuckled, "It was to be a surprise, darling, but we all have our futures at stake here!"

Tears misted her eyes. This surely had been a sensational climax to her parents' unexpected holiday. Happiness seeped from them as they knew, at long last, they could begin to take life just that little bit easier.

**

Christmas that year had been fun and quiet. Paul had joined them and although they had all promised not to buy presents, they had all made sure that Tony had plenty and watched as his eyes shone with sheer delight.

Ringing in the new year of nineteen seventy, they had all toasted, 'new decade, new joys and new hopes for the future'. Peace and nostalgia filled the home and it was perhaps one of the happiest times they had all enjoyed, with Tony a leading light in how little it takes to please.

Jim and Matthew had arranged to see a couple of young men, with a view to training someone. Ellen would be able to cope with the shop, enabling

Debbie to get on with her work. She was now longing for her wedding day, knowing she needed to be with Paul. Somehow it seemed to inspire her mind and the ideas would flow.

Debbie's designs and Matthew's photographs had been received with an abundance of enthusiasm. To her delight they had been sent off a full week before the deadline. Alma's voice bubbled with excitement, "Debbie, we are over the moon and the first week in March, there is a designers' competition in Paris. We would like you and Matthew to represent us. It'll mean another design, Debbie, will you do it?"

She became transfixed as Alma continued, "All expenses will naturally be paid and I will be joining you. We'll book a large suite in the hotel as we will entertain the odd client!"

Almost too shocked to speak, Debbie realised that this would be very lucrative indeed. Her voice was barely a whisper, "What about Paul? He'll be my husband, I'll have to ask him, Alma!"

A fleeting glance of herself in Paris with Paul somehow felt good. Alma imparted a warm laugh, "Of course Paul can come along if he can take the time off. I'll speak to you again of course, but I just wanted you to know, how absolutely thrilled we are with your work!"

The line went dead, yet she clung to the receiver. Her whole being shook, her mind rapidly thinking about the design she would try. Tears ran down her cheeks, they were tears of gratitude, she knew Paul would be elated, but it would coincide with their honeymoon, or part of it. Yet, somehow she felt he wouldn't mind sharing, especially as it meant success.

Her mind was racing, thinking that perhaps they could all end up working together and freeing Paul from Eric. "Debbie, what's wrong?"

Matthew's concerned voice had startled her. He was at her side, taking the receiver from her. His arm had instinctively gone around her shoulders. Her tear stained face turned to him as she poured out their success.

To say that he was pleased, would have been the understatement of the decade. He hugged her to him and then remembered what he was doing, hell he had nearly kissed the sensual, trembling lips. Gripping her hand, his voice filled with emotion, "Come on, let's tell your parents!"

She had aroused him so deeply that he could barely think straight, but realised there was no escape this time and gently led her in to break the news.

After the first burst of euphoria had died down, Matthew turned to Jim, "Perhaps we had better take on both of the lads to train. There's no knowing where all this will end, what do you think, Jim?"

Jim looked at his daughter, he couldn't and didn't even want to try to hide the pride her felt for her. How he loved her and she had done so much for them. One day he could tell her just how important that holiday had been for him and her mother. It had taken their minds off what had to be faced, yet it would happen all too soon and a shudder ran through him.

Taking her into his arms, they were joined by a tearful Ellen, both of them reaching out to draw her into the little circle. His heart happy, though heavy, he gulped, "I think we should also take on a young girl to help while Debbie is away!"

Debbie had decided against ringing Paul, she wanted to see his reaction for herself. In the safety of his strong arms, she told him. His kisses smothered her until he lifted his head and feigned a look of horror, "Do you mean that I have to share my honeymoon with an entourage?"

She knew he didn't mind as they hugged each other. This time though, the news had been broken to the media and again a series of interviews were booked. There was also an appearance of television, which she had to admit terrified her. One worry she didn't have, was what could she wear? She would simply wear something from her own collection.

The media had built up on her humble roots and this had worried her, but Ellen had assured her that there was nothing to worry about. She had started from nothing and worked hard and there was certainly no shame in the fact. At the moment, this Lancashire Lassie could do no wrong.

Debbie knew Paul was dreading his visit to Eric's home and wished with all her heart that they could have been able to afford to bring him into this new world that began to surround them. He would be a wonderful P.R. man, but as yet, she was barely underway herself. He seemed to be obsessed with a dread of the visit and she began to feel some of his dreadful apprehension.

Her arms looped around his neck, "Darling, Paul, don't worry, I love you too much to think you would touch Amanda. I know what she's like, remember? Let's go to our hill, I feel special there!"

They walked slowly, the wind blowing round and through them. Neither of them felt cold, just extraordinarily happy. There was grey everywhere, yet it didn't take any of the beauty away. Huddled closely, they watched the waves running in to lash the cliffs below. The fishing boats were bobbing about, almost angrily, thrilling and soothing them.

Debbie realised she would love to visit other countries, but for her, she was proud to be British. She was also proud to be a Lancashire Lass. Above all, she didn't think that the vista before them could be matched by anything overseas, grey or otherwise.

**

The publicity campaign was quite fun as the television cameras had been inside and outside of the shop. Every member of the crew had fallen in love with Tony, even allowing him to take a couple of shots with their costly equipment. Debbie began to feel exhausted as the shop had now become extremely busy, with more and more people flocking in to get onto television.

Her own personal appearance had gone well, indeed the cameras had seemed to flirt with her, drawing her into an almost full blown affair. Deep down though, she knew they would all be happy to get back to normal. Somehow she wondered what normal really was as each 'phone call brought some new proposition.

To her delight, Paul seemed to want her love more and more. Night after night they would return to the flat and glory in the gift of bodies. Although he tried hard to conceal it, she knew that he was near to despair as the dreaded weekend loomed.

She worried about the disturbances in her man. They had discussed that she keep her maiden name after marriage and she realised with somewhat of a jolt, that every article had spoke of Debbie Hudson and photographer, Matthew Ross.

Somehow, she knew that once she and Paul were married, they would both feel less restless and move permanently into the flat. They would then be off to Paris for their honeymoon, albeit a shared experience. Vanessa was taking over for Paul and life was developing with them all filled with inspired urges.

Debbie was very unsettled over the following few days and sleeping had been filled with nightmares. She was awakened suddenly from a fog like haze, a clammy sweat covered her body. There is was again, a feeble voice calling her name.

Swiftly, her mind came conscious. It was Tony, jumping from the bed she rushed over to him and stared in horror as he fought desperately for breath. She clutched him to her and called Jim. He took one look at him and called an ambulance. By the time it arrived, they were all up.

Fear clutched her heart as she dressed with haste. The dear little chap was hot and feverish. Ellen was in tears as she sat woodenly with them in the ambulance. Tony was being given oxygen to help him breathe. It was a tragic, horrendous sight. He had never hurt anyone, he was just a gorgeous little boy that asked for nothing in life, nothing except love.

Debbie found herself praying as a pressure so heavy, seemed to land into her chest. Upon the arrival at the hospital, he was diagnosed with acute pneumonia and instantly placed into an oxygen tent. A week later, there was still no improvement and they thanked God that they had taken on the extra help in the shop. Also for the fact they could afford to do so.

Her parents had practically lived at the hospital. Their eyes were haunted as they felt for their little one. Paul held her, "Debbie, darling, I'll tell Eric that I can't go for the bloody weekend. Christ, I couldn't think straight, my mind would be here with you, your family and dear little Tony," his voice wavered with sheer emotion.

There was no doubting the unbearable worry in him. He had come to love Tony as much as they all did. Matthew was almost beside himself as he bravely carried on in the bakery, with the trainees in tow.

Debbie worked just as hard, probably with a view to trying to ease her own hurt. The customers had queued many times over, "'ows little fella, chuck" That was the constant enquiry. The sincerity was overwhelming, and all Debbie could answer was a constant, "No change, but thank's!"

Helplessness hung around like a bad smell. Matthew understood Paul better than Debbie as he told her adamantly, "I wouldn't insist on Paul leaving at the moment, Debbie, he feels as hellish as I do!"

Matthew had spoken to them prior to their visit to the hospital and Debbie felt at odds with the whole blasted world. Her heavy eyes lifted to them both,

"I think Paul should go and get it over with. There is nothing to do here and Eric will only try and throw a curtain of gloom over our wedding. You go ahead, Paul. Tony will be alright, I feel sure he will!"

Little could she have realised that she would live to regret both of those sentences. On the Friday evening, the three of them had gone to the hospital to join her parents. They were all praying for him to regain consciousness, when to their horror his little life slipped away.

Gutted beyond belief, Paul and Matthew had both broken down. Ellen looked ill again and Jim sat in stunned silence. Debbie just shook with stark misery. She loved him so dearly and now felt the urge to run as fast as she could. Where she was going to, she hadn't a clue. But she felt if she ran fast enough, it would all go away.

Paul held her to him, not wanting her to run. Tenderly he whispered, "Darling, no matter where you run to, it will still be there. Please, dearest, try and calm down!"

His voice shook as much as his body and the dreadful truth began to seep into her addled brain. Matthew looked ill as they all took her parents home. She knew Paul didn't want to go away, but somehow she felt it was best to get it over and done with once and for all.

Paul took her into his arms and choked, "Darling, we will have to postpone the wedding. It would be too harsh on everyone, especially your parents. What do you think?"

There was no question about it, Paul was right. It would virtually mean the wedding taking place at the same time as the funeral. She loved him even more for his depth of understanding. "Paul, darling, we will sort it all out after the funeral. I can't think straight at the moment. I never, ever, gave a thought to Tony dying."

Sobs had torn from her, until finally he was able to kiss her with tenderness. Yet, at her insistence, he was gone. There was so much grief and they didn't have a clue as to how to begin and placate each other.

Never had she missed Paul so much. There had been so much to sort out, culminating in them all having a funeral to attend. For the first time in her life, Debbie experienced bitterness. Oh, she realised she must rid herself of the feeling, but Tony had loved his little life and just when she could have done so much for him, he had been taken.

He had behaved so very bravely and now, he would never benefit from anything she may have been able to do for him. Tragically, she felt her own life falling apart.

CHAPTER TWELVE.

Paul Howarth had never detested an evening so much. Maralyn had been filled with compassion for him, his fiancé and the tragic loss of her little brother. Eric had gone on like a never ending ticking clock. Amanda was much the same, almost as though they had rehearsed the double act of submerging him with pressure.

As he sipped his coffee in the tasteful lounge, a coffee that had almost been forced upon him instead of the inevitable nightcap, he felt the start of a sickly headache. A peculiar taste filled his mouth, making him sip frantically at the coffee, which also seemed to taste bitter. He cursed himself for not bringing his car, he could have left, no matter how late, but as the day had dragged on, he was so tired, a cab was the best option.

He had been escorted to his room by one of the servants, and with high hopes of not staying overnight, he hadn't even begun to unpack his small overnight case. But there was no doubt about it, he felt distinctly ill and loosened his tie.

Maralyn noticed his pallor, her mind immediately suspicious. Narrowing her eyes, she suggested, "Paul, you look bushed, how about an early night? You have discussed business all day and evening. I also know how saddened you are with the bereavement!"

Standing up rather precariously, Paul acknowledged the sincerity in Maralyn's words and swiftly excused himself. Upon reaching the bedroom, he realised he could see two of everything and a clammy sweat covered his body. Hell, he felt ill and began to rip his clothing from himself. The floor seemed to come up and meet him as he staggered, fell onto the bed at the same time as blackness enveloped him.

**

Amanda waited until everyone had gone to bed and smiled malevolently. She had waited for years to gaze on Paul Howarth's body, excited anticipation was near to choking her. There was no need to hurry, because she had all the time in the world. The slow movement sent erotic shudders through her. Gathering a handful of long silk and chiffon scarves, she crept to the room where Paul lay sleeping. Surges of lust charged through her as her eyes fell onto the unconscious frame. Christ, he was more gorgeous than she had imagined.

With the stealth of a panther, she took each wrist and tied them securely to the bedposts. Her heart beat fast as she took his ankles and tied them to the posts at the foot of the bed. He had not even stirred and now she gazed on his naked, spread eagled body and liquid fire burned in her passage.

Her eyes became transfixed on his flaccid penis, his golden pubic hair, his hair coated balls. She licked her lips as she imagined his cock rising up and dancing before she gave him the fucking, she had all but begged him for.

Before disappearing to prepare herself, she looked down on his youthful face. His lips were slightly parted sending a further infusion of heat through her loins. Before she could check herself, she moulded her mouth to his, knowing there would be no response, but she yearned for the taste of him. He would keep she promised herself, he would kiss her when he finally wakened and that would be in about one hour.

Pathos raged as Amanda bathed in the most expensive oils. Feverishly, she brushed her golden crop of hair and slipped into her translucent negligee. She gave a petulant pout into the mirror and understood why men found her so darned attractive. That was other men, but never, ever Paul.

Her breathing constricted as she re-entered Paul's room. Again she gasped at the sight of him. He was beginning to stir and she knew he would be more than 'mean' for a while. He would have a king sized headache, from the sleeping draught she had slipped into his coffee. A groan came from the bed, a husky, "What the …!"

**

Paul struggled to open his eyes. For a moment horror filled him, he had become paralysed. Moving his head gingerly, his disorientation soon vanished. He was tied hand and foot and a frothy cobweb of pink appeared before him. Raising his eyelids painfully, Amanda smiled down on him with a malicious smugness. "What the fuck happened?" He growled with anger. "I s'pose you think this funny. Untie me before I shout the whole house awake!"

"Shout, Paul, but you should dress first," she smirked.

Fury engulfed him as he realised the full impact of what had happened to him. He would try and appeal to Amanda's better nature, although that was a stupid idea, she didn't have one. His head banged as her hands ran over his chest. In spite of his anger he fought to control his temper, "Amanda, you win, you've had your fun, now please, untie me!"

Not yet, Paul. Not until I have what I want!"

"What's that?"

"A wonderful screw!"

"Never!"

"Tough, and you're in no position to chuck orders around!"

Smiling openly, she climbed onto the bed and knelt beside him. Very slowly, she allowed her negligee to slip from her. Paul couldn't help the gulp he swallowed. She did have a perfect body, her breasts were small with hugely engorged honey tipped nipples. She could have any man, why, oh, why, did she have to pick on him?

He closed his eyes against her, he was damned if he would watch her antics, she would soon get tired of playing to an audience that wasn't captive. An excruciating pain shot from his nose, making his head bang anew, Amanda had not only pulled, but twisted his nose. "Don't try to be more insulting than you are, Paul," she added caustically.

His eyes watered as he tried in vain to keep them open. Amanda wiped them with a tissue and then took her hands to her mouth and wet each middle finger. Like a work of art she allowed her hands to cover her breasts, running the wet fingers over and around her nipples. Without warning, she leaned and dragged her breasts over his mouth. At the same time she threw her legs over his body and sat on his abdomen. He clamped his mouth and allowed his anger to surface. "Get out, Amanda, for God's sake get out of here!"

"Open your mouth, Paul?"

"No!"

With amazing agility, she leaned towards the bedside table, for a wild moment Paul breathed a sigh of relief, she was obviously becoming browned off. How far wrong can anyone be? She took the narrow piece of rubber tubing and tied it onto his forearm. Then with a glint of sheer triumph, she picked up the syringe, squirting a little spray as she examined it.

Christ, was there no end to this woman's guile? Panic almost choked him, "Don't use that, Amanda, you are playing with something you cannot possibly understand. Please stop!"

Keeping a firm grip on the syringe, she pressed her breast to his mouth, "You have your fate in your own hands, darling. Stop trying to humiliate me, open your mouth!"

His eyes glued to the syringe, he began to suckle like a hungry baby, sending arrows of satisfaction through her veins. Allowing her to fall from his mouth, he jerked, "Okay, put that lethal thing down!"

Hearing the fear in his voice must had been like manna from heaven to her. Slowly she placed it back onto the table and pressed her nipples into his mouth. He would have to do as she bid, that was until she untied him.

A claustrophobic sweat covered him. Debbie had been very wrong to send him here. Then shame set in, how he hell could he blame her? Even he had never thought of this. Wondering what Amanda had been about to inject into him, had put the fear of God into him, especially after she had administered the sleeping drug.

Calming himself a little, he relaxed in the happy knowledge that even Amanda couldn't fuck a flaccid penis. He had no intention of becoming hard and if he *had* wanted to, there was an abundance of fear in his body, which must surely prevent him.

Amanda was wise when it came to seduction, her perception of Paul's attitude was quick and accurate. Her mouth moved over his chest, sucking in his nipples and moving down to his stomach. Deftly, she flipped her tongue into his navel, allowing her hand to enter the wiry bush of pubic hair. She groaned her satisfaction at reaching her goal, but Paul had not hardened. That would certainly have to change, she told herself and shot between his legs.

Paul felt fit to commit murder. He could barely lift his head, but he felt desperately vulnerable. This was how a woman being raped must feel and the thought sickened him further. Amanda was playing with his balls, taking one into her mouth, applying gentle suction and pausing. Taking the other one into her mouth, her hand closed around his cock and to his disgust he felt himself harden.

The hot tongue reminded him of a viper as it flashed in and out of her mouth, lashing the length of his penis. Hell, this bird knew how to administer a bloody good blow job, but then, she had enjoyed plenty of practice. Her hands now rolled his cock and her tongue attacked the tip of him, until his hips began to move, within the confines of his restriction.

Amanda had longed to taste this man. He was lovely and hard, she could take him when she was ready. She was salivating with greed and with tiny tickling movements, she eased her way back to his mouth. After teasing him with her breast, she knelt up, moved forward and placed her mound over his face.

He had closed his eyes as he felt her imminent approach. His hands were tied so tightly, he could scarcely make a fist of anger as her voice rose shrilly, "Don't close your eyes, Paul, otherwise …!"

His eyes levelled hers, "I know, bitch," he heaved. She was like something possessed, her and her lethal weapon. Her mound was a few inches higher than his head and he couldn't fail to notice the smooth fairness. She placed her hand between her legs and allowed a finger to enter her. Slowly, she extracted it and took it to her mouth, licking it with tantalisingly seductive movements, her tongue flicking as it had done against his cock and then she returned it inside of her pubic hair.

Paul's eyes boggled as she moved her finger in and out of herself. And then she brought her other hand down and parted herself wide. Her passage glistened with wet and she probed her clitoris as though she was about to bring herself off. He was beyond words and dare not even think about closing his eyes. She gripped his head and placed herself over his mouth, "Lick me, Paul, for Chrissakes bring me off," she screamed.

Hastily, he turned his head away. He was suffocating and needed air. She popped a kiss onto his lips and shot down the bed. She then launched an assault on his manhood that defied any man to ignore. He thought of his beloved Debbie, but that made him harder. One last endeavour, "Amanda, let me have my hand back, I will give you the fuck you want. Free me though!"

"Still think I'm silly, don't ye?"

Her voice filled with rapture as her green eyes glinted at him. She had wanted this man since they had first me, six years ago. No one had made her feel like Paul did, yet he had never shown her a flicker of interest which had hurt her deeply. Men fell at her feet, buried their heads into her bush, suckled her breasts, but one man had rejected her every move, a pill far too big for her to swallow.

She trembled with excitement as his cock flashed about like a fish out of water. He was the most beautiful sight she had ever seen. She would have him many times before the morning, but right now, she was so horny, she couldn't breathe. Raising herself, she took his shaft into her hands, steadied it and then with her other hand, she parted herself and sank down onto his erection.

A heavy sigh of blissful relief and beauty left her. He was inside of her. Paul's longed for penis was now enveloped deeply inside of her and she savoured the moment. Briefly, she dropped her head as her eyes longed to see where they were joined. Yes indeed, she wanted to watch herself being fucked, to see Paul's shaft giving her the one yearned for screw that had eluded her.

Paul could only watch as she finally flung her head back. It was obvious that she was thoroughly enjoying herself, feeling him inside of her filled her with luscious vengefulness. She closed her knees each side of his thighs, her hands fixed firmly onto his chest, she rode him, panting, gasping, whimpering, until he felt her passage tighten and pull his cock. Her orgasm was long and she moved faster and faster, her voice harsh, "Now, fuck me, Paul. Tell me you're fucking me,! She cried out in ravening triumph

He had clenched every muscle in his body to no avail If he could have freed his hands, he would certainly have fucked her and kept on till she screamed for mercy. It came on him with a swiftness that shocked him, his engorged appendage could take no more. He knew she had felt him tense, for she threw her hands beneath his buttocks and felt him come in bursts that made her heart light. And when he shuddered, she leaned forward and lay along the length of his body, making sure his cock stayed embedded in the heat of her hungry sheath.

Lifting her head she looked into his eyes and saw the stark anger smoulder there. He was fuming and she knew it. His voice told of his hatred, it's repelling rebuke hurt her, "Can I go now?"

"Don't be so bloody unkind. You got your fill, Paul. I felt you come in great bursts, so don't pretend you didn't enjoy it," she snarled.

He seethed, "A bloody animal would come if a crazed bitch prepared to bite it's cock off. Now fucking well untie me, Amanda and pray I don't tell your father!"

"Tell who you want, Paul. In fact, I would love to be a fly on the wall when you tell little Miss Innocent," she grinned with malice.

Paul thought about it and his blood ran cold. How on earth was he going to tell Debbie? She would be appalled, but then so was he. If ever he got his hands round this tart's neck, he would murder her.

She began to laugh, louder and louder, "If you could see your face, Paul. How would your beloved little woman react to seeing you sucking me off, to see you fucking me? Does she do that to you? By the way, dear heart, I filmed us at it, p'hps you could show her as you confess all. I'll pour us a drink, light us a ciggie and then you can please me again!"

Tears of sincere misery attacked the back of his eyes. He had never felt so god damn helpless in his life. He was too upset to feel the humiliation of being naked, of having his pride and joy poked about as though it was an animal seeking reward as he gulped his drink thirstily.

It was dawn when Amanda finally decided she had had her fill. Nausea swamped him and he was certain his cock would never rise again. She had made him come over her breasts, in her mouth, in her passage and humiliation had caught up with him. Feeling he could never sink lower than he already had, he rasped, "When I'm free, I'll kill you. One things for sure, Amanda, I never, ever, want to bump into you again. You're sick, depraved, a filthy little bitch with a greedy, grasping cunt!"

He bit his lip as he realised he should have waited before opening his big mouth. She strutted over to the door and for a moment, he thought she was going to leave him, but she took the key from the lock. Then with lightning speed, she cut him free and fled the room, locking the door behind her. Somehow, it gave him no satisfaction to know she was petrified of him.

Paul sat up with pain shooting throughout his body. He tried to rub his almost raw wrists, wondering if he would ever get away. Amanda needn't have run, he couldn't have chased her at the moment. His ankles felt they held no responsibility for his feet as anger almost suffocated him.

Desperate to get away, he began to dress with swift haste and pounded on the door until a bewildered servant freed him and he could rush outside.

A short distance down the road, he practically fell into the working man's café. The food was the last straw, he ran into the gents and wretched till his stomach was empty. With a stagger he arrived at the wash basin and sloshed cold water onto his face.

He had the sensation of walking on a bed of cotton wool. The cheerful bloke behind the counter asked, "Bit of a rough night then, guv? A strong black coffee should put lead back in the old pencil!"

"Ugh, ye, give us a coffee, sunshine. Could you call me a mini cab, please?"

Paul's voice was slurred as in drink. A rough night had to be a masterful understatement. He pinched himself to make sure he hadn't dreamed it all. Taking a swift gulp of coffee, he began to think how he could possibly explain to Debbie, 'dear, God, help her to understand', he prayed aloud, to the amusement of the counter assistant.

CHAPTER THIRTEEN

The tragic news of Tony's passing had leaked out. There were so many beautiful flowers for him. Even the television crew had sent flowers, with verses that tore at one's heart strings. It was the most hideous thing that Debbie had ever witnessed. The little white box that was to take him so far from them, made her feel violently sick.

There wasn't a dry eye in the little Church. The aroma from the beautiful flowers somehow felt wrong, they were bright and full of life and their little soldier had gone. Debbie watched with total amazement, the total composure that her parents were displaying. How she wished she could have behaved with the same decorum.

Misery laden and heartbroken, they all returned to the shop. Perhaps they could all talk some of the pain from their systems. Her parents needed each other, she wanted to be alone with Paul, he looked dreadful since his return from Eric's home. As if he read her mind, Matthew said, "I'll look after Ellen and Jim, so I will, you and Paul need to be together!"

His shaking voice belied the conviction with which he had tried so hard to muster. He was such a thoughtful person and full of deep understanding. Yet, who had he to comfort him? In spite of her twinges of sheer guilt, Debbie still found herself leaving with Paul.

Naturally and wordlessly they had headed towards their own private place, both gripped in grief as they finally arrived. Almost trancelike, they sat down, more or less before they fell down, the companionable silence still unbroken.

Paul lit a couple of cigarettes and handed one to her, again she noticed how downright ill he looked. Before she could ask, he gulped, "Debbie, my love, hell, I know this has been a dreadful and sad ordeal. I have been through an added, bloody shocking experience. Somehow, I can't believe it happened, but darling, oh, hell, Debbie, you've got to be told!"

Terror had joined them in their very private place. A hand of ice gripped her heart as somehow she knew, this was something connected to Amanda. Inhaling deeply, she turned to him, "What happened?"

Choking with emotion, he poured out the whole story. He left nothing out, not even the drugs. His heart ached as he saw the torment cross her lovely face. Paul had seldom been ashamed of his actions, but right at that moment, he hated himself as much as he hated Amanda.

Debbie felt prostrate with a new grief. For a brief moment she felt she had lost Paul too, she felt hurt, betrayed and very, very angry. "How could you, Paul? I believe all that happened to you and understand the shock of being tied up, but y .. you .. must ..." she broke off and coughed.

Taking a deep drag on his cigarette, his stomach churned as he knew exactly what she meant and responded, "Must have been hard. Is that what you mean, Debbie? Honestly, dearest, it is difficult for someone so pure to understand. A man will get hard if he is manipulated. .. Christ, Debbie, I knew you wouldn't understand, wouldn't want me to touch you again, I can't reverse what happened and I can't promise that she will not boast about her antics with me!"

His voice cracked with hatred, then he rounded on Debbie harshly, "You're so bloody sure it couldn't happen to you. For God's sake, if you were tied up and prepared for fucking, any bloke could rape you. Christ almighty, many people get their thrills out of bondage and humiliating someone. Think about it, Debbie, we're talking professionals here!"

He stood up and began to pace up and down, his hands plunged deeply into his pockets. He turned to her and saw how fragile she seemed. Instantly he felt himself harden and bitterness hit him. He had to make her understand, "Debbie, I know you probably don't realise this, but I only have to come near to you and my cock jumps up, right now its on bloody fire. And from the look of disgust on your face, I sure as hell am not in for a good fucking am I?"

Paul was at the end of his tether and horrified by the way he had spoken to her. Tears stung his eyes, "Hell, Debbie, I'm sorry. I didn't mean to speak to you like that. I forgot you weren't Amanda. Part of me wishes now that I hadn't told you, especially after the misery of the past week!"

"Why did you tell me then," she rasped.

"Because I love you. Because I couldn't hold you without guilt, not till you knew the truth and turned to me, because *you* wanted me!"

Her eyes rounded as like a flash it hit her. From the little she truly knew about sex, once aroused anything must be possible. She recognised her need for Paul alright, the moistness between her legs was a sharp reminder. And even when he was away, the feelings had still descended upon her. She admired the fact that he had been through such an embarrassing ordeal, yet seen fit to admit the truth to her.

She knew she must handle this, help Paul to handle this. Looking up at his profile as he gazed over the horizon, she knew she couldn't stop loving him, didn't want to. Humiliation had somehow bowed his shoulders, his tongue ran along his sensual lips and as he turned to her, she held out her hand, "Paul, let's go home to the flat!"

Was it her imagination? Was it a fact? It didn't matter anymore, because his love that night was so blissfully powerful as headily, they turned to each other many times over.

He couldn't believe how safe it felt to be locked into her wonderful silken sheath, it was so beautifully familiar and he thanked God for giving him the strength to be honest with her. He allowed himself a quick smile, this was certainly not what Amanda had hoped for. The woman he loved had understood and proved her own selfless love to him.

Lifting his head, his fingers traced the contours of her face. He kissed her with tenderness. Gently his hands roamed her body, pausing to kiss each caress. They both loved the after play, it seemed to add a captivating finesse to their union.

**

Debbie was relieved, if not more than surprised at the way in which her parents had accepted Tony's death. As they had all found themselves sitting around the table together one evening, Jim had gulped, "Debbie, well, all of you, you couldn't have known just how much that holiday did for Ellen and myself .."

His voice was strained as his Adam's apple flew up and down. He lifted his heavy lids to reveal the pain that still lurked in his eyes and continued, "When Tony was born, we were told that he was living on borrowed time. We knew you had a right to know, Debbie, but by not knowing, you could love and enjoy him without wondering when he would leave us!"

Taking Ellen's hand into his, the look they shared was too beautiful to describe, every nuance of their beings were as one. He seemed to gather added strength from his wife as he carried on, "The doctors thought he would have a year, maybe two, but being such a happy and contented little chap, he scraped by with a further year. He did die though, in the full knowledge that he was loved without question. Mum and I are happy about that, he had real guts, didn't he?"

Those deep brown, penetrating eyes had glazed over. Debbie felt claustrophobic, they had indeed made the right decision, she didn't think she could have carried on with such a sad secret on her mind. Tony had indeed been brave, but that streak had come directly from his parents.

Once the poignancy that had enveloped them began to lift, the topic was changed. The discussion centred on the Paris trip and everyone was eager for success in that direction. Ellen hugged her, "I know you will do well in Paris. All of you will and we couldn't be happier about it. Remember, Debs, you are still our child and we love you dearly!"

Tears blinded her as again she realised how brave her parents had been. Somehow she could accept that the holiday had been a real 'must'. Again Matthew intercepted her thoughts, "When we all return, you two will have another long weekend. I feel it in me bones, everything will be fine!"

A chuckle ran around the room, it was amazing that Matthew could always summon a quick quip to lighten any gloom. To her complete astonishment, Debbie found herself explaining what had happened to a still, deeply shocked Paul.

The words had just slipped from her lips, yet she knew she needed her parents to understand, knowing full well that if Amanda had her way, it would go round like wildfire, or her version of what had occurred.

An uncanny silence fell and then Jim turned angrily to Paul, "I realise you are having a honeymoon first, Paul, but I think enough time has been lost, we should fix the date of the wedding!"

Ellen jumped up, "It wasn't their fault they had to wait, Jim. I agree though, how about mid April? Bloody shame it couldn't be before Paris, yet we couldn't have foreseen Tony's death at the precise time of the wedding!"

Paul interjected, "It's no one's fault. It happened and you all know the truth. I'm so sorry!"

Jim's voice softened, "Once the pair of you are married, Eric will at least have to see sense!"

Paul and Debbie both doubted it, but Paul was only too happy to agree with Jim. Taking Debbie's hand, he stated, "I feel the sooner the better. It won't stop Amanda, or Eric come to that, but even he can't possibly be stupid enough to suggest bigamy!"

CHAPTER FOURTEEN

Debbie had never travelled out of Lancashire before, never mind out of the England. The thought of Paris was exhilarating as well as daunting and never having been close to a 'plane before, she was overawed by the sheer size of it.

Sensing her fear, Paul had taken her hand and Alma chatted to Matthew. Sitting into the comfortable seats, Debbie found her eyes drawn to the deft manner with which the stewards went about their duties. Like all true professionals, they made everything look so easy.

A chauffeur driven Limo was in attendance at Paris Airport, ready to collect their luggage and take them to the sumptuous hotel that overlooked the Seine. They were truly being treated as royalty, yet Debbie stubbornly felt, it all fell short of her beloved Morecambe.

The luxury suite was huge and several three seat long settees looked almost lost. The gigantic bay window was set up onto a low stage, so large that even the baby grand piano looked exceptionally lonely.

Three large bedrooms came complete with private bathrooms, and a pretty little maid unpacked their luggage while they all thirstily drunk the delicious coffee that had been served.

During the evening, Paul had suggested that he and Debbie should go for a walk. They were still smarting badly over the death of Tony, having promised to take him unlimited photographs back. They would still take them, or rather, Matthew would, but sadly not for the little fellow.

Wonder filled them as they walked down the Champs elyses, feeling the magic enter their hearts. It certainly lived up to its reputation. They seemed to take a step forward and pause to admire another item of beauty. Overhead a gorgeous midnight blue sky adorned them. Stars twinkled intrusively onto them. The full moon bathed them, sending erotic shudders through them, yet it was the same moon that glowed for them at home.

By sheer chance, they passed the exhibition hall, noticing the placards advertising the competition. Although most were written in French, there were sharp reminders written clearly in English. With a shock, Debbie realised fully, it was an international exhibition.

Suddenly, she felt sick with fright. Paul's arms went around her as he murmured, "Don't be scared darling. You would not be here if Haywoods didn't think you could cope!"

Somehow that just served to terrify her more and a strange tiredness washed over her. Arriving back to the suite, they found Alma's eyes danced with excitement, "Debbie, I've been busy on the 'phone. After the competition tomorrow, we are to attend an evening dinner dance. I've arranged for some dresses to be brought round, we must choose a cracker for you. In the afternoon, the press want to interview you and Matthew, we have a very full day lined up!"

Debbie was glad when Alma finally seemed to run out of breath and found herself shaking uncontrollably, tension was building rapidly in her. She didn't think she could handle all of this. Turning to Paul, she gulped, "I'm so scared, Paul, I wish I hadn't come!"

He held her to him, gently brushing the hair from her face, "You'll be fine, darling, won't she Alma?"

Alma still looked as fresh as a daisy. Her hair shone and her make up looked as though it had just been applied. She was like Paul, used to this kind of lifestyle, attending interviews and all kinds of special events. Debbie felt like a wilting daffodil, just wanting to climb into bed and forget.

Slipping between the rich grey satin sheets, Debbie felt her head spin with a feeling of luxury. Moments later, she forgot all about her fears as Paul transported her to another planet. His kisses seemed even fiercer than usual, her body an eager recipient of each caress. Gradually the tension left her.

After showering and dressing the next morning, they were served a typically French breakfast. Everyone was light hearted and tucking in with a rich hunger. To Debbie, each bite tasted like chaff as the lump of fear in her throat grew larger by the second.

She watched the complete composure that seemed to be Alma's main attribute. If only she could feel and act in the same manner, she thought as a representative called round with several designer dresses and shoes.

A short while later, she had been poured into a gorgeous dress, with the hugest shoulder pads she had ever seen. Apparently they had just come back into fashion again. The top of the dress was black and gold, with long sleeves billowing and nipping into her wrist. A plunging neckline almost exposed her naval, yet clung seductively over her bust. It emphasised her tiny waist, with the black skirt folding neatly over her slender hips and flowing to the ground, swishing sensually as she moved. Debbie stared into the mirror and scarcely recognised the person staring back at her.

Her feet gelled into a gorgeous pair of high heeled, gold strap shoes and the hairdresser would arrive to dress her hair. But first she had the interview, which was long and tiring. By the time it was finished, she felt more like climbing into bed than preparing for the evening.

Briefly she reflected on her design. Debbie had used the new cotton and had ironically placed small shoulder pads inside. Her inspired urge had led her to introduce several pretty colours into a fine lace design. She had then taken the narrowest of ribbon strips and threaded then through the various holes, ending up with tiny bows at the wrists and waist.

Alma thought it was exquisite, yet Debbie shook with fear as it was collected along with the photographs. The judging would be carried out during the afternoon and the results would be ready, prior to everyone arriving for the dance.

Paul and Matthew had been out together to photograph some of the landmarks. They reminded her of a couple of young lads as an atmosphere of happiness seemed to be everywhere, but in her heart, fear lurked relentlessly and her longing to sit and gaze over her beloved bay grew within her.

Debbie watched with fascination as the hairdresser began to 'teasel' her hair. His fingers and comb worked almost as one and she had to admit, that although she felt like a stick of candy floss, the style did suit her.

Paul had gasped his approval when he saw her dressed and ready. Matthew gulped and rushed to get his camera, making her giggle. His eyes sparked with mischief as he clicked, ensuring he had covered her from every angle.

They both looked dashingly debonair in their evening suits, both very handsome indeed, yet strikingly different. Alma as usual, looked as though she had stepped from a page in Vogue. All of them were infected with excitement, leaving her feeling sick and lonely inside.

A few short hours later, to her total astonishment, she was on the stage to collect her award. Her eyes glazed as she was named, 'designer of the year in the field of knitwear'. Her hands shook as she was handed the huge cheque, together with a contract to supply boutiques bearing her own label.

She could literally sell any of her designs to buyers to make up as 'exclusive' or general standard multi sales. Once again, the flashes of lights from the photographers were blinding. It was perhaps just as well that she had been asked to stay put, for she had become transfixed.

Profound joy was hers. The photographer with the most flair for detail was Matthew Ross. He was swiftly by her side to receive his award and a cheque for half of the amount that she had received. The applause was thunderous as he took her arm to escort her back to Alma and Paul.

The next couple of days rushed by in a haze of numb disbelief.

Debbie had been asked to design for several agencies around the world. Matthew was to continue with his photography and she began to wonder however she would cope, especially if she had to travel and Paul couldn't manage to get away.

**

Debbie didn't think she had landed back to earth before she finally arrived at the shop. Safely enveloped in her proud parents' arms, she wondered how she would possibly manage to complete the load of commissions. Her only salvation was the fact that they had managed to take on extra staff, yet even Matthew worried about the time in the shop.

Mercifully, one of the trainees was now ready to fly solo. Richard Blythe was a lovable character and obviously loved his work. At twenty two his energy knew no bounds. He was above five feet nine, a little on the thin side, but his personality was larger than life.

He sported a good head of light brown hair. His dark brown eyes held a deep sincerity, mingled with a heavy helping of playfulness. His ready smile could almost be interpreted as a cheeky grin. He had just married his childhood sweetheart.

Jenny was a real stunner, also thin and short. Her black hair was cut so short, it gave her an impish look. Her dark, almost black eyes, seemed to transfix everyone. She had worked in the shop since Richard had joined them. They were both saving hard for a home of their own.

They were naturals for the shop, both of them ready with a quick quip, accompanied by total courtesy towards the customers. Debbie felt they would do exceptionally well, neither of them fearing hard work.

Debbie was desperately trying to sort herself out, when yet again the 'phone rang. This time it was a television company asking her to do a series of knitting for beginners. It would be a regular weekly spot on an art program. The filming could take place within her home and she would be expected to answer the various letters that would no doubt follow. Hysteria reared as she had also been asked to produce a book to cover the series step by step. And that would all begin in about three months.

Rubbing her forearms in an act of soothing, she jumped as her mother entered the room and asked with concern, "Debbie, what's the matter dear? Would it help to talk?"

Swiftly she filled Ellen in and sighed heavily, "Mum, I feel bogged down. I know it sounds ungrateful, but sometimes I wish I'd never had an inspired urge!"

Ellen's arms went around her, "Debs, stop worrying, dear, I think that the five of us should sit down and have a meeting. Once you have a plan of action, you'll be surprised how quickly the weight will lift!"

Returning the hug, Debbie gave a watery smile, "You're right, Mum. It will ease when we have spoken together, I s'pose everything just overwhelmed me. At least there is no shortage of money and I would love to see you and Dad taking more of a back seat here!"

**

Later that evening, they were again sitting round the table. Having spread out all of the commissions, Paul said, "I think you should buy a large house and take on some secretarial staff. It must be done now, before everything gets on top of you. I will help you to sort that out!"

Debbie began to relax a little as he continued, "You do realise that 'White Castle' has not been sold. If you and Matthew both put your winnings together, I'm sure you could afford it comfortably. Funny enough, we all intended to see it anyway. It would be ideal and just far enough out of the way to be peaceful!"

A happy shudder ran through her, he was right of course, but she still wanted to buy something for her parents. In fact she was thinking of offering Richard and Jenny the chance to run the shop and use the flat for their home. As the idea developed she felt a rush of excitement, realising that they would be able to help a young couple find a home.

Mathew had again seemed to read her mind with an uncanny accuracy. He leaned forward, "Why don't we split the castle, giving Ellen and Jim their own private quarters? We could use a wing for offices, with a large communal lounge for entertaining or meetings. I could use a part to make myself an apartment and there will be stacks of rooms left for you and Paul to live there – that's if we get it!"

He feigned a mock collapse as he ran out of breath. Debbie knew that he, or indeed her parents would not want to sell the shop. It was probably in for the biggest season of its life, after all the publicity it had received.

After throwing many more ideas around, Jim said, "Well, let's go and see the place. Debbie and Matthew obviously can't afford to hang about for too long!"

**

Ironically, they had admired the building from the bottom of the hill. But as they approached, it was even more like a castle than ever as they espied the turrets. Sitting on the top of the hill, it nestled into trees and beautifully tended gardens.

Although it was well fenced in, they could see right across the bay and Debbie fell in love with it. Being so large, it had obviously been difficult to sell, but seemed tailor made for them and somehow she felt that their offer would be accepted, for the sake of a quick sale.

Filled with a new excitement, they all went through a small archway, above which was a large landing type room. A huge table with lines of chairs each side, was to be left and sold with the building. This would make an ideal boardroom, or just simply to entertain clients. They could add a couple of settees and secrete a small kitchen into the corner, to make hasty cups of coffee without troubling the staff.

Thinking of staff, intoxicated Debbie and she desperately hoped that they could retain them. They would never manage to cope with all of this. And she hated the thought of redundancies the minute they moved in, if they moved in.

One wing was L shaped and there must have been at least eight rooms that would not be needed immediately. But Matthew had fallen in love with the front room as it overlooked the sea. They could hear the waves as they roared and he wanted that room for a lounge, with two bedrooms, kitchen and dining room.

Debbie realised that they could just about afford the building and immediate alterations. It would use every penny that she and Matthew had won, yet she knew it would be well worth it.

Downstairs, they found that immediately underneath the same wing, the layout was exactly the same. This would be ideal for offices and she would probably share the huge front room with Matthew. They would need a couple of rooms for secretaries, leaving several rooms to be used as and when they could afford to have them converted.

Her mind raced with excitement as they made their way to the smaller wing. This would be ideal for her parents, they could have the bottom apartment, which would give them a spacious lounge, two bedrooms and a deliciously large kitchen, so nice and large that Ellen could ice many cakes without feeling cramped. A spacious dining room led from the kitchen.

Directly above them, the layout was identical. This was where she and Paul would ultimately live. There was no point in trying to renovate it yet, as they did have Paul's flat to start off with. At this point in time, it was vital for them to get moving on the bare essentials.

The staff quarters lay ahead of them in an attractive little building on its own. At present, there was a cook, a couple of housekeepers and a handful of maids. She felt giddy, it sounded so extravagant, but her time would be taken up with all of the work that was growing by the day. She also vowed that the staff would be treated with respect and not as scivvies.

Paul and her parents were seated at the huge table, going over exactly what had to be done immediately. It was going to be one mad rush. They really would have to start on the serious work without delay. She could still work on designs, until everything was sorted out. Jim managed to estimate what they could spend and Paul knew so many contacts, the work could be expedited.

Matthew was ecstatic about his new home. He and Debbie had wandered upstairs and noticed a doorway that appeared to lead to nowhere. They had caught each others' eye and opened the door slowly as a flight of steps confronted them. His grin was wicked as he chuckled, "Go on, let's see what's up there. I bet it's a secret passage!"

Giggling like crazy kids, they ascended to the top and found what must have been a patio, linking the two turrets, with a safety wall running across. They walked over to look out to sea and realised they could survey the whole of the bay. It was magical, even the sun had decided to shine, bathing it with an added beauty.

Debbie gazed out, not quite believing all of this. Matthew's arm fell loosely around her shoulder, "Look, Duchess, this is your own little kingdom and how you've worked for it. Ye, me darling, you've worked hard!"

The air was exhilarating up here and she felt it would be a very peaceful spot for the odd quick think. Giving her shoulder an added squeeze, he added, "You have a real head for business and a deep care for others!"

Filling her lungs with fresh air, she smiled, "I don't feel much like a business woman. In fact half of me feels terrified. Matthew, it is your empire too, you have worked just as hard as anyone!"

Somehow, her steps felt lighter as they descended to join the little circle. A list of urgent jobs had been drawn up and if Matthew sorted out the bulk of conveyancing, prior to engaging a practising solicitor, it would hasten everything.

Matthew had already elected that Debbie chose the décor for his flat and she knew she would pinch Paul's ideas, after all, she couldn't better them. Ellen was thrilled, much preferring this idea to a bungalow. Jim rubbed his chin, "Debbie, you want to give Richard and Jenny a chance to take over the shop and flat, don't you? As Matthew says, one of us can pop down there a couple of times a week!"

"I'd love that!"

She had never felt so restless in her life and knew that Matthew sensed this. She also knew how lucky she was to have him as her working partner. And Paul was more than happy for them to use his flat, till they could renovate the castle. Tossing her head with defiance, she vowed to pull herself together.

CHAPTER FIFTEEN

Debbie yearned for her wedding day which was only a month away. She knew she would have to be careful as they didn't want the media in. They wanted a small affair in Saint Peter's Church. When they had booked the new date, they felt they had entered a fairytale of their own.

The little church was set amongst the trees, overlooking the bay, with its beautiful Saxon west door and windows. Historians believed that it had been named after Saint Peter, who had himself been a fisherman.

Nostalgia had stifled them as they remembered why they had been obliged to change the date. The sadness of losing Tony was still very sharp. Yet, somehow she knew, that once she came out as Paul's wife, her happiness would be complete.

With unbelievable haste, they had bought the castle, chosen the décor and installed the offices. Debbie had found herself a secretary, instinctively knowing she would be invaluable. Everything could be dictated onto tape, with explanation as to where spaces for Matthew's photographs should be and then the whole lot sent to the printers.

Irene Binny, was a very efficient and professional person. At twenty four, she was five years older than Debbie and had 'capability' written all over her. She had a good figure, her fair hair was folded neatly into a pleat at the back of her head. Her cornflower blue eyes were direct as they seemed to flash sincerity and trust. Her make up was applied with care and she dressed the same way. In fact she was exactly the sort of person to meet clients.

She and Debbie had formed a close bond rapidly and Debbie realised she had been more than lucky to find her. Irene had made it crystal clear that she was looking for advancement, hopefully to an executive position. She had no plans for marriage and fully intended to be a first class career woman.

Debbie had readily assured Irene, that she saw her future as her own personal assistant. That had certainly put a huge smile onto Irene's face. She loved responsibility, which was the very quality Debbie had sought.

**

Two weeks before the wedding, they had all decided to move in and Debbie would sleep in her parents' spare room. The offices had been completed first, allowing Debbie to get Irene underway. At last things were well on the move.

Once the last of the details had been sorted out, they asked Richard and Jenny to come up to the flat before they finally left for their new home. Debbie noticed the way the young couple clung to each other as they were asked to sit down around the table.

Jim cleared his throat as he sat down. "We are very pleased indeed with your work. It is Debbie's wish that you should both take over the shop. She also thinks that the flat could solve your housing problem. How do you both feel about it?"

Debbie sat there in amazement, she had never realised just how much they had all listened to her ideas, let alone put them forward on her behalf. Richard and Jenny were absolutely flabbergasted. Jenny's eyes had filled as she gulped heavily,

"Christ, we expected – I don't know what we expected, but we sure as hell never expected this!"

Lighting a cigarette, Richard gripped her hand. "You mean, .. you mean, that you will pay us a wage and rent the flat to us? As Jenny said, we never expected this. We are totally shell shocked, what rent would you want?"

Matthew overflowed with enthusiasm and interjected, "The flat goes with the job. All we ask is that you keep up the good work!"

Debbie had never witnessed such gratitude and found herself adding, "This is not a gift. You have both worked jolly hard for us and have earned the right to live in the flat!"

Champagne was popped and poured, toasts ran into toasts and a couple of hours later, they watched two very happy young people leave them. Tears stung Debbie's eyes, it certainly was a lovely feeling to share one's good luck.

Paul could only grin as he put his penneth in, "If Matthew photographs all of the different types of cakes they could be displayed in the shop window, orders could be taken and 'phoned through!"

Delight ran through Debbie as she looked at her parents, they seemed so much happier and relaxed. They would never forget Tony, how could they? But at long last, they were all too busy keeping their minds occupied for long hours.

Every penny that she and Matthew had won, was being spent on the castle. They had even used some of the forward commission money for alterations. This had made good sense as they couldn't work in chaos, but now they would really have to knuckle down. The coffers would have to be watched until they were well and truly underway. Jim would keep his eagle eye in that department.

During the mad rush, Debbie had begun to feel a little under the weather. She was only too well aware they had taken on too much at once. But now they were organised, it would be less hectic. Not by any means easy and they had certainly sorted out their priorities.

Philosophically, she reasoned it was usually all or nothing in life. Just one short year ago, they hadn't a penny to bless themselves with, in fact six short months ago, they had been broke. Now it was coming from all directions. She vowed there and then, it would never, ever change her.

Handing over the shop to Richard and Jenny had been one very pleasant task and they had one more to perform. They called the castle staff into a meeting and reassured them, that providing their work continued in the same manner, they could be certain of retaining their jobs. It almost reduced Debbie to tears as she watched the anxious faces turn from worry to relief and she knew instinctively, the staff would be more than loyal to them.

There were two gardeners for the huge gardens and they were delighted to work for them. Although they didn't live in, they were kept very busy indeed. The beautifully kept lawns looked like freshly laid carpets. The herbaceous borders were coming to life and filling the air with the most exquisite aromas. Rose bushes were dotted about in pretty little beds and the hedges were cut to perfection.

The swimming pool had a couple of tables and chairs around the sides and sometimes she thought she was dreaming as her eyes misted over, 'all of this and the sea too'.

Wednesday morning, prior to her wedding on the Saturday, Debbie wakened feeling violently sick. Immediately, she realised she *was* pregnant. She had begun to think along those lines, now she was sure.. For a few precious moments she just lay there absorbing with love, the fact that Paul's flesh and blood was growing inside of her. How she loved him, how eager she was to see his face when the whispered the magical words to him.

She stretched herself almost cat like. It must have happened the night of Tony's funeral. Paul had been so down that night, almost desolate by Amanda's behaviour. Debbie had totally forgotten to take the pill while Tony had been so ill and since his death, she had been so busy, to the point of forgetting to collect a fresh prescription.

Tonight, she would make Paul the happiest man in the world. Perhaps she should have told him when she first suspected, but it could have been a false alarm, after all, they had worked so jolly hard. What a blessing she was to be married on Saturday. How thrilled her parents would be, a sparkle danced in her eyes as she realised that life was just about perfect.

**

Maralyn Morgan dressed with care. Her body was drained of energy after fighting with Eric and Amanda, she just couldn't allow them to put their plan into action, yet didn't quite know how to stop them. Vanessa Fairclough had 'phoned her the night after the firm's party. They both needed to get together again, both trying desperately to safeguard Paul, both for different reasons.

Vanessa owned a luxury apartment in a lavish block on the seafront in Morecambe. She also was dressing with care, her hands still managed to shake as she prepared herself to meet Maralyn. They met whenever they could, but took great pains to be cautious and discreet. She had married at the ripe old age of twenty two and by the time she was twenty five, had become widowed.

Work had been her only salvation and the only cloud on her particular horizon had been the constant 'come ons' from Eric. Eventually he had come to value her work and got the message that she was a very private property. She was never short of a man to satisfy her sexual needs, but never intended to become involved again. Then she had met Paul Howarth, a little young perhaps, yet everything she wanted in a man. Unfortunately, he was like her and wanted no involvements near to work. He had however, seen in her, a precious asset as a workmate as he had met and fallen in love with Debbie Hudson.

Try as she had, she found it impossible to dislike his young lady and his contentment seemed to make up for her loss. Like Maralyn, she was totally sincere to shield them both from Eric and Amanda.

Vanessa, now thirty five, threw back her shoulders and reflected on last year. She had gone to collect some documents from Eric's home. Maralyn had opened the door and placed an arm around her shoulder as she smiled in welcome, "Come in, dear, we have the place to ourselves – servant's day off!"

After leading her into the drawing room, Maralyn began to pour coffee into the dainty china cups. Vanessa noticed how very attractive the older woman was and a pang of pity hit her. "Does it bother you, Maralyn, I mean Eric and his affairs? I'm sure I'd be terribly hurt if I were you," the words were out without thought and she clamped her palm over her mouth.

"Don't be embarrassed, Vanessa, it is a well know fact and he always comes home to me. At times I wish we didn't always need a man, they think because they have a piece of surplus meat between their legs, that we are all ready and willing to part ours!"

Her voice held a low throb and Vanessa felt herself flush beetroot red. She was reading the sudden question in Maralyn's eyes. They both felt a charge of electricity spark between them.

For a brief moment, it was a though someone had pressed the slow motion button. Maralyn moved next to Vanessa and placed an arm casually around her shoulders. Dart like spikes seemed to pierce them both. Their eyes had locked, held and each were filled with questions. Maralyn had recovered first and gulped, "I've opened some wine, Ness, shall we take it upstairs with us?"

Vanessa sensed the older woman was nervous, frightened and at odds with strange sensations. Her own voice began to shake, her whole being had mentally entered the master bedroom. "I could murder some wine. Have you done this before?"

"Never thought about it. I swear if you don't like it, then we will stop and never mention it again," gasped Maralyn.

Gulping the wine and refilling their glasses, Vanessa felt herself led with a mysterious curiosity towards the bedroom. Her heart thumped with excitement as they walked into the room. Maralyn locked the door and followed Vanessa's eyes to the four poster bed.

Vanessa watched with wonder as Maralyn kicked off her shoes and began to wind her stockings slowly down her legs. Suddenly tiny throbs of ecstasy sprang between her legs, allowing an explosion of moist delight to run through her. Her eyes never left Maralyn as she removed the rest of her clothes. A soft moan left her as she gazed on those huge knockers. They were beautiful, billowing before her and the fair bush at the top of her long legs made Vanessa's passage spasm wildly.

Maralyn took Vanessa into an ethereal embrace. Enveloped in those frothy breasts, Vanessa felt as though she was suspended in an ever floating bubble of air. Swiftly, she divested every last garment from herself.

Holding Vanessa slightly away from her, Maralyn looked at the lovely ivory body, keeping a tight reign on her mounting passion. Unable to contain herself she bent and buried her face into the soft auburn mound, tasting the sweet smell of the woman labelled as the 'ice maiden'.

Standing up, Maralyn gazed at the full ripeness of the supple breasts, curving her hand over one and turning her face slowly, she kissed Vanessa on the lips. Their tongues met and both were lost in the wonder of exploration as they eased each other to the bed.

As far as Maralyn was concerned the younger woman's body felt indescribably sexy and curvaceous. The proud dusky nipples stood firm with expectancy. Tugging gently, Maralyn took each nipple to her mouth, allowing her hand to move toward the auburn bush. Fire raged in Vanessa and she threw her legs apart with a delicious agonised abandon.

Maralyn moved her mouth from the pin hard nipples and looked into Vanessa's eyes, clearly seeing the excitement in them. To see the pulse that beat in her throat sent her into frenzy and she ran her lips over the pulse lovingly.

Vanessa felt desire flood her as never before. A violent quiver shot along her inner thigh and joy upon joy, she felt the wet of Maralyn's tongue darting in and out of her pleasure centre. Her hands grasped air until they found Maralyn's breasts, easing them towards her mouth. And then the older woman was kissing her on the mouth and she Vanessa, could taste herself.

Dazed with erotic mystique, Maralyn lay calm for a moment and allowed Vanessa to bury her head into the billowing breasts. This act was one of undeniable beauty and suddenly she knew, this was something she had missed without realising. There was a sameness about their bodies, yet a real difference, each knew how to please the other.

Leaving a breast for Vanessa to suckle, Maralyn moved her hand down to the auburn bush. Slowly she ran her finger along the soft pubic hair, thrilling as Vanessa's hips began to swirl in response. Soft moans left them both and Maralyn inserted her fingers into the soft wetness of the younger woman's tunnel.

Vanessa had stopped suckling, allowing screams of delight to shoot from her mouth. Maralyn knew how to work with her fingers and when her thumb went to work on her clitoris, she knew she would come, everything around her had begun to swirl.

Maralyn returned her tongue to the burning softness, it was so wet and the work she had done on Ness's clitoris had made it swell and engorge and now felt like a small penis. Marvelling at the way Vanessa writhed with exquisite, painful greed, her own passage began to spasm and when her mouth was filled as Vanessa came in beautiful bursts, she cried out with her.

Swiftly she lay on top of the younger woman and rubbed her mound frantically against the auburn bush. They fitted together with perfection, breast to breast, bush to bush, arms tightly locked around each other as they clung with wild abandon, until they both exploded with a fire so fierce it could never be controlled, let alone extinguished. They shouted and shuddered as their bodies gelled as one, only able to guess who started and ended where?

At last Vanessa's senses began to return, her sight, her hearing, her sense, her sense of complete fulfilment. Turning her head she looked at the older woman, "That was the most beautiful experience I have ever had. In fact, I would like to think that this isn't just a one off!"

Tears slid down Maralyn's cheeks, "Ness, you'll never know how happy you have made me. I think in future though, I had better come to you. Hell, Eric and Amanda would have a field day should they find out. I love you, Ness!"

**

Maralyn shook herself, she had been so lost in the past, that she was now running late. Breathlessly, she applied her make up before stepping into her most beautiful set of satin undies. This was the part of her life she loved, her love with Ness had brought a new flush of life to her. And to her utter relief, Eric had not guessed. He came home and screwed her when the mood took him, but she wasn't dependant on him for sexual pleasure anymore, she was however, only too happy to have him as a breadwinner.

Later that evening she and Ness had made the most perfect love and lay in each others' arms. Ness noticed that Maralyn looked unwell and sat up to light them a cigarette. After pouring the wine, she grilled her, till her troubled eyes lifted. Her voice was strained, "Ness, I came her to see and love you, not to bring my problems!"

Fear gripped Vanessa as she stated, "Maz, we are lovers and take the good with the bad. This has something to do with Paul, doesn't it?"

There was a deep sadness as she replied, "I told you roughly what happened that weekend Paul stayed over. Something is warning me that there is to be a bout of blackmail, I can't warn anyone, because I'm not sure of the facts!"

Fury boiled in Vanessa, "How dare they upset you, my love? Tell me all you know, I may be able to pick something up!"

Maralyn then spilt her heart, telling Ness the secret she had promised Amanda to take to her grave. As she sighed heavily at the end of her revelations, she gulped, "You are the only person to know, Ness. I needed you to know, just in case I'm not around. I'm prepared to break my oath if Paul and Debbie are hurt again!"

Clinging together in solace, Ness said, "I'll take it to *my* grave, Maz. But as you say, should it need to be used, it will be. Come now, dear, cheer up!"

Still clinging in deep compassion, passion arrived swiftly and with great need. Much, much later that evening, Maralyn opened the front door to leave Ness. In the warmth of their embrace, they kissed and Maz was on her way.

She could never in her wildest dreams have guessed that she had been see, but unfortunately, she had.

CHAPTER SIXTEEN

Debbie found herself subconsciously rushing Paul to their special hill. She was breathless as they surveyed their own private piece of heaven. He crushed her into his arms, his kisses urgent and wild and she knew she must tell him, the news was literally bursting inside of her.

They slithered to the grass and for the first time, she noticed the heaviness around his eyes. In fact, he had been quiet over the past few days. With an element of panic, she wondered if it could be anything to do with her success. Hell, she would never allow that to come between them. And Paul had suggested almost every move she had made.

Paul felt her body close to him. Right now, he wanted her as never before. She could never have guessed the nightmare he had been dragged into. Somehow he had to tell her, he had to leave her, had to break both of their hearts.

He had deliberately left it until the last minute, hoping against hope for the proverbial reprieve. In spite of his hatred for Amanda, he had to admit that she had played her cards with panache. Her timing had been almost too accurate, her plotting would leave the most knowledgeable con artist, wanting.

Anger raged in his belly as Eric had broken the news to him, his tone had been one of contentment, "Paul, you will have to marry Amanda and take her to the States with you!"

"I'll have to do no such thing, Eric. I'm to marry Debbie!"

He had spoken more than caustically and with confidence. Yet never could he have dreamed what was to come. "Paul, you are the father of her child, my grandchild, I'm proud to say," he gushed and strutted proudly before adding, "Don't argue, old chap, she has assured me its yours!"

Horrified, Paul had gulped, "That's a fuckin' lie, Eric and you damn well know it. Once and for all, get off our bloody backs!"

"Time is running out, Paul. You must both be in New York, that launch has got its deadline. You can marry over there, a quiet little function and I do believe my daughter, Paul," added a sardonic Eric.

Sick to his stomach, Paul had argued until finally his mind was made up. "Sorry, Eric, you'll have to find another mug. I am going to marry Debbie and resign. There's plenty of work for me to do with her company. Forget it, Eric, I don't need you and you fuckin' well know it!"

Eric's face had turned puce as he played his ace. "Really, Paul, if you did anything so stupid, I could ruin her within a week. I could leak the information that she had tried to steal Amanda's chap, forgetting about the poor child. When I've finished with her, no one will want to know your poor little orphan Annie, I will also add the odd lack of morals, even edit the video of you and Amanda, grow up, Paul!"

Paul snarled, "You bastard, Morgan. You fuckin' bastard, I still will not be blackmailed. I don't even like Amanda. Get stuffed, you and your blasted magazine!"

Eric leered at him, "Sorry, Paul, you know the powers of the press and so forth. I know you will all deny the various allegations – probably prove them, but by that time, she will be closed down!"

Paul's fist landed across Eric's bemused face. Yet he knew, Eric could close Debbie down. At that moment the idea of suicide seemed attractive. Defeat swamped him as he realised that he would not only be closing Debbie down, but her family and Matthew, they would all be in serious debt.

With a terse snipe, he rasped, "Eric, I swear that Amanda has chosen the wrong person with me. I wouldn't go anywhere near her, she knows that. After all, she had to tie me up, or didn't you notice that particular point? Her life will be as miserable as mine, for fuck sake, can't you see that? There is and always will be, just one woman for me!"

**

Pulling himself sharply from his malaise, he had shuddered. He felt Debbie's arms loop around his neck. Her lovely mouth sought and found his. "God, give me strength to tell her," he prayed silently, it didn't work, his arms crushed her to him and he felt a new demand in her, almost as if she knew that evil lurked.

Debbie felt his frenzied kisses carry on as they gasped their way out of the furious passion. His teeth were biting her as deep guttural groans left him. In the safety of his arms and still reeling from his dynamic love, her eyes lifted to him, "Paul, dearest, Paul, I have some wonderful …!"

His mouth cut off her sentence as with a tormented sob, he tore himself from her. He was still shuddering and shaking with a violence that frightened her. "Christ, Debbie, I shouldn't have done that. Darling, I can't marry you. I have to marry Amanda!"

Debbie ricocheted from the statement, thinking it was some kind of cruel joke. Paul was visibly shaken and tears streamed down his face, dripping onto his rug like chest. Her voice was barely recognisable as she gasped, "What's wrong, Paul?"

Watching him light two cigarettes, she then listened with horror as he told her of the saga that was to destroy them. He ended, "I left it to the last moment, darling, but I have to leave first thing in the morning. The contract runs for five years, by then you'll be up and flying. Debbie, my heart is absolutely broken!"

That was almost laughable, *his* heart was broken, he should have felt hers. "No, Paul. You can't go, I won't let you, I love you and I know you love me. Tell Eric where he can stick his bloody job!"

She sobbed with him, his voice hoarse, "Don't you think that I have explored every avenue, Debbie? But Eric will see the scandal breaks in such a way, it will take you all down!"

Waves of nausea washed over her, "I don't want a business, not at this price. Darling, you know how much I love you!"

At that moment, she could have murdered Amanda. How dare she? Yet she *had* dared and she *had* won. Paul was right, it was not just herself, but her parents and Matthew.

The sea roared as her heart crumbled. Turning to him, she screamed, "No, Paul, I need you. Don't leave me, for God's sake, don't leave me," as sobs racked her body. Her fists were beating wildly on his chest.

Paul gripped them, "Stop it, Debbie, you'll make yourself ill. If only this had happened a year from now, he couldn't have hurt us. He wants my flat, but there is no way in which I will sell, the keys are with Vanessa, should you need it!"

Hysteria had taken over. Her fists still beat his chest, he cried out, "Debbie, you know I'll never love another woman. They may force me into marriage, but I will never touch the bitch. And she won't get to spike anything I eat or drink, because I'll touch nothing she's handled. Oh, God, Debbie, I'll never stop loving you!"

Her screams were carried with the wind and lost in the roars from the sea. Crazily she turned to him, "I can't wait for five years to see you, Paul. I cannot contact you, they will say I'm having an affair with a married man, my married man!"

Feeling the urge to run and jump off of their hill, she knew she was out of control. Her whole world had just toppled as she realised that if Tony hadn't died, the Morgans could not have done this, dear God, hadn't they already lost enough?

Even to herself, her voice sounded wild, "One things for sure, I'll never come here again, never, ever!"

Paul's heart broke anew as he saw the state she was in. Desperately he tried to calm her, but to no avail. She was like a wounded animal, doubled with pain as though she had been kicked in the guts. "Paul, please .. take me .. home. You'll have to tell the others, I .. just can't," she stammered through the sobs.

"I would do that anyway, Debbie. I know it will hurt them also, but I'm totally cornered, please say you understand?"

After seeing Amanda's performance at the Guild Hall, Debbie knew she had won and her heart shattered into a million little pieces. They walked home in silence, both gutted. What a brilliant start to a career, she thought. Tony's death, a lost marriage and a pregnancy. She didn't think that even Eric could top that little lot.

Although Matthew had a gorgeous lounge of his own, he spent most of his free time with her parents, mutually pleasing each other. Somehow it seemed natural to have him around and when Paul and Debbie walked in, they all jumped up. Fear must have risen in them when they saw the bedraggled couple standing before them.

Ellen's arms had shot around her daughter as Paul told them the unbelievable misery that had struck them. They were shocked to their nerve endings. Jim rallied first, "They can't do that, Paul. For God's sake, what about Debbie?"

Paul's face resembled a swollen red blob, his voice shook, "Jim, you really must see, Eric does have us all over a barrel. How the hell do you think I feel for, Christ sake?"

Debbie sat there as though watching a film, every ounce of her hoping for a happy ending. Many ideas were being kicked around and many more tears were shed. Finally it was time for Paul to leave. She couldn't see him off, she was too numb and didn't trust herself with him.

Matthew took him to the door and after a few angry words, he was back with his face black as thunder. Through the haze of fog, that had become her brain, she wondered how she would carry on, and if they weren't a success, all of this would have been for nothing.

Clearing his throat, Matthew asked if they wanted to be alone. Debbie felt herself slump further down the settee, her tone flat, "Whatever happens, it will affect us all. I would rather you stayed for now. We all have so many things to sort out!"

Ellen poured them all a drink and choked with bitter sobs, "Sadly, I can understand Paul's predicament, he must feel even worse that we do!"

Jim and Matthew seemed stunned into silence. Debbie could feel her face swelling up and her eyes felt like slits in a puffy mass. At long last she thought about the little life inside of her.

Realising everyone was already upset, she thought she may as well break that news also. Her voice somewhat a couple of octaves higher, she gulped, "When I left here tonight, I don't think I had ever felt happier. You see, I had some wonderful and special news for Paul!"

Three pairs of anxious eyes were on her as a feeling of hysteria rose again. Her eyes spilled over as she remembered how happy she had been. Inhaling deeply, she blurted, "I never told Paul, but I am just over two months pregnant. I think it happened the night of Tony's funeral, I had forgotten about the pill. I was so happy .."

She broke off as sobs tore from her, "I know Paul isn't the father of that Morgan woman's child, proving it is another matter and time sure ain't on our side!"

Jim walked over to her, "Debs, none of us are seeking to lay any blame dear. I think I speak for us all when I say, we trust Paul, but if you had told him about the baby, he would never have left. Sorry, Debbie, I think you owed him the right to choose, don't you?"

Still sobbing, she knew he was right and mumbled, "I know, Dad, but Eric would break us all and even if I didn't care, Paul does. Its not just me, its all of us and I sure wouldn't want to stoop to Amanda's level!"

Having studied the contents of her glass, she drained it, feeling it begin to warm her ice cold heart. Ellen choked, "You will have the babe, won't you, Debbie? We'll stand by you, just as you stood by us, you know that!"

Seeing the sadness in her mother's eyes, only served to upset her more. Casting a quick glance around the room, there wasn't a dry eye to be seen. She knew that she could no more have an abortion than fly. This baby had been conceived in a very deep love.

Defiance entered her, "There is no way in which I will not bear this child. There may be a small scandal, but it will not be from Eric. The little mite didn't ask to be put there and already I feel responsible for it!"

Matthew was still sitting at the table, his chin cupped in his hands. His black hair was ruffled as his fingers had run through it. Raising his eyes to her, "Debs, I sure have the perfect solution, so I have. Marry me? We are always with each other in our work!"

They all turned to him with utter shock. Finding her voice, she gasped, "I couldn't do that, Matthew. You know I'm in love with Paul and it wouldn't be fair, but thank you!"

He stood up and walked over to her. Would she ever know how much he loved her at that moment. She was devastatingly vulnerable and every inch of him yearned to comfort her, yearned to take her pain from her. Somehow he had to convince her that he could make her happy, but subtlety was called for, he mustn't scare her. He had hardened beyond words and swiftly sat down beside her.

Gently, he turned her face to him, "Debs, we could be happy. The baby needs a father and I have loved you from the day we met. In fact, I just told Paul that now he is out of the running, I would try and court you, even try and win you. Although, I admit, I wouldn't have rushed like this!"

Taking his drink from him, Debbie promptly knocked it back.

Surely she was hearing things, but then, the whole evening felt like a charade. Her father's voice drifted through the haze, "Think about it, Debs. It is and has been obvious to us, that Matthew does love you!"

Her mind swung like a pendulum, back and forth, bumping as it swung, until her head throbbed. She had not accepted losing Paul, or being pregnant and now this. "Dad, I don't know anything anymore. I just feel ill and frightened. I can't marry a man just because I'm pregnant!"

"Debbie, I didn't mean it to sound like that, dear. Of course you can't, but you and Matthew already share so much. Once you get over the shock, you may see everything in a different light!"

He had paused several times, his voice torn with emotion. Looking into those kind eyes, Debbie could see grief and anger in them. Ellen broke down again, "Jim, what have we done wrong? First we lose Tony and now our daughter's heart has been broken. She didn't deserve this!"

Jim's arms went around his wife, "Come now, darling, let's go to bed and leave them to chat. Nobody can blame us, we did our best, perhaps it was never enough!"

Debbie jumped to her feel, almost falling back down again. The drink was making her a little heady. It was farcical, one upset led to another. "Don't dare blame each other. You couldn't help what happened to Paul, none of us could. Go to bed and get some rest, tomorrow is another day!"

Standing where she was as her parents left the room, her whole body shook with shock, fear and total confusion. Matthew had paced the room, lighting them a cigarette and handing one to her, his voice as unsteady as everyone else.

"Debs, my proposal wasn't one of kindness. I fell in love with you almost when we met, so I did. But you were Paul's girl and I swear I'd have taken the secret to my grave, but everything is different now!"

He paused to pour a further drink and continued, "I couldn't bear to leave, so help me, yet it hurt like hell to stay, me darling, I know you and I are close. I love you, Debbie!"

Squinting into his eyes, she could see they finally betrayed his feelings. Instinctively, she knew he would never hurt her. Yet what about the baby? What about making love with another man? It was certainly ironic that all through their pieces of success, it had always been him beside her.

Feeling sick with fear and worry, she gulped, "Matthew, I can see that love. Hell, I've always thought the world of you, but not in that way. Yet, I don't even know if that's true, I've never thought about it. God, Matthew, I'm so muddled, what about the babe, it wouldn't be yours."

He pulled her gently into his arms. Suddenly, she felt safe again. She could hear his heart thumping, making her cry. As he soothed her, he whispered, "I'll bring the babe up as my own. Everything would fall into place. I know it's a hell of a rush, but right now, little one, the church is booked, I think we should use it!"

Holding her tenderly, his rich Irish lilt was even more pronounced under the huge deluge of emotion. His entire body ached for her. A desperate need to lighten the air of tragedy, sent his voice into a hoarse growl, "I'm not such a monster to put you off entirely, am I?"

In spite of her misery, she found that made her laugh, he always seemed to lift her spirits. He was such a dear person, confusing her even further. A shudder ran through her, "Matthew, everyone will know you were second choice. I couldn't do that to you. I know you would be a superb father, I watched you with Tony, but I have nothing to offer you, nothing apart from my undying loyalty!"

"As the saying goes, who could be asking for more? I don't mind what order I come in and people don't know much about us outside our immediate circle. I love you, Debbie!"

Sincerity fell from his lips, his breath felt hot on her forehead. His body shook violently and she put her arms around him to comfort him. Feeling his grip tighten, she mumbled, "Matthew, if we did go through with this .."

She stopped and gulped as the words she had just uttered hit her. The fact that she could even think about it at the moment, spoke volumes. Her mind was in a chaos that she could not have believed. Lifting her eyes to him, she gasped, "I never, I never thought of us, I mean, not like this!"

Momentarily, he had to release her, he didn't trust himself at all. Pouring further drinks and handing one to her, he gave a little moan, "Look at the state of me and I have only had you in my arms!"

They looked at each other, his arousal blatantly clear. He was in a dreadful state and not knowing how to handle such a situation, she gave a little giggle. He smiled, "Do you remember asking me if I had found a nice girl? I meant that I had all I want and that me darling, is how much I love you. When Tony died, my arms longed to hold and comfort you, to comfort me, but I couldn't. You designed my flat for me, now it can be for us both. I swear I'll never give you a moment of heartache and the babe will be mine!"

Tenderly, he pulled her back into his arms. Again she felt safe as he kissed her eyes softly. Never had she needed to be held as much as she did right now. She felt his lips searching hungrily for hers and headily, lifted hers to him and felt her mouth being brushed. Slowly he moved over her eyes and back to her mouth. Only then did it deepen and his arms folded about her, holding her against his hardness. Yet she knew he would not take advantage of her, but found herself responding to the tenderness he offered. In fact she was shocked to find she didn't want him to stop. Never had she felt so much confusion, perhaps she had drunk a little too much, she did however, feel safe.

Somehow she felt she would have no problem living with him. She would always love Paul, but she would have to lock that love deep into a corner of her heart. If she did marry Matthew, she would be loved, poor Paul was left with Amanda.

Matthew felt her beautiful confusion. His heart leapt at her responses to his kisses, but he knew she was in shock and very vulnerable indeed. Her body leaned trustingly into him, he could not betray that trust. With a tortured groan he pulled her away from him, "Debbie, go to bed and think this through. I love you desperately, but right now, if you stay here, I'll not be responsible for my actions."

"Sorry, Matthew," she gulped.

He turned from her, he mustn't pressure her, but he could pray.

Clearing his throat, he choked, "I don't need to think about this, Debbie, but *you* do. You're in deep shock and I mustn't take advantage. We'll talk tomorrow, so we will. Goodnight, precious!"

CHAPTER SEVENTEEN

Debbie drifted somewhat trancelike into her room. Without question, she had obeyed Matthew after he had left her in the room alone. She fully realised he had left her with great difficulty and warmth seeped into her.

Her life had ended and started again during the course of a day. She just lay there, her mind racing as she realised that she would have been devastated had Matthew left the home. He mixed well and had a rich sense of humour, he had also had his own heart broken. It was probably crazy even to think of marrying him, what if she ended up hurting him?

Tossing and turning restlessly, she asked herself, would she want to wait for Paul even if he were to be free in five years? The she realised she shouldn't have to ask, she should be only too willing to wait, yet she wasn't. Her thoughts tumbled around her mind, yet in her heart she knew, she could make Matthew happy.

Her mind concentrated on how they had worked together, both in the shop and with this latest rush of success. They had formed a perfect partnership, appearing side by side, almost as though they were a couple. She also recalled that it had been he who had encouraged her and knew that without him, she would be lost. She had just had a slight taste of the depth of his love. Thinking back she knew, she should have realised how he felt.

She now had a choice, she could either pull herself together and carry on for all of their sakes, or, she could go into a decline and break them all, just as Eric intended and she vowed there and then, one day she would overtake his empire, she had people around her who would willingly help.

Like a flash it hit her, she would marry Matthew. She would never cease from trying to keep him happy, to show him the love he had selflessly hidden from her.

Next morning she awakened feeling sick and ill. Dragging herself reluctantly from her bed, she showered and dressed and still managed to look and feel as though she had completed ten rounds with the heavyweight boxing champ.

Matthew was already down with her parents, he looked very strained and tired. Her parents had sadness written all over them, obviously they had talked for the best part of the night.

Guilt stabbed her as she realised that she had brought so much misery into the home. Granted it hadn't been her fault, not even Paul's fault, but sad faces were all about her. Ellen broke down again as Matthew stood up and led Debbie to the table.

His voice trembled, "Debs, I've explained to your parents. I think they would be happy if we married. They know I love you dearly and will bring the babe up as my own. Its now up to you, me dear one!"

Ellen sniffled as she went into details about offering a man a full marriage. Debbie felt frustration, her voice almost terse, "Mum, I do know what I must do. You brought me up to understand that marriage must be all or nothing. Matthew and I have always been photographed together and no one knows about the baby. If the wedding is kept very quiet, no one need know, apart from Alma and Irene. I owe them both the truth!"

Matthew had subconsciously crossed his fingers. He had also been forced to cross his legs, a happy Debbie gave him an almighty hard-on – a sad Debbie, incited a riot in his loins. He bloody well knew he could love her pain from her. That was when it hit him, she was accepting his proposal. And he couldn't even stand up to envelop her into his arms. Instead, he buried his head into his hands and wept, "Debbie, you're saying 'yes' aren't you? Oh, me wee darling, what can I say? I'll never hurt you," he gulped.

Jim was on his feet, "Debbie, we are happy with your decision. I hope you haven't felt pressured into this though. We will always love Paul, but Matthew is family!"

Her eyes lifted to him, her heart went out to Matthew, "Dad, I'm sure this is what I want. I'm bloody lucky to have someone like Matthew to love me. Meanwhile, I must go and explain to Irene and Alma, there is so much work to get through and the sooner this is sorted the better. We'll talk later, Matthew, if that's alright with you. We're all weepy at the moment," she swallowed the sob that had risen in her throat.

Mercifully, the staff didn't know whose girl she was. So they would accept what was happening without question. Alma and Irene knew about Paul and as Debbie expected complete loyalty from them, she felt it was a two way street.

Fact one, she was pregnant, fact two, she was supposed to marry Paul on Saturday. Not only had she changed the name of her husband overnight, but she could hardly have become pregnant with the same speed. It was farcical, but she felt the need for honestly. After all, it would become apparent soon.

Irene jumped up as Debbie entered the office, "Gosh, Debbie, you look dreadful, what happened?"

Balling her hands with determination, her controlled voice belied her inner fear, "Irene, everyone will think I'm sick in the head. However, I do want you to know the whole truth, in the full knowledge that it will be treated as confidential!"

Debbie went through the story and as she ended, Irene had tears dripping from her blue eyes. "Thank you for taking me into your confidence," she stammered through choking sobs, "You could've kept quiet, although I would have wondered what was happening. Golly, Debbie, I feel so much respect for you and for Matthew. For what its worth, I really feel that you're doing the right thing!"

Irene hugged Debbie with real affection and returned to her desk. A couple of hours later, Debbie began to wish she hadn't bothered to tell Alma as she waffled on about the marriage, forgetting she had honeymooned with Paul.

Massaging her throbbing temple, Debbie gasped, "Alma, I don't want anyone to know yet. When my babe is born, you can run a feature that Matthew and I have had our child!"

The silence was deafening as Alma, at last grasped the full implication of what was being said. Her voice now serious, "Debbie, I'm so sorry about Paul, but I must admit that Matthew is adorable!"

Exhaustion had begun to set in, yet Debbie knew she had been right to take the bull by the horns. She was more than lucky to have Matthew and she did owe everyone their jobs. A sort of peace began to descend on her, she was beginning to accept the situation herself.

Within the hour, Alma was back on the 'phone, "Debbie, I have arranged a television contract for you. They want you to design a 'modern mother layette' and feature your diary of events during your pregnancy. They will hold the last program over until after the birth. And then, Debbie, and then you can show the babe dressed in your designs. Oh, they automatically thought that you and Matthew were already married, so I didn't give the game away!"

In spite of herself, Debbie smiled. With an assurance she was far from feeling, she replied, "Yes, I would love to do that, providing that the wedding is kept quiet. I know Matthew would agree with me and it must be this way, Alma, for the baby's sake as well as his!"

Alma was emotional as she said, "Fair enough, Debbie. Incidentally, I think you have coped with your trauma magnificently. We all owe you, it must have been such an easy option to allow everything to drift away. I for one, would like to thank you and should you ever need any help, don't hesitate, promise?"

Her mind raced, she was due to start on the knitting for beginners series. The diary of events would run parallel, finally linking together with the layette. Golly, she would be busy, already this little life was bringing its own luck with it. Fortunately, whatever she had to tackle would include Matthew and that fact alone reassured her.

Debbie was completely overawed as everything began to feel real to her, especially by the fact that having a baby could enhance, rather than hamper their joint careers.

Paul's departure still hurt like hell, but she was far too busy to dwell on it and instinctively knew, that Matthew would help with the pressure. Little by little she was subconsciously relying on Matthew's strength and she began to feel relaxed. Her parents would indeed love the babe, yet this time last year, they would have all worried how to afford it.

That evening, Matthew took her down to walk along the beach. It had been a long hard day, yet the puzzle was falling into place. She felt dreadfully tired and knew it would be quite a while before the shock left her system.

Although it was only April, the weather was reasonably warm. The night was perfect with a sky that was almost navy blue. Stars winked their approval, while the moon shone as though it had been switched on especially for them.

They had slipped their shoes off, meandered to the edge of the shore to allow the water to lap their feet, strangely soothing them.

Chatting over the events of the day, Debbie told Matthew of her discussion with Alma. She had emphasised the fact that she had sworn Alma to secrecy about the wedding. He gathered her to him, "Ye must have some love for me, Debs, otherwise it wouldn't matter to you. Debbie, me darlin', Debbie, I just know what we are doing is right!"

His voice held a tantalising low, with an added spurt of Irish brogue. His lips sought hers and with an ease that surprised her, she looped her arms around his neck. Feeling his kiss deepen, she felt his hands cover her buttocks, pulling her tightly to him, filling her with a heady excitement.

To her amazement, she found herself tingling from head to toe and felt his throbbing manhood against her abdomen. Stunned with shock, she realised that she wanted this man, yet how could she? Was this a rebound from losing Paul? Her heart thumped painfully against her ribs as her breast pressed into the hard wall of Matthew's chest. She could feel the tremors in his body as his lips moved over her face, brushing her lips apart and kissing her again and again, expounding soft moans of sheer delight.

Matthew could feel her responses and knew only too well that she wanted to be loved. But for the moment he was content with her responses. He had to keep reminding himself that she was still in shock, still lonely, still a very frightened young woman.

After assuring her of his love, he finally left her outside her parents' flat. One thing was certain, she felt a darned sight better than when she had woken that morning and when she crawled into bed, she felt so much better than the previous night, which strangely felt light years ago.

The important factor within her, was that Matthew was never hurt. It was very important that she felt able to give herself to him. Suddenly, she felt fire roar in her belly, her skin burned and crazily she found herself blushing. She recalled the sweetness of his kisses, feeling arrows of desire spike into her. She could scarcely breathe as she wondered how his hands would caress her naked body. Her nipples hardened, oh yes, he would take them into his mouth. She groaned aloud as she envisaged herself locked into his arms, she did want him to touch her, to enter her body and join them forever.

She shuddered and felt the familiar warm moisture arrive between her legs. Turning towards her pillow, she dragged herself into the foetal position and allowed the important thoughts to flow. And when they finally stopped whirring around, she felt the merciful kiss of sleep engulf her.

**

Debbie awakened with mixed feelings on her wedding day. Part of her felt pain, the other elation. Every nerve in her jerked as she prepared herself to walk down the aisle with her father.

She had chosen a cream, chiffon, knee length dress, the sleeves billowed, before gathering into a tight cuff at her wrist. The bodice was breast hugging and tightly nipped into her waist. Her feet gelled into dainty, cream, court shoes. A pert little hat, complete with veil, to cover her face until after the ceremony, added the finishing touches.

A small posy of spring flowers had been made for her to carry. Matthew had asked if she would like a weekend in Paris, but they both preferred Morecambe. They had however, booked into a hotel for one night. They both had hectic schedules, which had slipped slightly behind as a direct result of the upsets.

Arriving at the church and hearing the organ playing softly, she took her father's arms and felt her body cover itself with hefty goose bumps. Walking up the aisle, she gasped as she saw Matthew. His lithesome body, clad in a smart silver grey suit, gave him an air of devastating elegance. Her heart flipped as she felt herself being deposited beside him.

Momentarily, she thought of Paul, especially hearing herself making her vows. It still felt strangely right to be saying, "I, Debbie Hudson, take thee Matthew Ross." His eyes never left hers as he made his vows loud and clear, it was obvious he was proclaiming to the world that she was his wife.

The service ended and he lifted her veil, "You look gorgeous, Mrs Ross. I love you so much, so I do!"

Tingles of joy ran through her, his hand had shaken as he had placed the exquisite gold band onto her finger. He had chosen it himself, the deeply engraved leaves intertwined all round the circle, an unbroken circle and she knew, he had chosen the design as he saw their future.

Photographs had been taken of their secret day and Jim had booked a table in a quaint little pub in Old Heysham. Glasses of champagne were clinked and they also toasted the future of the business they had all embarked upon.

Debbie had already moved her belonging to the upstairs flat. She knew Matthew had longed to make love with her, yet had restrained himself, somehow endearing himself even more.

Leaving the castle later that evening, he took the overnight bag and instinctively they made their way down to the beach. His smile plucked at her heart strings, tingles of desire ran through her, coupled with a little trepidation about their first night together. At all costs, she must make Matthew happy, make sure he never regretted marrying her.

He watched her with love. The breeze lifted her lovely hair and made it bounce around her shoulders. She positively enchanted him, yet he sensed her nerves were on edge, wishing he could think of words to reassure her, whilst at the same time keeping his own feelings under control. They sauntered along, drinking in the beauty of the bay. The air was rich with ozone, intoxicating them. Suddenly, he stopped, his arms folding around her, "Can I kiss my wife?"

His kiss was filled with tenderness and her heart began to skip beats as he led her towards the hotel. It must have been around ten o'clock and for the very first time, she signed 'Debbie Ross'. Matthew checked that champagne had been sent to the room and when she stepped into the lift, she had a strange feeling that some type of heaven awaited her.

CHAPTER EIGHTEEN

A very embittered Paul had collated all of the events leading up to his much fought against marriage. Every detail was filed with his solicitor, to be opened in the event of his death or sudden disappearance. Many people would think he was over the top with his extra precautions, but he was the one caught up in the Morgan trap.

The haste of the wedding had struck him as ridiculously odd. The absence of Maralyn was perhaps the thing that frightened him most of all. She was a loyal wife and mother, yet her non attendance had been totally self imposed. Paul had felt sorry for her when he had 'phoned, her voice was tired as she said flatly, "Sorry, Paul, there are certain conditions with which I cannot agree to. Should I ever be able to help you, don't hesitate and so forth ..!"

Paul had never felt so incensed and when he sat down and analysed his reason for calling her, it was to make sure that she had not mysteriously vanished. Hell, he was becoming paranoid, but Eric's explanations had left him remarkably suspicious. He had strutted, rooster style, "Let's not bitch, Paul. You have more than landed on your bloody feet. Your salary has trebled and Amanda has found the most sumptuous apartment for you both!"

Anger engulfed him, "Oh, the apartment's fine, Eric. At least I can lock myself into my room and keep out of her bloody way!"

Paul was in no mood to play about with their stupid, cruel and dangerous games. He had made his vows, choking on every oath he uttered. There had been no option open to him, other than to allow Debbie to be ruined.

His heart ached for her, he should have made his vows to her by now. A pain so sharp it doubled him, shot through his body, tugging him with yearning, rocking him with misery.

He had been obliged to move in with Amanda, that was part of the deal. But he had chatted up the maintenance lads and persuaded them to sink a huge double mortise lock into his door. A spare 'phone line had been installed, together with a radio and television. He almost managed a wry smile, Amanda would fume when she realised she hadn't won him after all.

Amanda had indeed appeared radiant in the registry office. She had lost no time at all in making an exhibition of a new bride in the lavish restaurant where Eric had decided they would dine. Paul felt weary and longed to get home, he was fortunate to have his own bathroom, but no kitchen. He only intended to use the apartment to change and sleep.

At least Eric had been forced to dash off to the airport. Amanda wound herself around Paul's neck as the car drove them to their Manhattan apartment. "I'm so happy, Paul. To think we can spend two full days honeymooning. I've wanted you for years," she purred.

Her words sparked off a fury he had never felt in him. How dare she? She had wanted him, he wanted Debbie, Debbie had wanted him and his fists clenched and unclenched as they arrived outside of their new home.

Stepping into the ridiculously gigantic lounge, she threw her arms around his neck. "Darling Paul, shall we go to bed? Would you like a drink first? Her voice was eager, excited and decidedly expectant.

How he loathed the very air she breathed. He would fuck her at his own convenience, but he would leave her needing so many times, she would look outside. And then, he smirked inwardly, he would smack an adultery suit on her.

She stripped her clothing without removing her eyes from him. She stood before him, clad in an ivory suspender belt, the suspenders clipped to her skin coloured stockings. Her blond mound glistened between her legs and he watched without a hint of arousal. He just wanted to dive into the whisky bottle he had planted into his room, but he had to pretend, at least for a few more moments, otherwise she would become suspicious of his next move.

He watched again as she wet her fingers and circled her rigid nipples. He longed to rush into his room and leave her stranded, but he intended to play her body, to the rhapsody of his own choosing, under his own directorship.

As he removed his jacket and tie, he saw the light of excitement glint in her green eyes. Her breathing was erratic as she offered her lips to him. Swiftly he brushed her mouth from him and bent his head to suck harshly on her hardened nipple. Seeing her wince with pain, his cock hardened. Well, she could suck him off, by golly she could suck him off. If he had to, he would make her come, but his cock would certainly never enter her greedy bush.

Although deep down, he doubted he was the father of her child, he had made an appointment to have a vasectomy for the future. He shuddered as he vowed to make sure that something like this, could never happen to him again, although he would always be childless, unless …Easing himself down into the armchair, he watched Amanda performing. Slowly and deliberately he clasped his hands behind his head. With the speed of light, she was on her knees, "Paul, hold me. You know what I want!"

He knew alright, he also knew what he wanted her to have, a severe case of strangulation. If only he could oblige, but his time would come, he needed to be free as soon as possible, yet realised at least a year would have to elapse. His prayer was that Debbie would be well underway and would take him back. Until he was in such a position, he didn't even want to hear how she was, temptation was more than he could bear.

His cock was pressing against his fly. Amanda was on her knees, her hands tearing at his trousers until, with a contented groan, she took his hardness into her hands. "You're ready to fuck, aren't you, darling? Get out of your clothes and take me to bed," she breathed into his neck.

For a moment, he was tempted to leave her there and then, but he had to be more subtle than that. Sort of gradually make her see his true feelings. Right now, though, she could get rid of his hard-on for him. His fists clenched to stop him from slapping that spiteful, greed filled face.

Easing himself to the edge of the chair, he gripped her head and pushed it between his legs, her mouth instantly taking in his hardness. He leaned back slightly to watch her, and her tongue did dart with the speed of a viper.

She did not, however, have the power to arouse him and he was nowhere near ready to come. He must somehow train himself to this routine for a while, he absolutely must. Her eyes lifted to him, "Let's fuck, Paul," she gasped.

"Make me come first then!"

He knew only too well, he could have gone to his room and masturbated, but there was still a role for him to play. He felt her part her legs and take his hand to place onto her bush. She was saturated and with resignation, he rubbed his finger over her clitoris until she screamed out.

Paul felt the bitter line of contempt form around his mouth once more. With a degree of sheer spite, he removed his hand and she screamed for its return. He had had enough, he wanted to come and get to bed. Pressing down on her head, he controlled his cock and pushed it further into her mouth, back and forth, in and out, feeling her suck for all she was worth.

Only then did he return his hand to her bush and seconds later she came into his hand. Now it was his turn and again he supported his cock, until he shot spurts of semen all over her face. He then replaced it back into her mouth to allow her to suck him dry.

Feeling the benefit hit him, he looked down at her. Her mouth pouted, "Paul, come to bed. I want to feel your cock right inside of me, you on top of me. For chrissakes, Paul, will you fuck me?"

Resisting the urge to tell her, 'never in a million years', he pushed her roughly from him. She lay there, her legs already parted for him and he stood up, zipped up his fly and much the same as Bill Murray had done, said, "Goodnight, my dear!"

Amanda watched with horror as he slammed his door shut. "Paul, what about food? What about a drink?"

She realised he had locked himself in and heard acid drip from his voice, "You are, of course, joking. Last time we ate or drank together, I was drugged!"

Amanda screamed out, "You must eat. I wouldn't do that to you again!"

He gulped heavily, "I know you won't. If I ever eat in this apartment, it will be something I have brought in!"

Paul thought he would hate the person he was turning into, but it was impossible to change. He didn't see why he should. Hearing Amanda's pitiful pleas, only served to incite him further, how many people had she hurt? How many men had run scared? How many marriages had she tried to ruin?

Amanda had to admit that Paul had won this particular round. The son of a bitch had used her without mercy. He would suffer for this, she vowed, never realising he was already suffering, just being away from his beloved Debbie.

CHAPTER NINETEEN

The lift stopped and Debbie and Matthew stepped out. Reaching their door, Matthew swung her into his arms to carry her over the threshold, a cry of exaltation left him as he set her down as though she was a priceless gem.

His deep blue eyes smouldered with unspent passion, his body shook as his lips searched for hers. As his kiss began to deepen, he groaned and crushed her to him. Little squeals left her as his tongue slid silkily into her mouth.

Half crazed with passion, he felt her eager welcome, her tongue met and then gloried with his. The urge to strip her there and then had become a desperate need. With a violent shudder, he whispered, "Don't be frightened, dearest. I won't do anything you don't want me to. I'm the chap that loves you, remember?"

Having uttered the hardest sentence of his life, he let her go. He noticed her hands shaking as she collected her nightwear from the case. Her eyes were moist as they lifted to him, "I'll have a quick bath, Matthew. You could pour us a drink!"

Closing the door behind her, she leaned heavily against it. At last she could release the breath she had inhaled so deeply. Turning on the taps and watching the water swirl into the bath, she realised that her mind was very much at home. With a surge of sorrow, she wondered how Paul was coping.

Questions tumbled about her mind like acrobats in a circus. Had her love for Paul been a shallow love? Could she have been in a shock so deep not to know what she wanted anymore? Could she just be seeking solace?

Whatever the answers were, she knew she did want to make love with Matthew. Tentatively, she slipped into hr seductive, pretty black lace nightgown. Tying the tiny black ribbons on her shoulder she knew she was ready to face whatever the night held.

Matthew had gasped as he saw her framed in the doorway. She looked adorable in that flimsy piece of nonsense. Her hair hung deliciously around her shoulders, little damp strands fell softly around her lovely face and his hand shook as he handed her a glass of champagne. Watching her gulp it down and handing it back for a refill, he poured it and smiled, "I'll just have a quick dip, darling. Incidentally, drink that slowly, or you'll be sick!"

In spite of his warning, she still knocked it back, feeling it sending her spiralling with excitement. Apprehension now made her throat constrict. Forcing herself from the spot, she made her way to the dressing table and sat down on the long stool. She then commenced to brush her hair.

Hearing the bathroom door open, her hand froze. Through the mirror, she watched the easy sway of his body as he hung his suit into the wardrobe. He had popped on a white bathrobe and she asked herself, why hadn't she realised just how handsome he was before now? It was unbelievable, last week Paul had broken her heart and so very quickly, Matthew had picked up the pieces and mended it. He must have found a piece that she had never recognised.

The light from the promenade shafted over him. His black hair shone like jet as it fell over his forehead. The sea had begun to roar as slowly, deliberately, he walked towards her, taking the brush from her and continuing to brush her hair.

Matthew was regarding her as if she was the most feminine, most beautiful, most precious of women. Lifting her hair, he dropped his kisses onto her nape. Pulling her head gently back, he parted her lips with his mouth. "Debbie, you are a beautiful woman and I love you with all of my heart!"

His throaty groan set her off, feverishly she turned to him, her arms eagerly folding around his neck. Their eyes met and locked in the mirror, sending fire through her. He placed a knee onto the stool beside her, his mouth now searing a path to the pulse in her neck. Never had anything felt so erotic as she gripped the sides of the seat for support.

She saw the pulse in his throat throb beneath his skin, saw his eyes smoulder as they fixed on his destination. Tenderly, he ran his hands over her breasts, cupping them over the thin layer of material. A deep guttural groan left him, "Debbie, I can't believe I'm doing this to you!"

Again their eyes met in the mirror, both smouldered with passion as his hand slipped inside of her nightdress and wended its way over her naked breast.

Her mouth turned to him and after he kissed her, he moved his mouth to her shoulder. His teeth gently tugged at the ribbons and as they opened, the garment slid to her waist and she was exposed.

Swiftly, he sat next to her, his back to the mirror. No one could have warned her that the sight of his dark hair against her breast would send her wild. Watching his head move from side to side was more than mind and body could stand. He suckled each nipple until it stood firm, opening his mouth just a fraction to take in more of her breast. Mortified with exquisite desire, she watched with wonder as her nipple stood engorged as he moved to the other side.

With a deep sigh, Debbie melted softly against his chest as he carried her over to the bed, laying her gently onto the white satin sheets and straightening up to gaze upon her. "You're so beautiful," he whispered, as he bent over her and slipped her nightdress from her.

She was naked in the moonlight. He drew his breath, marvelling at the slim contours of her body, the high, firm rounded breasts, the dark triangle at the top of her gorgeous thighs. Her hands reached out to him, and he moved so that his body lay full length against her as his robe slid to the floor and she felt his hardness swell against her thighs, firm and deliciously insistent.

Matthew pulled away, cupping her breasts in his hands, "I want you so much, me darling, but not yet, not just yet," he murmured, taking one erect nipple between his teeth and tormenting the hard bud with his tongue. He flicked it across the surface of her nipples, sending golden darts of desire coursing through her veins, tugging cords connected directly to the heart of her body.

Debbie groaned with longing and wrapped her arms around his neck, trailing her hands along his skin. She tangled his hair, pressing his mouth firmly against her breast, writhing beneath him as she felt his manhood rearing against the soft flesh of her inner thighs. She was incredibly aware of the wet moisture of her own arousal, straining her body further and further towards him.

He paused and lifted his head, "I love you Debbie," he said, his gaze unwavering, "I've loved you from the minute I met you, so I did!"

Debbie returned his gaze. She yearned to give herself to Matthew, to surrender herself to him completely and have him know her absolutely, to have him deep inside of her. He saw her face flood with desire, happiness and need. Her sighs of pleasure whetted his already heightened appetite and his body burned.

Suddenly, he was filled with a yearning to possess her, to be inside of her and lose himself within her. He gazed down on her face, her eyes wide and her lips soft and quivering, "Tell me when, me darling," he gasped, barely able to conceal his longing.

"Oh now, Matthew," she gasped. Her legs had opened instinctively and then he was inside of her, filling her with his manhood driving into the depth of her. Debbie moaned and clung to him, burying her face in his shoulder, trying to stifle her cries as he moved rhythmically within her. Every part of her body seemed to fit perfectly with his; her shoulders against his chest, his stomach against hers, her legs wrapped around his body, embracing him again and again.

Waves of delight ebbed and flowed within her, lapping along her veins and surging through the muscles in her arms and legs, around and along her stomach. Every inch of her stiffened, then relaxed as the pulses of desire flowed through her. She tensed and shivered alternatively, vividly aware of the forces within her gathering momentum.

Matthew paused momentarily, before applying his hands under her buttocks, raising her so that he was deeper within her. She gasped, feeling as if he were burying not into but through her.

And swiftly, she lost all conscious thought and was aware only of the relentless surging inside her. The pressure now reaching an intense quivering peak. There was nothing but Matthew thrusting into her body, nothing but endless pleasure surging through her. Nothing but the two of them as they became one and poured themselves into one another, coming together until they were totally spent.

For a long time neither of them moved. Debbie remained safe in the hollow of Matthew's arm. She was aware of having experienced an intensity of love she had never even envisaged. Her absolute surrender to Matthew had given her a new freedom. She felt strangely complete on every level with him. His vulnerable strength and love, matched her own.

As he finally rolled from her, she felt stunned by the deep joy that filled her. A divine lethargy settled into her and she realised, with somewhat of a shock that she hadn't thought about Paul once, how could she? Matthew had filled her with vibrant life, leaving her replete, satiated. Yet already, her passions were beginning to stir again.

Debbie knew she would never forget Paul or his love, he would always remain embedded in her heart, he had been her first love. Right now though, she knew that she was *in* love with the man beside her. Never had she felt so treasured as she did at that precise moment.

Turning to him, she felt the natural urge to touch him. His arms crushed her again, but she pulled away. Stroking the ensuing frown from his brow, she gasped, "Matthew, I want you to know, I don't regret my decision one little bit. I do love you, more than I ever dreamed was possible!"

Matthew revelled in her words, almost as he had revelled in her love. He had prayed for her to respond to his love, but he knew she had never felt as she did now. His wildest dream had come true and he would never cease to thank God.

Turning her towards him, they lay naked and facing each other. "Debbie, I want you all over again. I know I'll be very demanding, you must tell me to stop, me darling," he whispered into the ear he was nuzzling.

"Just demand, Matthew. Just demand, my dearest." And he did, and she did and both landed just this side of paradise.

When the last utter of love, the last tasteful caress, the last tender kisses had been administered and received, they clung to each other, his penis still penetrated her and an infinite peace filled the room.

She knew her parents loved Matthew and would be thrilled when she told them how happy she was. She had indeed been given a second chance of happiness and knew that whatever lay ahead, she could face with Matthew beside her. The peace that settled into her, seemed to grow, warming the very bowels of her being. They did have a heavy workload and it would be faced together, who could possibly ask for more?

CHAPTER TWENTY

Over the ensuing months, Debbie and Matthew had been rushed off their feet. They often worked late at night, but like any couple crazily in love, they found time to express their love. It never seemed to matter what time it was, a look, a touch, a word, would lead them to plateaux new.

They worked in a kind of delirious awareness, inspiring each other. At times Matthew would catch her alone and they would turn to each other, their kisses driving them into ecstatic wonder and he would suckle her breasts as she would release his throbbing manhood, wriggle her skirt upwards, until he could penetrate her.

The charges of electricity between them never ceased to amaze Debbie. Every time Matthew was ready so was she, at times they almost had to rush or be caught. That, she felt sure, was the most erotic daring of all and Matthew teased her without mercy, "You and your beloved inspired urges. Me, wee, darling, I didn't think it possible to love you more, but daily you make me love you till I feel I'm going completely mad, so a do!"

"Me too, mmmeee too," she gasped.

The layette was proving a huge success. Debbie had knitted every stitch with a huge portion of love, making sure both boys and girls were catered for and Matthew had lovingly photographed each garment, prior to her placing them into her case, ready for their own baby.

Debbie had taken to the cameras like a duck to water. At times it was as though she was having a passionate affair with the camera. It loved her, idolised her and portrayed her as a real beauty. Her early nerves had seemed to vanish and confidence filled her as she recorded the details of her pregnancy.

She had worked out that flat seams were vital for a babe's comfort. And designs that would be easy to pop on and off were essential. In fact, being pregnant had helped her no end with the constant ideas.

The knitting series was exceedingly popular and the sacks of mail told them that she was a smash hit. She was also in the middle of designing a booklet for winter garments, a further request from Alma. Right then though, the weather was sweltering and thinking of winter was somewhat difficult. They were all lucky indeed, to be able to work in the fresh air.

Irene was in seventh heaven as she had a small typing pool working under her guidance. Jim had arranged to have a room converted into an office for them. He also needed to convert a further room as he also needed his own domain and extra help with the accounts.

Matthew was in demand more and more, his latest commission had come from a well known magazine. He had been asked to cover the 'miss Morecambe beauty contest', which was a very prestigious highlight in the summer. He was extraordinarily happy and like her, looked forward with immense curiosity to the birth of their little one.

Debbie then received a request to write a book to accompany the pregnancy series. She and Matthew had taken that particular assignment with reservations. They always talked every detail thought, bouncing ideas from each other and usually arriving at the same conclusion.

Tension built in them both and suddenly Matthew's eyes lit up, "I know, darling, why don't you have a chat with Brian? Get him to check the details through, I'm sure he would be only too pleased to help. Like you, I feel that we can't be too careful about any advice we may offer!"

Her ebony eyes lifted to him and he knew they held the key to many questions as their mail indicated. There was a rich understanding about her, a caring thoughtful understanding and people found it so easy to relate to her. They made a perfect team, both equally concerned that any information should be checked and doubly correct.

Brian Jessup had been their physician since they had first moved to Morecambe. He was more of a family friend than a doctor. Debbie had great faith in him and he was well pleased with the progress of her pregnancy.

He was in his mid thirties, happily married with four children. His brown hair was always unruly, yet somehow it managed to add to his air of understanding. His tall, six foot, slightly portly frame, explained his obvious love of food. Hazel eyes sparked, 'confidence and trust'" It would have been impossible not to have felt ease in his company.

After confirming what she already knew, that she was positively blooming, she explained her plight to him. Sitting on the corner of his desk, his arms folded, a mischievous grin covered his face. "I would be honoured to read it through for you, Debbie. I feel sure that you can help many young couples. You are very easy to identify with. If only other advisors took their work so seriously .. if ever you need me, I'm always around," he chuckled warmly.

Leaving Brian, she felt as though an albatross had left her shoulders. It was a beautiful day and Debbie decided to wander down to the shop, which as expected, was now a roaring success. Orders for Ellen's cakes were arriving thick and fast. Richard and Jenny were coping well and had taken on extra staff.

Debbie always looked forward to popping in, especially to have a chat with them. This day, Jenny had taken her up to the flat and nostalgia had flooded her as she went up the familiar stairs. So much had happened here, the birth of Tony, the birth of her romance with Paul. Conversely, there had been the death of Tony and he death of her romance.

Shuddering all over, she realised that she had met Matthew here. Yes, so much had happened here, but Jenny's eyes danced as she guided Debbie around the various rooms. Suddenly, this place bore no resemblance to her memories.

Jenny and Richard had decorated the place throughout. It looked beautiful and modern, with Jenny's personal stamp placed fully onto the premises. Seeing Debbie's obvious look of approval, she had instinctively hugged her, "Debbie, we owe all of this to you. Richard and I couldn't be happier!"

113

Debbie felt her mouth become dry. Her eyes had filled with such gratitude. It certainly was wonderful to be successful, but even more wonderful to be able to share it.

**

Turning back into the busy promenade, she had almost bumped headlong into an excited Matthew. Clutching her to him, he gave her a cock eyed grin, "Darling, there is someone ye gotta meet. I was miles away with me thoughts and I realised I owed someone a great big thank you!"

She was clueless as to his ravings, but nevertheless, his joy was infectious as he guided her towards the fairground. The music plucked at both their heartstrings, Matthew had remembered just what Rossita had told him and he not only wanted to thank her, but allow her to see the girl she had seen in her crystal ball. The raven haired beauty, was his wife.

Winding their way through the happy holiday makers, Debbie noticed the three dancing girls as they waved in eager recognition. Matthew waved back and placed his arm around Debbie and mouthed 'my wife' as he patted her bulge. Turning to her, he explained, "Darling, they used to take care of my sexual needs. Suzy on the end there, she loves a different bloke for all seasons!"

Her startled look made him chuckle as did her sharp reprimand, "You shouldn't kiss and tell!"

"I know and I don't, but you're me wife. All men screw around till they find the right woman. Anyway, women are no different, look at yon Amanda!"

She shuddered, "I know, Matthew and I believe I felt a stab of jealousy. Of course you owe me no explanations. If you cheated on me now though .. I couldn't ..!"

His arm tightened around her as they approached the palmistry tent. Rossita was unusually quiet and sitting outside. Her old eyes lit up as she saw them approach. "Matthew, this is ye woman. Tis the very one I told ye about. Ye wasted no time by the look of things," she smiled and patted Debbie's lump.

Debbie's face was a mixture of confusion and pride. "I didn't know you took this seriously, Matthew! I mean, did you have a reading? Oh, do tell me what was said?"

The old gypsy gave a little chuckle, "Him believe, stuff and nonsense. He always laughed. I told him about you, luv, and take it he has cum back to thank me!"

Matthew leaned forward and kissed her cheek. "Yeh, I did, but I wanted you to meet my wife, Debbie. Our babe is due in November, thanks a lot, Rossita!"

The gnarled hand gripped Debbie's hand. The tired old eyes searched Debbie's palm and she gave a titter, "I knew I was right about you lass, he'll never make ye sad. You'll 'ave many, many children, yer a fertile lass. Good luck," she smiled as a queue began to form.

114

Passing the dancing girls on their way home, Debbie found no problem, she was proud that Matthew could have these beauties and had chosen her to marry. Wisely, she decided not to refer to it again, but Rossita had made her happy. Her eyes lifted to her husband, "So, sunshine, we'll have many children, so we will," she mimicked and chuckled.

No matter how busy they were Matthew and Debbie always took a walk along the sandy beach. Almost ritual fashion, they would down tools about nine thirty in the evening. The air was always nice and cool at night and the various shapes of the moon would bathe them from a navy blue, star spangled sky.

Headily, they would return and walk up to that secret staircase and onto their own private balcony. Together they would survey their little domain, of which, according to Matthew, she was the duchess. His kisses would suffocate her with love, their infant kicking with a sharp reminder of its presence.

**

Debbie had completed the winter batch of designs for Haywood. The first series on knitting was drawing to a close and a further series was scheduled. She must have answered a good few thousand queries and realised her help was invaluable.

The pregnancy series was also drawing to a close and Debbie found people stopped her as she waddled along to the shop, eager to know how she was getting on. They would often run and catch her up, Brian was right, people did identify with her.

Matthew was just as popular and had invested in a very sophisticated camera to enable him to video events for himself.

Many film stars had asked for special photograph sessions, either for themselves or their children and he had the wonderful gift of bringing the best out in everyone.

At long last, the series on her pregnancy had ended, apart from the final show which would be held over until they could present their baby, dressed in the layette for the cameras. Having entered her ninth month, she longed to oblige as she felt somewhat like a beached whale.

Ironically, each program she had been involved with, had been accompanied by her being hailed as the lassie from Lancashire and she just prayed that she could make them as proud of her as that adorable lady from Rochdale had done.

Debbie was having great trouble sleeping as her huge body turned from side to side. Matthew was so tender with her, almost feeling her exasperation. He had never loved her more, she looked inordinately feminine in her role of mum to be.

His words were filled with love as he held her to him, "I bet you never want to go through this again, do you, Debs? If only I could take some of the discomfort from you!"

Stroking her head, he asked, "Have you decided what we are going to have yet, me darling? After all 'D' day is only a couple of weeks away!"

Leaning onto her elbow, her fingers ran over his mouth. "Matthew, darling, I truly don't mind what we have, providing it is healthy. Somehow though, I feel it is a little girl and I bet you want a boy, don't you?"

His smile devastated her, "I don't mind either. In fact, I think I would rather like a daughter. Maybe, in a couple of years or so, you might just consider trying for a boy, but you have given me so much pleasure, I'll leave that decision with you!"

Her mouth covered his, "I will give you a son, Matthew, no matter how many times we have to try. You have given me so much love and made me feel permanently safe. I love you!"

Ruffling her hair, he chuckled, "No matter *how* many times we try? That sounds more like a threat. Darling, we could end up with half a dozen daughters. After all this discomfort, would you really want to go through this again?"

"Providing you are with me," she sighed contentedly.

The following night, Debbie had awakened with excruciating stabbing pains. Excitement and an element of fear surged into her, at long last they were going to meet the little life she had carried for what seemed to be forever.

Trepidation hovered as she lay quietly for a moment, she wanted to be good and sure. Holding her stomach and stroking the bump, her heart brimmed over with love. This was a little girl, of that she was sure and now realised why she had craved a daughter. She wanted to name her Kelly. That had been Matthew's mother's name and he had adored her.

Turning to look at him, her heart thumped with love. His mother must have been a truly lovely lady to have brought up such a wonderful son. In a funny sort of way, she felt it would be a thank you to him. He had cosseted her though all of this and taught her the true meaning of a selfless love.

Almost as though he knew she was watching him, his eyes flickered into awareness. Another pain engulfed her, he was out of bed and making her giggle, "Is it the babe, darling? How often are the pains? Don't panic, me love!"

She didn't need to panic, he was doing her share for her. As he jumped into his clothes she felt herself smile. He was terrified, yet excited. The strength and frequency of the pains told her she should be reasonably quick.

Matthew ran to put a note under her parents' door, then rushed to start the car. For a moment she feared he would leave without her, but he returned. His beloved face was etched with concern and flushed with eager anticipation. Safely locked in his arms, she felt confident, relaxed and beautiful as they finally entered the hospital.

They had decided to book a private room, to ease the pressure from the staff and a nurse took the case from Matthew as Debbie was examined. The doctor was reassuring as she was swiftly taken into the delivery room and gowned in a white shapeless tunic.

Perspiration poured from her as the next pain almost knocked her out. The instructions were clear, "Push, good girl and another one, come now love, one more big push!"

Matthew lovingly bathed her face with one hand, the other hand was there for her to grip. Suddenly the nurse came round to her and lifted the gown from her. Her smile was warm as she said. "You do want baby placing onto you, don't you, dear?"

Her head nodded as she turned to meet Matthew's eyes, which were moist in his tension filled face. He couldn't bear her pain and a desire to get up and run from the room was increasingly difficult to ignore. Again, he felt her nails dig into him and knew she needed him.

Through a haze of pain, the magical cry heralded the arrival of their baby daughter. The squealing little bundle was beautifully clean, the tiny mouth instantly finding Debbie's nipple and began to suck ferociously. Matthew's tears ran unchecked down his cheeks as his finger stroked the soft little face and he gulped, "Debbie, she's a wee darling, so she is!"

Over awed by the birth and totally exhausted, Debbie found tears of gratitude run freely down her face. Matthew leaned over to kiss the babe as the nurse took her to be bathed. His arms went around her, "Debbie, you've done us proud, she's a real beauty and I love you both!"

A sob caught in her throat, "Matthew, I couldn't have done this without you." Perhaps the maternity staff were used to all of this reactionary behaviour, to them however, the moment had been so personally intimate. Temporarily, they had managed to exclude everyone from this moment.

**

Half an hour later, Debbie had been changed into her own pretty nightdress and sat up in the rather luxurious ward, her arms eagerly stretching out to receive their child.

Profound love engulfed her as she took their babe. Matthew placed his arm around Debbie as they both gazed in wonder at the cause of all the pain. They scarcely breathed, just watched spellbound as their daughter's eyes opened, large and blue. Her miniscule amount of hair was pure blond. Her lashes were long and curled upwards, her fists flaying around the petal mouth. For a moment, Debbie thought of Paul, how could she not?

The thought disappeared as her eyes lifted to her husband. He had nursed her through all of this. Although her labour had lasted about four hours, only two of them had become unbearable. Yet Matthew had filled the birth with a rich happiness.

His arms enclosed them both, a cocoon of love engulfed the three of them, "Matthew, thank you for pulling me through. She is adorable, in fact, she is so adorable that I think there could only be one name for her," she choked with emotion.

"What's that, me darling. What'll we call our babe?"

They were both still in shock. His body not quite in control, yet his eyes smouldered into hers and she read in them, the love she felt for him. Her hand reached to touch his face, "Matthew, I prayed for a daughter, you see, there is only one name she can have, darling, it has to be Kelly!"

Those moments had been filled with poignancy and it deepened as a cloak of emotion gripped them and tightened. Matthew's Adam's apple flew up and down and she knew, beyond any shadow of doubt that she had paid him the highest possible accolade. And his eyes spilt over again. "When did you decide on her name?"

Debbie sighed happily, "She has been Kelly ever since we married. I prayed it would be a girl, we may have had boys from now on. To me, Matthew, it was important that this one should be Kelly!"

He feigned mock surprise, "What's all this about boys? After all you've been through, the fact that you can even think about more, fills me with amazement!"

Taking his hand to her lips and kissing it, she whispered, "How about you ringing Mum and Dad? They must be frantic after receiving our note. Then, my darling, you can nurse your daughter!"

Matthew had dialled the number and begun to speak, "Ellen, you and Jim have a grand daughter, Kelly...," he gasped and broke down. Debbie then realised just how much of an ordeal it had been for him. Her naming the baby after his mother had choked him beyond words.

Taking the 'phone from him, she heard her mother in tears. "Congratulations, Debs. Dad and I are thrilled for you both. We can't wait to see her, love," Ellen's voice wobbled on a funny note between high and low and part of Debbie still wobbled, "Matthew will be home to change soon, Mum, he will bring you both back with him. I'm so happy and our little girl was also born under Scorpio. If she's half as lucky as me, well she will be a happy little lass!"

Matthew looked so natural with Kelly sunk into the crook of his arm. Part of her just wanted to remain in the cocoon of private, intimate wonder, loving the gentle caresses from her husband as he used his free hand to run over her face.

It was therefore, with a sting of reluctance that she rang Alma. She then smiled as she heard the excitement rise in Alma's sleepy voice, "Debbie, heartiest congratulations to you both. How about the press release? How do you want it to read?"

Debbie pulled Matthew close to the 'phone, a smile broke over his face as he heard Alma's infectious excitement. Gripping his hand, she sighed, "How about, Debbie Hudson and photographer husband, Matthew Ross, announce the safe arrival of their baby daughter, Kelly?"

Replacing the receiver after Alma promised to visit late in the day, she looked into Matthew's eyes, "Debbie, it sounded so wonderful to hear to tell the world that her name is Kelly. To me, me darling, that was the jewel in me crown. If only Mum could've seen this day, she would've been so proud!"

After kissing them both with tenderness, he was ready to leave and collect her parents and she stared after him as though a limb had suddenly gone missing.

She felt very emotional as she gazed upon her little daughter and thanked God for her safe arrival.

Kelly was the most precious thing that had ever happened to her. Already she knew she would be Paul's double and felt a stab of sympathy. He would never know her. He was still locked away safely into the corner of her heart and he would always be there.

The love they had shared could never be totally forgotten. Yet, she knew, if Paul were free tomorrow, she would find Matthew's love to be irreplaceable.

CHAPTER TWENTY ONE

Debbie's malaise was broken into by the opening of the door. Her husband was back with two very proud grandparents in tow. Ellen hugged Debbie and then took Kelly into the safety of her arms.

Jim had taken his own daughter into his arms, "Mum and I couldn't be happier, dear. Matthew is delighted with his daughter and you can take it from one who knows, she will always be very special to him!"

Returning his hug, Debbie knew exactly what he meant. She had been lucky enough to be his daughter and had never doubted his love for her. In spite of one's love for both parents, there seems to be a added bond between father and daughter.

Filled with his own emotions, Jim walked over to see his grand child, his arms around his wife. "Ellen, she is beautiful, dear, it feels just as it did when Debbie was born. She was gorgeous and it is hard to believe that so soon, she has grown up and become a mother herself!"

A short while later, baskets of flowers began to arrive in shoals. Carefully removing the cards from most of them, in order to send their thanks, Debbie then asked for them to be distributed throughout the hospital. Nothing gave them more pleasure than to share their joy.

Debbie's cup ran over when the doctor confirmed that she could return home the following day. There was a load of work to be sorted out, plus the final Chapter of the book. Debbie had stressed the advantages of breast feeding and to her delight, found that Kelly took to suckling with natural ease.

The Lancashire Post had been in for photographs and a few words on their joint feelings. Debbie still couldn't believe that Kelly had arrived, although losing the lump felt good. She felt exceedingly well and knew that it had been Matthew's care throughout her pregnancy and the birth, that had relaxed her.

Excitement at going home almost choked her, yet the night seemed to stretch unendingly. Never had she felt such a deep loneliness as when Matthew had kissed her goodnight and left.

Her arms had closed around Kelly, her nose nuzzling into the tiny neck, smelling the sweetness of her babe. Debbie lowered her face to the tiny mouth, smelling the soft breath and savouring anew the magic. Kelly responded by turning a suckling Debbie's chin. How very trusting new born babies had to be, had sent further pangs of love through her.

Bright and early the following morning, Alma arrived in sparkling mood with the television crew. Much to Debbie's surprise she wanted to cuddle Kelly. A smile reached her eyes, "Debbie, she's a beauty, well done to you and Matthew!"

Cameras clicked wildly and then she was asked to dress her babe into the layette that had made them famous. Being a new mum, she was almost afraid of hurting her babe. Her hands trembled as she slipped on the tiny dress, bootees and bonnet. And suddenly the designs came to life, ideas pouring from her mind and into her fingers and inspired urges began anew. The camera followed each stage, zooming in closely to pick up the pattern and design. After popping on the little cardigan, Debbie wrapped Kelly into the shawl. "All your own work, me darling," Matthew chuckled as they beheld Kelly.

Their darling daughter looked just like a princess and they were then asked to sit on the bed with her. To everyone's delight, Kelly opened her delicious eyes and a fresh wave of clicking began as the cameras zoomed in to pick up the bright blue. Those pictures would now wind up the final program of that particular series.

Apparently, a chap called Ron Murray had taken over Paul's place in Ventura. Vanessa had been invaluable to him and he had chanced his arm with a request to take photographs and run a short story for the magazine.

Resisting the urge to tell them to get lost, she heard Matthew reason, "They are the Morecambe branch, darling, it would be silly not to have them cover the story!"

Of course, he was right as usual. Ron wound up the interview and added, "I think the New York branch is folding soon. There has been nothing but trouble over there. The Boss's daughter is playing up again, she doesn't care a jot about the magazine and I think Paul Howarth has had enough!"

Debbie felt the ricochet, why hadn't she thought of that? Simple really, she had been frantically busy. Amanda must have got good and fed up with a man that didn't want her, and Debbie had believed Paul when he said he would never touch her.

Lifting her eyes to Matthew, she noticed his face had closed. Amanda would never know the happiness Debbie now felt. Turning to Ron, she asked, "Has she had her baby yet? What did they have?"

Ron grimaced, "She was never pregnant, she is too damn clever for that. It appears that she made it up, to enable Eric to help her trap Paul!"

Her heart raced with sympathy for Paul, if only they had known. She now felt confusion, knowing she would have been happy with Paul. Yet she would never have known the beauty of Matthew's love. If she had never known about it, she could scarcely have missed it, she reasoned.

However, she did know. And she wouldn't change a single thing. She was truly happy with Matthew, feeling honoured by his selfless love. Poor Paul, he had lost so much, yet there was nothing anyone could do for him.

When Ron left, Debbie felt Matthew's unease, feeling he was sorry for Paul and instinctively her hand went out to him. He sat on the bed, "Debbie, has that upset you, love? Are you sorry ye didn't wait?"

His voice dripped with emotion as the lilt accompanied each word. Her eyes rounded, "Matthew, it may sound shallow, but I swear to you that I wouldn't change a thing. Obviously, you know Paul and I would have been happy, we were very close, but after …!

Her voice faltered as she saw the naked pain in his eyes, and continued with a gulp, "Had Paul not left for whatever reason, I would never have tasted your love. Having done so, I've become a total addict, craving more and love you from the bottom of my heart!"

They were in each others' arms, his kisses rained down on her. Crushing her he groaned, "I must be the happiest man in the world, so I must. Forgive me, Debbie, I should never have doubted your love!"

Alma had popped back to say cheerio, before she left. Debbie got the distinct impression that there were many plans on the horizon. There was no doubt about it, Alma had definitely taken on the role of personal representative. Debbie's designs had certainly done a lot for Alma and indeed Haywood. Their yarn used in her designs and Matthew's photographs were a double advertisement for them.

They had all been enriched and Debbie felt a warmth towards Alma. The two of them seemed to have a bond, much the same as Irene and herself. Mercifully, she had taken them both into her confidence and in turn, they were making sure she would never live to regret it.

The summer designs would have to be ready by the end of January and she knew she would have to make a start in just a few days time, but right now, her husband was ready to take his little family home.

The staff lined up to welcome them on the bitter cold November day. They all longed to see the wonderful daughter that Matthew had raved on about. She looked like a little pink flower, with an almost rose petal mouth as champagne was served by the proud grandparents.

Debbie felt the need to visit their balcony, albeit for a very short time. Matthew took Kelly from her and together they climbed the steps. She needed to see the bay, to savour the fresh, crisp air. Matthew kissed his daughter's face and whispered, "This is our wee empire and Mummy is Duchess!"

The word 'mummy' felt strangely good and sounded perfect. Suddenly weakness flooded her as Matthew gripped her, "Come on now, love, time to get those feet up, while I make us a coffee!"

Sipping her steaming drink a few moments later, she knew there would be many hands to help them, but she and Matthew would bring up Kelly in the warmth of a real family, knowing that Ellen and Jim would always welcome their little cherub.

**

Paul Howarth had been sitting in his office when the news came through. He groaned with grief as he read the tel-e-printer. His beloved Debbie had married Matthew and had given birth to a daughter. A fire burned deep in his belly, what in the name of God had he done? He counted the months on his fingers, was it only just over six fucking months since he had left England?"

His hand went to the intercom, "Hold my calls please and I don't wish to be disturbed, Beth," he instructed his secretary.

He locked the door and returned to the printer and cursed its very existence. Lost in his misery, he had made sure he heard precious little from England and Vanessa had promised to keep any news of Debbie from him.

Unfortunately, he had forgotten the blasted printer, which spread the news of all interviews, giving the editors the full starting price of life.

Reading the print again, his eyes blurred. Truth be told he was pleased that his beloved was with Matthew, but a little girl, hell that hurt. Searing pains gripped his head as though a vice were being tightened. Nausea rocked him and racking sobs riddled his body. The pains in his chest almost stopped him breathing. His heart had already broken, but the pieces seemed to grind deeper, the raw, jagged edges piercing his chest.

Desperately, his fingers tore through his hair as he wiped his wet face with the back of his hands. His legs had become hollow, barely able to keep him on his feet. Clutching his desk, he moved slowly around to his seat, opened a drawer and poured himself a good stiff drink. Nothing could ever hurt as this was hurting. Hell, that bitch was going to pay for this. Amanda would wonder what had bloody hit her, that was if he ever calmed down.

The rumours were indeed correct. The magazine was under severe pressure in New York. Paul had and continued to fight tooth and nail, but with Amanda's perpetual parties and subsequent hangovers, everything was slipping away.

It was a natural instinct for him to try and salvage what he could, that was his way of working, aim for the top, give one hundred percent and then more. His life became more meaningless, yet Eric knew he still held the trump card where Debbie was concerned. In fact, her success had put her in greater, temporary, danger. Eric had lost no time in telling him, "The higher they are, Paul, the greater the fall."

Paul just savoured the thought that a further year would just about put Debbie and Company in the clear, but right now he had to toe the proverbial line.

His mind raced back four months, when Amanda had given the performance of her life. She had staggered into the apartment, her voice cracked with seeming despair, "Paul, darling, I've been in hospital all day. We've lost your child, but I'm assured we can try again!"

Not able to feel sorrow as he had never believed it was his child, he had nevertheless checked the hospital only to find that she had never been pregnant. He had raged into the apartment, "You lying bitch, you were never pregnant. And there is no way in which I will rectify the matter, I have no intention of us remaining together!"

Eric had been on the 'hot line'. "I won't have my daughter upset. If you leave her, I'll inform the press pronto."

Paul had the distinct feeling that Eric had a new angle to blackmail him with and a shudder ran up his spine as Eric added, "Amanda is a beautiful woman, what more do you want!"

"Beautiful, maybe, Eric. The way she puts it about is shocking. She must have had more men than I've had hot fucking dinners!"

He had ultimately cooled off and tried hard to discuss his wayward wife's behaviour with her. In spite of his determined effort, his voice had been clipped, "We must try and pull our weight Amanda, after all, neither of us wants to see your father going broke. How about you keep your affairs under raps?"

Her smile was filled with guile, "Fair enough, Paul. I'll be discreet. If you screwed me, I wouldn't need to go out!"

Somehow the vasectomy had given Paul complete peace of mind, he had reasoned that if he should be lucky enough to return to Debbie, he could probably have the procedure reversed, how bloody ironic, he thought bitterly.

When he did want a good screw, he paid for his pleasure. The classy whore house was spotlessly clean as were the girls. All of them eagerly tended his needs and at the end of the day, he had no commitments.

Dragging himself from the reverie, he knew he could cheerfully murder Amanda. He had thumped his fist onto the desk so many times, he felt a pain shoot through his hand. He shouted to the empty room, "How the hell am I supposed to come to terms with all of this?"

His whole being was bereft, it was as though Debbie had died and left him forever. Paul had never known such anguish and hatred filled him. He needed to get home, get stoned and get to bed. On the other hand, he needed to feel his hands around Amanda's throat. His fists clenched and unclenched in spite of the pain. Over and over, he told himself to 'grow up'. But he did intend to hurt and knew just how to humiliate her.

With an assertive jerk, he went over to the sink in the corner of his office. After slooshing his face thoroughly, he poured himself a strong cup of coffee, the intercom sounded, "Paul, I know you said no interruptions, but your wife is waiting!"

"Okay, Beth, I'm free now!"

After unlocking the door, he opened it to admit his smug looking wife. It dawned on him that she knew about Debbie's babe, realising that Eric must have been onto her. Locking the door behind her, he waited for her to speak, "You've heard the news then!"

She had made the statement as she stared at the torn message from the printer. Inside she felt a great envy for the woman she wanted to destroy. She had managed to own Paul, followed by Matthew Ross and had a child to proclaim to the world. As far as she was concerned, Debbie Hudson was the luckiest bitch of all time and she would never stop in her efforts to destroy her.

Paul watched surreptitiously as the dainty figure admired herself in the long mirror. She was wearing a soft woollen suit in a pretty jade. It matched her eyes to perfection, the lust in them totally naked and undisguised.

Amanda could see the distress in Paul and to her astonishment, he allowed her to touch his face, press her fingers onto his chest, rub her knees around his cock. She looked at him with a somewhat dazed expression.

She knew he would never kiss her, never had, but she could see his cock straining as a wild bulge appeared in his trousers. "I knew I could turn you on,

Paul. In fact, I had a funny feeling that you would want somewhere to nestle your cock!"

Paul replied caustically, "Good."

He wasn't one bit surprised when she threw her arms in the air, taking her jumper with them, her breasts firm and bare for him to gaze upon. His eyes narrowed as she flushed with delighted expectancy. His hands gripped her breasts, twirling her nipples until she winced with pain. Hearing her sharp gasps of pain sent ripples through his engorged manhood. With one swift move she stepped from her skirt, leaving her clad only in suspender belt and stockings.

She then sunk to her knees and began to free his cock. It delighted him to see the subservience, the greed on her mouth, the lack of shame in her whole demeanour. Slowly, he eased his stiffness from her mouth. Today, he would allow her to expect the full treatment. He looked down on her patronisingly, "Lean over the desk. Show me what you want?"

She breathed heavily, "You know, darling!"

He winced at the endearment. A cruel line replaced his mouth as he watched her lay flat on the desk. Her hands began to play with the fair pubic hair and slowly, she parted herself to him. With practiced expertise, she brought herself off in front of him. A bemused grin spread over his face as her breathless pleas, "Fuck me, Paul," served lustful excitement up to him.

Soon she would feel silly, used, humiliated and he wanted to enjoy every moment. She sat up, her arms reaching for him. His need for Debbie sent his penis into flames and Amanda slid from the desk, again sinking to the floor. "Bend over the fuckin' desk," he commanded.

Much to his surprise, she obeyed and power as well as fire surged through him. She leaned forward onto her elbows and parted her legs, until he could witness for himself the wet seeping from her. He gripped her buttocks and thrust with all his might, almost knocking her off desk. She clung on and moved herself back and forth on him.

Mercilessly, he pumped. He had never entered her since that fateful night and never would again, but right now, he wanted her grovelling to him. Sharply he withdrew and she screamed out for him. Every sense and thought centred around his stiffness and taking it into his own hand, he rubbed it back and forth until he was ready to burst. His whole body was inflamed and swiftly he rammed himself back into her, ramming at her 'till he was empty.

Pulling himself out, he relished the knowledge that she was waiting for him to make her come. With a sadistic smile of satisfaction, he levelled his voice, "I think we had better get on and run Daddy's magazine, don't you?"

Her eyes turned to him and anger blazed, "Paul Howarth, if I live to be a fuckin' hundred, I will get even with you. You and that little whore who picked up and married the first sucker to come her way," she spat.

His reply was terse, "What a good job that I'm in a good mood, Amanda, otherwise you might just about have had that nasty, dirty little mouth slapped!"

CHAPTER TWENTY TWO

Debbie had suspected that Alma had been at work again. Now it became evident. The television company had asked for them to run a spot each week, keeping a diary of Kelly's development. Matthew would take care of the filming and together they would offer any helpful hints from their own point of view.

Matthew had certainly been right when he had told Kelly that they had their own little empire. It was rapidly becoming colossal, as Irene now had her own personal secretary and yet another room was converted into an office.

At times Debbie would pinch herself to make sure she wasn't dreaming. Not long ago, no matter how hard they had worked, they had been so desperately short of money and now, although working non stop, they had enough money to keep them in reasonable comfort for the rest of their lives.

Somehow they had captured the public's needs for a knitting series and judging by the sacks of mail, they had taken them to their hearts. Apparently viewers had watched the pregnancy programs and waited eagerly to finally see the end product.

The run of public demand had certainly been with them and having Kelly had opened many more hearts. Yet, they both realised that they had to be very careful to check various ideas. After all, they would appear in many living rooms throughout the Country and owed total trust and responsibility.

One thing that dear Amanda had made them sharply aware of, was to make them vow that Kelly would not be spoiled. If she did show any interest in Debbie or Matthew's work, she would start from square one. Money could not be appreciated unless it was earned, often with blood, sweat and tears. Amanda had already learned that money couldn't buy love.

Debbie must have been home for about a week or so and gazed from her office window, her eyes resting lovingly on the gorgeous carriage, where every morning, Kelly slept after her feed. Yet again, she saw the telegraph boy cycle towards the building.

They had received so many cards, telegrams and 'phone calls, it seemed almost impossible to think that there was anyone left to warrant another delivery.

The telegram was from Paul, "Heartiest congratulations to you both. Gorgeous baby. Hope all is well. Always thinking of you. Fondest love, Paul!"

Her eyes filled as she read the words. Her heart went out to him, especially as she knew of the trouble that had become part of his miserable life in New York.

She had been so lucky, she thought and although life was hectic, perhaps their favourite part of the day was the evening. They would bathe Kelly and prepare her for bed and as she fed so well, she slept well and contentedly.

They would then put in a couple of hours of solid work and hopefully pop up to the balcony to savour their little empire.

Although Debbie had been pleasantly surprised when they were approached with a view to writing their own story on pregnancy and birth, she burned with an added excitement. She knew that her beloved Matthew had an unfulfilled ambition – to own their own magazine.

He knew exactly what he wanted. A magazine to feature family life, to be aimed at the very people who had enjoyed their series so much. Something new, something that everyone could identify with. They had already spoken to Ellen and Jim and Matthew wanted Ellen to write a cookery column as Jim said, "I think it would go down very well indeed!"

Many rumours were circulating about Ventura being taken over, or indeed, closing down altogether. Many times they all thought if only Paul had been over here, perhaps he could head the type of magazine they wanted. They would also want to keep Vanessa.

There were so many magazines aimed at the richer end of the market. They wanted one, full of ideas for people on a smaller budget and ideas to help them enjoy their lives. There was no shortage of ideas, but they would have to wait and see what transpired later next year.

Matthew had been down to arrange a small christening on the Sunday prior to Christmas. Debbie had made time to design a special robe and bonnet for Kelly. Realising they would undoubtedly be asked for the pattern, she had written it down carefully, together with a version for the short dress.

Her fingers had practically come alight as she deftly made a very pretty, soft lace pattern with tiny ribbons scattered around it. Matthew had photographed it and he would also cover the occasion with photographs and a video for release after the event.

Irene and Alma were delighted when asked to be Kelly's Godmothers and Richard was to be Godfather. He and Jenny were thrilled to be coming to the castle. So many times they had been invited, but time had always been difficult. The only day they had was a Sunday, which had worked out perfectly.

Returning to Saint Peter's Church, had unleashed a riot of nostalgia. She and Matthew had been married here and her parents seemed to have a little difficulty in breathing as they once again admired this beloved old building.

Kelly had been handed round like a parcel for the rest of the afternoon. She was now able to give semi windless smiles and her nature was one of sheer contentment. Richard and Jenny were besotted with her and when Debbie showed them over their own apartment, Jenny had turned excitedly to Richard, "Darling, when can we start our family? I'm sure we could manage, Debbie still works. What do you think Debbie?"

Watching the love between them, Debbie smiled, "As far as I'm concerned, I found Kelly enhanced our careers. I don't believe there is such a thing as a right time. You have your home, you're obviously in love, why not let nature take its course!"

"That me love, is very sound advice," came Matthew's enthusiastic and teasing voice from the doorway.

Richard guffawed, "We didn't hear you coming, Matthew, but it is a fact you two are never far apart. I can see how happy a child has made ye and feel that Jen and I could cope!"

His arm reached for Jenny, her eyes danced with joy, "Rich, ye mean it, don't ye?"

Matthew slid his arm around Debbie, his Irish lilt dominant, "The shop receipts are great, we're here to help, just let it happen!"

Debbie allowed herself to lean into him. He seemed to grow more handsome each day. Her eyes lifted to him, "I think we had better go and rescue our daughter. Her aunts have had quite enough time to cuddle her!"

**

Debbie wakened a little later that night and as usual, she and Matthew were locked side by side like a pair of spoons. She was aware that over the past few days she had felt exceedingly horny. She began to be blissfully aware of Matthew's hardness throbbing against her back, just above her buttocks.

Stunned with desire, she feels his hand reaching around to tenderly cup her breast. The warm breath close to her ear, the gentle kisses at the corner of her neck and shoulder, stroking her softly, making her groan. She feels her nipples harden like rough uncut diamonds. He toys with them like precious jewels, circling, rubbing them between his fingers.

Still unable to move, she feels the familiar pull between her legs, feels him spiralling downwards, his hand soft like magic. Slowly, from behind, he slides his fingers between her legs, gently, insistently, stroking from back to front, circling, opening, widening, probing, until she heard him catch his breath.

Gently, he turns her face towards his and kisses her with deep, dizzying kisses. Erotic, symbolic surges fill her as his hands grip her buttocks. Matthew breathes into her neck, "Dearest, can I take you from behind? Christ, I feel crazed with need!"

"Me too, Matthew, how we never .. I want you to …," she cried.

Beside himself with agonising desire, he grips her lower cheeks hard, lifting her bottom upwards. Gulping helplessly, he chokes, "Oh, Debbie, kneel on all fours. Ride with me, darling!"

As if in a dream and certainly in a trance, Debbie obeys the delicious command. Stifled and breathless, Matthew parts her and flicks his tongue in and out of her vagina. Her heart pounded when she felt his penis replace his tongue. The most exquisite sensations shot like arrows as he pushed into the hilt. Then his hands reached for her breasts and he squeezed their opulent fullness, softly, with gentle torment.

Matthew panted with pain to avoid coming instantly. He held still and moved his hands down between her legs, running his fingers through her pubic hair, easing into her to join his penis.

Debbie had never felt anything so erotic, so intimate and moaned with ecstasy. Matthew placed his hands onto her buttocks and began to move within her, her response sending fire down to his primal roots. Then they were moving fast, her head spinning as she heard the luxurious slapping of skin as his body slammed against hers.

She felt her breasts begin to fly about like unidentified flying objects, thrilling her until he gripped them. Matthew shouted out, "I'm losing it me darling, stop for a minute!"

"Lose it, Matthew, hell I love this," left her lips.

Without slowing down, he took both breasts and held them firmly and with strong fingers he found her clitoris and caressed it wildly as the slapping continued.

Nothing had ever made Debbie feel as she did now. She didn't want it to end, but liquid fire exploded and she felt herself come in torrents of beauty. And with expert timing, she knew he was pouring into her, she slumped forward onto her arms, revelling in the shudders that still ran through Matthew.

His mouth moved over her back, reaching her nape with kisses that were still filled with passion. Gripping her shoulders, he whispered, "Let me turn you over, love. I'm still hard, only this time I want to be on top when we come!"

With the speed of a whippet, she turned, opened her legs wide to receive him and then closed her legs around him. Moments later they poured into each other again, both crying out, until the passion finally began to ebb and she knew she hadn't been dreaming at all.

Matthew held her crushed to him. "Debs, I wasn't too crude, was I? You must tell me if I'm ever after hurting ye. Its been so long since we could do it like this and we shouldn't have done it prior to your check up!"

Her arms tightened round his neck, "I don't believe anyone does wait for a check up. I loved what we did, everything was wonderful," she gasped.

Rapture seized her as she realised that this was the very first time they had made love without her being pregnant. Every move had been like manna from heaven. Gasping, biting and tasting each other, they shuddered from the plateau that knew no name. Somehow, they must stagger from the hurricane that had swirled and whipped them into its spiralling wake.

Debbie suddenly felt treasured again. Cherished beyond words, loved beyond bounds. With a deeply contented sigh, she knew this was where her happiness lay, anywhere in the world, as long as they were together.

**

Christmas that year was a very emotional time for all of them. Nostalgia hung in the air as they mourned the death of little Tony, remembering just how happy he had been last year. They also celebrated the birth of Kelly, instinctively knowing that Tony would have been enchanted with her.

Matthew had taken reels of photographs, some of them for the series and some for their own private album. It seemed impossible to realise just how far they had come in such a short time. And all of this from a design that Debbie had been almost too shy to submit, that was one thing they all had Paul to thank for.

The shrill bell of the telephone broke into her thoughts. Lifting the receiver she almost dropped it again. "Hi there, Debbie, I couldn't allow Christmas to pass without speaking to you. How are you all? How is Kelly?"

Paul's voice sounded strained, not at all as she remembered. "Its Paul," she called out. Her hand had begun to tremble, he sounded dreadfully despondent, "Happy Christmas to you, Paul, we are fine and Kelly is adorable," she couldn't keep the natural pride from her voice.

"Was she born early, Debbie?" He broke in making her flush as an element of guilt stabbed her, "Slightly, Paul," she gulped.

He sounded sad, wretched even, "Debbie, Matthew told me he was going to try and court you. I'm so pleased that you are both happy. He really is a great guy!"

Confusion swamped her as she felt bound to ask about his life, she couldn't bear him to know that they knew he had been duped. Inhaling deeply, she gasped, "How is everything over there, Paul?"

She heard the catch in his throat as he confirmed, "I was a bloody fool, Debbie. Amanda was never pregnant, but at the time, oh, well what's done is done!"

He then added, with a choked resignation, "We will be divorced by the time I return to England. Thank goodness I kept the flat!"

Debbie knew that he would never leave her heart, the very heart that went out to him, but Matthew was well and truly rooted there and she worshipped him. After her parent had wished Paul well, Matthew took the 'phone.

They were then both discussing business as they always had. Matthew's face pensive, "I'll be after speaking to Debbie, so I will. We are all keen to start up a magazine and if you're free, Paul, we'd all love to see you at the helm!"

The sheer trust from Matthew brought tears to her eyes. Her parents were caught up in a euphoria of excitement and Matthew was ecstatic. Suddenly, she knew it would work, they would all work well together, Paul held much the same code of ethics as Matthew.

She smiled with contentment, "If he is free and Ventura does fold, I think we would all benefit a thousand fold by his expertise. Yes, it would be just the way it was and Paul would have something to look forward to. He must be dreadfully lonely out there!"

CHAPTER TWENTY THREE

Early in the New Year, Debbie received a call from Alma. She was excited as she explained that an American head of network had just arrived in England and was exceedingly impressed with all of their series.

Apparently, he didn't want to buy those versions, but wanted them all to go into America and film brand new series under his own direction. Excitement buzzed down the line as Alma chatted, "I think he wants us over there after Easter and I can plug our yarns in the States, apparently the Americans love anything that is British and in particular hand made."

Debbie felt goose bumps break out over her skin. She had been right about the Christening outfits, requests had poured in and she also realised that in America and the continent, needle gauges varied. It would be vital to get that right and learn to talk to them in a jargon they were used to.

Her mind was on overdrive as she felt the receiver slip through her clammy hand and gripped it. Exhaling in short bursts, she gulped, "Alma, I can't believe this, are you sure you've got it right? What's his name?"

Alma chuckled, "His name is a long, fancy one, something like Henry Arnold Marcowvitze, known to everyone as Hank. He does sound like a nice guy. Can I bring him out to meet you all? He definitely wants a true British slant on whatever he intends to do!"

Debbie had to smile, Alma was almost an American just by conversing with him. Still shaking, she replied, "Yes, I suppose we can at least meet him. Matthew wouldn't agree to leaving Kelly behind, neither would I. Oh, hell, Alma, life is complicated. I would miss my parents .. I just don't know!"

Nothing seemed to deter Alma as she bubbled, "Of course we can't leave Kelly behind. I think Hank intends to take us all over there. He was on about a ranch type place, big enough for everyone. We may not like his plans, leave all the questions 'til we meet him, eh!"

Her body was still shaking when Matthew entered the room, "What's wrong, love?"

His voice was filled with concern, somehow she must calm herself down, yet it would be a golden opportunity for them all. As she explained it to him, his face lit up as he took her into his arms. "Debbie, me wee darling, well done. We'll all be together, you've worked darned hard and now they want you in America!"

She turned to say emphatically, "No, Matthew, they want us both. We are a team darling, one just as important as the other!"

Taking her hand to his lips, he ran his lips over it, "Come on, let's sound your parents out. The shop couldn't be in safer hands, Irene is quite capable of handling everything here. Oh, Debs, I love you so very much!"

As expected, her parents were delighted and Debbie was adamant that she should manage to feed Kelly for a while yet. Matthew swiftly assured her that schedules would have to be arranged around their infant and Debbie felt reassured that they would all discuss any anxieties with Hank. He was apparently eager to please everyone.

**

Hank and Alma were due to arrive later in the morning. Debbie decided to wear one of her own suits. She had to admit that she was happy with her figure, her tummy was nice and flat, her waist neat and tidy again. Even her bust was nice and firm and she was certain that feeding Kelly had played a huge part and although that information had been given out during ante natal classes, she had proved it for herself and would be happy to enter it into her book.

Matthew came up behind her, "You look ravishing, what a figure!" He gave a cheeky wolf whistle, but she loved his banter, never did she want to lose his appreciation and love of her body.

Alma arrived with Hank. Her eyes danced with pride when she saw her protégé. From the moment she had met Debbie, she had felt a bond between them. She loved the frank simplicity of her and was happy to see that Debbie hadn't changed one bit. Yet she had come so far in such a short time.

Many girls had been through her hands, most of them allowing success to go to their heads. And Alma had felt relief when their contracts had ceased. She loved Debbie as a young sister, admired the way she had played the cruel cards she had been dealt. The frank truth with which she had confided in herself and Irene and the complete competence with which she worked, in fact her complete dedication to them all. It was therefore, her pleasure to introduce Hank to Debbie and Matthew.

Hank had watched her place her babe into the carriage. He had seen her on camera, but she was a true English rose. He found her direct look more than appealing, she was absolutely adorable and he knew then, that his fellow countrymen would fall in love with her. Her love for her husband was obvious and seeing her parents enter the hall, he felt a deep family warmth fold around him like a cloak.

His hand was outstretched as his voice boomed, "Hi there, Debbie, gee you sure are a clever girl. Hi, Matthew, love your work!" He paused and went over to shake hands with her parents, "You must be very proud of your daughter, and this must be Kelly!"

He had walked back to see Kelly in her pram, waiting for Debbie to push her through to the garden for her sleep. He smiled, "She's a real beauty," as Kelly gave him a beaming smile and Debbie realised that she would probably break a few hearts later in life.

Debbie was pleasantly surprised, he was much younger than she had thought. He must have been around thirty five and seemed to look like an American, with a voice full of warmth and rich with friendship. Somehow his body was not unlike a mop, tall, very lean and his fair hair was closely cut. His eyes were a deep brown and his sincere smile lit up the whole of his face.

His rich charisma seemed to infect everyone around him. There was also a restlessness in him, giving the impression that he said what he wanted and

132

meant it. Debbie also felt that like themselves, he never worked normal hours and never settled down until every last detail was taken into serious account.

Alma broke in, "Shall we go up to the boardroom?" Ellen turned with a radiant smile and added, "I think that is very formal, Alma. I have coffee on the go, we can use our front room!"

Debbie pushed the pram into the garden and fixed the brake firmly into place. Pensively, she walked back into the castle. Ellen had surprised her, they had all seemed to take a shine to Hank and entering the room, she noticed he was sitting comfortably in one of the huge armchairs, his legs stretched easily in front of him. She smiled and asked, "Have you any children, Hank?"

He gave her a wicked grin, "I sure hope not, Debbie. I'm not married, well, I suppose I'm married to my work. No woman in her right mind would be happy with the hours I put in!"

Feeling the flush creep up from the belly of her and landing squarely into her cheeks, she gasped, "I'm sorry, I shouldn't have asked!"

His smile was disarming as he looked into his cup and laughed, "I wish I could find someone to share my work with. You and Matthew are a rare combination. Everything you do is shared, that's why I know they will love you in the States!"

He then let rip in that deep American drawl. "Alma has filled me in with details. My station would like you to be our guests. Our idea would be to settle you all into a private ranch type home in Long Island. The air is also gorgeous there," he grinned as his eyes fell on the baby carriage. "We would like you to plan on a six month stay, you will have all the clerical and housekeeping staff you need. Any problems with that?"

Debbie's mind had flown into turmoil, but everyone else was delighted. She worried about her time with Kelly. Almost as he knew of her inner confusion, Hank said, "Don't worry about Kelly, truly, Debbie, we can shoot a lot of the shows from the ranch and I'm sure that Matthew can help us there. But we would expect you both to attend the various publicity functions!"

He broke off to refill his cup, after drinking thirstily, he continued, "There are also several 'chat shows', but at all times provisions will be made for the babe. C'mon now, we sure are a very friendly bunch over there!"

Although deeply affected by such enthusiasm, she adored Morecambe, especially in the summer. Then again, she had read that Americans loved anything to do with family unity. Realising that she and the whole family had received so much from life, she knew they must now give something back and Matthew would make sure that they spent time with Kelly.

Once business was out of the way, Hank had them all in fits of laughter as he related his various experiences. The contracts were duly signed and they would all be leaving for the States in mid April.

Feeding Kelly that night, Debbie reflected that Irene would stand in for herself and Matthew would sort everything else out. His arms were around her as they both stared at the big blue eyes as Kelly suckled happily.

"She grows more like Paul every day, so she does," said Matthew and dropped a kiss onto the little one's forehead.

Taking Kelly from her and placing her into her cot, she asked him, "Matthew, you once said you wanted lots of children, I know I do, have you changed your mind?"

"No. me darling, but there is so much work to do and I don't want you under more pressure. One day though, hopefully, I will be in a position to oblige and make you pregnant!"

She snuggled into him, "How about we carry on making love as we do now, I mean, when Kelly finishes suckling. Who knows? Maybe I'll get pregnant straight away!"

He inhaled heavily, "Whatever you say, darling and as soon as we want to stop, well, I can be doctored, so I can," he chuckled and clung to each other.

**

Life continued to be hectic and by the time February was through, Debbie began to look forward to going away for a while. A delicious headiness filled her as she allowed her mind to luxuriate in thoughts of the beautiful gowns she would have to wear. Although she would have to wear her own designs for the knitting programmes and had succeeded in her thorough research into gauges and other snippets of interesting information.

Rushing around shopping for items to take to America, she had been startled to realise that there was a severe gap in the market. There was nothing really fashionable for babes around three to nine months. Arriving home, she had sat down and willed her inspirational urges to come to her aid.

Her hands fled through the pretty cotton yarns and before she knew what had hit her, she was designing pretty dresses for Kelly and that had taken her into the realms of crocheting. Having made several little dresses and bonnets for her daughter, she had also made contrasting jackets to pop on when the sun went in.

Those designs had gone down so well, that she had been asked to prepare a series on crocheting for the following year. She had also paid attention to nice and trendy outfits for boys. There was never a large variety for them. Again, gratitude filled her as she realised, Kelly had enhanced their careers beyond belief.

Irene had studied the new designs, "Debbie, I almost envy you. You love your work, husband and child, I couldn't cope, wouldn't want to. In many respects I'm like Alma, we get on so well!"

Debbie smiled, of course she was lucky, but she couldn't understand either of her friends and asked, "Irene, you do like dating though, don't you?"

Instantly, she thought she had overstepped the mark. But Irene chuckled, "Of course, I love to be wined and dined and I love to be bedded. Does that shock you?"

"Not shock, Irene, you're a very attractive woman and you obviously have normal horny attacks. You and Alma are both dark horses, but I wouldn't change either of you," she chuckled.

"And we wouldn't change you, Debbie," Irene added with deep sincerity.

CHAPTER TWENTY FOUR

Hank called to ask them to extend their stay from the end of September to the end of October, even to early November. His publicity marketing campaign was showing much more than a little interest. He wanted all of the American mums and grandmas to have their needles clicking.

He had also apparently learned that the knitting would be helped on by running the programme on pregnancy alongside it, just as they had done in England. Again, she would have to talk her way through her pregnancy with Kelly, using her to wind up the series and truth be told, Debbie didn't really understand why he didn't use the British series.

A couple of days later, Hank was back on the 'phone, "Hi there, Debbie, Alma tells me that you are doing a crocheting series over there. Would you consider doing one for us? The designs sound fantastic!"

Somehow he was carried away in a euphoria that she found hard to keep up with. Almost wearily she added, "Hank, I'm booked here for next year's series. I suppose we could return for your next season. I'll chew it over with Matthew and see what we can manage!"

After hanging up, she realised that she did feel very tired. Tears welled, although hours were long and deadlines had to be met, she felt an element of guilt to be earning so much for doing something she loved. She also wondered if others felt as she did.

Realising she was overawed, she balled her hands with determination. They had all been through so much worry, hardship and loss, yet she had never once felt unloved. She had been blessed with loving parents and it hadn't seemed dreadfully hard at the time. In fact, had things been easier, the advertisement would never have gone in for Matthew, now they were husband and wife, working together as one. Her parents shared their success and were invaluable to the running of the little empire.

During March, Debbie and Matthew had to sort out the visas and make sure that Kelly was added to their passports. Jim and Ellen had been for check ups with Brian, so had Matthew and today was to be Debbie's turn.

Brian seemed to pummel away for quite a while, a frown forming on his forehead as he asked, "Do you feel well, Debbie? No problems with feeding Kelly?"

"No problems at all, Brian, Why?"

Her voice had shaken as unease crept into her. Brian smiled, "I think I'd better do an internal, just to make sure that all is well, nothing to worry about!"

After summoning his nurse, he proceeded with the check. A few moments later, a little nod dismissed the nurse and he told Debbie to dress and sit down. Feeling concerned she gulped, "You do think it safe for Kelly to travel, don't you? I know she has had her first lot of injections, but I do feel a little worried about boosters. It will be strange to see another doctor sticking needles into her!"

After gabbling like an idiot, she felt irritated with him as he sat there writing down the details of Kelly's injections. His eyes raised and his voice was teasing slightly, "Kelly will be fine, but I think your timing could have been a little better, don't you?"

Her obvious blank look must have indicated to him that she hadn't a clue what he was talking about. His hand covered hers, "Debbie, you're nearly three months pregnant. You didn't know, did you?"

Shock registered, it hit her that had been the reason for the internal. Staring at him in total disbelief, she gasped, "Brian, I can't be, I'm still feeding Kelly, you're teasing me, aren't you?"

Taking up his usual position on the corner of his desk, he spoke seriously, "You've fallen for the oldest myth in the world. You thought you couldn't get pregnant while feeding, didn't you?"

Her head nodded stupidly. She couldn't absorb this at all, her first thought fell from her lips, "Brian, thank goodness that isn't in our book. I must cover the point in Kelly's diaries. Many young couples could find themselves in this situation, many of them sick with worry about it. Matthew and I were going to start trying for one as soon as I finished feeding this little madam!"

She had hugged Kelly as she had spoken. Turning back to Brian, she asked, "Are the hospitals good over there? Brian, I feel such a darned fool. Matthew will be shocked, yet I'm certain he'll be over the moon!"

"You'll be fine, Debbie. You show them over there, just how to give birth and come and see me when you return."

Once outside of the surgery, a stunned Debbie placed Kelly back into her pram. A rush of love shot through her, at least her condition wouldn't show until after the publicity launch. There was no doubt about it, she couldn't and didn't even want to conceal her condition for long.

In fact she made up her mind that if Hank didn't like the news, they would have to put off the trip. Matthew's child came first, yet this one, just as Kelly had done, would probably bring its own luck with it. She scarcely remembered going home, yet worked hard alongside Matthew all evening. Even as she fed Kelly that night, she still felt shell shocked.

Matthew had noticed her mind wandering, in fact he felt worried about her. Her face held an almost wistful look about it, her eyes seemed to turn to him constantly as somehow, she appeared vulnerable and more precious than ever.

Her sensual body swung from the bed, giving him an almighty hard-on. His original idea had been to allow her to unburden herself then, well, he would love the life from her.

He followed her to the cot, his arms closing around her. "Debbie, somthn' wrong? Are you sure you're up to all this travelling?"Lifting her smouldering ebony eyes to him, she deliberately allowed her nightdress to fall, forming a soft pool around her feet. Every nerve in her jerked as he took her hands tightly into his. His mouth covered hers and slowly, tantalisingly, he began to devour her mouth.

She tried to loosen her hands in order to torture him, but he interlocked their fingers and took her hands straight down to her hips. His mouth moved over her eyes, ears and back to her mouth. His body closed in on hers until her pearl like nipples dug into his chest. Mindlessly she rubbed her mound into his hardness, feeling the wet flow into her loins.

Matthew teased her nipple with his mouth and whispered, "Climb onto the bed darlin', I won't let you fall," his voice was low with delicious intent.

Trancelike, she felt her heels digging into the bed as she eased herself into the centre. Matthew followed her without disengaging their fingers. His eyes locked hers and as her head reached the pillows, his body covered hers. Erotic fire sparked through her, she had no control of her hands, yet her body burned with desire.

His knee parted her legs and with ease, he entered her. His mouth went down to the pulse that beat in her neck. Neither moved, just gasped at the sheer joy of being one. Suddenly, he spread eagled their arms and swept them in a semi circle above her head and moaned with deep desire. Her beautiful breasts were taut, allowing the nipples to stand so firm they nearly left her skin.

Slowly, he moved his mouth downwards, allowing his teeth to scrape the swollen buds until she screamed out and writhed beneath him. "Debbie, there's something extra special about you tonight, you're even more adorable, so ye are!"

His rich dark voice was driving her wild and she felt his grip tighten on her fingers, keeping her arms high above her head. Matthew could feel the heat within her and never wanted this moment to end. If he stayed where he was or moved an inch, he would explode and he didn't want to, not yet. She was beautiful and seeing her breasts stretched and taut was perhaps the most erotically exciting pose he had ever seen.

Gently, he eased himself from her. "No, Matthew," came her frenzied cry. Biting each nipple as her head tossed from side to side, he ran the tip of his penis along her lower lips, groaning his love. Without warning, her legs closed around him, her heels forcing him back into her. Blindly they moved as one, until they both burst into a crazy series of orgasms.

As the shuddering began to slow down, Matthew looked at her and saw the love in her face, "That was beautiful, well its always beautiful, but tonight, you set me on fire, darling, Debs!"

Debbie just lay there throbbing from the ferocity of his love. Her hands had gone numb as she felt Matthew trying to prize their fingers apart. Then it hit her, she had some very important news to impart, after all that was the idea of this wondrous situation in the first place. A shudder ran through her, rocking her body. Her eyes lifted to him, his black hair had fallen over his forehead, his deep blue eyes were moist, his breath was decidedly laboured and she had never loved him more.

Fearful of him separating from her, she gasped hoarsely, "Hold me in your arms. Oh, Matthew, whatever came over you? I thought you were absolutely…"

He had freed his hands and gathered her to him, crushing her as though she were about to escape. "Whatever came over you, Debs? Hell, you drive me wild, so ye do!"

For a brief moment, she felt a silly little shyness. Her fingers were just coming back to life and she raised them to hold his head. Gulping back the suffocation that threatened, she whispered, "Matthew Ross, you not only made me love you, but you also make me pregnant!"

Golly that felt good. It was the first time she had said the words aloud. She watched the different expressions cross his shocked face. He buried his face into her neck, "You can't be, me precious one, you're still feeding Kelly!"

They stared at each other momentarily and she teased, "Don't ye want me to have it?"

"When it does happen, promise you will tell me just like this. Oh, darling, I love ye!"

"That's just as well. Brian told me today, Matthew. It is due early in October. Apparently we both fell for the so called myth. I wanted to tell you, just like this!"

Rolling from her in a shocked stupor, he stared at the ceiling. He had sensed something extra special in her, even felt her added need. How tastefully beautiful her love was. How happy she had made him, how madly he loved her. He felt her move beside him, "Are you sure you will be fit to travel? I can't get over the way you have accepted this," he gulped as his lilt rose excitedly.

"Most women don't enjoy the conception as much as I did and there is only one way to accept it, as far as I'm concerned. Honestly, although I feel dog tired, I have no sleep in me. All I can think about, is the fact that your flesh and blood is growing within me. It fills me with a wonderful sense of love!"

They gripped each other like young lovers and Matthew said, "I admit, sleep is the furthest thing from my mind, let's go into the kitchen and have a hot drink!"

As he poured the hot chocolate into the mugs, his eyes held hers, his voice shook with emotion, "Debbie, do you think Hank will want us to cancel?"

"I don't know, darling. I think at worst he could possibly want to postpone. Fair enough, we didn't intend this to happen, but as it has I'm afraid it will have to be considered during the schedules," she smiled and touched her stomach.

He didn't have to ask how she felt about it all. Her lovely eyes spoke of her love and yes, his very own flesh and blood. Taking her hand, he ran his thumb over her wedding ring, "Debs, when we married, I prayed for your love, then I knew I had it. When Kelly was born, I felt just as special. Now we have another one on the way and you are happy about it. Honestly, I have never felt so bloody special in my life!"

His voice trailed as emotions gripped him. She was feeling much the same and whispered, "I will ring Hank and tell him about our baby. Its midnight here, so it must be early over there and we can make the official announcement tomorrow, at least we will know one way or another!"

As she dialled the number, she could see Matthew was still stunned. Within seconds Hank picked up the 'phone and hearing her voice, fairly gabbled, "Hi there, Debbie, how is everyone over there? Sure hope you're looking forward to seeing us. You'll love the place we have taken for you all!"

He broke off to impart a rich guffaw. Every word he spoke seemed to add difficulty to her news. Inhaling deeply, ready to cut in, he raced, "Its getting wild over here. You will be booked solid for the first couple of months and then we can run the t.v. series. Hope you're fit and well. Golly, it sure must be late over there, hope there's nothing wrong!"

A hint of panic appeared to have entered his voice, almost matching her own. Shrugging her shoulders back, she stated, "Nothing's wrong, Hank. But Matthew and I have just found out that I am pregnant and we are delighted. If you feel it would be better to postpone, well, we will understand!"

Suddenly, she realised that she had spoken with a confidence that springs from contentment. Hank's booming reply, nearly made her drop the 'phone, "Gee, Debbie, that is fan tas ...tic. It will be so much more realistic. That's g r e a t, we can hold our last episode until after the birth!"

Matthew's arms held her as she had turned the receiver around. They both managed to pick up Hank's infectious mood, "Gee, I couldn't have asked for more. This will double the ratings. We'll start on the publicity campaign immediately!"

"See you soon, Hank and cheers!"

Sweeping her into his arms, Matthew nibbled her ear, "Mrs Ross, tis time to go back to bed. If we do have any problems, they're not coming from America. Hank is thrilled with our news, so he is, nearly as thrilled as I am, I love you!"

"Just as well. I s'pose you want a son this time?"

"I don't mind what we have, another daughter will be more than welcome. In fact, I wouldn't mind half a dozen like Kelly!"

"Mr Ross, you're incorrigible, half a dozen indeed," she chuckled and sunk into the delicious warmth of him.

Long after Matthew had fallen asleep, Debbie found herself wide awake. Her hand held her tummy, this was really like a miracle, first of all Kelly had enhanced their careers and now this one was doing just the same. In any language, it seemed that people loved hearing about little ones.

She had been absolutely certain that she could not conceive whilst feeding. They were lucky indeed, they could afford to have children, but many mums would be frantic and this news must be given over as quickly as possible, she thought dreamily.

A restless Debbie was up early next morning. She knew her parents would be thrilled with the news and was certain they would be a tremendous help. She must ring Alma, who was just as delighted as Hank, when she finally came fully awake.

Irene swiftly predicted many more children as Debbie was almost certain she carried another daughter, but kept quiet for the time being. They were all feeling restless, partly due to the fact that they would be leaving Morecambe, partly due to fears of the unknown.

**

At long last they were ready to board the 'plane. Debbie did feel a little sick wondering if it was an attack of nerves. They had flown to Paris without problems, but this was altogether a different proposition.

The hostesses couldn't have been kinder, again drawing her to the deft way in which they went about their duties. Their total professionalism making their work look easy.

Eying her parents, her heart flipped as they were shaking with excitement. Ellen's eyes were almost popping from their sockets. It was obvious that they were happy being altogether and not having to miss the arrival of their new grandchild.

Alma was her usual self, smart, calm and happy to chat to anybody about any subject. Matthew was holding Kelly who was shamelessly beaming at anyone who spoke to her.

Lunch was served and everyone seemed to relax. Debbie managed to feed Kelly and had decided to change after her next feed. She had taken the precaution of packing a lightweight linen suit with matching court shoes, making sure she was nice and cool for their meeting with Hank.

Matthew had taken the sleepy little cherub from Debbie. Her eyes had closed, the long lashes brushed her rosy cheeks. Her hair had begun to grow and was forming into tiny curls. She was a truly adorable child.

Lost in the crook of her husband's arm, Debbie felt the kiss of sleep taking her into a dreamless and much needed rest.

As she wakened, she felt slightly disorientated, but Matthew had ordered coffee for her and never had it tasted so good. After changing and feeding Kelly, she hurried to prepare herself for what lay ahead. The pale blue suit looked and felt decidedly fresh and cool, filling her with a new confidence.

CHAPTER TWENTY FIVE

Debbie's heart was in her mouth as the 'plane finally circled and touched down in New York. As they alighted, she noticed that Hank and the press were there to meet them. He hugged her almost violently, "Gee, Debbie, it sure is good to see you, hi there, Matthew," he called and carried on throughout the rest of the little entourage.

He then called out, "Let them through, we have a room ready to hold a press conference and then we must allow them to settle." He was in total command of the situation, knowing exactly what he wanted. In fact he was a true professional, in many ways, he reminded Debbie of Paul.

Hank had watched her descend from the 'plane, he marvelled at her cool composure and the suit seemed to enhance her body. The shoes certainly showed off her gorgeous legs, she was just like a magnet, drawing eyes in her direction, yet she was totally oblivious of the powers she held.

The photographers were having a field day, her whole family were delightful and he felt the buzz of excitement from the press. He had felt drawn to her from the moment he had first met her and with a shock, he realised that she was the sort of woman with which he could easily have shared his life.

His arm draped the shoulder of her almost fragile body. Everything about her attracted him. The way she held her head, making her hair bounce around her shoulders. Her lovely eyes were always frank and direct, her sensual mouth …

Carefully, he took her arm and jerked himself back to the present. He could almost feel her assurance in him as he led her from the airport and into the waiting room.

Debbie gulped as she saw the huge table, with chairs all around it. One side was full of press men and women and the other side was reserved for them. She felt covered in confusion, not knowing what to say.

Frequently she had listened to people landing in England and expounding its virtues, yet had never visited before and vowed she wouldn't make the same mistakes.

Again, she had worried unnecessarily, most of the questions were about their own country, especially Lank a shire, as they pronounced it. Her mouth dried as she chewed her lip, her voice sounded a little shrill, "Yes, Lancashire is a lovely place, yes, we did start with nothing and worked our way up and yes, we are expecting another baby!"

Matthew was answering the same questions, his accent had somehow warmed the hearts of the Americans. Although his answers were almost identical to hers, his lilt made everything seem more exciting. Alma was able to plug her yarns and explain that she and her company were deeply grateful to have Debbie and Matthew as ambassadors.

Finally, Hank interjected, "That's all for now, they must be feeling hungry and we must get them settled. You will be given plenty of time to get to know them, they are here for the next few months!"

Their luggage had been checked through and a huge batch of 'diapers' had apparently been sent to the ranch, together with a request for Kelly to model them.

A cheery chauffeur, complete with Limo., collected them, they could retain him for their own use. Debbie realised that Kelly was getting a little restless and realised it would take her a few days to get used to the new time zone.

The traffic was almost bumper to bumper and it did seem odd, driving on the other side of the road, but after a seemingly long time, they suddenly found themselves on a country type road. A cool breeze now circulated through the car as they all tried to gaze out and absorb their surroundings.

Deftly, the driver swung the car into a long driveway of leafy trees. Lazily, they swayed in the delicious breeze, wafting it by them, reminding them sharply of home. The car slowed right down, enabling them to take in the breathtaking beauty.

Directly ahead, their eyes fell onto the massive 'ranch'. Encompassed in a setting of trees, with gorgeous flower beds, it stood in a panoramic vista. The rambling two story building had little balconies leading from the various rooms and ripples of excitement ran through them.

Having already passed a couple of tennis courts in the driveway, they were spellbound. One minute they had been in the heaviest of traffic and just seconds later, had almost arrived into another world.

Stepping from the car, Debbie palmed her hand over her eyes. The sunlight streamed down, her eyes taking in the greenery that stretched far away into the horizon, meeting the perfect blue of the sky. Somehow, she could imagine herself and Matthew roaming through the fields, perhaps stopping to kiss under the many huge oak trees.

Headily, they entered the spacious hall. Highly polished, non slip floors were scattered with sumptuous rugs. A large kitchen led from a tiny corridor, where a couple of cooks were happily at work. Debbie felt Matthew grip her hand, "Darling, isn't this absolutely beautiful. Just look at your parents, they seem thrilled and so does Alma!"

Her head nodded as they entered the massive dining room. A rich mahogany table ran down the centre, displaying a row of beautiful flowers, tastefully arranged in tall vases. The chairs were exquisitely carved, with tapestry covered seats and back rests and a carver stood at each end, reminding them a little of the boardroom at home.

Practically the whole of one wall was taken up with serving space. A gorgeous white stereo unit, complete with speakers, ran down the other side. Huge French Windows led out onto a patio, with several tables and chairs decked around the lovely, rich blue swimming pool. The sun depicted the sheer sparkle from the water as the odd cloud was pure white, almost like cotton wool, frothed up and placed neatly into the sky.

They were all overawed by the view and Hank, now excited himself, with their obvious delight, suggested they move on and see the rest of the place.

Matthew's arm was around her as they entered the elegant 'reclining room'. Several settees were filled with pretty pastel scatter cushions. A log fire, set and ready to light, seemed to beckon them to sit around the huge stone fireplace.

Slightly set away from the ground floor, was a games and pool room. It had been cleared for now, to make room for desks and typewriters, not to mention telephones. Debbie felt deeply moved as she realised just how much thought had gone into all of this.

Ascending the large staircase, they found about seven large bedrooms with private bath and dressing rooms. Each one was designed with very English overtones and each one led onto a small balcony.

Hank was smiling as he watched their faces. Taking Debbie's arm, he led her into the bedroom chosen for herself and Matthew. A large landscape of Morecambe Bay hung over the bed. Her eyes filled as the many gestures to make them feel at home, finally choked her.

Their own dressing room had been turned into a nursery with a new cot and 'stroller' for Kelly. Debbie didn't think that one tiny detail had been overlooked and walking over to the balcony, she gasped her sheer appreciation.

Hank watched the different expressions cross her face. It was clear, she took nothing for granted, and certainly didn't hide her delight. He noticed the loving way with which she had taken Kelly into her arms, her eyes falling onto the rather large building ahead of them.

Clearing his throat, he explained, "That's where the staff live. They know their various chores, but should you wish them to work differently, just explain to them. Well now, how do you like it here?"

Totally overwhelmed, she turned to Hank and gasped, "I think it is truly beautiful, Hank. Thank you for the thought that has obviously been put into the whole idea. Let's just hope that we can earn your station plenty of money!"

"You will, Debbie, believe me, you sure will!"

He walked over to the door and called over his shoulder, "As soon as you are both ready, we will have coffee by the pool and go over your itinerary!"

Debbie suggested that Matthew go along with Hank whilst she fed Kelly. Afterwards, she placed the babe onto the bed and realised she was as tired as her sleeping child. The bed was beckoning her, willing her to lay down and sleep. Tossing her head defiantly, she collected her sleeping child and headed off to join the others.

Matthew had placed the stroller into the shade and instantly jumped up to take Kelly from her. Debbie sank into a chair, gratefully drinking the coffee. Hank's face lit up, "Gee, it sure is great to have you all here. The news of the babe is great and we have given you a couple of days to settle. Then we have the first of the evening receptions. Alma, perhaps you would like to partner me, we will both have to attend!"

Alma bubbled as she said, "Yes, Hank, I would love to partner you, but what about Ellen and Jim?"

Ellen interjected sharply, "Alma, Jim and I will be fine here. We would much prefer to be here with Kelly. She would fret if one of us wasn't around. Anyway, Jim and I can catch up on some reading!"

Jim squeezed her hand and Debbie knew, already they were beginning to enjoy themselves. That in itself gave her a deep joy. Her head had begun to ache, never had she felt so down right tired. Gulping her coffee, she poured a second cup, willing her mind to concentrate on Hank.

Although he was totally relaxed, his strange restlessness seemed to be part of his make up, infecting everyone around him. He spoke with ease as he explained that he had arranged for someone to come out to the ranch with dresses and accessories. He had already decided that many of the series could be shot from the ranch and then explained about the chat shows.

Pausing only to drink his coffee and refill his cup, he went on, "That seems to take care of the first three months and then we will commence the series on pregnancy!"

Standing up, he paced up and down and after lighting a cigarette, he sat down again. Watching the smoke rise, he carried on as his hands gesticulated the various shots he envisaged. He seemed to have an inexhaustible flair, his mind ticked with the regularity of a clock. It all scared her a little, sounding almost too simplistic.

Debbie knew it would be hard work, in fact she was happy about that. Perhaps she would begin to feel better after a couple of nights sleep, she also realised that Kelly would take a few days to settle down.

After eating the evening meal, it was time for Hank to depart. Matthew bathed Kelly and asked, "Would you like to go for a walk, darling? You sure you feel alright? You seem a little quiet!"

"Matthew, I feel fine, just very tired. I'm longing to walk over that gorgeous greenery, but right now, I just want to shower and fall into bed," she almost snapped.

Stepping from the shower, she felt a stab of guilt. Matthew had been so eager to take her out and explore. She had all but thrown his excitement back into his face. Clenching her fists, she walked into the room and as the moon shafted over his shorts clad body, wildness ran through her.

She knew he thought he was being too demanding and raised her face to him, "Matthew, I don't think you could ever be too demanding for me. It takes a great lover to make one keep coming back for more. You are that lover and I could never picture not wanting you!"

Again his arms engulfed her, his body throbbed for her. Once more their bodies could glory together. With a happy little sigh, she knew she could sleep. A healthy lethargy had enveloped her, replacing the dreadful tiredness. Her man had made her feel complete and whole and incredibly cherished.

CHAPTER TWENTY SIX

During the following three months, Debbie went from wearing gorgeous gowns, to beautifully knitted suits for the series. The mail had begun to pour in by the van load. Relief surged through her as she could pass the work through to the typing pool, headed by her new secretary, Grace Fielding.

Grace was a middle aged, jovial lady, ever eager to work. Her blond hair was obviously dyed as the darker roots just peeped through. Her grey eyes were warm and friendly, at times almost motherly. She had a knack of coercing the typists in a manner that made them want to please.

Debbie found that staff treated her with the utmost respect and in many ways, Grace's competence matched that of Irene. Very quickly she had come to understand Debbie's requirements and was able to sort out main sets of queries into different compartments. She also handled anything that Matthew might throw at her. In fact, no one could ask for more. The four main queries mirrored the ones in England and Debbie swiftly decided to print an answer sheet to stop people going off the idea, before they got started.

Reports on Kelly's progress had been kept up to date and sent off to Irene for the diaries. There always seemed to be so many little items to pop in them. Funny little items, like cutting teeth and sitting up unaided, but they all added to the excitement and Matthew's filming was truly exotic.

He had managed to capture her crawling and her clumsy attempts at trying to stand. Often she would land on the floor and as she laughed, her little teeth gleamed delightfully, they were so proud and looked forward to their new arrival.

Debbie felt something niggling at the back of her mind and found it impossible to put her finger on it, that was until they paid a visit for her check up at the large maternity hospital.

Confident that her birth would be uncomplicated, she had turned to her husband, "Matthew, I only want to book into the hospital for the actual birth and then go straight home. I don't want us to be apart for even one night and I couldn't bear not to be around Kelly," she sighed with love.

"I won't argue with that me darlin'. Providing the doc gives the all clear, I'll take you home, so I will," he grinned roguishly.

Arriving at the hospital, they had both been treated like royalty. The staff had been eager to show them around, from the delivery room, to the premature baby unit. Just as in Britain, they found that medical research had been developed to save the tiniest of babes. It was a magical experience, seeing the incubator clad, small bundles with a real chance of survival.

A few babies had been removed from the incubators and just lay in little cribs. In spite of being dressed into the smallest garments on the market, the clothes just drowned them. Many had sleeves rolled over so many times, they looked dreadfully uncomfortable.

Nearly all of Debbie's urges had come to her in a flash and today was no exception. This is what had been niggling her, these babes had nothing small enough to wear, poor little mites, they needed something to fit them now, needed to be comfortable, which they certainly could not be feeling.

There was a serious gap in the market for the premature baby and Debbie felt that this was a priority that must be tackled immediately. Realising it would take time to sort out, her inspired urge was to alter some of her existing designs to fit. It would mean scaling everything down and she would do that as a temporary measure.

It hit her again, had she not been pregnant, she would not have been drawn to this problem. She had slotted the ideas into her next programme and the response had been unbelievable. Hank had been delighted when he rung, "Debbie, that sure was a great idea, honey, our switchboard was jammed. Good job you have ample staff out there. I'll be over at the weekend, that's if you can put up with me and some new ideas!"

She had smiled to herself, somehow she felt totally at ease with him, at times he reminded her of an older brother. With a little chuckle, she replied, "Of course we can put up with you, Hank, but I get the distinct impression that you want us to do something more for you!"

"Debbie, how could you think of me having ulterior motives?" He also chuckled as he feigned indignation, but she knew they would all enjoy his company.

Her parents were lovely and bronzed, well and remarkably happy. Jim would often sit by the pool and work and was rushed off his feet with the huge amount of bookwork to wade through. Debbie loved to sit and have a chat with him, they had always been close and looking at Matthew with Kelly, well, she was sure they would have the same heart warming bond.

Alma was constantly in and out sorting various details on Debbie's behalf and loved being treated as a celebrity, but took a tremendous amount of pressure from her protégé. All in all, life was just about perfect.

**

They had all settled easily into their new way of life. Kelly now slept through the night and the hospitality was so sincere it almost suffocated them. Matthew had nevertheless insisted they make time for a couple of hours together every day.

Sometimes they would go for walks over the fields and Kelly loved that, stopping every few seconds to pick up a blade of grass as she crawled along. Her hair was growing more quickly, it was very curly and the auburn tint indicated she would be the same colour as Ellen. That time was so precious to them and they knew that was one of the many reasons for their total happiness. The simple matter of making time for each other and their babe, led to such a rich and full life.

Some nights Debbie and Matthew would walk over the fields, lost in each other's arms. The moon shining from a star spangled sky, filled them with nostalgia. Matthew revelled as she led them hurriedly towards their favourite oak tree and hidden from the rest of the world, they would make exquisite, mind blowing, passionate love.

Her beautiful ebony eyes were always filled with moisture, betraying her needs. She would often just pop on a sundress and leave herself naked beneath, knowing it drove him crazy. She knew how to please and to his utter joy, she loved trying new ideas and as yet, he found she not only responded, but often instigated their love making.

Stroking the damp tendrils from her face, he would thank God for guiding her to him. At times, he would shudder, just thinking of life without her love. Holding her with one arm, he would slip his hand between them and feel his flesh and blood kicking with ferocity. Kissing her sensual lips, he whispered with a deep tenderness, "Darling, there's somethin' so ethereally special about the moon light, so there is. I love you so very, very much!"

**

The chat shows in America were at first glance, somewhat horrifying. It seemed that everyone was placed onto the stage, where not only the host, but the audience joined in to ask the many questions.

One such hostess was Joanne Day. She was a real natural and they had enjoyed her shows more than anything else. To Debbie, Joanne was not just filling a slot, but was genuinely interested in her guests. Every appearance they made, no matter where it was, the music of 'She's a lassie from Lancashire', heralded their arrival.

Joanne had seemed to take an instant liking to Debbie and Matthew, virtually hailing them as the perfect couple. They were, and the Americans loved them. Debbie found herself able to relax more and more and Matthew conducted himself with his usual panache.

They were then approached for Kelly to advertise various baby foods and cereals and as their little girl loved people around her, they so no harm in it, providing of course that she did like the things that would carry her name.

Matthew and Debbie both realised that many American parents trusted them entirely. It somehow made it more important than ever, that everything attached to them was thoroughly tried and tested.

Debbie's body now told the world that she was with child. Having turned six months, she felt full of good health and happiness. The knitting programmes were rocketing in the ratings. The pregnancy series was running almost alongside and just as popular. They had succeeded in England and had managed to capture the hearts of the American public in a big way.

Grace had come in one morning, carrying a request from 'Ventura', to conduct an interview. Matthew was invited to tend to the photography and Mr Paul Howarth would conduct the interview. Thanking Grace and promising to deal with the matter, Debbie turned to Matthew. A grin spread over his face, "How do you feel about it me darlin'? I must admit, it would be great to see Paul again. Perhaps he'll know more about the magazine. We may still be able to pull him in with us!"

Debbie had to agree, it *would* be lovely to see Paul.

She did wonder what he would feel, when he saw the bliss that she and Matthew shared. Giving him a hug, she nodded, "Darling, Matthew, if you think we should to the interview, we will!"

**

When Paul finally arrived, Matthew bounded out to meet him. Debbie's heart flew into her mouth as she noticed he looked even more handsome, yet there was a real sadness about him. Hugging her warmly, he smiled, "Debbie, you look good enough to eat, being a mum to be certainly suits you!"

Paul's heart had almost stopped. He had watched her on the box so many times, seen the cameras caressing her into vibrant life. Yet never had she looked more beautiful than she did now. Never a moment went by without him remembering her love. Christ, he had taught her to love and what a delightful pupil she had been.

Time and again he had kicked himself for losing her. There was a radiance about her, a kind of expectancy. Of course there bloody well was, he admonished himself sharply. He had longed for and dreaded this day. But it didn't take a mastermind to see how happy Matthew had made her. His loins ached with longing as is cock served notice of its impending misbehaviour, he would have to sit with his legs crossed again, he mused.

Once everyone was seated and drinking coffee, Debbie produced Kelly. His eyes widened and she knew, he had worked it all out. Yet, it hadn't been Paul they had kept the secret from. Standing up, he held his arms out and like her usual, happy little self, she beamed at him with his own smile.

Debbie felt tears sting her eyes, he knew alright, dear God he knew and she knew there was no threat from him. There was no denying Kelly was delicious. Paul looked across to her, revealing the love in his gorgeous eyes, "You have both done her proud. She's a delightful little girl, no wonder you are happy to have more!"

Once she was placed into her stroller, one of the staff came to take her for a walk, normally they would have taken her together, but this was a rather special occasion. It seemed rather stupid for Paul to interview them, he had started the ball rolling and he knew everything about them.

Matthew then asked, "Is the magazine folding then, Paul?" Debbie watched him closely, he had aged dramatically in just over fifteen months. His face was literally etched with misery, she thought sadly.

Lighting a cigarette, his tone was flat, "Yes, I think the magazine will close. There's some talk about Eric amalgamating with another magazine, anyway I've already told him to count me out. Everything should be wound up by this time next year. If the Morecambe offer still stands, I would love the job!"

Matthew's eyes lit up as he literally bubbled, "Wonderful, as soon as that branch comes onto the market, we'll buy it. Thank goodness you kept your flat!"

150

He paused to light his own cigarette, "I think we need a magazine that deals with family life. Handy hints and knitting designs, we could also run an agony column," he enthused.

As the many bright ideas were thrown around, Debbie noticed that Paul was looking better by the minute, that old familiar smile had returned and instinctively she knew, they could all work together again. Ellen, who had just been sitting quietly, chirped up, "Why not come for Christmas, Paul? You could spend it with us, even a few days would be fine, you need a break, son!"

Happily they had all latched onto the idea as Paul said, "I would love to, but I will have to watch Amanda, she is hell bent on destroying Debbie, well, all of you!"

His eyes had clouded, he had been through hell and it showed. Pouring himself a further coffee, he grimaced, "I've filed for divorce, but I know she will contest it. Somehow, I think it will end up being very unpleasant and that's if I'm lucky!"

Leaning his elbows onto the table, Matthew frowned, "I would watch that, Paul. My advice would be to wait till you return to Britain and file from there. Keep a record of events, Paul and allow me to help you from home. You certainly found the queen of bitches with that one. You can 'phone me day or night and I'll help you, we want to see you happy again, so we do!"

Paul nodded his gratitude, "Honestly, she has caused the collapse of this end of Eric's business and there's nothing more that I intend to do to save it!"

Debbie could see the dark smudges under his eyes, he looked worn out as he said, "I think you're right, Matthew, I'll wait till I return home and would value your help, God, she's a real bitch," he scathed.

There wasn't one of them that didn't feel his pain. Debbie felt close to murder inside, he had not deserved all of this, but then, Eric would have broken them all. She wondered just how many sacrifices he had made, needless sacrifices and confusion gripped her. What if she had told him about Kelly? No, their fate had been sealed when he left her.

Although Eric's huge empire was beginning to crumble, Debbie could find no pleasure in the thoughts of his come uppance, indeed her heart went out to the people who would be made redundant. On the other hand, she truly believed that God did pay debts without money.

Granted, she would have been married to Paul and would never have known Matthew's love. Her mind was spinning in all directions, her confusion again to the fore. Shaking herself sharply, her loyalty for Paul was being swayed by his blatant misery.

Kelly was back with them and for the rest of the afternoon, she kept them all amused. Paul enjoyed seeing her bathed and hugged her as she waved him a cheeky goodnight. After a lazy evening meal, a very reluctant Paul left them. At least he had Christmas to look forward to, a new bounce seemed to have entered his step.

That night, Matthew held her closely, "Debs, you do know that Paul is still in love with you, don't you? Hell, I know his feelings, can you handle that, darling?"

Dropping kisses along his cheek, she whispered, "Yes, darling, I can handle it and I know you're right. I've never tried to hide the fact that my love for him is locked away deep in my heart. I also know Paul realises how much we love each other!"

Passion consumed them and they continued to fuel the fire. How lucky they were to have each other, to want and need each other, to be able to enter their own private paradise.

CHAPTER TWENTY SEVEN

Amanda Howarth hated Debbie Hudson so much, she now felt an intense desire to harm her. She was sick of seeing the very homely bitch and her pathetic little efforts to teach others how to knit. She hated the body that even she had to admit, moved sensually to allow the camera to capture her bulge.

An anger so deep had raged within her as she learned that Paul had gone out to conduct an interview for her father's magazine. Paul had treated her as promised, either completely ignoring her or using her for the sole purpose of humiliating her. Each time she had set up a ploy to win him over, he had seen through it. Worse still she knew had she left him alone, he would have only been too pleased.

The trouble was that she couldn't leave him alone. Her body burned for him. She craved he would love her as he had the Hudson bitch. Often she closed her eyes and pretended his mouth was on hers, his hands caressing her body until her breasts and passage screamed out for appeasement. He had never ever kissed her and since that day in his office, he had never entered her again.

Amanda had quarrelled with both her parents about her lack of enthusiasm with the magazine. Why should she keep her mother in luxury? Why should she work to make her mother's life easier? They had never got along and Maralyn had told her that is she didn't pull herself together, there would be trouble. A sneer crossed Amanda's face, her mother was a glorified bag of wind, so was her father come to that, it was as if she somehow blamed him for Paul's attitude towards her.

Something had led her to believe that Paul would come back to the apartment after his day with darling Debbie. She would give him one last chance to alter his attitude towards her. It had taken her ages to understand, but she now had to admit, he must have truly loved her rival after all.

**

Paul's knuckles gleamed through his skin as he gripped the steering wheel. The depth of gloom had almost claimed him, but he did have something to hang onto, to begin to look forward to, to savour. He could ultimately return to Morecambe and work with the Hudson company. He even allowed himself the luxury of contemplating his future, knowing full well that Debbie would never again be on his agenda. Yet he was happy in the knowledge that he could be around her, her family and his old mate.

He realised that he would have to push it all to the back of his mind until the time came. Nobody must even have a hint of their future plans, what wasn't known, could scarcely be scuttled.

Entering his apartment, he was mildly surprised to find a puff of pink chiffon heading in his direction. Amanda had obviously gone to great effort and he had to admit, had succeeded in looking beautiful. If only she wasn't filled with so much relentless poison, he may well have fucked her in the past, but after the way she had trapped him, he detested every hair on her head. He had developed an almighty hard-on during his drive home and had he not been so tired, he would have called into his favourite home for the 'needy'.

Amanda smiled at him and whined softly, "I know where you've been, Paul. How was it? Did you tell them we were happy? I mean, you wouldn't want them to know you could have lost out, would you?"

"I left them in no doubt whatsoever as to our lifestyle, Amanda. They were all well and pleased to see me," he added, stifling the urge to enthuse.

Her hands moved around his neck, her body pressed itself along his hard length and for the first time, it didn't annoy him. Debbie was now well under way, he didn't have to pretend anymore, he could assure Amanda that soon he would be leaving. At times, he barely recognised himself, he hated his role as user, but he had been taught by the very best.

His eyes narrowed as he noticed the body beneath the transparent garment. Yes, Amanda did have a beautiful body, she was a show stopper, that was until one got to know her. His cock was posing a problem for him and he didn't feel like resorting to jerking himself off, not when there was an eager mouth before him.

She would never know the thrill it gave him to see her on her knees, yet she persisted in her quest for sexual gratification. With a mocking gleam in his eyes, he opened his fly and released his manhood, "D'ya wan it?"

His voice was harsh, abrasive, but this bird did know how to give a bloke a good blow job. Her mouth closed around his wanton staff, his hand pressed down hard on her head, his other hand controlled his greedy wand and then, inhaling deeply, closing his eyes and thinking of Debbie's tantalising body, he came in excruciatingly long spasms, allowing Amanda to suck him 'till he was drained.

Amanda took him, swallowed him, enjoyed him. He had come swiftly and with seeming fulfilment and now it was her turn. Her body shook as she stretched her arms to him, her passage already wet and eager, "Paul, come to bed now," she panted.

Paul's mind had flown back to Debbie, to Matthew, to Kelly. He knew he would never want Debbie to know of his present behaviour, yet felt she would understand, he just couldn't push the bitterness from him. He zipped up his fly and imparted a stiff smile, "I *am* going to bed, Amanda!"

"You bastard, Paul. If you leave me like this, I swear you'll live to regret it. I know you fuck around at the whore house. In fact, you would fuck a bloody lamppost if it had a skirt on," her voice rose shrill and harsh.

"Goodnight." He mused and headed towards his room.

**

Amanda would have stabbed him had she had a knife handy. Well, she had warned the sod and as the hatred rose within her, she would put her plan into action, he had gone too far this time.

Seething with malice, she slipped into a black leather mini skirt. Carefully, she dragged a fine silk blouse over her body, allowing her nipples to protrude beneath the material. She placed her bare legs into the highest court shoes she could find and slipped on a black leather waistcoat.

Five minutes later Amanda entered the infamous wine cellar. It was dimly lit and filled with smoke, but this was where the many tabloid press reporters hung out. Several of them knew her and this was part and parcel of her plan.

Many couples were snogging in the tiny booths and after collecting herself a double vodka, she moved swiftly into an empty booth. The place was crowded as usual and she was as horny as hell. Watching the couples touching each other up didn't help, her nipples felt like rocks and her pleasure centre craved appeasement.

She had met most of the head hunters at some of the parties. No matter how damaging the tabloids were, their reporters were usually given a fair hearing, otherwise they would print what they chose and hang the possible embarrassment.

Her eyes ran along the several men hunched at the far side of the bar, until the dark haired, red shirted, middle aged chap gave her a look of appreciation. He lifted his glass and nodded, having read her message, he ordered further drinks and approached the booth, "I thought it was you. What brings you down here then, toots?

Aggravated by the term of toots, she lit a cigarette and seductively blew the smoke across the table. "Could be you, if you played your cards right," she purred.

His eyes suggested a good screw as he asked gruffly, "Fact or fiction?"

"Mainly fact, I s'pose," she replied huskily.

He eyed her up and down, obviously having already fallen into instant lust with her. Hell, his cock reared, this was some bird and he needed to land a good story. If she was teasing him, he would print that and he knew she was jolly well aware of that. Her knee rubbed against his leg, her hand took his under the table. Slowly, she placed it onto her inner thigh and he knew she was wearing nothing under the short skirt. "I don't like being taken for a sucker, are we on or not?"

Keeping her eyes on his, she allowed the waistcoat to open fully, exposing her rosy nipples. Hearing his gasp of greed, she parted her legs and pulled herself to the edge of the seat. "Does it look like I'm teasin'?"

His hand felt the soft pubic hair, his fingers slid into her slippery passage. Hell, this cookie meant business alright. She rubbed herself frantically over his hand, her lips grimaced into a tight line, somewhere between pain and ecstasy and she came fast and eager. "Now its your turn," she groaned, "Let's get out of here!"

Once outside, she pulled him into the ally. His cock was huge and hard as she took him into her hands. Using her elbows, she wriggled and pulled her skirt up to her waist. His mouth felt dry as his eyes dropped to where she had parted her legs. The moon shafting over them gave her mound the appearance of silvery gold.

With a frenzied moan, he knelt and licked the wet from her bush. Standing up again, he stuck his fingers back into the moistness and felt her hands driving his cock into the throbbing furnace. As though demented, he began to pound into her as she wrapped her legs around his waist. She had placed a nipple into his mouth and pumped with him. He felt her come again and this time, he flowed into her. Choking from the unexpected pick up, he gasped, "This is the best shag I've had in a long time, I want more of this. I thought you were going to pull my dick off, darlin', oh, yesserree, I want more!"

"Mee too, but first, you have a real scoop. If we go back to your place, you can write it, 'phone it through and for the rest of the night ...," she giggled with spite.

Paul and Debbie had asked for this. Now she knew they would be shown no mercy and just for good measure, she had picked herself up a good screw. Yes, this evening was turning out even better than she had first thought.

**

Debbie wakened the next morning, with the strong arms of her husband tightly locked around her. She could never have dreamed of the horror that was waiting to greet them.

Matthew carried Kelly and held Debbie's arm as they descended the stairs and entered the dining room. The happiness died on her lips. Her heart froze as many pairs of stunned eyes faced her. Ellen's gentle eyes overflowed, Jim looked furious and Alma seemed to be impersonating a jelly that wobbled violently.

Swiftly moving to her mother's side, Debbie followed the sad gaze to the table, where the tabloids were displayed. The headlines leapt out, "Debbie Hudson meets with ex lover!"

Blinking with disbelief, she felt the comfort of Ellen's arms and pulling out a chair, she sat down clumsily. Matthew was beside her as she read on:-

'Amanda Howarth, daughter of tycoon, Eric Morgan, was said to be heartbroken last night. She and husband, Paul, editor of 'Ventura' magazine here in New York, had settled happily after facing difficulties in England. A close friend revealed that after a serious miscarriage last year, Amanda and Paul were trying desperately hard for another baby. Amanda sobbed as she told reporters that Miss Hudson had tried to halt their marriage in England, forcing the ceremony to take place in New York. Paul had felt exceedingly uncomfortable as he had been more or less obliged to visit Miss Hudson, it is widely rumoured that she wishes him to return to England with her'.

The room seemed to sway as a wave of sickness washed over her. Matthew's grip tightened, "I'll swing for that fuckin' bitch, what the hell does she think she's playing at for chrissakes?" He punched his fist onto the table as an attack of anger so great almost choked him.

Vaguely, he was aware that he would frighten Kelly and had not realised how bad his language was, he was blinded with hatred and sick to his stomach. "It sounds as though Paul and Debbie spent the whole time alone. What a twisted mind she's got, anyway, nobody in their right mind takes

156

notice of the soddin' tabloids," he choked on the words and seeing his deep distress, Debbie felt worried sick for him.

**

Hank had just turned his car into the drive. He had never felt so much fury. Having met Amanda briefly, the opinion he had formed of her, left a lot to be desired. At first he had suspected that Paul must have married her to further his eminent career, but having seen his work, it spoke for itself. Paul was brilliant and until now, he had thought nothing more on the subject.

His eyes fell on Debbie standing dejectedly on the lower balcony. Although her body was heavy, he still found her deeply attractive. She was too direct to be involved with anything of a sordid nature. Anger filled him as he brought the car to a shuddering halt and rapidly disembarked.

Debbie had walked out onto the balcony, she had never seen Matthew in such a temper and as the telephones began to ring non stop, she had slipped out. Her mind had been miles away, until Hank's gangly figure presented itself before her. He boomed, "Hell, Debbie, whatever happened here? I'm so sorry for the headlines!"

"Its not your fault, Hank. Paul came out yesterday and spent the day with us all," she gulped.

"Did you know him in England, Debbie?"

Inhaling deeply, she gasped, "It isn't anyone else's bloody business, Hank. I do, however, feel that you deserve and reply. Paul and I were once engaged. I'm not prepared to explain the details, but Amanda and Eric Morgan placed so much pressure onto Paul, he had to leave. It was a time of profound sadness, we were just starting out and knew that Eric could and certainly would break us!"

She paused, "Let's find a seat by the pool. I'll ask the others to join us and bring some coffee out. Hank, we will understand if you wish to cancel the rest of the trip. Right now, I would love to be on the way back to England, to Morecambe!"

Her words were filled with sincerity, her voice strained, a sort of resigned misery seemed to fill her. Hank had caught the stifled sob as she called out for coffee and asked the family to join them. He felt near to murder himself. Watching the little entourage walk along, he could feel the warmth from them and after bidding them all 'good morning', he sat down.

Just seeing the way Matthew's arm had gone protectively around his wife, seeing the misery in all of their faces, he became incensed, "There is no way in which this will interfere with the trip. I'll arrange a chat show, Joanne would love to have you back. You can then put your own version across!"

Debbie felt sicker by the minute and almost screamed, "I don't want to put my version. There's nothing to put, I feel so upset and this will hurt Paul dreadfully, I want to go home!"

Hank rose and paced up and down restlessly, "We'll cover this with the truth, a proper story. Come on now, Debbie, you can't just run. Seems to me,

157

you sure as hell have fallen on hard times in the past, you never ran then, did you? I know you won't now. What say you, Matthew?"

Matthew gripped her hand, "Its up to Debbie, Hank, honestly I could murder that woman," his eyes smouldered with anger and suddenly, she knew, she owed them all and if it took a show to give them peace of mind, then a show she would do.

Pouring himself a fresh coffee, Hank said, "Debbie, too many people love you as you know by the amount of mail. Our viewers identify with you, we're not such a fickle bunch over here!"

In spite of herself, she had to smile and taking all the varying factors into account, she conceded, "I'll do a chat show, especially if it is Joanne's show!" Her baby kicked as if to jerk her back from the doldrums and Hank swiftly sorted out the details. With a warm and relieved hug, he finally left them to discuss the future privately.

CHAPTER TWENTY EIGHT

Debbie wore one of her new designs for the show, at least she had something pretty to wear for the unexpected appearance. After popping the soft blue, cotton top over her head, Matthew came up behind her, "You look gorgeous, keep your hair loose and don't worry about a thing. We're together, so we are and I feel that we both owe Paul as well as ourselves!"

He knew just how to relax her and as she turned to kiss him, she gulped, "You know, Matthew, I did think it funny, sort of odd – you know, the fact that Paul had not contacted us. Now we know why. Somehow my heart aches for the misery he has endured," she spoke as her mind felt, confused and hurt.

Prior to the show, Joanne had chatted to them, her smile warm and reassuring, only served to relax Debbie further. Joanne could see they had been devastated, having taken more than enough flack from the tabloids herself.

Once more they found themselves sitting on the stage, with a sea of faces staring at them. The questions, although coming in thick and fast, seemed to be about England, or the new babe, not to mention the series they were making.

By the time the first break had arrived, Debbie felt that people were more interested in them and their way of life. She was relaxing more and more. Her eyes had stopped searching, for they had already fallen on dear Amanda, reminding her sharply of the reason for their visit. She felt sure, that the wicked lady was just biding her time before pouncing.

The pounce arrived with her question, "Isn't it true that you were engaged to Paul Howarth? You never forgave him for dumping on you, did you? Her drawl was as though she was a born American.

Debbie felt her mouth dry as Matthew took her hand and gave it a gentle squeeze. A gulp of water, "Yes, Paul and I were engaged. In fact, if my little brother hadn't died we would have been married. But as you know, it was postponed. I was lucky enough to find Matthew and feel it was perhaps God's wish that we should marry!"

"You didn't want Paul to leave you though, did you?"

The question was caustic and Debbie drunk some more water as Matthew gave her a reassuring wink. She inhaled deeply, "Anyone knowing Paul would find it very easy to love him, surely *you* know that. He is a very sincere person. When he came out to Long Island to conduct the interview, we all felt as though he had never been away. You should have come along with him, he was his usual honourable self. Paul will always be a very welcome visitor to our home!"

Defiance had entered her as a thunderous roar of applause burst forth. She had broken into a clammy sweat, but knew that she had spoken with truth and obviously the rest of the audience felt her sincerity.

In spite of Amanda trying to change the subject, it kept returning to knitwear and pregnancy. It was then Matthew's turn for the next attack. Amanda almost purred, "How do you feel, knowing you weren't the first choice? If Paul hadn't dumped her, she would not have married you!"

For a brief moment, the desire to cut that vicious tongue from its spiteful mouth, tempted Debbie. Lifting her eyes to Matthew, she was drawn to his total composure. His Irish lilt became more pronounced, "If you knew Debbie, you wouldn't mind what order you came in. No, I can say with complete honesty, so I can, I have never felt second best!"

He paused until the applause died down, and added, "Paul and I are very close friends. He is perhaps the most trustworthy and honest person I have ever had the pleasure of meeting!"

Debbie was choked beyond words by the way Matthew had spoken. She knew he loved her, but to admit that he didn't mind which order she had come to love him, humbled her.

A standing ovation ended the show. A day that could have been a disaster had ended up doing nothing but good. Debbie felt in her heart that they were totally unscathed. By golly though, she had felt like spitting the words she felt for Amanda, from her mouth. She had longed to tell of the blackmail, but felt she had gained far more respect by not sinking down to that level.

Hank joined them backstage as they drunk a very welcome cup of coffee with Joanne. He had felt exceedingly moved, both Debbie and Matthew seemed able to draw strength from each other. They thought and acted as one, it was beautiful to behold such faith. Turning to Joanne, he smiled, "You must be well pleased with the way the show went. Jolly well done, Jo, and thank you for your belief in our British pair."

Joanne flashed him her famous smile, "Tell the truth, Hank, it gave me a great deal of pleasure. Debbie, you and Matthew must promise to come onto the show next time you visit the States. You made many more friends out there today!"

**

Eric Morgan had persuaded Maralyn to fly to New York with him. He was more than worried about his magazine and for the first time in his life, he began to think that it was his daughter's neglect that was the problem. Arriving into their hotel suite, they had turned on the television, both agog at what they saw.

Maralyn slumped into the sumptuous armchair and watched with total admiration, the way Debbie and Matthew handled themselves. And with horror, she realised it was her own daughter casting the stones of evil. "Eric," she gasped, "Ring down for the papers please, I do believe our precious daughter is up to her old tricks again!"

Without question, Eric did as he was bid and swiftly poured them both a stiff drink. As they stared at the tabloids together, Maralyn felt tears run freely from her eyes. "Eric, I truly think we should go over and see Paul and Amanda. God almighty, Eric, I should've told you everything long ago, but I thought I was doing the right thing. Hell, its patently clear, I was horribly wrong!"

"Told me what, Maz?"

He fumed, yet two hours later, they entered the Manhattan apartment and Maralyn felt she would break down when she saw the misery written all over Paul's face. Her daughter was sitting on the floor and painting her toe nails. Barely lifting her eyes, Amanda called, "Hi, what ye doing here?"

Paul walked over to pour them a drink, "If you have come to tell me about your airhead daughter's neglect, you can forget it, Eric. I'll stay till you sort out the magazine and them I'm off. Even I didn't think that your precious brat would pull a fuckin' stunt like this. If I were you, I would insist she withdraws any further statements," he added coldly.

Maralyn was close to tears as she gulped, "Oh, she'll withdraw them, Paul, won't you, Amanda? You see, I'm ready to spill the beans. I prayed you would never force my hand, but enough is enough. How can that poor couple be feeling?"

Amanda looked up and seeing the expression on her mother's face, picked up the varnish bottle and screwed the top back on. "If I were you, Mummy dearest," she emphasised the words with a malevolent smile, "I would guard my own secrets, I mean, does Daddy know of your preference?"

For a moment, Maralyn felt a wave of sickness cover her. No one could possibly know and she must at all costs protect Nessa. She would have to take the gamble that Amanda was bluffing. Deliberately and slowly, she placed a cigarette into its holder and began to puff as though her life depended on it.

Scarcely able to control her breathing, she sat down. For the first time in ages, she saw fear in Amanda's eyes. Turning from her, she stated, "Eric, I owe you an apology. Do you remember when Amanda was sixteen and again at seventeen? I mean she went away for a while!"

"S'pose so, but whats that to do with anything?" Eric mumbled impatiently.

"Nothing at all. Mother, shut up," squealed Amanda.

"Will someone have the decency to tell *me* what the hell's going on?" Paul insisted.

Maralyn lit a further cigarette and inhaled deeply, "Sorry, Amanda, but you have gone too far this time. Each time she went away, it was to give birth to a child, both of which were placed for adoption!"

"No, oh, my God, no. You mean I have a couple of grandchildren somewhere out there?" Eric asked in stunned shock. "Hell, I was so bloody happy when she was pregnant by Paul," he gasped as pain seemed to grip and twist his heart.

"Yes, Eric, we both have grandchildren, but we will never see them," sobbed Maralyn.

Paul looked at Amanda as though she had grown two heads. "D'ye mean to tell me that you gave two children away? How could you? You've never been pregnant since, have you?"

161

"Yes, she was, Paul. When she was nineteen, she became pregnant again and that time I refused to help. She went to a back street abortionist and he messed her up for life. She can never have a child and what's more, she *does* know that!"

Maralyn fell silent, disgusted with the whole situation. She knew that Eric had craved grandchildren, yet at the time it had been almost natural to help her daughter. Deep down she had never forgiven herself for not helping out that last time and pain stabbed into her almost doubling her, she had never wished to betray her daughter, but had obviously seen fit to betray her husband. Her eyes rested on him momentarily and words stuck in her throat.

Eric fought to regain his composure. Tears fell from his eyes, "Amanda, I see no reason for your mother to lie. If this is true, you lied to me about Paul, how could you? We have given you all you want and more, we had a bloody right to see our grandchildren!"

Obviously seeing the utter loathing in Paul's face and the grief and shame in her father, Amanda spat at her mother, "You're a fucking liar, you've thrown up this smoke screen to cover yourself, to protect that saintly no hoper, Vanessa!"

"Let's all calm down for a moment, its been a shocking day and we all have funny little foibles we wish to be kept secret," said Paul, sensing danger.

Sadly he did believe what Amanda had done, but seeing the sadness in her mother, brought him no joy. If Debbie had known of the way *he* had treated Amanda, she would have been ashamed of him. It was common knowledge that Eric screwed anything that moved and now he felt sure, there was a deep secret between Maralyn and Vanessa.

Lighting a cigarette himself, he gave Amanda a long, cool look. "If I stay with your for a while, will you help with the work? Will you also sit on these secrets?"

"First its protect Debbie. Now its protect fucking Vanessa, who the hell do you think you are? You see, you pompous, jumped up son of a bitch, I intend to disappear in a couple of months anyway," she laughed as her eyes glinted with malice.

She swallowed her drink and began to laugh helplessly. Paul knew she was hysterical, but his spine chilled at the thought of her causing more trouble for Debbie. The hysteria continued and not daring to smack the stupid, spiteful face, he couldn't trust himself not to kill her, he suggested that Maralyn administer a sharp smack around her face.

It stopped the laughing alright, but her hatred was naked, her mouth twisted into a tight line, "Thank you, Mother. Does Father know you love pussy as much as he does? Indeed you prefer it to cock, don't you?"

The deadliest silence reigned. Everyone sat in a state of shock, until Maralyn asked, "Who told you that, Amanda?" Her voice was strangely calm as sickness swirled in her mind.

"I saw you. I was so ashamed that I kept quiet. You have told somethin' you vowed you would never tell and now its your turn. How can ye bear another woman to touch ye? Can't Daddy satisfy you? Or is it that you're sickened by his behaviour? After all, neither of you have been fuckin' roll models," she shuddered as though revulsion covered her as a second skin.

Eric watched with horror and suddenly felt very insecure. He had always enjoyed screwing his wife, could it be possible that he hadn't managed to satisfy her? Shame began to mix with his horror, "Is this true Maz, don't I satisfy you? You always seemed to enjoy that side of our marriage. Are you really a lesbian?"

Maralyn ran her tongue over hr dry lips, "In spite of your carryings on, Eric, you always had plenty left for me. I am also deeply in love with Vanessa, but that's not the issue here, Amanda has caused enough trouble and if I had known the story you told Paul, I would have spoken up about her barren state!"

Slowly, she took out another cigarette and turned to her wayward daughter, "What have you gained, Amanda? You're not happy and neither is Paul, and whatever you may think, I didn't relish having to break your news," she choked, visibly shaken.

Paul took the older woman's shoulders, "If you had known about the story when I was told, when I was told," he paused as an excruciating pain, not only entered his heart, but wrung and pummelled it, 'til tears filled his eyes. With a deep swallow, he continued, "It would have made a difference then, Maz, but my precious Debbie is happy with Matthew now. I think that the revelations of tonight can stay within these walls. Amanda, you wish to leave, fair enough, but do it with an element of decorum, it will help no one to know of any of our individual sexual prowess!"

For the first time in his life, Eric had remained silent. Not only did the revulsion sicken him, but by Christ, he owed a sincere apology to Paul. His eyes were that of a tortured man as he went over to his son in law, "Paul, I truly am sorry. I did think that Amanda expected your child. It was almost like a dream come true when I was told. God knows, I have been as guilty as the next man as far as playing around, but it sickens me to think of my wife with Vanessa!"

Maralyn sat there stunned. How on earth was she going to break this news to Vanessa? Would she feel betrayed? Her own world felt as though it had toppled, held still, before finally shattering.

Her eyes lifted to Eric, "Do you want us to split up then? I have found much happiness outside of my marriage and am not prepared to let it go. Its up to you, Eric, I'm happy to carry on as we are, with you screwing around as before. Indeed for many years I've known you were playing around, but you always wanted me, didn't you?"

"You're right, Mazza. I don't want us to part. I know homosexuals are more open about themselves now. They are entitled to their way of life, I just never thought about it in my family. After the way Amanda behaved, you my dear wife, are a paragon of virtue," said Eric, feeling some sort of pride return.

Amanda was fuming as she saw everything slipping away from her. She would never stop trying to destroy Debbie, had it not been for her, she would at least have had a chance with Paul. Now, thanks to her mother, she had nothing and in spite of everything, she didn't want her own behaviour to become public.

Filling her glass with neat Vodka, she shouted, "I agree with Paul about keeping it all in one room. If you ever betray me again, Mother, I'll release to the world that you are a fucking pussy sucker!"

"I do know that, Amanda. I think I'm past caring about myself, but Nessa has never done you any harm," said Maralyn wearily.

"At least she doesn't know of my past, or have you told her?" Amanda flared.

"No one else need ever know," sobbed Maralyn.

**

Arriving back at the ranch, Debbie and Matthew felt exhausted. To their delight, Paul had obviously managed to escape to his room and ring them. His voice choked his apologies.

"Paul, it was nothing to do with you. Everything Matthew and I said stands, we love you!"

Hearing his relieved sigh, she knew his mind was now at peace and snuggled into the crook of hr husband's tender arm, where solace claimed her.

CHAPTER TWENTY NINE

Debbie entered her ninth month and although she felt huge and clumsy, her mind was literally on overdrive. So many ideas were spinning around, after all, she had to be ready for the new series in England and for their next visit to the States. Pregnancy did make her mind more active as creative urges for her own babe were uppermost and she realised that other mums would feel just as she did.

Somehow she suspected that Hank was about to come up with a new idea. His rich American drawl had provoked an enigmatic smile as he leaned over to impart his usual peck upon his arrival

He found himself agreeing with Matthew, she did look devastatingly serene and tormentingly sensual as her body moved heavily. Watching her smile, he prayed she wasn't able to read is mind. Restlessly lighting a cigarette, he gulped, "Debbie, what brings such a smile to you? Gee, do you know something I don't?"

Her little chuckle enchanted him as a gleam entered her eyes, "Sorry, Hank, I just guessed you had something up your sleeve and just wondered when you would deign to tell us!"

Carefully shaking the ash from his cigarette, he also smiled, "I think with the diaries being so successful, it would be a brilliant idea for Matthew to do a series. Many men would want to learn to take good, sharp photographs. How about a series on 'photography for beginners'? I would like to run it through on your next visit, could you work on that, Matthew?"

Matthew couldn't have been more excited. His voice rose with eagerness, "Hank, there is nothing I would like better. I'll work out a format with Debs for our return!"

Alma suddenly piped up, "We could do the same in England, but then, I suppose you will run that through the magazine once Paul returns. I think it's a wonderful idea!"

Debbie rose to her feet, the dull ache in her back seemed to be getting sharper. Seeing the joy on Matthew's face had pleased her more than anything and she silently vowed that her name would be absent from his programmes. He worked darned hard, they all did, but it was always under the Debbie Hudson umbrella, now it was the turn of Matthew Ross. Her eyes sought his with love, "It seems we all have so many ideas, we are lucky to be able to share so much!"

Hank interjected warmly, "Gee, folks, I sure feel privileged to work with you all. I was thinking seriously about a party, somthin' like the week before you return to England. If we hold it here at the ranch, the camera crews would love to come and I feel sure that Joanne would love to attend. If I make the arrangements, how about it?"

Her parents were nodding in agreement as Ellen said, "We would love a party, Hank, but Jim and I would love to prepare some English fare. We will go over it together. You would be happy with that, wouldn't you, Debs?"

Having taken in a deep breath, Debbie now blew it slowly out. "I'm happy with anything you all decide, but right now, I think Matthew and I will have to leave!"

Her face contorted with pain, Matthew was on his feet, his expression one of concern. "Debs, are you sure it's the baby, it isn't due for three weeks!"

"Tell her that," she smiled.

All of them looked at her, Hank's eyes held a mixture of tenderness and fear. Her whole body had tightened as the next contraction arrived. She dropped a kiss onto Ellen's head, "We won't be long, Mum, give Kelly a hug when she wakens!"

If Debbie could have had one wish granted about her babe, it would have been that she be life her father. The thought of a boy never entered her head and as they arrived at the hospital, she found she had already broken out into a clammy sweat.

The portly Doctor Jarvis greeted them. Sister helped her onto a trolley and after holding her tummy through a further contraction, Doctor Jarvis smiled, "Take her through to the delivery room, Sister!"

His tone was brisk and business like, yet his eyes were soft and gentle. Turning to Matthew, Debbie saw the naked love in his gorgeous eyes. The pains were non stop as she heard the instructions to 'push'. Matthew dropped a kiss onto her forehead as she was told to 'pant', "We will call her Verity," the words came out with the pant.

A magical, yet familiar cry, heralded the arrival of their new daughter. She was also placed onto Debbie, the babe turned her little mouth and began to suckle. Matthew's tears fell unashamedly onto them both. His hand went out to stroke the petal cheek, and yes, the baby did have a lot of hair, Debbie's wildest dream had come true. Her husband's mouth was on hers, "Thank you, darling, she's gorgeous. I like the name, Verity, it means truth, doesn't it?"

Within half an hour and still not believing how quick the delivery had been, she was ready for home. Verity was bathed and dressed and was handed into her eager arms. Almost in a daze of sheer unadulterated bliss, she examined every inch of the new arrival. The tiny rosebud mouth. The button nose. Deep blue eyes. The mop of soft black hair, made up the picture of Verity. It was almost like holding a miniature clone of her beloved husband.

She felt a true contentment, Matthew's arms had gone around them both. Doctor Jarvis sat on the bed, "You sure mean business when you start, don't you? She is a beautiful baby!"

Pausing to gaze with wonder at the tiny bundle, noticing the lashes were almost black, she choked. "I can't believe this tiny cherub came so quickly. Thank you and your staff, as you know, Matthew and I would like to make a donation to the hospital, but would like to make sure it goes where its most needed!"

Doctor Jarvis smiled, "There is no need to make a donation, you have been charged the normal fees," his voice boomed with kindness.

Matthew piped up, "That is fine, but it is something Debbie and I would like to do!"

Rising to his feet, Doctor Jarvis was very serious, "Well, we are sifting through plans to open a new neo natal unit. The fund is badly in need of a boost, I'm sure that any donation would be more than welcome," and added, "If Debbie is alright in an hour or so, you can take her home. I must pop off now!"

Alone at last, her eyes lifted to Matthew, "I love you, Mr Ross and I think I rather like the babies you make. Let's not ring home, let's just get there!"

His arms crushed her, his mouth bit her, "I love you, Mrs Ross. He could see the strain in her face, it had been a very quick delivery, but dreadfully painful for her, yet she hadn't complained once, just got on with delivering the gorgeous bundle that now slept in her arms. How many times can one fall in love? How many times could he explain his love for her? How often could fresh waves of love attack a man?

Debbie choked as the car pulled up in front of the ranch. Matthew jumped out, collected Verity and placed her into Ellen's arms. Love shone from him as he took Kelly from Jim, kissed and said, "Come and find Mummy, my precious one and we can all play with our new baby, so we can!"

Alma rushed to hug them both and Hank followed suit. He had watched Debbie climb from the car, she looked almost ashen beneath her sun tan, she looked so very fragile, so very, very filled with joy, yet she was sensual beyond belief. The love for her husband shone from her gorgeous eyes as she took Kelly from him.

Once inside, coffee was served and Matthew joined the crew for photographs. Ellen still held Verity as Kelly clumsily explored her sister. Her little fingers kept straying towards the bright eyes, obviously wondering how they worked.

Reels of film were taken of those very special moments, for themselves as well as for the diaries. Matthew had bought a carry cot as a temporary measure until they arrived home. Irene had been asked to order a new cot, to be delivered in time for their return. Debbie knew she must rest, she felt exhausted, but before she did, she needed to ring Irene and give her the facts first hand.

It was obvious that Irene was working flat out when Debbie finally got through to her. She gave a happy little squeal, "Debbie, I am so happy for you both, who's she like? What does Kelly think of her?"

Debbie felt herself drawn into the euphoria of excitement, momentarily bringing a wave of severe homesickness. Having given Irene all of the details to release to the British press, she sighed, "Irene, I only had one wish to be granted and by golly it was!"

"I bet you wanted her to look like Matthew," chuckled Irene.

"You know me better than I know myself, Irene. I know we are all looking forward to coming home. How's everything over there?"

Still chuckling, Irene replied, "We've had several requests to extend Kelly's diaries for another year, coupled with one of the new arrival. Honestly, Debbie, so many things are going on over here. I'm longing for your return, its not the same without you, we miss you all dreadfully!"

"Me to, Irene, I'm longing to come home, although everybody over here's so friendly. Anyway, must dash!"

"Take care now, give my god-daughter a big kiss and one for Verity," gulped an emotional Irene.

She almost staggered back to the pool, where the rest of the family were enjoying the late summer sun. Matthew had made a barrier, fearing Kelly getting too near to the water, she loved him being with her and was rapidly turning into a daddy's girl. Seeing Debbie approach, he jumped up, "Now, Mrs Ross, put your feet up and get some rest!"

Kelly climbed onto her knee and Debbie knew the mite wondered where the excess baggage had gone and smiled to herself. That evening, Matthew bathed Kelly and as Debbie fed Verity, Kelly snuggled to them both and watched.

They knew that together, they had learned so much and were only too happy to share the little lessons. Paul had rung, his voice soft and gentle, "I'm almost scared to contact you after the last episode, but I needed to wish you all the best. Take care, Debbie, I'll see you all at Christmas!"

Climbing into bed that night, delight filled her. Matthew's arms could now encircle her. It felt so good, so right, so beautiful. His kisses rained down on her, arousing the very heart of her as she eagerly returned his kisses, until sleep finally claimed her exhausted body.

Offers for commercials seemed to pour in. Debbie had made sure it was an issue at their regular meetings. Jim was beginning to be bogged down with the accounts and would need help when they returned home. He had considered the offers for commercials, always serious where work was concerned, but his grandchildren, well, they were personal to him. His eyes were filled with tenderness, "I can see no harm in them advertising. As you say, they do endorse the products you allow them to model for. And if the money they earn goes into trust funds for their future, I think its wonderful for them!"

The close family bond seemed to grow stronger. Never had they had disagreements, or even altercations. They thought as one and even without the regular meetings, Debbie thought they would all have come to the same conclusions.

The many, many floral gifts that continued to arrive were also directed to the hospitals, just as with Kelly, and the toys went to the children's wards. It was now beginning to look that it would be at least a year before they could return to the States.

How she thanked God for Matthew, he knew how to calm her as he went through her ideas, ideas that had sprung readily to mind, had come from thinking about her own babes. She had felt the urge to make a pretty circular shawl, a hooded cape and ponchos, each idea adding further excitement, yet time to make them all was very tight. Somehow though, she knew with Matthew beside her, she could and would cope. Hank was right, mums did identify with her.

CHAPTER THIRTY

Preparation for the party was well underway. Jim and Ellen had asked permission to take over the kitchens for a couple of days. Jim literally revelled as he plunged himself into baking bread, rolls and scones, feeling a healthy nostalgia tug at his heart. The tug was undoubtedly due to the fact that Ellen was beside him, somewhat as they had worked in the early days.

Her hands were still more than deft as they iced various fancies. Yet she was just warming up to the big cake, one that would salute America, with a view to thanks for their wonderful hospitality. His eyes prickled as he went involuntarily over to her, took her into his arms and whispered, "This reminds me of the day we met, how we began to work together, how we fell in love and married. Darling Ellie, I love you as much now as I did then. Mind you, I don't think either of us would want to struggle like that again, would we?"

"No, Jim, yet we were just as happy then. I wouldn't wish to go through losing Tony again, seeing Debbie's heart break and mend. Shut up, you fool, I'll cry in a moment," she gave a bewitching little chuckle and allowed him to kiss her long and hard, without the privacy of the bedroom

Hank had popped in to make sure there was nothing further he could do, and to all of their delight, Paul had also turned up, his smile covering his face as he saw the startled, welcome surprise from them. Hank had shaken his hand warmly, "Hi there, Paul, you coming to the party?"

His eyes rested on Debbie, "I suppose I could come, but although Amanda has buggered off, I think I'll wait till I get back to England to celebrate. Although I could refuse to come back to tie up loose ends, it really isn't my style, but in six months, I'll be free!"

Having espied the carry cot, he had gone over to look at the latest arrival. "Matthew, she is the double of you, she is gorgeous," he exclaimed with sincerity and filled Debbie with his sadness.

Standing up to leave, Paul shook hands with the men and hugged the women, "I look forward to Christmas," was his parting shot. Debbie's eyes followed his car down the driveway. He had always been an ardent lover, she couldn't help wondering how he satisfied that need. It reminded her of the time they had first become lovers on their 'hill'. She shivered as she realised just how lucky she had been in the love stakes.

During the next day, the typing pool was emptied and turned into a dance and party room. Everyone had enjoyed helping, leaving early to prepare themselves for the evening ahead. Trestle tables were set out, with enough delicious food to feed an army. Debbie could feel the sheer excitement radiate from her parents, filling her with an added joy.

Once the little ones were settled, she had decided to wear a flared mini skirt. It nipped into her tiny waist, folded softly over her slender hips and fluted out for easy movement. In just three short weeks, her figure was almost back to normal, so she selected a modestly cut, low neck top to cling seductively, in fact she felt rather special as she laid them out ready to step into.

After showering, she popped her black lace panties and matching bra on. She rubbed her arms as little bursts of excitement filled her. Feeling delightfully feminine, she sat down at the dressing table to apply her make up.

Matthew was in the shower and she couldn't help but giggle, he was singing his lungs out. He returned with a small towel draped over his lean hips and gasped as he saw her, "Debs, you look de li cious, so ye do."

Her throat constricted as he stood behind her, his eyes smouldered into hers through the mirror. Lifting her hair, he bend and kissed her nape. She felt her body shake, "Matthew, go away, this reminds me of our wedding night!"

Turning her mouth to him, his lips brushed hers apart and his tongue gently invaded her. Heat radiated from his body, his voice deep and sensually low, "It reminds me too, only I remember something more like this," he groaned as he unclipped her bra, taking it slowly down her arms.

Again, he moved behind her, "And this," he gulped with throaty intent, cupping her breasts and kneading them. "And this," his mouth moved down to claim them, extracting an eager groan from her, "Matthew, we .. must .. get ..ourselves," he just swallowed her words with hunger.

Mindlessly, she pressed herself into him. Her hips began to move, seeking relief from the burning ache which now consumed her. His teeth nibbled the delights of her throbbing nipples, sending arrows of desire through her. Feverishly, she pulled the towel from him, "Oh, God," he murmured, responding ferociously to the provocative movement. His arms went around her, "Debbie, I want you, hell, I need you!"

"Mmmee too. Matthew, make love with me and keep hold of my hands," her voice rose with the impassioned plea.

Lifting her into his arms, he stood her beside the bed. He had aroused them both to torture level. Second thoughts, had there been any in the first place, flew out of the window. His hands gripped hers as she allowed herself to climb onto the bed.

Her eyes glued to the swatch of black hair that trailed his lower abdomen. Suffocation choked her as she took in the beautiful sight of his penis, it was deliciously thick, wonderfully rigid, it seemed to stand with pride, up and out from the black tangled copse and before her eyes left it, the end had begun to pearl in erotic anticipation.

Liquid fire surged between her legs as his body covered hers. There could be no banishment of the sensations that ran untamed through her. He knew how she felt, because he felt the same, as her body squirmed sensually beneath his. Sweeping their arms above her head, he gloried in the tautness of her breast, she was absolutely gorgeous and her body raised to allow him to surrender to her blistering heat.

For a brief moment they held still, his ecstatic groans as he assaulted her breast with his mouth, sent her into a crazed frenzy. They began to move, slowly at first, building to a rapid pace, as with a scream, her legs wound around him, trapping him into a bliss he never wanted to leave.

Debbie felt as though she had left her body and was watching two people making mad, passionate love. Every nerve in her tingled as she gazed in wonder, at the magical manner with which the couple sought to please each other. Matthew's taut buttocks seemed to gleam beneath the tightly locked ankles of his partner.

The couple were lost entirely from the outside world, tears dripping from their eyes. He pounded into her and an infusion of heat flew upward within her. Suddenly, without warning came the almighty explosion, the blasts recurring over and over as they arched to each other. Mercifully, she re-entered her body to receive the exquisite burst and enjoy the eruptions that showed no signs of slowing down.

Gulping, shuddering and tasting each other, they shivered onto a plateau that knew no name. Matthew lifted his head, his moisture filled eyes smouldered into the mist that filled her eyes. "Never have you tasted more delectable," he gasped, biting her ear.

Locked in the sweet ebb of passion, she felt a divine lethargy wash over her. Turning her mouth to his, her lips suckled his, "I can't feel my hands, darling!"

"I love them where they are, so I do. They can't interfere with what I'm doing," he whispered softly.

Slowly, he unlocked their fingers and brought his arms to close round her body. No one would guess she had given birth to a child less than a month ago, her responses were as eager as a newly married girl and like him, she couldn't stop her need, her urge, her love.

Reluctantly, he withdrew from her, knowing they would continue later in the night. He just couldn't envisage himself handling a situation where she didn't want him body and soul.

**

Finally, they were ready for the party and Debbie had slipped her feet into her high heeled sandals. Suddenly, she was back in Matthew's arms and he groaned, "Darling, you look fantastic, like a young teenager, every man will envy me tonight, any night!"

She wound out of his arms deliberately, knowing it would take the tiniest peck to land them back into bed. He looked devastatingly handsome, his blue jeans clung tightly and seductively over his sensual hips. She almost envied the way they seemed to caress his masculinity, knowing that she had the powers to arouse him at any given time.

She loved his short sleeved shirt, which was tastefully open at the neck, the multi colour mix depicting the bronze of his body. Swiftly, she pulled him outside and arms locked around each other, they entered the party to the welcome of 'Lassie from Lancashire'.

Debbie felt herself flush, she could feel her eyes dancing after the love they had shared. Stupidly, she thought that everyone would know, yet they could only envy her. Watching Matthew, she allowed herself to briefly luxuriate in the sacred knowledge that she knew every ounce of her man's body. Knew his every thought, knew how his muscles flecked in passion.

After receiving hugs from Hank, Alma and her parents, Jim smiled, "Matthew, would you mind if I danced with my daughter?"

"You may dance with your daughter, Jim, providing that your wife will dance with me," throbbed his Irish lilt, telling the world of his obvious happiness.

Hank watched her, she radiated her beauty as her lithesome body moved rhythmically. Alma followed his gaze, "Its difficult to remember that she won't be twenty one until we arrive back in England, isn't it?"

He desperately wanted to dance with Debbie, yet feared her nearness. Admonishing himself sharply, he finally led her onto the floor. Her body was light, her feel followed his steps to perfection. For the first time he could remember, he found conversation impossible, the words seemed to stick in his throat. After drawing a deep breath, he finally managed, "Debbie, we sure will miss you when you return to England. Hopefully, I'll be over there early next year!"

Her gorgeous eyes lifted to him, "We will all miss you, Hank, but if you do come over, we would love to have you stay with us!"

How very simplistic she was, how easy to understand, how very easy to fall head over heels for. Returning her to the table, he walked over to the doorway. Lighting a cigarette, he knew he needed the air. Even where he was standing, her eyes drew him like a magnet. Suddenly, he saw Matthew take his wife into his arms, her arms looped so naturally around his neck and he noticed the way her mouth lifted to his. Never had Hank envied anyone, but right then, he envied Matthew. Yet, he was perhaps one of the nicest men he had ever met, it was easy to understand why Debbie loved him so very much.

**

All too soon the time came for them to say farewell to America. The 'plane took off amidst a flurry of press and arrived back in England the same way. And, at long last, they were heading along the promenade, feeling the nostalgia and the invigorating ozone that reeked through the air.

America had certainly been wonderful, the warmth and friendship knew no bounds over there, but, there was still no place like home. It was a glorious feeling to be approaching their castle on the hill and Irene's outstretched arms, put the final seal onto their happiness.

Irene had done a superb job in making sure that everything was up to date. Cards for Kelly's first birthday, together with many gifts had also arrived. Swinging Kelly into the air, she smiled, "She's even more beautiful and so happy. Golly, its really great to have you all home!"

There was no concealment of Irene's excitement as she went over to gaze on Verity. Her eyes saucered, "No one could ask who *her* daddy is. She is absolutely gorgeous and the image of you, Matthew!"

173

Kelly's cot had been moved into the spare room and Verity would sleep in the corner of their bedroom. Once their children were safely in bed, Matthew's arm went about Debbie and without a word, they walked up to the balcony. Nostalgia flooded her as they surveyed their little empire.

His mouth nuzzled her ear as he whispered, "Those lights flashing 'Ventura', will soon be dimmed. Its gone up for sale and we can make a bid immediately. Honestly, Duchess, life is so rich and full at times, it scares me!"

The ensuing few weeks flew by in a flurry of activity. The series for television was scheduled for early March. The diaries for Kelly and Verity would still continue and Matthew had put in a bid for 'Ventura' which had been accepted, with a completion date for May. Again, life was just about perfect.

Excitement ran rampant, with just a week to go until Christmas. Paul would be arriving in a few days time and Ellen was rushed off her feet with special cakes for Christmas. Poor Jim was working non stop with the books, he came in to join them, "The shop receipts are excellent. Richard and Jenny must have worked like demons," he added with delight.

Matthew was looking out of the window, "Debbie, I think we could have a trip down to the shop tomorrow. We could take the children to see Richard and Jenny, we could also call into 'Ventura' and reassure the staff that Paul will be back!"

Jim smiled, "I think that would be a lovely, thoughtful idea. I would have gone myself, but I think they would probably like to see the children!"

Out of the blue, and taking Debbie completely by surprise, Ellen asked, "Aren't you supposed to have a check up, Debbie? Verity will be three months old soon!"

Matthew piped up, "We have to take the updated book into Brian, he can examine you also, Debs!"

Debbie turned to Jim, "You are looking tired, Dad!"

Matthew jumped in, "As we are having a couple of rooms prepared for the kiddies, I think we had better have another couple of offices converted. Jim you will need a new accountant to work with you, plus some more clerical staff. How's about it?"

"I couldn't agree more, Matthew. There is so much going on at once and the magazine itself, could keep one accountant busy," said a serious Jim.

**

Matthew had bought a little chair to clip onto the pram. After Verity had been fed the next morning, Debbie placed her into the pram, briefly allowing her mind to wander back to the night of the party. Every inch of her tingled when she thought about the first time Matthew had loved her that evening.

The whole of that time had been a series of heady orgasms, until the foreplay and after play became indefinable, the varied positions were beautiful, erotic, awkward and sensually scintillating. It was as if they had just married, neither able to pass the other without bouts of searing passion flaring.

As she wrapped Kelly up ready to place into the seat, her mouth ran over the little pink cheeks, "Oh, Kelly, all I can ever wish for you, my little one, is that you meet a man like I did. Mummy feels sure she has a surprise Christmas gift for Daddy, but it's a secret till then," she sighed blissfully.

Walking along the almost deserted promenade, Debbie had never felt so much peace in her heart. The angry sea still soothed her and Kelly squealed her delight at the seagulls, sharply reminding them of Tony. Although everywhere was grey, the vista was still one of the most beautiful sights. Even the air seemed to belong to them alone, bracing and invigorating them.

Brian had greeted them with his usual warmth and after a brief chat, he examined Verity with gentle hands. Breathing a sigh of relief, Debbie continued to dress her babe. "They are lovely and lucky children," added Brian.

Proudly and hastily, she collected her handbag and noticed that Matthew hadn't moved. A slight irritation ran through her, "Come on, Matthew, we must call into 'Ventura', Verity will need her feed before we know where we are!"

Stubbornly he sat there, he knew she was ducking the issue. His vivid blue eyes challenged her, "Brian hasn't examined you yet, Debbie. Don't be after telling me you've forgotten," he stated with raised eyebrow.

Brian gasped, "Are you telling me that you haven't had a post natal, Debbie? Come on now, we must make sure all is well, hop up onto the bed!"

Flushes of indignation swept her as Brian completed the internal behind the screens. He looked at her, "You knew, didn't you, Debbie?"

"About the end of July, I reckoned," said Debbie.

Tossing her head defiantly, she went back to Matthew and knew he knew. His look was one of total bewilderment. Her voice was strained and defensive, "I wanted this to be a surprise for Christmas, Matthew and you have spoiled it for me!"

"Sorry, darling, but you can tell me again at Christmas. As long as you're happy," he said emotionally.

After wishing Brian the compliments of the season, they left. Once the babes were placed safely back into their pram, Matthew took her into his arms, "God, I love ye, so I do. I should've guessed when I felt that added delicious need in you," he said and kissed her soundly.

"Matthew, I am so deeply happy. We did say we would have four. Perhaps after this one I will go on the pill for a couple of months and try again as we leave America!"

Pulling themselves apart, she tingled at the sight of her handsome hunk, she could have jumped on his there and then and knew he would respond. They were perfectly attuned in every single part of their lives.

CHAPTER THIRTY ONE

Matthew and Debbie just about floated into 'Ventura' and were met with the warmest of greetings from Vanessa. She was preparing to nudge forty in a couple of years, but apart from virtually being married to her job, it was easy to see that she was happy in her personal life as well.

Every time they had seen her, she always wore a smart trouser suit. It was as if she was making a statement by doing so, yet she was a very feminine lady, her grey eyes were soft and gentle, at times revealing her pain at the loss of her young husband.

Surprising them both, she had billed and cooed over the children and after making coffee, sat Kelly onto her lap. "Obviously, I have heard the rumours and sincerely hope they are true. Really, it's the only reason I stayed on here, to work with Paul again. You are taking over 'Ventura' aren't you?"

A frown had puckered her brow, but Matthew's excitement was infectious, "Yes, every word is true, Vanessa. We only popped in to confirm it for you. We also thought it would make a pleasant Christmas bonus for the staff, you know, to understand their jobs were safe!"

The rest of the staff gathered and had indeed been worried. They all cheered when Matthew confirmed the situation. Emotions spilled over as relief surged through them, many had already worked with Paul and it was obvious they looked forward to his return. And then it was time for them to leave as happiness settled once again in the magazine offices.

Nostalgia flooded them as they entered the shop. To their delight, trade was good and brisk, it really was making a huge profit now. Granted, Debbie, Matthew and her parents had sown the original seeds of hard graft, the vast spate of publicity also helped, but it was the care that Richard and Jenny had continued to ply, that had kept it high in the popularity stakes.

Jenny saw them enter and called excitedly to Richard. Seconds later she threw herself into their arms. "What a wonderful surprise, how are you?"

Her dark eyes danced as Richard joined her. He had even hugged Matthew, before his arm found its way around Jenny's waist. Both of them stared at Kelly in amazement, Jenny gasped, "Golly, she's grown, she's adorable!"

Richard bent down to cuddle her, she was a very friendly little girl, used to having people milling around her. As long as she knew there was a familiar face with her, she was quite happy to receive the many hugs.

Jenny moved round to gaze into the pram, "Richard, come and look at Verity, she's absolutely gorgeous, look, she can smile, oh, Richard, I just can't wait …!"

Debbie looked at Matthew, realising he had seen that 'look' in Jenny's eyes. There was also a new maturity about Richard. Matthew smiled, "And when is your little one due?"

"Middle of June, how'd'ye guess?" Jenny interjected as radiance bubbled from her.

Seeing the table in the corner become empty, they all headed to sit down. Jenny asked for coffee to be served and a glass of milk for Kelly.

Richard sat down and turned to Matthew, "I'm so pleased you came in, we needed to speak to you both. I have taken on a part timer, to train as a baker, I do hope that's alright. I mean, we're happy to pay him, because I don't want Jenny doing too much, especially in the lifting department!"

Matthew took the words from Debbie's mouth, "No, you have earned the need for help. You must both enjoy this pregnancy and the wee one when it arrives. Pop the slips through and subtract it from the banking. Jim will alter the books, so he will. You've both done a fantastic job here and deserve the extra help!"

Two eager faces turned to him, Richard gulped, "Are you sure, Matthew? We are earning bloody good commission and our happiness is complete with the news of the babe. We have been trying since Kelly's Christening!"

"Richard, you earn the commission with hard graft, why should you work hard to improve takings, if you have to pay it out again?" Matthew reasoned with sincerity.

Verity became restless and Jenny jumped up, "Is she ready for a feed, Debbie? Come upstairs, can I lift her up?"

Richard watched as Jenny clutched the baby to her. Turning to Matthew, he suggested, "How about you coming through to the kitchen? Bring Kelly and we can talk, I know Jenny is longing to chat with Debbie, we tape all the shows and watch them at night. You both make it look so easy, so you explain the birth to me!"

Following Jenny back up the familiar staircase, Debbie's heart thumped excitedly. Almost grudgingly, Jenny handed a very hungry Verity over for her feed. Then she literally bombarded Debbie with questions about everything to do with child birth and feeding.

Dropping a kiss onto Verity's forehead, it hit her hard. Fair enough she knew many people identified with her, but right then, Jenny stood beside her, literally drinking in any vestige of advice she could possibly gleen. Mentally, Debbie thanked God for guiding her to seek Brian's valuable advice.

Changing the babe to the other side, she felt stunned as she looked at Jenny and gasped, "I never realised just how much notice people were taking. The mail sacks are always full, but you are the first person to ask face to face. I'm used to all sorts of questions in the post, but being with you, seeing your trust, hell, Jenny, it's a huge responsibility and it frightens me!"

"It shouldn't, Debbie. I've made lots of friends at the clinic and in the shop. They all thirst for any details you can give out. You manage to impart the knowledge in language we can understand, it's true, everything does look easy," enthused Jenny.

Wandering back along the seafront, she cast a sidelong glance at Matthew. He was in a very pensive mood, his jaw set, if not rigid. Concern filled her, "Is anything wrong, darling?"

Kelly wanted to get down and walk and without thought, Matthew had lifted her down and taken her hand. Turning to Debbie, he spoke softly, "Nothin's wrong, Debs. Are you sure you are happy about *our* baby?"

"Of course I am, in fact, I'm thrilled, especially now that Jenny is pregnant. Mind you, the way she hangs onto my every word makes me feel even more responsible, why d'you ask?"

"Didn't you want to tell them about our little one? I almost did, but it seemed like stealing their thunder!"

"Exactly, Matthew, exactly," she smiled.

He should have guessed, but this day had been filled with surprises. Her face was flushed as the wind whipped the colour into her cheeks. His heart almost burst, two little daughters and a baby on the way, a wife that always wanted his love. How could he ever tell her just how much she meant to him? How could he ever let her know the deep happiness she had brought into his life? Simple, he couldn't, there were no words to explain the deep rooted security she had given to him.

**

Debbie wakened early on Christmas Eve morning. A strange tingle of excitement shot through her. Turning towards her husband, she watched his eyes flicker into awareness. Instantly, his mouth covered hers as he gathered her into his arms. They both felt the passion flare, yielding eagerly as they were transported to paradise.

Later that morning, long after Matthew had left to pick Paul up from the airport, Debbie noticed Jim heading in the direction of his flat. Unease crept into her, hastily, she called to Irene, "Call me if you need me, I'm just popping in to see Ellen!"

Having tapped gently on the door, she entered. Her parents were locked together, Jim soothed, "I'm sure they will tell us, dear. Perhaps there *is* nothing wrong and they want to tell us whatever it is together!"

Stunned beyond words, she realised they must be talking about her. "Mum, Dad, whatever's wrong?"

Ellen's tear filled eyes turned to her, "Debs, I'm sorry, dear, its just that," she gasped in the air, "Just that, well you went for your check up and neither of you have mentioned it. Dad and I think you look pale and a little drawn. If there is something wrong, dear, pl ... please don't try to shield us," she ended swiftly on a sob.

Running into their outstretched arms, Debbie hugged them, "Mum, Daddy, golly, I'm so very sorry. We were keeping a secret for Christmas. What with the new of the shop, the happiness from Richard and Jenny, we have all been so busy. I never dreamed you expected a report from me and feel dreadfully sorry!"

She paused, sad to think she had been the reason for upsetting her beloved parents. With a little gulp, she added, "Our news was sensational, Brian was very pleased with me and Verity, but he did confirm that we would have our own little stranger sometime in July!"

Jim kissed them both and exhaled heavily, "Thank God for that, Debbie. We were so worried … we had no business sticking our noses into your business, but we were so worried!"

His voice had shaken with emotion as he ended with a painful gasp. Guilt flooded her, "I truly am sorry. Matthew is very thrilled and would agree with me, its very much your business!"

They chatted for a few more minutes and then Jim said, "Must get on, otherwise we won't be ready to welcome Paul!"

**

Paul arrived with Matthew and Kelly, having learned to run, shot straight into Matthew's arms. She had also begun to link several words together and in her own language, managed to welcome Paul. Confusion filled Debbie, here were the only two men she had ever loved, both under the same roof and she had born a child for each of them.

Chewing her lips, she shook off the threatened guilt. Poor Paul, he had never known the happiness that she herself was bound into. His eyes told her that he had never stopped loving her. And in spite of his certain knowledge of Kelly, he hadn't so much as mentioned the fact, let alone hurled recriminations.

They had all arranged to have a quiet Christmas, Ellen and Jim wanted to prepare the meal. Van loads of cards and gifts had arrived and been forwarded to hospitals and life was just about perfect.

Christmas morning, they all elected to walk to the church. Many people ambled along the sea front, the rich, vibrant ozone filled them with intoxication. Nostalgia ran rampant as they watched the sea rushing in to lash the sea wall.

Carol singers assaulted their ears as their voices broke into the crest of the waves, stirring the very hearts of them. Saint Peter's Church was packed and Debbie sensed they would all be thanking God for their luck, plus helping them to achieve their desire never to change. They would also be offering prayers for Tony, still sadly missed by them all.

After a splendid dinner, they all sat down to listen to the Queen's speech and then it was time to sit and watch Kelly open her presents. They all roared with laughter as although she had toys in abundance, the paper and string were her main fascination.

All too soon, it was time for the children to go to bed. Paul kissed them and chuckled softly, "I still can't move after that huge dinner, but I'm certainly looking forward to discussing the launch of the magazine!"

Returning to the front room, it seemed as though Paul had never been away. Matthew was just as eager to sort out the various details and turned to

179

Paul, "Is there any chance of you arriving before June? Honestly, Paul, I think we should Launch in July!"

Lighting a cigarette, Paul smiled, "I think there is every chance of me arriving back by late April. Are you all sure though, that you want me to head the magazine?"

Debbie chuckled as Matthew said, "Paul, you know the format we are looking for and we trust your judgement entirely. Remember, you put us on the road to success!"

When Paul finally left for the States, they all felt much happier, knowing he would soon be back for good. He seemed far more relaxed as he kissed them all farewell. He lingered briefly as he hugged Debbie, "Take care, love, see you," had been his parting shot.

CHAPTER THIRTY TWO

The castle returned to the hectic work load and it truly was hectic. Somehow though, Debbie felt confident that they would cope, a deadline hadn't been missed yet. In fact they nearly always had at least a couple of days to spare.

Debbie no longer doubted that she and Matthew would have been successful, but knew that having babies had given them another dimension and although entirely separate, they seemed to intermingle perfectly. It was one thing just led to another, bringing even more success. At the same time it enabled them to fulfil their desires to have a family.

She had worked extremely hard on the booklet for the end of January, which now included the pretty circular shawl. She had made it for the new babe and was thrilled with the result. She also thought that a hooded cape would look sweet, having made a lacy one for girls and a little plainer for boys, or both.

Her mind raced on and on. When she did tackle the second series on crochet, she would put them into that programme, thus giving a choice. Looking at her own little ones, she felt a poncho with coloured tassels would look exceedingly gorgeous and would also include a version with a hood. Living by the sea had alerted her to the sudden bursts of wind.

Needless to say the wool company had been ecstatic with the new designs that were to hit the fashion scene for Easter. Matthew had taken some beautiful front cover shots. Verity had worn the cape and they had laid her down beside Kelly, who was sitting and wearing the poncho. After placing them together, they spread the shawl in front of them.

Intoxication often seized Debbie as she knew that every single inspirational urge came to her as she dressed her babes. It gave her far more scope with which to enter the front rooms of the public. They were the ones that craved her ideas on such a regular basis.

Realising they had polished off their work load early, Debbie and Matthew decided to give themselves a couple of days off. A couple of days in which to indulge themselves and their little ones. Debbie was feeling a little tired and they had worked non stop since their return from America.

The following day was bitterly cold as Matthew helped to get the children wrapped up. They had decided to walk around Old Heysham, simply because it was such a pretty place. The cobbled back streets all led towards the bay. Kelly loved to walk, or rather stagger over the cobbles as Matthew moved closely to her, ready to catch their fearless little off spring.

Debbie watched them together, her heart at times fluttering into her throat. Many people congratulated her on the way she brought up her children, but without Matthew's devotion to her and the little ones, she never kiddied herself that she could have even begun to manage.

Jenny and Richard were delighted as they entered the shop. Instantly, they broke off to join them for coffee. Jenny's eyes danced, her bump now very visible. Verity was wide awake as Jenny peered into the pram, "Oh, Debbie, she's beautiful, can I hold her?"

Richard piped up, "She is a lovely babe, Jen, but I think I prefer them around Kelly's age. I'll be too scared to hold our one!"

Matthew chuckled, "It comes naturally, Richard, so it does. You'll make a super dad. Oh, while I think about it, should Jenny go into labour and you are tied up with the shop, be sure to ring us. I'll take over, or I'm sure Jim will. You mustn't miss the birth, for both your sakes!"

Draining his cup, Richard smiled, "Thanks, Matthew, I knew we could rely on ye. Granted there's plenty of time before it happens, but it's good to know that every things under control!"

Love choked Debbie as she noticed the calm manner with which Matthew managed to reassure. She knew he was desperate to impart their own news and gulped, "Aren't you going to tell our friends about our news, Matthew?"

Startled expressions faced him as his gorgeous grin grew broader. His eyes penetrated hers as he replied, "Yes, we have some good news, so we have. Debbie and I are expecting another one, sometime in July!"

"How wonderful," gasped a dreamy Jenny.

**

As they walked back, Debbie turned to look at Matthew, he really was devastatingly handsome and her body burned with desire. As they passed 'Ventura', his eyes lit up, "It won't be long now before we have Paul back. I've been thinking, how about we call the magazine, 'Lady Kelly'?"

Tossing it around in her mind, she frowned slightly, "It's nice, but somehow it doesn't seem to ring, not for everyday families, the ones we specifically want to aim at. We don't want it to even remotely resemble the present format, do we?"

"Fair point, darling," he acknowledged.

Kelly was very busy trying to catch a seagull. Matthew's watchful eye fixed onto her, "Madam, don't run too fast, come and hold Daddy's hand!"

Brushing away the mist of love that had sprung suddenly to her eyes, it hit her, "Matthew, how about 'Miss Kelly'. That encompasses the younger end of the market. I also think that the readers would like to send in snippets from their own children's diaries. It would keep them stimulated and it really is a magazine for them.

"Debs, that's great, what gave you the idea?"

"You calling Kelly, madam. My mind just latched onto she's a Miss!"

Guffawing richly, he picked Kelly up and slipped the pram brake on. Turning her to face him, he allowed his mouth to cover hers, his free arm drew her tightly towards him, right there in the middle of the promenade.

For the rest of the way home, they had chatted happily, both exhilarated by the bracing air. Once inside though, real tiredness overcame them. Matthew smiled, "Let's get the babes to bed and then I'll go for some good old fashioned, Lancashire fish and chips!"

"That sounds super duper," she sighed.

They were not going to follow their normal routine tonight. For the next couple of evenings they were going to spoil themselves and watch a little television, probably kissing and cuddling as they relaxed.

Their normal routine was to take the bedtime ritual seriously and play with the children. Once they were in bed, they would work flat out for a good three hours, and somehow manage a quick stroll along the beach, but always made time for their climb to the balcony.

Debbie sometimes felt that they cleared more work during the evening than they could accomplish during the day. Their love and children were almost a sacred way of life. In spite of the money they could have spent when and how they wished, they found that all they would ever need was under one roof.

Important things in life cannot always be bought, things such as love, happiness and health, no one could ever buy. It was as if every moment was measured and every second counted. They had to make their priorities work and so far they did.

Debbie's mouth watered hungrily as she smelt the fish and chips. Almost childlike, she and Matthew delved into the steaming hot food, using their hands and wincing as it burned them. Ironically, they could buy fish and chips where ever they went, but nothing tasted as good as they did in Morecambe.

Lifting her eyes happily to Matthew, she gave a contented little sigh, "Darling, when Paul runs the magazine, I think we should run various competitions. We could run them for knitting and crochet," her voice began to rise with excitement, "If the series is a success, we could offer vouchers for Haywood yarns. Oh, Matthew, that would share our money and I know when Mum was expecting Tony, I could truly have done with some financial help towards the wool!"

Licking his fingers, he found himself caught up in her enthusiasm, she was delightful and he adored her, "That's a good idea, they'd all feel very involved if they were taking part!"

Adrenalin pumped around her, "What about photography? That involves the whole family. I think you should do a few articles on that subject. We can run competitions and really bring everyone in!"

Matthew chuckled as he teased, "Yes, boss, I tink those are all wonderful ideas. And here was I thinkin' we were supposed to be off duty!"

They were, but it was almost impossible to ignore the ideas as they sprung to mind. Still chuckling, he added, "The beauty of all of those ideas, is, we can give them to Paul and he can take it from there, so he can!"

Smiling happily to herself, Debbie realised she had begun her career with adult designs and still had to continue with them, but now felt a distinct preference for baby wear. That led her naturally into things for the mum to be, not just to wear during pregnancy, but also for their stay in hospital.

She could design pretty bed jackets, which would make lovely ideas for presents for the elderly. The list was endless as the requests for the crochet tops had come in like wildfire. It was almost worth being pregnant as the ideas seemed to tumble from her mind and straight into her nimble fingers.

Still teasing her, Matthew ruffled her hair, "Woman, get up to that balcony, there's something special I have to say to you!"

"Oh, have you now," she giggled as hand in hand they reached the balcony. Eagerly she turned to him, "I know what you want to tell me and I love you just as deeply, she sighed as a deluge of desire captured her.

"Debs, y're a precious work of art, so ye are. I was right, you are a duchess. Hows about a shower and …"

Pure joy was theirs. He knew her every whim, her every thought, her every desire. What was more he knew exactly how to fulfil each and every part of her body and soul.

**

Delight ran rampant when the 'Ventura' deal was completed. Paul would definitely return to England late in April, with the hopes for a June launch. Vanessa seemed to live for his return, he had always treated her as a capable friend, never needing to pull rank. It was also Mazza's wish that she stay in Morecambe. Between them all, they realised they could take their magazine to the very top.

The first crochet series had taken off, even better than they had dared hope. They were also in the middle of producing a book to accompany it and to her further delight, Debbie had managed to make a start of the new winter collection.

As expected the diaries were still very popular in both countries and thanks to Brian's notarised version of their book, the sales were rocketing in both countries. They had also confirmed their return to the States the following February-March. This time though, there would be three little ones.

Kelly and Verity now had their own bedrooms. Debbie had used soft lemon, pink and white for the décor. Pretty chintz curtains matched the bedspreads, all ready for them to grow into. And once more, the corner of her room waited a little impatiently for the new arrival.

Again the press had seized the news. Debbie now found it easy to talk to them. They had all come to a sort of mutual agreement, if she kept them up to date, they would leave her alone.

**

Paul Howarth finally felt his 'plane bank and land. He could just envisage the excitement that would buzz around the castle and Matthew was to meet him at the airport. They were surrounded by press, the burning question, "When do you hope to launch the magazine?"

With crystal clarity, Paul stated, "The magazine, which will be named 'Miss Kelly', is to be launched in June. We will have to work flat out, but we *will* launch in June.

Jim, Ellen and Irene were standing beside Debbie as the news was broadcast. Jim smiled, "Well, he couldn't be more positive than that. It's all very exciting indeed, I somehow feel the success already!"

Paul would stay at the castle and occupy her parents' spare room. He had so much to sort out with his luggage and work, it would mean he could take his time before he returned to his own flat. Many long hours of discussion were to be put into the venture, but there was now no doubting, it would be ready for June.

CHAPTER THIRTY THREE

Summer arrived at last and promised to be good and hot. Jenny had taken to chatting with Debbie, via the occasional 'phone call. She was very nervous indeed as her time drew near. Debbie would try hard to reassure her, try to build her confidence by taking her through the breathing routine and promising to be around as soon as her labour began.

Each time Debbie hung up, she knew that Jenny felt a little easier, for a while at least. It did, however, frighten her to hear the implicit trust being placed onto her.

As she and Matthew surveyed their little domain from the balcony, she snuggled into his body, her voice filled with a choking love, "Matthew, I want to have this baby here. I want to be near to the kids and any 'photo's must be taken by you!"

"Debs, that's a beautiful idea. We'll check it out, so we will," he breathed into her neck.

Brian could see no reason why not and suggested he send Megan, his midwife to see them. She was in her early forties, a little plump, but her movements were deft and sure. Debbie felt instantly safe with her and they soon became firm friends. Megan's eyes were hazel and seemed to change colour with the light, but they were always very soft and gentle.

Just a week prior to the launch, the 'phone had broken the still of the evening. Picking up the receiver, she heard the sheer emotion in Richard's voice, "Debbie, Jenny as gone into labour. I'll ring when we ave sum news, but just in case, would Matthew pop and start on the baking?"

"Of course Matthew will be there, Richard. Give Jenny our love and the best of luck," said Debbie catching the excitement.

Matthew placed his arms around her bulky body. "If you've arranged for me to be down at the shop for four thirty, we'd better catch forty winks," his lilt was heavy with anticipation of Jenny's big event.

Quietly, deep in thought, he led her up to the balcony. His kisses rained down on her, his voice was soft, dark as he murmured into her ears, "Hell, Duchess, doesn't it warm your very heart to see the lights flashing, 'Miss Kelly'. I sometimes have to pinch myself to make sure I'm awake. Come on, little lady, bed," he sighed with contentment.

Climbing into bed, they chuckled with happiness, she kneeled to loop her arms around his neck. Having succumbed completely to his caresses, the sharp shrill of the telephone interrupted their would be oblivion. Matthew cussed, "Damned 'phones!"

As his hand hastily retrieved the receiver, his face became serious. Richard's stunned voice shook with emotion, "Hi, Matthew, I'll be back in the morning after all!" Debbie was able to hear clearly as Matthew had placed the handset between them.

They searched each others' face with concern as the silence was almost deafening, until at long last Richard spoke, "We 'ave a little lad. Hell, I, I just can't believe it. Jenny's fine …"

Suddenly they realised that Richard was in tears. Matthew, understanding fully the emotional stress as well as pleasure, prompted gently, "How was the birth, Richard? I know how you feel old chap, it took me a while to absorb the fact that our babes had arrived!"

Thank God, I never dreamed of the emotion involved. Jenny said to tell Debbie, their discussions worked, our lad weighed in at nearly eight pounds!"

Debbie felt her husband's arm slide around her shoulders, her eyes filled as she realised that he had felt much the same as Richard and was managing to put his reactions over. She watched his sensual lips move, "What are you going to call him, Richard?"

An emotional Richard managed, "We were going to name a daughter Debbie, but we have called him James Matthew, after the two men that made it possible for us to go in for him. Ehhh, I don't think I'll ever sleep!"

Matthew's eyes glistened as he hung up, he was choked as he turned to her, "Debbie, I doubt if anyone knows just how a man feels during and after the birth. Perhaps we should remember that during the series. I know how it affects me, but hearing Richard, well it sort of brings it home!"

"That's a truly important point, Matthew. You're right, we must explain how the new father feels. I think Richard was ready to crack up tonight, until he spoke to you. Let's go and tell Mum and Dad, they will be thrilled," she added as she gripped his hand tightly.

As expected, her parents were choked to hear that the babe had been named after Jim. Holding her bump, Debbie smiled, "I suppose if this one's a girl, we'd better call her Ellen!"

"Never in a million years, I wouldn't like that at all. Anyway, it would be too confusing," came her mother's swift retort

They were all emotional, after all, Richard and Jenny did feel like family. All in all though, they felt that their luck was rubbing off onto others. And as Debbie gazed at her husband, she hugged closely to her, the knowledge that once they returned to bed, they would indeed carry on where they had left off, if not start all over again, when once again she would melt into the sanctity of his arms.

**

Happiness radiated from Jenny as she sat up with her brand new son in her arms. Debbie had taken a swift hour from work to pop and see her friend. Her heavy body tired rather quickly these days, but her face lit up as Jenny eyeballed her and shot an arm in her direction, embracing her as a dear sister.

There was a wonderful serenity about her as she gulped, "Debbie, you were right, it wasn't as bad as I thought, but it does hurt at the end, doesn't it?"

Nodding in wry agreement, Debbie held the little male bundle in her arms. He was adorable, his mop of black hair suggested he would be like Jenny. His huge blue eyes were dark and would definitely turn into a lovely rich brown. Hugging baby James tightly and dropping a soft kiss onto his forehead, she handed him back to Jenny. As she did so, she felt her own child kicking her, almost possessively. Instinctively holding it, she knew, this one was not a little boy, yet love surged through her as she longed for its safe arrival and as she finally walked home, she mingled with the happy holiday makers.

She smiled happily as her eyes took in the beach where she and Matthew loved to walk. At times it was truly exotic, they loved their new home in this beautiful old town, and to them, Morecambe was Lancashire.

**

Paul and Vanessa worked jolly hard with them on the magazine and the launch had gone down better than they could possibly have hoped. Everyone seemed to like the idea of having a magazine that they could contribute to. They couldn't have asked for a better response and the ideas were coming in thick and fast for the next issue.

It was good to see Paul happy again. He was almost back to his normal self, insisting on a Christmas layout, to include the whole family. He had a wonderful flair and the restlessness, that had always been a vital part of him, was well and truly back. In fact, he reminded Debbie of Hank, his mind darting from layout to layout.

Alma had been delighted with the magazine, after all her company was receiving a lot of free publicity. Her voice bubbled as she rung Debbie, "When you leave for the States, Debbie, I will be able to accompany you, but then return for a short while. So much has come from your designs and ideas, it has put me under more than a little pressure!"

"Sorry," chuckled Debbie, acknowledging the jocular jibe, as perspiration dripped from her, "I think this is one of the hottest summers I can remember. Sleep is almost a novelty, anyway, see you soon, cheers!"

After popping her babes down for a nap, just a couple of days later, Debbie knew her time had arrived and swiftly rang Megan and called out to Matthew. Her tender hands shook as she made up the cot and when Matthew joined her, there was a wicked grin accompanied by concern on his face.

Megan breezed in, her happy smile dying as she held Debbie's tummy. "Come along, Debbie, hop onto the bed, dear. I'll be with you in a second," she smiled and hastily placed on her apron.

Apart from searing pain, the cold flannel was the only thing she sensed, until the faint cry. It seemed to travel around the room, overwhelming her with the delicious sensations of love and their new daughter was placed onto her, the tiny mouth instantly suckling.

A very stunned Matthew kissed her, his finger rubbed tendering over his new daughter's cheek. Although this was the third time, it was still filled with wonder, sheer wonder of the gift of life, sheer wonder that five minutes previously it had been just a bump and now the most perfect little body. Debbie felt her tears prickle, for she was firmly convinced that no matter how many times parents went through this experience, it never ceased to be charged with new emotions.

She looked down at her babe, her hair was dark and she seemed to have plenty of it. Again a button nose, but as yet, she hadn't opened her eyes, poor little soul, she was probably still in shock with the speed of her arrival.

Matthew kissed Debbie's eyes and sought her mouth, his own eyes moist as they met hers, his voice choked with deep tenderness as he whispered, "You were marvellous, darling, you really were!"

"I wish all my babies came like that. What are you going to call this one?" Megan asked as she bustled about.

"Lucy! Yes, I think that is a pretty name, Lucy," she said again as if trying it on.

"Tis a lovely name, darling. I'm sure going to be out voted when they grow up," chuckled Matthew.

Megan left them almost as quickly as she had joined them. Debbie sat up feeling good and fresh after the nurse left, her arms now engulfed the new arrival. Matthew held them both into the safe haven of his own arms. Brushing his lips over Lucy, he almost grudgingly pulled away, his eyes lingering on his wife as he said emotionally, "I'll go and bring her grandparents to see her. Then I think the girls will be up!"

Ellen nursed the latest addition to the family. Jim dropped a kiss onto the little head as he commented, "I really thought this one would be a boy, but she is a beauty, Debbie, well done!"

Matthew had gone quite naturally to bring the other babes. Kelly held her arms out and managed her own version of 'Kelly hold her' Verity just gave an odd poke and lost interest.

Paul appeared in the doorway, his eyes lighting up as he glanced over Lucy and took her into his arms. He looked so natural with her and Kelly and Verity simply adored their Uncle Paul. He always chased Kelly as she loved to run, Verity would crawl over to him, pulling herself up to stand, holding his expensive trouser leg for support as she waited patiently for him to pick her up.

Debbie's heart went out to him, he would have made a wonderful natural father. He chuckled, "We almost have our own little dynasty, a couple of more should do it!"

His blue eyes were gentle and Debbie knew, he would always regret leaving England. Irene had run up to join the congratulations, "I'll give out the press release, Matthew, let me have a photograph as soon as possible. Debbie, just rest. There's nothing even remotely behind schedule!"

With both babes bathed and ready for bed, Matthew brought them in to watch Lucy feed. Kelly looked on momentarily and left her to it. Verity did just as Kelly had done with her, poked and prodded and lost interest as she went back to Matthew.

These little points were all vital information to be included into the diaries. Debbie knew that her children weren't jealous, yet she had just followed the most natural of instincts.

Over the next few days, Matthew had taken reels of film to release to the press and run a video through for the television studio. Alma had trotted over for a quick peep and added, "Debbie, everything is so hectic, our company is having to look for new premises, your hard work has done so much good for so many people. I know you'd be the first to admit, you couldn't have managed so much, not without Matthew!"

"Alma, I don't think I could have managed anything without Matthew. He is totally involved with the children, we do just about everything together. No one in their right mind, would underestimate Matthew!"

After she left, Matthew came in and rung Joanne. Debbie heard her now famous little whoop of joy, "Matthew, congratulations, give Debbie and the children my fondest love. We sure look forward to seeing you all next year!"

Granted the news would have reached the States, but there was a little item named courtesy. With that in mind, Debbie decided to ring Hank, especially as he had been nominated for an award for his valuable art programmes. He was good at his job, rising to Station Controller at such an early age. She realised with a happy little shudder, that the work they had done with him had pushed him into the high ratings category.

She heard his gasp as he recognised her voice, "Hi, Hank, we have just had another little girl. We wanted to tell you before the news breaks!"

Debbie couldn't have guessed just how much her news moved Hank. He could envisage her serenity as his mind flashed back to Verity's birth. Gulping, he spoke with total sincerity, "Heartiest congratulations, Debbie and thanks for letting me know. Gee, babe, we sure are looking forward to your visit. Take care and keep in touch!"

He had more or less had to hang up, blinding envy seemed to have caught him it its merciless grip. Debbie replaced the receiver and thought she must have caught him at a bad time, she hadn't even had the chance to congratulate him on his nomination. Oh well, the world wouldn't stop turning, she thought sleepily.

Ruminating pleasantly, her mind relaxed and became alive at the same time. Alma had asked for several new designs, apparently Haywood had brought out a new chunky yarn and it was Debbie's job to tempt customers to buy it. It was beautifully soft and she must hastily design patterns to accompany the launch.

When Brian bounced in for a quick inspection, Matthew asked, "Will you leave a prescription for Debbie to go onto the pill? I want her to take it before we return to normal. We do want another child, but not until we return next year!"

Debbie's mouth gaped open as Brian grinned. "I think that's a good idea, Matthew. Debbie, you can start to take the pills in about ten days or so. Let me know if you have any side effects!"

His eyes were quizzical as they met hers. She smiled a little stiffly, "Matthew is right, Brian, I hate the thought of it, but we do have commitments from next February, we owe a lot of people our total responsibility. I wouldn't mind conceiving while we are away," she jutted her chin in a small act of defiance.

Later that evening, they stood together on the balcony, Matthew's arms now able to reach around her. "Debs, are you upset with me for asking Brian about the pill? I think our love is too important to risk spoiling, but it does affect us both, so it does!"

Suddenly, she realised how worried he must have been. Whatever was the matter with her? She was being childish and a little selfish, Matthew had taken the situation from her hands and she felt rebellious. He loved her dearly and she should damned well be grateful for his care.

Turning into his arms and holding him in a grip that practically sapped all her strength, she whispered, "Where would I be without a wonderful husband to watch over me and our children?"

**

Eric Morgan placed his hands behind his head and stared at the ceiling. His heart had almost broken as he watched helplessly, the closure of the New York based magazine. Deep down he had come to terms with the fact that it was his daughter's behaviour that had cost him so dear. He also realised, had he treated Paul with a little more respect, or any respect at all, he might have been able to stay on with him and between them, put up a good rescue attempt.

He was still in bed in his luxury apartment in Blackpool. Weariness, shame and disappointment filled him as he wondered for the thousandth time, if he could ever forgive Amanda. Paul and Mazza had been right, she would and did lose him a fortune. It was not a matter of pulling her own weight in the business, it was the way she treated members of staff. A flush covered him, had he not been guilty of the same?

Maralyn came into the room, having showered and wrapped herself into a large bath towel. She smiled softly and said, "I didn't mean to waken you, Eric. You looked so peaceful for a few moments, how d'ye feel?"

"Angry, Mazz, bloody angry!"

His words had all but stuck in his throat as he watched her walk over and sit by the dressing table. Amanda's cruel revelations seemed to have brought him and his wife closer, in fact, ever since he had discovered that she had a lover, albeit another woman, he found her even more desirable. She was the one that had stood firmly beside him, without recriminations, as they watched the sinking of his empire.

They had spoken quite frankly about her feelings for Nessa and she had been adamant when she said, "Eric, if you want me to stay with you, I will, but I will not stop seeing Vanessa. She intends to stay outside of your world and I agree with her. We both must understand that Amanda hasn't finished yet and as soon as her money runs out, she will be back!"

Eric had felt his throat constrict, he knew she was right, but since they had managed to stand firmly together and face whatever came up, he felt he could somehow cope. Pouring them a drink, he turned to her, "Mazza, I'm so sorry about the collapse of some of the magazines. If only I'd listened to you, treated you as my partner …!"

Maralyn gulped her drink, her heart heavy at the hurt that had been inflicted on her husband. Her voice softened, "Eric, money isn't everything. We gave Amanda too much, too soon. The only thing you need to regret is not telling me about her and Paul, because we destroyed his life. He knows Debbie is happy with Matthew, but we robbed him of his love, simply to meet our daughter's selfish demands!"

She stared at the amber liquid in her glass and sighed, "I know that Paul will bid for Preston, you know that also, but how about we keep the London branch? We could concentrate your vast knowledge and wisdom down there!"

"Yes, I think that would be worthwhile. One thing's for sure, Amanda won't receive another penny from me. She deprived us of any grandchildren and I feel you should've told me about them!"

She saw the hurt in his eyes, "Yes, Eric, I should've told you. I was wrong, very, very wrong. I just hope her mouth has stilled, at least long enough to get us back onto our feet!"

**

Amanda Morgan felt the 'plane bank before landing at Manchester Airport. She had heard rumours that Preston was up for grabs, oh, yeseree, this was her chance, she needed money and needed it fast.

One hint of refusal and she would take the lot of them down, together with Vanessa, Paul and above all, Debbie bloody Hudson. She had nearly pulled it off in New York, but her mother had thrown a spanner in the works. This time, unless they all agreed to her demands, they would all fall.

She was still not prepared to have her own secret revealed, but once she had finished, the limelight would be well and truly off her. Taking her gold compact from her bag, she smiled with evil at the face that stared back.

**

Debbie and Matthew looked forward to the next board meeting. It was really more of a family gathering, Paul being included as such, although it still had to have minutes taken properly. Irene now had her own personal secretary and had taught her how to set everything out in a business like manner.

Rumours had certainly been running rampant and this meeting opened with Paul. He spoke with his usual eloquence, "We have all heard that Preston is to close, I think we should buy it. The demand has been astonishing and we can't contain it all at this Branch. I have a couple of blokes who could well take over. One of them in particular, well, he would certainly be ready in about a year!"

Everyone had nodded with an air of profound pride. Their magazine was a roaring success. The mums loved sending in their own personal hints. That in itself now warranted a double spread.

Ellen had begun writing up recipes for cheap and cheerful meals, making sure they were filled with nourishment. In fact, Irene was already interviewing candidates to work as secretary, to ease Ellen's burden of response. Yet again, another room was converted into an office.

Debbie found her head spinning, the whole meeting reeked of success and excitement, with more than plenty for all. She leaned forward, "I love the idea of opening in Preston. What did you have in mind, Paul? A launch in a year from next Easter, I hope. I'm certain Matthew wouldn't have time for a Christmas launch, that is if we have our offer accepted!"

Contentedly blowing smoke rings and watching them lift and disappear, Paul agreed, "Yes, I think a year from Easter would give us all time to sort the job out. As I say, it will take me that sort of time to train the lads!"

They knew Irene was delighted to head the company during their absence. In fact they would have felt sick without her. She was adept and hardworking, yet little could Debbie have realised just how much Irene had striven for such a position. Anyway, the meeting ended on its usual happy note.

Alma and Irene sometimes popped to a show and enjoyed a meal. Alma said with a deep sincerity, "We are so lucky to have been able to jump onto this bandwagon. I know we work darned hard, but Debbie has never changed, not one ounce of her success has marred her simplistic approach. I don't know how she manages to design and raise a family, but I do know she appreciates us fully!"

"If they weren't as they are, the public would not have taken them to their hearts. I don't think anyone realises just how hard Matthew and Debbie work. They are a wonderful family and her parents are so natural. Yes, Alma, we are lucky indeed," smiled Irene and lit her cigarette.

**

Verity had just learned to walk by the time her first birthday arrived. As Kelly would be two in November, Debbie decided to have a party for them both in October. Ellen had arranged with cook, to lay out a large buffet in the board room.

Paul arrived with Irene and Vanessa and Alma wouldn't have missed it for the world. Debbie had deliberately chosen Sunday, to enable Richard and Jenny to come alone with little James. Although it was basically the children's party, the adults were to stay and have drinks, probably dance, but most of all to talk.

Matthew had suggested that James went into his carry cot in the room with Lucy and Debbie had never loved him more. Both Richard and Jenny wanted to stay on and were quite relaxed to know that the intercom would alert them, should James waken.

Time zipped along, with work coming from around the world. It was challenging, even fun, but so utterly hectic. No matter how busy they were, they always made time for their stroll along the promenade. The sea sent shivers of delight through them as it lapped around the shore, or, if it was angry, it was possible to hear its rage being taken out on the sea wall.

Matthew turned her in his arms, "Do you know, Mrs Ross, I can't wait to take you under that lovely old Oak tree, how about a definite date in …about … March? I'll eat every part of that delicious body, so I will!"

Debbie knew she would miss Morecambe again, but as Hank had said, the Americans were a very friendly bunch of people.

To everyone's horror, Debbie had gone down with a virus in February, just a week before they were due to fly out. Brian ordered her to bed for a couple of days and Matthew had been like a mother hen, worried about his chick. She had never been confined to bed before and hated every moment, but her legs just refused to support her.

Panic talks had taken place between Matthew and Hank, but mercifully she recovered quickly. Matthew had nevertheless asked Hank to cut the load during their first week. Hank was only too happy to oblige, he truly didn't know what he would arrange to take their places. Many couples were clever, but his countrymen loved the English couple and he could understand only too well.

CHAPTER THIRTY FOUR

When they finally landed in New York, Hank almost crushed the life from Debbie. He then swiftly continued along the line to welcome each member of the family, before coming back to her, "Gee, Debbie, you sure gave us a scare. Are you sure you're fit now?"

Kelly was now holding reasonable conversations. Verity walked with confidence and Debbie dressed them both alike. They looked like princesses as the photographers had a field day with them. Kelly loved posing, having no fear of cameras as her Daddy's hugest fan. If Verity had been any further laid back, she would have fallen over. She was a real Irish Colleen, the double of Matthew, her deep blue eyes were stunning, beneath her lovely, wavy, almost black hair. Lucy was more like Debbie, her eyes were a beautiful brown velvet, her hair was light brown and curly, still very short, but her smile would have charmed the devil himself.

After all of the usual rituals and formalities had been completed, they arrived back at the ranch. Nostalgia filled them as once more they appraised this gorgeous place. Hank had done them proud with his choice and if they hadn't loved Morecambe so much, this could well have been a second home. Matthew turned to her, "I think we should come here for a complete holiday as soon as time permits. This truly feels like home!"

Just looking at him, Debbie felt herself suffocating with love. Never did she cease to be thankful that he had answered the advertisement. She did truly hope that their little ones would benefit from all the hard work that had gone into their success. They had been very lucky, yet knew they had earned this success and managed to provide many jobs for others. In their book, they worked with staff, not over them, a happy atmosphere was essential and for them, it was obviously working well.

Grace had bustled up to hug them all. She and her little band of typists were all ready for the hopeful onslaught. At least this time, they didn't have to explain the work from scratch. Indeed they had all looked forward to returning and settled down quickly to their new lives again.

Ellen still sat for them when they did have to attend a function. Hank was a well respected man of the media and many functions were in aid of charity. It was something they could endorse wholeheartedly and relate to personally.

Matthew and Debbie found themselves intoxicated by the atmosphere in the Big Apple. They gasped with amazement as they were driven down Broadway. There was always a buzz of excitement as everywhere seemed to throb with life and razza ma tazz. It was impossible not to be affected by the gaiety as they drove through.

Sometimes Debbie would feel like a film star as she was placed into some of the gorgeous dresses that were sent out to her. It made her feel that they must be back before midnight, or just like Cinderella, it would all disappear.

Drifting headily into her fairyland, she had her very own prince charming by her side, he was dashing and certainly her hero. In his eyes she was beautiful, in her eyes, he was stunningly handsome. They were hailed as the perfect couple from Lancashire, and she had to admit, they were. They had never fallen out about any aspect of their life or work. They always talked everything over and as they thought so much alike, invariably came up with the same ideas, they *were* perfectly matched.

As Hank had predicted, the crochet series had been eagerly received and already rocketed in the ratings. The diaries were even more popular, in fact, whatever they did, the public seemed to lap it up and Matthew's photography for beginners was an incredible success.

Debbie had expected the new designs for the premature baby to be popular, but she had never guessed just how many babes were born with dreadfully low birth weights. Many letters flooded in from various hospitals, all with requests for more. The letter that had come from the hospital where Verity had been born, had touched Debbie deeply.

They had not only asked for more ideas, but had sent profound thanks for the donation she and Matthew had made. The budget draft had been enclosed for the new Neo Natal wing. A phenomenal amount was still needed, but the building was about to be commenced.

Gripping the details into her hand, she decided to find her father. He was in his usual place by the pool, he loved the calm of the water, just as he did back home. She tripped over to him and handed the budget draft to him. His tender eyes lifted to his beloved daughter as he moved his books away to enable her to sit with him.

She noticed every flicker that crossed his face as he read. And not able to contain herself further, she blurted, "Dad, I would love us to send part of the amount that is still outstanding. We can more than afford it and I did have Verity there. We've given large donations in Morecambe, somehow, I feel a real affinity with this project!"

"Here, here," came Matthew's happy lilt.

Jumping from her skin, not having heard the approach, she turned to see Matthew standing behind her with Hank. "You two nearly gave me a heart attack," she jested.

Hank had heard her conversation with Jim, not an ounce of what she had said surprised him. It was typical of her, yet he felt a deluge of anger with her, he couldn't free his mind of her. Even when she was in England, she managed to haunt him.

Her body still reminded him of a young, innocent teenager, yet she had given birth to three babies. No wonder she looked so young, she was young, still only twenty two. He was fifteen years her senior, but she bewitched him and his manhood tormented him beyond belief. If only he could begin to dislike Matthew, but he was a swell guy and obviously deeply in love with her.

He watched as Jim answered her, "I think we could arrange to do this, dear, providing Matthew and Mum agree with us. We can send a personal donation, just as you did last time!"

"Great," she gulped and hugged him as she rushed away. Her lovely hair bounced around her slight shoulders, her every movement, a torment to any man and unfortunately, Hank was no exception.

Matthew had seen no reason to contain his feelings and ran after her. Catching her arm, he pulled her closely to him, "Darling, I think that's a wonderful thought. We've been lucky with our babes, but if we had to watch one struggle for life, I don't think I could bear it. The hospital needs that money, so it does!"

His arms crushed her to him, his mouth covered hers. She was beautiful, everything he would ever want and more. He loved to watch her work, her fingers deftly handled the yarn as she turned it into something of beauty. Her body was always ready for him, her very vivaciousness enchanted him.

Desperately trying to regain his composure, after all, Hank was waiting to discuss photography, he feigned shock, "Mrs Ross, it's the end of April and we had a date in March, have your forgotten the pledge we made?"

"No, but I thought you had backed out," she added seductively.

Watching his reluctant return to continue his discussions, she allowed the weakness to flood through her. She would definitely take him there tonight. There was a very special reason to take him under the huge old oak tree, she knew she was once again pregnant. Joy filled her as she recalled how it had happened. She had been forced to stop taking the pill during her illness and simply forgotten. A sigh left her, it would be due around Kelly's third birthday.

Having spent the evening working hard, Debbie was ready for their stroll. To their astonishment, it was pouring with rain. She giggled at Matthew's stricken face and said, "That puts an end to our date, darling. And I was so looking forward to it!"

"It's not funny, I wanted to go there, Debs!"

Suddenly, they both chuckled and she raced to their room. He was hot in pursuit and when his arms engulfed her, she could feel his arousal, hard against her thigh, he groaned as his lips parted hers, "I want you so much!"

Allowing her body to sink into the hard wall of his chest, her knees had grown week. Fire coursed through them as the cry came from the dressing room. "Oh, no, Matthew, we'll have to wait, although I must admit, I feel like making her wait!"

Moments later, she was in his arms. He inhaled swiftly and gasped, "Debbie, there's something about you. I've noticed it for the past few days. Your beautiful eyes have an extra glow, in fact everything about you seems to glow!"

Her heart raced as she felt his was positively pumping. With a shudder, she whispered, "You know how I want you to love me. Matthew, I've waited all day for this moment!"

Each time felt like a first for him as she managed to draw him till every ounce of his passion was truly spent.

"Debbie," he groaned as his arms gathered her shaking body to him.

They waited for the sweet ebb of passion to ease. Gasping painfully, biting and tasting each other, his hand lifted her chin, his eyes glistened. She knew she was drowning again, just surrendering to the depth of those huge pools that reflected so much love. His voice was still hoarse, "You have something to tell me, don't you, darling? I felt that added need in you!"

As she nodded, her eyes never glowed more than they did now. His heart thumped with love for her and a claustrophobia seemed to cover them. Clutching each other, they knew, they had everything they could ever want and more. At times this frightened Debbie in a silly kind of way.

**

Ellen lay in Jim's arms. They had just made the most perfect love and he held her closely. He blew into her ears, "Something's bothering, Ellie?"

She sighed wistfully, "You read me like a book, Jim. I think Debbie's pregnant again, she seems to radiate. They are so happy, do you think its too much for them, dear?"

Jim pulled her to him and kissed the top of her head. He smiled softly, "Ellen, I thought just the same earlier. They will tell us when they have time. I wonder about taking on too much, but they are deliriously happy. In fact they remind me of our marriage, I love you as much today as the day we married!"

He felt his wife mould into him. He had fallen in love with her almost the first time they had met, somewhat the way Matthew had fallen for Debbie. He felt good in every way a man can hope and wrapping his free arm around Ellen, he murmured, "I'm so happy that you told Debbie the importance of a full union, no matter what happened to us, you always wanted my love, we have passed that on to our daughter!"

**

Debbie could never have known of the conversation, but she would have been thrilled to have done so. She knew her parents placed major importance to a marriage of love and fulfilment and one day hoped to be in a position of passing it onto her own daughters.

Before breakfast the next morning, Debbie trotted into her parents and challenged, "Guess what?"

"You're pregnant again," they replied in unison.

The programmes were still enjoying great popularity in both countries and Debbie instinctively knew that once they were home again, their schedules would be just as hectic.

They had decided to keep the news of her condition quiet for a while. That was until Joanne called, to Debbie she was a real friend. It had been Joanne whose friendship had been invaluable when those dreadful headlines had appeared last year. It was indeed she, who had turned a probable nightmare into a day full of fun and excitement.

After hearing her famous whoop of pleasure, Debbie caught her enthusiasm and said, "Joanne, Matthew and I never really got a chance to thank you for that dreadful day last year. It could have been the end of us, anyway, we have some news, if you want to break it first on your show ...!"

"What news?" Joanne was now chomping at the bit. Debbie took a deep breath and told her about the new arrival.

The proverbial deafening silence followed. Debbie could almost see Joanne's face and hearing the squeal of delight, only served to reassure her that Joanne deserved this news. An excited gasp, "Debbie, please let me announce it on the show. Please keep it secret, it's only a couple of days away!"

Debbie chuckled, it never ceased to amaze her that something so natural could become a scoop, inhaling her own happiness, she simply replied, "I give you my word, Joanne. You can announce it on your show!"

**

The day of the show arrived and the first half had been fun, with questions coming thick and fast. After the interval, Joanne bubbled as she imparted that infectious little squeal, that now preceded her fame and walked forward, "You have all asked how they cope with their lovely children and they do make everything appear so easy, but I'm delighted to announce that they are expecting another one in November!"

The whole period of time in the States had been one glorious success after another. They all felt tired, in a healthy, fulfilling way. Their next visit was still under discussion, but they had so much work in both countries, they had requested to leave the dates open.

By the end of August, Hank accompanied them to the airport. Having hugged them all a fond farewell, he reserved an extra big hug for Debbie. He still couldn't free his mind of her and seeing her with child, only served to make her even more sensual. He had dreaded today, knowing he would miss her, yet realised even if she stayed, she was in love with Matthew.

Boarding the 'plane, Debbie looked around her and waved to the press, everyone was so friendly in the States, but she knew they would all just catch the last of the summer holidays in Morecambe. And for good measure, their castle was waiting for them and she knew, she longed to get into it.

CHAPTER THIRTY FIVE

Debbie clutched Matthew's hand as the car sped them along the seafront. Paul had met them at the airport together with a multitude of press. Hugging her to him, he teased, "I don't think I'd recognise you without a bump!"

Kelly knew exactly where she was, her squeals of delight began to affect Verity, both of them filled with excitement. Nostalgia choked them all as the sea air wafted through the car windows. Suddenly, it was as if they had never left Morecambe.

The tumultuous welcome from the staff almost overwhelmed them. Irene had greeted them as though they were long lost relatives, in fact that was just how they felt. Paul was eager to begin to discuss the future, now that the Preston deal had gone through without so much as a hiccup.

Matthew stretched, a huge yawn sprung from him, "Paul, we have a full board meeting in the morning, so we do. There's so much to discuss, but I think we all need an early night!"

In spite of the excitement, they had no problems at all getting their little ones to bed. Kelly and Verity jumped into their own beds, almost asleep before their heads hit the pillows. Lucy now had her own room and once again, the cot was in the corner of their own room.

Although dog tired, Debbie and Matthew still made time for a brief wander own to the beach. They had removed their shoes and walked out, to allow the water to lap over their feet, relaxing them to perfection.

Fresh and cool air caressed them. The moon shafted over the sea, turning it dark as pewter, contrasting with the baked orange sands. They walked along in the intoxication of sheer beauty, filling them with poignancy.

Somehow, they had managed to climb up to the balcony, to capture once again, the stifling, panoramic vista. This was their special domain, private and only for them. Wearily, Matthew held her, "Home at last, Duchess. I can't wait to jump under the shower, get into bed and sleep for an eternity, after I've made love to my wife, of course!"

"Oh, you remembered them," she chuckled.

Shuddering their way back from the plateau that knew no name, his eyes locked hers, "Debbie, darling, I always want our love to be like this. As soon as this little one is born, I think I ought to ask Brian about a vasectomy. I know the pill upsets you, and I think four children are enough for you, my love!"

"Matthew, what if its another girl? I thought you would want a son. Unless you object strongly, I'm happy to try at least once more!"

She leaned over him and traced the contours of his beloved face and whispered, "Matthew Ross, I know it's a tall order, but I also want a son and we will just keep trying. If I go onto the pill for about six months before we try again, we could try at least twice more. After all, I'm young and healthy and we did have eight rooms to convert!"

His arms crushed her. He knew she meant exactly what she said. At times he could scarcely believe his luck, she was his life, his love, his partner. Never would he cease to be grateful for the gift of her love.

**

Whilst in the States, they had decided to give Irene some shares. Although she did have a big say in the meetings, she would be able to vote as a shareholder and it had been decided that Jim would announce their decision at the next meeting.

Despite her obvious delight, Irene's eyes had filled as she thanked them, "I love my work, but this is the icing on my cake," she choked.

Paul had then become very serious, "Matthew, we will have to rely heavily on you to settle one of the lads in at Preston. We need everything put together by February, ready to roll by April. It has been scheduled to launch the magazine with an Easter block buster!"

Sipping his coffee, Matthew replied, "Of course I'm willing, but it'll put a lot of pressure on us here. I think we should meet the lad I am to work with as soon as possible. It's obvious that you and Vanessa will be well tied up after launching the Christmas competitions, yes, that's fine with Debbie and myself, Paul!"

Suddenly, Irene piped up, "Golly, with all that excitement, I almost forgot. Debbie, the television station want you to fit in half a dozen episodes on pregnancy. They also want to film the birth to end the series!"

A stunned silence fell over the meeting. Momentarily, Debbie felt embarrassed, yet somehow, she felt this would help many young mums. Mothers did identify with her, but more importantly, fathers identified with Matthew. It was only too clear they would have been successful, but the series on children had been real winners.

Coming at a time when it was important to draw the family into the joy of birth, she and Matthew had been there, just as the markets had opened out, ready to receive all of this information. There humble beginnings had warmed the hearts of the public, making everything they said even more realistic. That image was important to them both and they were honoured to be in a position of such trust.

Matthew's indignant voice broke into her malaise, "I'm not having cameras in, its very private for us both!"

Debbie couldn't help chuckling, she had never heard Matthew put his foot down, but he seemed adamant. Paul leaned forward, "I'd feel the same, Matthew, but *you* could film it. Start up the camera and no one need intrude!"

Looking around the table, Debbie could see that the others seemed to agree with Paul. Jim spoke up, "I think this is something far too private to go before the board. It would help many young parents, but we must respect their wishes, how do you feel about it, Debbie?"

"I would be happy if Matthew did the filming, but whatever he wants to do, must be his decision," she added with sincerity.

201

Matthew took her hand, "Darling, its entirely up to you. If they do agree, perhaps we can film it. Many women have and probably will tread this path, I think it will help. When it comes to giving birth, well you're a natural," his voice shook with sheer emotion

"You could be an inspiration to the fathers, Matthew, we'll do it!"

Returning to the rest of the meeting, they were delighted with the shop receipts and Debbie and Matthew would pop down to see Jenny and Richard. Matthew would take up training the new lad with Vanessa accompanying them part time. After calling a meeting just prior to Christmas, they were able to adjourn.

**

Megan beamed when they asked her about filming. Patting her hair as though she had become an instant star, she smiled, "You sure you want me to deliver your baby?"

Still patting her hair, she went on, "I'd be happy to be filmed, seriously though, seeing Debbie give birth with you at her side, Matthew, could do nothing but good. How about filming me doing a routine check up? If Debbie is too quick again, I won't have time to explain much on the day!"

That was a very important point and Matthew agreed readily, "I'll set up two cameras and angle them to pick up the important points. You're right, Megan, we'll film your next visit!"

Watching Megan being filmed was in itself almost comical. Her face beamed into the lens as she made her points clearly. She was extremely thorough and Debbie felt that they couldn't have found anyone better than Megan. There was a real motherly charisma about her, reassuring vibes just seemed to bounce from her, her hands soothed as well as examined.

**

Alma's voice held urgency as she spoke to Debbie the day after Kelly's birthday, "We have a new chunky yarn, could you quickly design a couple of ideas for them?" Her voice was filled with enthusiasm, it sometimes made Debbie laugh, the way she emphasised 'quickly'.

Debbie felt tired and heavy, but assured Alma that she would commence almost immediately. Suddenly, she felt the old familiar pain, "Alma, I have a pressing engagement right now," she gasped.

"Good luck, Debbie, let's know what you have!"

Hastily, she 'phoned Megan, found Matthew and delivered the children to her parents. Her nerves were beginning to show, balling her hands, she realised this because of the importance to parents everywhere and not just herself and Matthew.

Matthew held her to him, "Darling, forget about the cameras. If you don't like the end production, it can always be ditched. There's no way in which I want you upset!"

"I know, darling. Everything about you is tasteful and I trust you entirely," she gulped as perspiration broke over her.

Moments later, the little squeal heralded Emma's arrival. The little mouth instantly began to suckle as her daddy stroked her little cheek. It was perfect and with that, Matthew switched off the cameras. They had accomplished all that had been requested of them.

Megan handed Emma to the nurse, "What a beautiful way to give birth. If others watch that, it will take away so much of the normal fear. Debbie knew she was right, she also knew that she would be questioned about it when it was shown. This was the end of the series and mentally she thanked God for giving her the strength to provide such a useful 'aid' to parents.

Her parents were overjoyed with Emma. Kelly came in, "Why did we have to have another little girl, Mummy?" That thought Debbie was a very good question and realised why she hadn't wanted Matthew to have the vasectomy.

Irene and Alma would deal with the publicity, having popped in to see the new arrival. Matthew had 'phoned Joanne and somehow, Debbie had been left to notify Hank.

She noticed a tenseness in his voice as he greeted her, "Hi there, Debbie, bet you had another girl!"

"Trust you to guess, Hank. Yes, her name is Emma and when the videos are ready, we'll send a copy over," she chuckled.

"Gee, Debbie, thanks, I'm .. I'm so pleased for you!"

Debbie picked up the stutter, a frown developed, "Hank, are you alright? You sound strained, are you working too hard over there?"

Hank felt dreadful, she had just given birth and still found time to be concerned about him. He longed for her to return, whilst at the same time, wished he would never have to see her again.

Shame flooded him, yet he could not come to terms with his feelings. Just for good measure, he had lost the urge to go out anymore. In fact, he began to wonder if he should allow someone else to handle their next visit. Biting his tongue, he gulped, "Thanks for calling, Debbie, congratulations and take care!"

Replacing the receiver, he literally swept the papers from his desk. Watching them flutter to the floor, he knew, he did want marriage, he did want children, he did want Debbie. There was no way in which he could head the next production.

**

As Debbie had said 'cheerio' to Hank, she had felt there was something wrong with him. Perhaps he was under severe pressure, but when Matthew came to take her into his arms, she forgot about any nagging doubts that may have threatened her delight.

The children had gone to bed and he handed Emma to her. Together they watched her suckle. She was unlike the others, just a small amount of hair, but not instantly identifiable. Yet there was something special about her.

Debbie snuggled up to Matthew, "If I wrap up warmly, will you take me up to the balcony? We won't stay long!"

203

His arms held her tenderly as they surveyed their wonderful, yet not so little kingdom. The evening was grey and they could see the lighthouse flashing its friendly light for the many fishermen. Matthew's voice choked, "Well, Duchess, it just keeps growing, doesn't it? So does my love for you!"

"Why do you all me Duchess when we come up here, darling?"

"That's how I see you when we look over our wonderful bay. To me, darlin', you are majestic!"

Hearing the lilt so strong with emotion, choked her. She was the happiest woman in the whole world.

The little nursery school had written to say that Kelly and Verity could commence morning school, directly after Christmas and Debbie was grateful they had managed to fit Verity in, they both looked forward to attending. She did feel pride with her little ones, they were reasonably well mannered, very secure and loved by their grandparents, not to mention uncle Paul, who doted on them. They were happy anywhere, providing one of the family was present.

Sometimes the amount of work stifled them. Ellen had been a huge success with her baking series and was asked to put further ideas forward. It was now obvious they would not be able to return to the States until the following year.

Matthew would soon be very tied up with the magazine, which had raced into the top ten ratings. That had really thrilled them all, for it had sunk the figures of 'Ventura', who, although merged, still didn't come into the top twenty.

**

Brian had teased them unmercifully about their four daughters. After checking Debbie over, he smiled, "Well now, you're fit and well again, Debbie. I know the pill upset you last time and should it upset you again, let me know and I'll change it!"

He had perched on his desk as usual, his arms folded over his chest. His eyes sparkled with fun as Debbie assured him, "If I have any problems, Brian, I promise you'll be the first to know!"

It had been easy to laugh and joke with him, he was more like a family friend than a doctor. He was proud of the success they shared, and pleased they saw fit to share their happiness.

Having waved a cheery goodbye to him, they proceeded down to the shop. She and Matthew had been meaning to get down there, but there was always so much to do. Nevertheless, Richard and Jenny welcomed them with eagerness.

Although the shop was busy, Jenny had taken them upstairs. Debbie noticed the way Jenny held Emma. There was an added gleam in her eyes and Debbie guessed. Jenny announced, "We're expecting our second one in June. James will be two by then, oh, Debbie, the children are beautiful, I'd love a little girl this time!"

Richard had gone to get James, who had just wakened from his nap. Golly he had grown, he was almost a clone of his mother. Huge eyes, black hair and a really winning smile. He began playing with the girls instantly, all of them shrieking with excitement.

Matthew watched with gentle eyes, "Richard, you and Jenny will need an extra pair of hands, you can interview anyone to assist, you know exactly what you want!"

"That would be great, Matthew, Jenny will need help once the season starts. I'll place an ad."

Debbie chuckled, "Richard, you talking about placing an ad., has so many happy memories for me, if we hadn't placed our own ad., I'd never have met Matthew. Its incredible to think that I could have missed so much," she added wistfully.

Her eyes went to Matthew, his grin broadened, "You make me sound like a mail order product, I never thought it meant so much to you, Debs!"

"You *are* my male order, it was such a surprise when you walked in, I nearly put you off entirely!"

Turning to Richard and Jenny, he guffawed, "If she hadn't been such a brilliant designer, she would have made a brilliant cross examiner for the Mafia. She had my life history out of me in a couple of seconds flat!"

They all laughed happily and as they left, Matthew once again stated that should Jenny need help when her time came, they would be on hand.

Once outside, they decided to walk back via Old Heysham, through the countryside. There was an abundance of greenery, although the trees were decidedly bare. The branches, somehow managed to sway and dance to the soft breeze. It filled them with peace and tranquillity, flushing happiness through them as they arrived back onto the promenade.

Life had treated them well, especially after all of the shocks they had endured at the start of their partnership. Turning to Matthew, she noticed that he was deep in thought. She loved him so much and in April, they would have been married for four years.

Instinctively he had turned to her, right there and then on the deserted promenade and taken her into his arms. "Darlin', I never realised that you remembered so clearly how we first met. It was the happiest day in my life, till I found out about Paul. Somehow though, just being around you made me feel complete!"

**

In spite of their hectic schedule, the meeting had to be attended. Paul had already circulated the details of Mark Thompson, the young man that was to travel to and from Preston with Matthew. Debbie felt a strange loss, almost resentment, she needed Matthew with her. They did have such a hectic workload, yet Matthew had always wanted the magazine and needed her support. After all, once the launch had taken place, he would be back with her and the children.

Debbie could almost take a back seat at this meeting, yet seeing the young man enter, she felt a stab of sympathy for him. Mark Thompson looked distinctively nervous, although the rest of the board knew it was a mere formality, to him, it was make or break day.

She watched him, he was in his mid twenties, with dark brown and slightly unruly hair. His jaw was angular with a rather generous, though sensual mouth. Warmth exuded from his lovely hazel eyes, his smile began there and lit up the whole of his face. There was also a restlessness about him, reminding her sharply of Paul and indeed Hank.

He was smartly dressed, in a silver grey suit, with spotless white shirt. He looked well turned out and was obviously thrilled with the chance he was being interviewed for. There was a large flat above the Preston branch and Debbie felt that he had worked just as hard for the flat as he had done for the job itself.

Paul's report on him left him wanted for nothing, he had a natural aptitude for the work and was totally committed. He knew that the hours could be long, especially before a deadline, but apparently, he took all of that in his stride.

Debbie liked him and asked, "Are you married, Mark?" She knew full well he was, but felt strongly that in this type of work, a man needed a wife to share his job with. Not actively sharing, but to understand when work became urgent.

Paul had been brought down by a demanding Amanda, yet it had been the reason for her success with Matthew. There is no way in which one can work well, not if their partner is constantly pulling in another direction. As Hank had explained that kind of partnership was very rare and she felt Mark realised this.

His eyes filled with pride, "Yes, my wife's name is Sally. We're expecting our first baby in April. She loves my work and often comes up with a few good ideas herself!"

Seeing Paul shake his head, it was as if they all realised that Mark would do them proud. Although, they were all mindful that he couldn't have chosen a worse time for the birth of his child.

Debbie smiled wryly, thinking of the times when her own timing had been well out of sync. They would all be able to help him through. He was a very likeable young man and she also felt they would like Sally.

His swallowing was more frequent than usual and taking a gulp of his coffee, he vowed, "If you give me this chance, I swear you'll never regret it. I'll have to work with Matthew until the launch, which makes me even more grateful!"

This type of interview was really about giving the candidate impetus. He now knew the people he was working with and hopefully would realise their motto to be that of the three Musketeers.

It had been agreed to allow Mark and Sally to move into their flat before the launch. Although Sally wanted to have her baby in Morecambe and be near to her mother, they could at least decorate it prior to moving in.

Never had she felt so much gratitude as they now received from Mark. His eyes were full, but he had begun to relax a little. She didn't want him to be humbled, or indeed grateful, he would do very well. Turning to him, she added, "Mark, we're not doing you any favours. You've been offered this pose because you worked darned hard. Once you settle in with your babe, we'll come over to celebrate with you and Sally!"

He had obviously worked himself up waiting to meet them. Now it seemed, he liked what he saw. Turning to Debbie, he gulped, "Sally is a real fan of yours. She's learned to knit and crochet for our child and she loved the diaries. I think she's longing to be able to send her own hints in, like the other mums!"

Watching him leave, they all felt that once again, they had shared another part of their empire. Paul stood up, rubbing his hands with pride. He was well pleased with his latest protégé and promised to release Vanessa for a couple of days a week as Matthew made a point that Debbie would need help herself.

Suffocating with love for him, she knew she had many eager hands, but she couldn't rid herself of this strange unwelcome feeling that had descended upon her. In spite of her determination to pull herself together, the feelings still persisted, frightening her.

CHAPTER THIRTY SIX

Amanda Morgan had all but begged her father for money, but the miserable sod had refused point blank. He had also refused to give her part of the action in the London magazine. In fact, he had made it pretty obvious that he didn't care about her future one way or the other and after selling off her jewellery, furs and contents of her apartment, she was truly broke. She had tracked down a tabloid reporter in a pub just around the corner from Fleet Street, who had made it plain, if she came up with the goods, he would print.

Filled with spite, she had confronted her parents in their Blackpool apartment. For the first time in her life, she had been horrified by their stand of unity. Lighting a cigarette, she almost spat the words, "I'm going to give the story to the press, the one about Mother and your ex empire builder. Vanessa would hate to be humiliated, we all know that. Think it over, folks, I want fifty thousand quid by Wednesday, or I'll collect from the press!"

The cruel words had fallen swiftly from the pouting mouth. Eric smacked his daughter across the face, "Don't you dare bring anymore problems upon your Mother. You're a bitch, Amanda and I can promise you, we'll pay nothing. Maralyn and I will face what has to be faced," he flashed, suddenly realising that for the first time in his life, he had slapped his daughter.

Her hand had gone to rub the mark, "You'll be sorry for that, you bastard. Paul and Vanessa will feel the humiliation, so will the fuckin' Hudsons. I mean, how can they pose a magazine for the family, when their behaviour leaves so much to be desired?"

She screamed the words as her face contorted with ugliness. Eric turned to her, "Amanda, you have nothing to blackmail any of us with now. Go home, grow up and
find yourself a job, something to keep that evil little mind busy!"

Amanda rolled her eyes, "Everyone will feel sad for my plight. Look what I've had in my life, a father who has screwed everyone that has ever worked for him, including a lesbian. And as if that's not bad enough, I find out my mother is screwing the same tart!"

Eric was on his feet and she feared he would hit out again. Backing away slightly, she watched his face turn puce, "I've never stuck one on Vanessa. Don't you dare run her down, she's a bloody good and loyal worker. She and Paul, together with the Hudsons, know exactly what the public want, what's more, they work hard to prove it."

Even as the words left his mouth, he realised he had done the worst thing possible. He had spoken of his daughter's imagined enemies with warmth, pride, envy and passion. His eyes had noticed the horror in his wife's eyes and fear knotted into his stomach. He breathed in slowly, "Amanda, why do you want to hurt the Hudsons and Vanessa so much? They've done nothing to hurt you, even Paul didn't set out to hurt you, he just didn't want to be married to you. You're still a beautiful woman, why not channel some of that bitterness into something worthwhile?"

Neither of them noticed that Maralyn had left. Maralyn needed to see her beloved Nessa, with Amanda in this destructive mood she feared for Nessa's future. She drove from Blackpool to Morecambe and let herself into her lover's flat.

**

Once inside the spotless apartment, Maralyn walked slowly, fingering delicate objects, holding lingerie to her face, before kissing and caressing the soft folds, recognising the sweet smell of Nessa's body. Her eyes filled with pain as she wrestled against tears. Never would she allow this woman to feel the pain she now felt, to feel the threats dangled over her head. There was only one answer for them and for Eric and she was the only person in a position to stop Amanda.

Maralyn showered and slipped into one of Nessa's soft negligees, she breathed in and closed her eyes as the folds enveloped her skin. Suddenly, she was like a young fawn, ready to prance about, ready to meet her mate. Her body sunk into the large mattress and a swift tiredness seemed to pick her up and carry her on it's wings.

As though floating on a cloud, her mind became aware of the woman beside her. Tender arms enfolded her as she gasped, "Nessa, darling, I had to see you. I just fell asleep," she moaned as she came awake.

"What a wonderful surprise, Mazz," smiled Vanessa allowing her lips to be taken She lay in the arms of her lover, her breath jerking with an overwhelming desire. Maralyn breathed into her mouth, her ears, her eyes and back to her mouth. The moment she had seen Mazza sleeping, she had been eager to prepare herself, showering and slipping naked next to the blond, fair creature.

Together they has discussed the various probabilities of Amanda's threatened actions, Vanessa hugged Maralyn, "Stop worrying, my love, let her do her worst!"

Maralyn crushed her, longing to believe it would be as simple as Vanessa made out, but it wasn't. Running her fingers through the soft hair, she gulped, "Thanks, Nessa. Eric is comfortable with us and has played havoc with Amanda, but I think she wants this public, to humiliate me, definitely you, because Paul respects you and because he loved Debbie. She is sure she can bring us all down and make herself rich into the bargain, the newspapers would have a field day ..," she choked.

"I can't stay over, if I don't sort this out tonight, I'll lose my bottle!"

Seeing the question in Vanessa's eyes, she realised she had almost given herself away. Swiftly she smiled, "Let me love you once more, let me love you before I leave!" And she did.

Vanessa felt lost when Maralyn left. She had never tasted love like she had tonight and with a jolt, she realised there had been a strange finality about the love Mazza had shared with her. Horror filled her as she ran to the 'phone and

209

hastily dialled Eric. Hearing his strained voice, she almost screamed, "Eric, for Christ's sake, I think Mazz is in danger, for God's sake, find her!"

**

Maralyn drove her car to the edge of the cliff. Tears poured from her misery laden eyes as she thought of Eric. He had finally acknowledged his love for her and she truly believed him. Vanessa had taken her into a new and beautiful world, yet she knew, it was a first for them both. They had stumbled into this scene, both probably having thought about it before, even desiring to try, but it had been together they had found the beauty they had shared. Mazz would never allow her beloved friend to suffer.

Her only hope now was that her wretched daughter would show respect for the dead. Her mind danced to every tune, from the samba to the tango, with intricate steps and smooth steps, but when each dance ended, trouble always lurked. Inhaling onto her cigarette, she flicked the remains into the sea and climbed back into the car and released the brake. The explosion was the last she heard.

**

Vanessa hadn't even thought of going to bed, she had just about smoked herself hoarse and was trying to drink herself into some kind of blissful oblivion, when the bang came on the door. Her stomach was a knot of pain, she knew what was coming as she ran and flung the door wide. Almost falling into the grief stricken Eric, she screamed, "Oh, no, I'll kill your bloody daughter!"

Eric lifted her and carried her into the apartment and without a word, placed her gently onto the settee. Biting his lower lip, he walked over to the cabinet and poured them both a d rink. Vanessa looked at the pathetic picture, he was dressed all in black, giving him an almost slim look. Maralyn had spoken of his change of attitude and momentarily, Vanessa forgot to be bitter.

Her voice was barely audible as she lit a cigarette, "What happened, Eric? She did kill herself, didn't she? When she left me, her words drifted back to me, 'once more before I leave'. Hell, Eric, I got the message too bloody late. She was terrified of me being destroyed and ... and .... And she didn't want you to suffer. She didn't want anyone hurt, Paul, Debbie, all of us!"

Breathlessly, she looked at Eric. Tears dripped from his cheeks as he held the woman who had given his wife so much. He could scarcely believe the devastation in her. "Yes, she did kill herself. I've left a message for Amanda to call me, but I'm sure it was her that finally pushed Mazza over the top. She was so loving towards me before she left, this was no accident," he sobbed.

**

One week later, after the papers had been filled with the new of the Morgan's tragic 'accident', for that was what Eric and Vanessa preferred, an army of reporters had gathered to attend the funeral.

Paul had been absolutely gutted and had gone along with a distraught Vanessa. Debbie, Matthew and family had sent flowers with their condolences for the sad day. Paul just told Vanessa to take what time she needed, not

210

wishing to be indiscreet, after all, he wasn't supposed to know the whole truth.

Amanda had stood in the crematorium stunned. Never had she thought of this, but it didn't alter the fact that she needed money.

When everyone had gone, Vanessa pounced, "Right, you bitch, listen to me and listen bloody good. Nothing will be printed about your mother, she was a fine, kind, generous woman and I will not have her name tainted. It was thanks to you, you filthy, lying bitch, that she died!"

"Shut your mouth, Vanessa. I didn't know she would die. Anyway, I can still break you. I can tell the press about you, you're the filthy cow around here. How could you do that to my mother? Can't you take a man?

There was only one thing that stopped me before, but now I'm free," she smirked.

"Sorry, bitch. I know your bloody filthy secrets, you go to the papers, dear. And when you tell them about your mother and me, I will simply explain that it was yourself and me, much as the thought appals me," she gasped and carried on, "Your mother was highly respected, you're not. Once I break the news of how you tried to destroy Debbie, the game will be up. No, Amanda, this is the end for you. I'm prepared to pay your fare out of this country, providing you never come back!"

Vanessa almost broke down as she finished her mini speech, but she was determined to defend all the people that Maralyn had died for. Her chest stabbed with agonised pains, as the grief, the argument, the language of her own threats had left her exhausted.

**

One month later Vanessa had found no solace from her grief. She had thrown herself into her work, but misery stalked just about everywhere. She had been heartbroken when her young husband had died, how she had loved him and just as she had found love again, it had been ripped from her grasp.

Fortunately they had been rushed off their feet and she gradually lost herself as she and Paul worked side by side. Every now and then, she would remember how she had fancied him and realised with somewhat of a shock, that although he was ten years her junior, he could still bring a burst of moisture to her loins.

One evening as they worked in silence, Paul had looked at his watch, "Good Lord, its gone nine and my stomach is feeling as though my bloody throat's been cut!"

Vanessa couldn't stop the little chuckle that sprung up in her, "I never gave the time a thought, Paul. Come to think of it, I feel quite peckish myself. How about I pop up to the kitchen and make us an omelette?"

"Why should you cook? I've a better idea, you go and open a bottle of wine, I'll slip out and bring in fish and chips," he grinned.

"Great," acknowledged Vanessa.

After they had eaten the meal with an element of greed, they didn't sip the wine, but knocked it back unceremoniously. Paul's eyes wandered over

211

Vanessa, she was still a very attractive woman, if only she wouldn't wear those sexless trouser suits. A sudden urge to take her into his arms and kiss her shook him.

It had been a long time since he had kissed a woman. When he had visited the high class, yet illegal brothels, his need were completely attended to by the girls. Sometimes there would be two girls making love to set his pulses racing, then he would be given a superb blow job and usually left there, complete in body and mind. Seldom did he seek to touch or join in, simply lay back and give himself up to whatever delights were administered, his mind focussing on Debbie as he came.

Realising the urge to kiss Vanessa was still with him, he felt himself grow. His manhood had become so hard, he felt pain. Embarrassment covered him as he noticed her eyes travel his body. Desperately searching for suitable words, he jerked, "How would you fancy a shag, Nessa?"

He felt the blood rush to his head and pound against his temples as she shrugged off her jacket, "If that's what you'd like!"

"Is it what you'd like though?" He sought to confirm as his cock reared in desperate expectation.

Vanessa felt a thousand arrows shoot from her body, her mind flew back several years, tugging her heart as she had once longed for moments like this. Then her conscience became uneasy, "Paul, I would like us to … but there's something you, you should …"

The soft gasp left her as he finished the sentence for her, "I know, Ness, we all have secrets and they are too personal to discuss. Don't be afraid, love," he moaned as her body folded into him.

His mouth found hers, soft and warm, opened slightly to receive his tongue. Overawed by her response, he realised he hadn't kissed anyone, not since Debbie. Without words, they kneeled up and began to undo each others' buttons. Ness ran her fingers over his hair coarsened chest, breathing in the musky smell of him. Throwing her arms around his neck, she trailed her hand down his heavily muscled back and shoulders.

Trembling with wild anticipation, she placed her hands behind her and undid her bra, allowing her breasts to be free, needing Paul to gather them into his strong, firm hands. His hand was trying to enter her trouser band as liquid fire burned between her legs. With a long groan, she ripped her trousers, panties and hose from herself. Paul looked at her youthful body, it was not far from perfect. The dusky breasts, with honeyed nipples were firm, her stomach was flat and her bush was almost the same colour as his own pubic hair.

Crazily, she moved her hands to circle around his straining cock. His mouth was chewing on her nipple, filling her with exquisite delight. And then he buried his face into her bush and moaned, "We should have done this before!"

Paul couldn't believe the depth of his arousal. This woman was so very feminine and seconds later he had stripped himself. He had always been proud of his manhood and enjoyed having himself brought off, but he felt a need for this woman to take hold of him, caress him, knowing that ultimately it would sink deeply into her and without warning, he began to leak.

His hands covered her soft creamy buttocks as he pulled her against his impatient, demanding weapon. Suddenly, his hands moved between her legs, his fingers searching for the most secret passage. Her hands gripped the distended penis and he found the opening. Holding his breath with excitement, he allowed his finger to enter the fiery heat. This was the first time he had ever wanted to participate in this act, this was the first time he sought to fulfil the woman in his arms, not since Debbie. Mentally, he thanked God, he needed this back in his life again and he moaned soft and low.

He eased her carefully down onto the rug. Inhaling deeply, he opened her with one hand and entered her with one steady push, for she was so ready for him that there was no resistance. Vanessa hadn't felt so good for ages, yes, she did indeed enjoy the excess meat that hung deliciously between his legs. And the way Paul was delivering himself to her was as beautiful as she had once thought.

Although the need on her face matched that on his own, he stopped and held steady. In spite of being inside of her to the hilt, he still didn't move. He looked into her eyes, passion now unmistakable and bright in his own eyes, "Are you sure about this, Ness?"

"Oh, Paul, I'm so very sure," she breathed out her desire.

At last he was liberated, strongly in command, thrusting deliberately and knowingly, Paul Howarth gave Vanessa the long, piercing climax that she was so ready for. Waiting until she was in the middle of her frenzied release before he allowed himself to grind into her body without holding back and join her own spasms of the first mighty, relentless strokes of his masterful orgasm.

They lay in silence. Paul was shocked from his skin, he never thought he could ever find a rich fulfilment, not after Debbie, but this had taken him into realms he had never bargained for. His penis still penetrated Vanessa as he brushed her lips with his, "Fancy, you and me. Ness, that was beautiful, I can't believe this happened!"

"I'm glad it did, Paul. I know you'll always be in love with Debbie, but any time you feel a need to indulge, feel free," she shrugged her shoulders and savoured the passion they had shared.

Suddenly, he understood her loss. Understood her need to be loved. Understood her offer. They were two lonely souls, each searching for something they had found together. He moved from her and poured them a scotch each, "Stay the night, Ness. I'm still in a state of shock about this, but it was the most wonderful experience I have enjoyed for a long time. Don't jump down my throat … How would you feel about us being lovers? Or are you looking for commitment, Ness?"

Vanessa took a huge gulp of her drink and peered over the top of the glass, "I used to dream of you and me like this," she admitted and flushed. "It was as wonderful in my dreams. There's no need to feel uncomfortable, Paul, I know you don't want commitment and I must admit, I don't wish to alter my lifestyle, but I do like the idea of a regular lover!"

They made love many times that night. It wasn't a question of being in love, more a question of sharing work, worries and most important, sharing good, satisfying, passionate sex, both holding each other with the deepest respect.

CHAPTER THIRTY SEVEN

February that year was freezing cold and Debbie found herself tiring easily. Matthew was travelling in and out of Preston with Mark. He was thoroughly enjoying the challenge, but she worked with Matthew all evening and he also began to look very tired and drawn.

Kelly and Verity had settled well into the nursery school and mixed well with the other children. Debbie would pop in to kiss all of them goodnight and feel herself choke with love and again, admonished herself, she was still dreadfully uneasy about Matthew being away.

The onset of irritability had driven her to see Brian. He had checked her over and smiled, "Debbie, there's nothing wrong with you, but you're obviously allergic to the pill, seems to be making you depressed!"

Exhaling the breath she had subconsciously held, relief flooded her, why the hell hadn't she thought of that? Brian chuckled, "I can give you another type of pill, but it will be ten days before you can take it, as it takes that long for the old one to be free of your system!"

"Oh, no, Brian. I don't want to mess Matthew about now, he has far too much on his plate. Surely there's something I can take now," she pleaded.

Brian watched her anguished face. Asking her and Matthew to refrain from sex, was almost like asking them not to breathe. Sitting down to write the prescription, he chuckled, "I know ten days is a nuisance, but I can give you some pessaries as a temporary measure, so you can cheer up!"

Leaving the surgery, she literally bumped into Paul. Hugging her, his face held concern, "What are you doing here? I must admit, you do look a little peaky, Debbie. Come on, let's pop and have a coffee together!"

Checking her watch swiftly, she replied, "Well, it'll have to be a quick one. I'm snowed under, the children miss Matthew at bedtime and I feel browned off!"

Paul looked at her, his concern growing, he had never heard terseness in her before. She did look a little fragile and guilt flooded him. Somehow, he knew how she was feeling, after all, he had never stopped loving her. Finding a quiet corner, he ordered coffee and sat down. "What's wrong, Debs? Is there anything I can do?"

To his relief, she smiled, "Sorry, Paul, it's almost farcical. I've been feeling wretched, but Brian put his finger on it straight away. The pill has given me a depressive side effect, I never gave that a thought, but he had changed it for me!"

He gave a hearty guffaw, "Thank goodness. Why doesn't Matthew do what I did? I mean I had a vasectomy, it took me ages to begin dating again, but I don't want to take risks!"

Her eyes saucered, somehow she had thought that Paul would ultimately marry and have children, but how wrong could she be? Leaving the many questions alone, she said, "Matthew did offer, but I want us to try at least once more, I think he would love a son and I *know* I would!"

His eyes fixed hers, "Surely you don't want more children? After all you could have more girls, mind you, I love your daughters, they are as *we* used to promise, unspoilt," he spoke wistfully and then continued, "You always said you wanted lots of children, mind you, you'll have four weddings to pay for!"

He had spoken in jocular mode, making her giggle. He was funny at time, she certainly would have four weddings to pay for, but thank God, they could afford that. The girls were very close to Matthew and she felt, if they looked for his qualities, they would be guaranteed happiness. They were also close to Paul and he would have made a wonderful husband.

Noticing the time, she jumped up with haste, "I must get back, Paul. Although I've made myself late, I did enjoy our chat and feel much better, but it will be a relief once the launch is well and truly over!"

Arriving home, she found herself tucking into the work with a new found delight, after all, it would only be a couple of months till Matthew was home again. Suddenly, it didn't feel so far away and she felt new, inspired urges begin to flow from her brain, reaching down into her fingertips as ideas seemed to spring from nowhere.

To her delight, Matthew arrived home early. In fact he would be able to read the kiddies their bedtime story. Although he played with his daughters and reassured them that he would soon be home for good, Debbie noticed that he was visibly upset.

Panic stirred in her as she waited impatiently for him to eat his meal. Pushing the plate away, he choked, "Debbie, Mark was called to the hospital earlier, Sally was rushed in and he was devastated. Paul popped over to pick him up, we've just heard that she'll be alright and so will the babe, but she must stay in hospital till after the birth!"

He stared into space, the strain showing on his beloved face. Heaving painfully, he gasped, "I couldn't have faced that. Had that been you, Debbie, I'd have gone completely to pieces, so I would!"

Mercifully, it wasn't her, but nevertheless, he had still gone to pieces. Making him a coffee, she ran to ring Paul. His voice was gentle, "Hi, pet, is Matthew more settled? He was stunned, almost as if it had been his own wife. If he still feels rough in the morning, I'll take Mark across!"

Paul's very thoughtfulness made her catch her breath. He was a kind friend and she asked, "Is the babe going to be alright?"

"Yes, Debs, apparently, if it were to arrive early, it has a good chance of survival. Mark will return to work tomorrow, he's better with his mind occupied!"

Typical Paul, speaking with utter concern, yet allowing common sense to prevail. Normally Matthew would advise the same recipe, but this had sent him reeling. Paul then suggested, "I know you're busy, pet, but, I wonder .... Could you manage a quick visit? It would buck Sally up I'm sure!"

"Of course I'll go, Paul!"

His voice tremored, "You're such a dear person. Give Matthew a large dose of t.l.c. he'll soon be fine, cheers, love!" Replacing the receiver, she smiled, how well Paul knew her.

Matthew seemed calmer when she returned. Sitting on his knee, she whispered, "Darling, there's no reason why Sally should lose her baby. She's healthy, her blood pressure is a little high and let's face it, they've both had a lot of pressure, we all have!"

Crushing her to him, the colour rapidly returning to his ashen face, he began to kiss her eager lips. Her arms went around him, "Paul suggested that I give you a large helping of t..l.c. Come on, as soon as Emma's fed, I'll seduce you, my darling!"

She had intended to send him wild, never dreaming of the erotic frenzy that was to grip her. Her hands now sought to fulfil her almost obsessive need to touch, to caress, to bite and savour, till he groaned to take her. A cocoon of love wrapped itself around them, locking into the beauty of their love as they fell asleep.

**

The next day, as promised, Debbie went along to see Sally. She took Lucy with her as Ellen had promised to keep an eye on Emma and the girls were at school

Debbie's heart went out to Sally, when she finally found her. She looked so lost and frightened, her gorgeous blond hair framed her pretty face. Her large blue eyes were almost lost in the pallor of her skin. As Debbie walked over to her, Sally's arms rose in greeting.

A smile lit up her lovely face, "Debbie, I'm so pleased to see you. I want to thank you all, not just for Mark's job, but our home and everything!"

"Mark earned that position and freely admits, he couldn't have done it without your help and support. I think you two are a little like Matthew and myself!"

Sally flushed, making her look even pettier, "Debbie, I do hope so. But look how hard you work and all of those lovely babies you has so quickly, aren't you exhausted?"

Debbie realised that Sally felt embarrassed to have asked such a very personal question. But really, there was precious little that was personal in her and Matthew's lives, everything had been run through the media and they had done that themselves, with the diaries and pregnancies, the books and now the film of Emma's birth.

Even as she thought about it, she could not begrudge one piece of information they had given. They knew, beyond all doubt, that many couples had found their experiences had helped them. She didn't feel exhausted, tired sometimes, but a happy tiredness that comes from true contentment.

Smiling at Sally, she spoke gently, "No, I'm not tired, just lucky enough to have good health and healthy babies, just as you'll have. When your labour starts, someone will bring Mark to you, it'll be from him that you draw your strength and both enjoy the birth!"

To Debbie's horror, Sally burst into tears. "Sally, what's wrong? I came here to cheer you up, what have I said?"

She felt absolutely dreadful as Sally had thrown herself into her arms and sobbed, "Mark and I have followed everything you and Matthew have told us. We've gone through the video, but now Mark doesn't think he'll be able to be with me!"

Pausing to grab a handful of tissues, her body still shaking, she gulped, "Debbie, he'll be tied up with the launch and all that is going to happen. I pray it comes at night, but then, it won't be fair for him to be up all night and going to work!"

Looking at Sally made her feel sad, taking her hand, she urged, "Listen to me, Sally. I give you my word, that the minute our labour starts, Mark will be on his way. No matter how busy they all are, he can take a cab, Matthew would insist!"

Sally managed a watery smile, "Debbie, Mark will be cross with me for this. He'd never ask, although he would dearly love us to share the birth. But we must be practical, the job means everything to us!"

Her sobs had now subsided into little sighs, Debbie felt that Sally had been bottled up for quite a while. In the first place, she had worried about Mark's job and now this. No wonder her blood pressure was high and squeezing Sally's hand, she soothed, "No one will tell Mark. I'll ask the hospital to ring Paul or me, we'll then leave it to Matthew, so Mark is outnumbered!"

They both chuckled as the sadness left Sally's lovely eyes, to reveal a gorgeous sparkle. They chatted for a little longer and as she left, Debbie knew that Sally would be fine for a while.

Just thinking how uptight Sally had been, made her feel a little more than shaky. Opening her bag to take out a tissue, her eyes fell upon the prescription. What had she done now?

Tingles of joy ran through her as she thought of the night before. She had been so obsessed with Matthew's distress and had forgotten completely. Oh, well, she thought, que sera sera. She even admitted to herself that she would be thrilled if she had conceived once more.

Realising that she had made Sally happy, had made Debbie feel good. She must pop in and put Paul into the picture, after all, they must be in agreement to make sure that Mark was released.

Paul swung Lucy into the air, smiling with affection when she squealed with delight. Turning to Debbie, his face turned serious as he breathed his relief, "Debs, what a good job you went, Mark would never have asked for time off. Yes, it'll be hectic, but for one day, I'm sure we can manage!"

Levelling Paul's eyes, she replied, "I don't think we should tell Mark about Sally breaking down!"

He guffawed loudly as he tussled her hair, "Don't worry, Debs. Mark will have no problems!"

**

By the end of March, Debbie desperately wanted Matthew to be finished with the Preston runs. More and more offers were still pouring in and the demand for the premature baby garments was growing rapidly.

They had also received a letter from the hospital in America. Apparently they had been so touched by their last donation, they had decided to name the new wing, 'The Debbie Hudson Unit'. Matthew had been thrilled about it and they had been asked over the following year, to unveil the plaque. It seemed the more they did, the more they were in demand.

The film on Emma's birth had gone down so well that Debbie found herself sitting with hundreds of enquiries, all wanting her views and feelings towards the various aspects. She remembered only too sharply how Sally trusted her. Also how Jenny had taken everything she said as gospel. Nevertheless, she and her husband continued to be exceedingly happy.

Her parents, although worried about her work load, were still happy to plough their way through their own respective jobs. And Ellen was always happy to keep her eye on the children, to enable Debbie to pop and see Sally and invariably pop in to see Jenny.

Walking home along the seafront, she allowed the breeze to whistle around her. She could feel the air being drawn deeply into her lungs. Somehow she was drawn to the sea rail and leaned heavily onto it. The sea was calm, filling her with tranquillity and engulfing her with happiness.

In just two more weeks Matthew would have seen the launch through and be back with them. Together they would celebrate their secret wedding anniversary and shudders of joy ran through her. She knew she was pregnant again and would have just turned two months by then. Watching the foam like lather being deposited on the sands as the sea flowed and ebbed, she rubbed her forearms. It was almost as a caress from Matthew.

This would be another November birth, but this one, she felt sure, was going to be Matthew junior. She had now convinced herself that this was the reason for the pill upsetting her, she was carrying the son they both craved.

Although bursting with excitement, she had decided to keep the news to herself. She would break it to Matthew on the night after the launch. There was to be a small party that night, but when she finally climbed into bed, she would whisper the news to him.

Her body seemed to love being pregnant as already she felt inspiration flow through her. Dragging herself reluctantly from the sea rail, she felt as though she was floating on her way back to the castle. Somehow she found she could begin to dispel the niggling doubts that had haunted her of late.

**

The day prior to the launch, Mark had been summoned to the hospital, where he had helped Sally to give birth to their son. Matthew was choked with emotion as he rung Debbie, "Darling, I have invited Mark over for a drink and a bite to eat. He's over the moon with his son. Paul is calling in and I suppose Irene will stay back. He needs s to share his joy, but we must have an early night, so we must!"

219

Replacing the receiver, she realised her hand was shaking. If Matthew was overjoyed with Mark's son, however would he react to one of his own? Tears of happiness stung her eyes, she knew that Matthew would have guessed, had he not been so busy. Bliss was hers, she would tell him tomorrow night.

Ellen had insisted they all eat with her and Jim. She had opened a couple of bottles of champagne, they had been for the party the following night, but could soon be replaced. The market research had shown that the new magazine would be welcomed and again life was full, even overflowing.

The whole evening was perfect, Mark could now relax and enjoy the launch, knowing his wife and son were safe. As Debbie's eyes rested on his youthful, happy face, she said emotionally, "I think Sally must have had a word with junior, sort of reminded him not to hang about!"

Mark bade them all a fond farewell. As he left the castle, an ethereal peace seemed to have settled. It was as if everyone's nerves had been on edge and at long last, the waiting was over, it was about to happen, yet an eerie tiredness claimed Debbie.

CHAPTER THIRTY EIGHT

Matthew's love that night seemed to have an even greater urgency. His arms had gathered her, "I'm so happy for Mark, so I am. It seems funny to have a little Matthew in the business!"

Trembling with ecstasy, she almost blurted out the news there and then. Yet after tomorrow, he would be able to absorb it to the full. His mind would be at peace and they could savour the joy slowly. Succumbing eagerly to him, their love seemed to reach out and find an unknown plateau. Quivering and panting tender words of love, they found they didn't know where one kiss ended before another began.

Morning arrived to find Matthew leaning over her. His hand gently brushed her body, bringing instant response from her. "Debs, let me love you before I leave," he groaned into the depth of her neck.

Crushing her to him, "Hell, Debs, I can't wait for tonight. It has been such a strain for you over the last few months. The way you turn your beautiful body to me sends me wild, so it does!"

She watched his sensual body as he slipped the knot in his tie into position, their eyes caught and held in the mirror, and her insides turned somersaults. "Matthew, I think I'm completely addicted to your love. I want you again already. Yet, looking at your smooth composure, nobody would guess the extent of your passion, but would envy me for being the one to receive it!"

"If they know you, they'd realise how easy you are to love!"

She giggled happily, "In the morning, you and I are going to stay in bed for two solid hours, before the children get up. Just think , we can make love without you having to leave me!"

His kiss was filled with hunger, "I must be off now, me darlin'. As you say tomorrow …, hell, I love ye, Debs. Can you be ready to start the party around six? If the kiddies are too much, I'll help, so I will!"

Dropping a kiss onto Emma's head, he was ready to leave. Her eyes misted as he closed the door behind him. Her throat constricted, how she loved him, how she longed for tonight, how she looked forward to the rest of their lives together.

She was jerked swiftly back to earth, Kelly got up with the miseries because her daddy had left too early to kiss her goodbye. That seemed to set Verity off and Debbie began to feel the pressure. Trying to control her anxieties, she said, "If you're good girls, Daddy will take you to school tomorrow. After today, he won't have to go to Preston anymore!"

Although she had spoken sharply, she had to turn away to resist chuckling at the two defiant little faces before her. Kelly still whined, "Mummy, will Daddy be home in time to read to us tonight?"

"Of course he will try, Kelly, but you are going to bed early. You'll have plenty of time with him over the weekend," she spoke firmly and ended the argument.

Paul rung around four, "Debbie, its been a huge success. They'll leave shortly and we'll meet round there about six. I think Matthew has just about had enough travelling, but they couldn't have managed without him. So many ideas were his!"

Giving a light hearted chuckle, "He has had enough, Paul and so have I. The children were quite naughty this morning, they miss him being here. Anyway, thank goodness it was all worthwhile. See you later!"

**

Jim left his office early, again they were to use his front room. Ironically, these occasions were planned for the boardroom, but nearly always ended being held downstairs. It was easier with the children's alarm system being set down there.

Entering the lounge, he rubbed his hands together, "I've come to offer my services. The table looks wonderful, Ellen, I suppose we can help Debbie with the children now!"

Ellen's copper head had turned to him, "Jim, I'm so relieved this is over, the strain is showing in Debbie as well as Matthew. Everything's ready, yes, we can help get the children to bed!"

After a hectic rush, the children were all settled and Debbie prepared to dress for the evening. She had chosen a pretty woollen suit and brushed her hair till it shone, leaving it loose, just as Matthew liked it.

Adding the merest hint of make up, she noticed the rich sparkle in her eyes. Matthew would surely guess if she wasn't careful. She had planned exactly when she would tell him and indeed, how. Shivering with a wild anticipation, she tripped down to join her parents and Irene.

Having rushed around so much, the lads were now late in arriving. Debbie began to feel a little edgy, although she realised that with them leaving early, they would undoubtedly catch the rush hour traffic.

At long last, the doorbell rang, Debbie jumped up smiling, "I bet he's forgotten his keys," she flung over her shoulder with fun. Running to the door, her heart raced with love and then almost stopped.

Standing before her, were two police officers. A young man and a woman officer, who asked, "Mrs Ross, may we come in?"

As she had spoken, she had taken Debbie's arm and led her to a chair. Her parents, together with Irene were at her side. The officer's voice was strained, "Mrs Ross, your husband's car has been in a serious accident. We are so sorry to bring this news, apparently the car is a total wreck!"

Debbie felt terror clutch at her heart as she almost screamed, "I don't care about the car. How bad is it? Where are they? I want to be with my husband!"

Jim's arm had gone around his daughter as the officer continued, "We believe the driver was killed instantly. One passenger is said to be in a serious condition, but we don't know any further details as yet. They've been taken to hospital!"

She heard a scream, realising it was her. "No, dear, God, make me wake up. I don't like this dream!"

Blinded by tears, she vaguely recalled saying, "Mum, listen for the kids, ask Paul to let Sally know he'll be late!"

In spite of the many arms trying to hold her, she just ran and ran, so fast she thought she would collapse. Not knowing where she was going, she just continued to run. Her mind was screaming, "No, not Matthew, what about his son? Not my beloved Matthew!"

On and on she ran, she couldn't stop, feeling that if she ran fast enough, it would all go away. She would not and could not live without Matthew, her whole being shook, till she could run no more. Collapsing onto the grass, she found herself back on that hill. Again she was staring across the bay, watching the sea, seeing the view she had never seen for exactly four years. She had been two months pregnant then.

**

The anger of the sea penetrated Debbie's fog like mind. Her own anger surged with the waves. Someone was screaming, "No, no," and it went on and on. Her body felt bruised, her mind severely battered. Time held no importance whatsoever, in fact, she doubted she knew this person at all.

A movement beside her made her jump, it was Paul. His voice shook, "I had a feeling you might be here, at least I prayed you would be!"

Slowly, he turned her to face him. She could see he had been crying, her throat felt raw, yet she felt like laughing hysterically. Paul had cried the last time they were here, her voice now hoarse, "What are *you* doing here?"

Paul had watched her before going over to her. Her screams had curdled his blood. He couldn't stand her pain, if only he could take some of it for her. His arms went around her, "Everyone is worried about where you could have gone. I told them that there was one last place you just might be. I don't know why, but I had to check!"

She sobbed in his arms as he stroked the hair from her face. He had placed his jacket around her shaking body. His voice was riddled with emotion, "Dearest one, we're not certain as to who was in fact killed yet. One person was killed instantly, one seems to be severely hurt and they are in Lancaster hospital!"

Feeling the anger of the sea again, she lashed out at him. "Well, they said the driver, Matthew *was* the bloody driver. I want to die with him, I can't live without him," she sobbed.

He held her tightly through the whole of the tirade and finally soothed her, albeit temporarily. Still holding her, he spoke quietly, "Debbie, I told the others that if I hadn't rung in about twenty minutes, they could assume that I'd found you and would take you home!"

Suddenly, she realised that the heaviness in her breast meant that she had missed Emma's feed. Paul's voice drifted in the wind, "Come on, dear, let me take you home. There could well be some more news. The children will need you, Debbie!"

She became transfixed as she remembered the promises to her children. They would never trust her again, but in spite of that she felt herself being led towards the car that Paul had parked at the bottom of the cliff.

Running indoors with Paul hot on her heels, she could hear Emma's screams. Ellen was pacing up and down with her. She looked dreadful, her eyes had become slits in a red puffy mass. Her voice croaked, "I've changed her, dear, you must feed her!"

Disregarding privacy, Debbie took the screaming bundle. Emma's little mouth searched and instinctively Debbie released her breast. Instantly the frenzied suckling began. Her arms felt like crushing her babe towards her as guilt flooded her, she had thought of no one but herself.

Her heart near to breaking, she watched the naked trust in the dear little face, hearing the milk running into her hungry little tummy, the urge to squeeze the infant almost overcame her, she wanted her to know she was sorry.

Finally, her eyes roamed the room. Mark was there, looking bruised and strained. "Does Sally know you're alright?" She rasped the words ungraciously as the soreness in her throat reminded her of the shouting she had done.

She felt like a spectator watching the tragedy that surrounded this little family. Jim took over, his face ashen, his eyes swollen, his voice reminded her of the time he had discussed Tony's condition with her. "Debbie, listen to me, dear, Matthew is still alive. His condition is very critical, his legs are badly crushed and at present he is in theatre!"

Realising she was about to get up, Jim held her, "Feed baby, dear, then Mum will put her down. The hospital will ring if there is any news. They want you to ring about five thirty. Apparently they will have a better picture when Matthew is out of theatre!"

Looking at his beloved face, Debbie could see he had been to hell and back himself. His velvet brown eyes were full, she loved him so much and found comfort from his nearness.

Stunned and totally confused, she heard Paul gasp, "Thank God, I'll stay with Debbie till she 'phones. I know she won't go to bed!"

How well he knew her, she thought once again as bewilderment registered. Her throat hurt as she spoke with hysteria, "Will someone tell me, what did bloody well happen?"

Mark's voice faltered, "Debbie, I was thrown clear and after treatment for shock and bruises, they allowed me to come home. I've been to see Sally. Honestly, it was dreadful ….!"

Fighting not to scream at the disorientated lad, she gulped, "Who's dead then?"

Still riddled with shock, Mark tried, "We were driving along, all of us happy with the world, when a huge truck skipped the lights. Matthew had no time whatsoever to stop. Vanessa is definitely dead, I think for a while they thought she was a third male, her trouser suit …!"

He broke off and Debbie could see he was distraught with grief. Vanessa was a wonderful person, mercifully she had no dependents. How dreadful that such a potentially wonderful day had ended in tragedy.

Hearing Paul's gasp, Debbie instinctively knew that he and Vanessa had been more than work mates. Although she was quite a bit older than him, they had obviously been close at work. That must have spilled over as they could manage to fulfil each others' sexual needs. She shivered, Paul must be feeling gutted.

Paul walked over to sit beside her on the settee, her eyes held the apology for his loss. She seemed to know he had never loved Vanessa, nor she him, but they had been good together, of that she *was* sure. How was he going to manage, work or play without her? She was a very endearing person, yet right now, Debbie needed his strength.

Mark stood up to leave, "I'm dreadfully saddened by today. Please let me know how Matthew is? Don't worry, Paul, I'll go into Preston tomorrow!"

Taking his car keys from his pocket, Paul threw them to Mark, "Take my car, old chap, Debbie and I will use the chauffeur. I'll get on to Don Prescott to stand in for me here!"

Numbness reared again, as she realised, Don was another young protégé that Paul was ready to release, but right now, she needed his comfort and he also needed hers.

Irene sat still, riddled with bitter shock. Jim saw Mark off and returned, "I think we could all use a drink," he stated and commenced to pour. Debbie downed hers and felt it hit her stomach with a thud. Irene did the same and added, "I think I'll get myself home, ring Alma and we'll both return about six. The press will be onto this and we can answer their many questions!"

Jim rallied, "That would be a tremendous help, Irene, but I would rather you went home by cab. It'll take enormous pressure from us, knowing you are safe!"

Placing Emma onto her shoulder, Debbie rubbed her back automatically. Her voice still unbearable hoarse, "I think we should notify Richard, he'll be up around four thirty. I'd hate Jenny to hear the news, either over the radio or in the papers. At least Richard can tell her gently!"

Paul's eyes fell on her, she never ceased to amaze him, here she was in the middle of her own crises, worrying about Jenny and her baby. Irene walked over to kiss them both goodnight, "I'll be back around six, I'll pray as never before," she gulped and left.

Ellen came over and took the sleeping babe from her, "I will put her down, dear. Jim, I think we should sleep upstairs, just in case the children waken," she sighed heavily.

To everyone's horror, Debbie began to laugh uncontrollably, "I promised the girls that Matthew would take them to school. Mum, they must go, if I'm called to the hospital, perhaps you could let them think that I've gone to meet him. Well, I will have done, won't ....!"

Her voice broke as the laughing turned to tears, "Tonight was to have been so special. I was going to tell him that, th .. that we are going to have another baby in November. This time I know it's a boy, he'll be so ..!"

Jim's hands held her shoulders firmly. "Debbie, stop it, you'll make yourself ill. Are you sure about the babe, why didn't you tell Matthew?"

Spluttering helplessly, "Of course I'm sure, Dad. Tonight had so much for s all, I was going to wait till after the party. Normally, he would have guessed, but he was so tired. I I longed for to …, to …, tonight," the sob caught in her throat.

Jim turned to Paul and gripped his hand, "If you need us, come and get us, Paul. I agree with Ellen, we will sleep in Debbie's room!"

**

Having hugged their daughter, Jim led his wife up to Debbie and Matthew's flat. Watching her place Emma into the cot, his mind flew back to when she had first placed Debbie into her cot. His arms were waiting for her now, as they had been then.

Holding her shaking body, he stroked the flame coloured hair. Tears filled her eyes as they lifted to him, "Jim, what have we done, darling? First we lose Tony, then have to watch Debbie handle her break up with Paul and now this!"

Choking with hurt himself, he whispered, "Ellie, we've done nothing wrong, dear. Both of our children were born out of and into love. We have four gorgeous grandchildren and another one on the way. I didn't say much to Debbie tonight, but I think poor old Matthew's chances are dreadfully narrow. Hell, it'll just about crucify her."

He felt Ellen's body crumble into him. Her tear stained face lifted, her mouth sought his. Their love was so beautifully familiar, and for a while at least, they could lose themselves to the misery around them.

**

Somehow, Debbie guessed what was taking place upstairs. At least she felt gratitude knowing that her parents could find a deep solace within themselves. She obviously took after them, it was the way she handled her own life.

Right now though, there was just Paul and herself, both of them left to try and make some sort of sense out of the totally uninvited and thoroughly unwelcome nightmare that had descended upon them.

Paul poured them both a drink and handed one to her. She broke down again, this time with relief that Matthew was still alive. How closely linked were those two impostors, happiness and grief. Both seemed to cause tears to be shed.

Again Paul held her, "Try not to cry anymore, Debbie, it'll make you ill, my precious. We'll ring the hospital at five thirty and somehow I feel he'll be alright, I couldn't sleep till we know!"

"How did you know where to look? I'd never thought of where I was going. I just landed there. I haven't been there since …," her voice trailed away.

"Since I let you down, is that what you mean, Debbie?"

He walked up and down, his face looked haunted as he added, "That was the only place I could think of. I'd been all around Morecambe and felt frantic with worry. Thank God, I was right. You could have caught pneumonia out there!"

Debbie watched as he paced, the relief of finding her was now crystal clear. She then remembered something else, "Paul, I'm so sorry about Vanessa, you and she were .., special, weren't you?"

"*She* was special, Debbie. Neither of us wanted commitment, but we both needed sex. That sounds crude, doesn't it? But that was how we both saw our relationship. I'll miss her dreadfully, both at work and play!"

She saw him grimace at the memory and sadness filled her. His voice was strained, "She was the first woman since you, Debbie. We trusted each other and somehow ended up as lovers, she was filled with warmth and I had a deep regard for her," he sighed.

"Paul, forgive me, I had no right to ask!"

For a moment, silence had fallen. He then turned to her, "Debbie, if we had lost Matthew tonight, would you have allowed me to stand in for him, as he did for me? I've never stopped loving you, but then, you know that!"

Feeling giddy under his gaze, not to mention the drink, she noted his face, he was a devastatingly handsome man. How cruel he must have thought she had been, "Paul, it was never like you make it sound!"

Taking her glass, he refilled it with his own and gulped, "Debbie, when I last saw you on that hill, you were pregnant, weren't you? I just didn't give you a chance to speak. I feel so darned guilty and sad. Why didn't you tell me? Debbie, I truly wouldn't have gone!"

"You had to, Paul, we had no ammunition against dear Amanda and the magazine, anyway its in the past!"

Her body began to shake again. The drink went straight down, she felt it warm her. Refilling her glass, she realised she rather liked this feeling of floating. She didn't really want to tell him. Yet it did need to be sorted out and she knew, Paul already knew.

Tossing her head defiantly, she added, "Paul, whatever you feel, Matthew adores his children. To me, a father is the one that brings the child up!"

He looked shocked, hurt, his eyes filled, "Debbie, you don't think I would tell anyone? I love you and Matthew too much. But, I do know, that Kelly is my flesh and blood. Why ever didn't you tell me?"

Had he shown anger, even spite, she could have coped with that. She felt wretched, he had known for a long time and not once tried to cause trouble. He was a dear person and it must have hurt him. It can't have been easy for him, watching the sheer adoration from Kelly to Matthew.

He choked, "I can understand why you love Matthew so much. I watched the film of Emma's birth over and over, I saw the strength you drew from one another. I wondered how he must have felt, going through all of that, for someone else's child!"

Swirling the amber liquid around his glass, he continued, "I broke my heart as I watched, just wondering if I could have been so supportive. Worse still, I wondered how the hell you would have managed alone!"

Tears ran down his cheeks and desperately needing to comfort him, she placed her arms around him. His lips found hers, this kiss was frenzied and full of bottled up emotion. Her body shook with his, his breathing was rapid as his hand began to caress her body. Again his mouth found hers, rushing her back to four years ago.

Her heart pounded as to her shame, she found herself responding, feeling a thrill run through her. The aggressive invasion of his tongue, only served to remind her that he had been the first man to have known her intimately.

Totally lost in the past, she remembered how she had loved these kisses, yearned for these caresses. Fire shot through her, "Darling, Debs, I love you!"

Suddenly, a dreadful confusion swamped her. She wanted this man, but he was not Matthew. Her body writhed for him as she realised with horror, just what she was doing. With a strangled gasp, she pulled away, in much the same manner, he let go of her and broke down completely.

Sobbing bitterly, he gulped, "Debbie, why didn't you smack my face? That's what I deserve, I wanted you so desperately and felt that need in you. But in your mind I was Matthew. Darling, please forgive me, it was as if we had never been parted. That was how we eased our pain after Tony's funeral. And that, my love, was when you fell for Kelly, wasn't it?"

His body was racked with sobs, Debbie just held him, "Paul, I was going to tell you. All during that particular day, my heart had sung and I couldn't wait for your love that evening. In fact, I remember, I was the instigator so great was my happiness. After we made love, I turned my head to whisper the news, but you jumped up and ... Paul, I'm truly sorry!"

She could feel her body shaking as he stared into space. They had meant so much to each other in the past. Right now, she knew their emotions were in a state of devastation, both needing comfort, both turning naturally to the other. His eyes held hers, "Please tell me what did happen that night. Matthew did tell me he would try and court you, he had loved you from the start!"

Shock at her behaviour still filled her. Granted she had drunk too much, granted she had once been in love with Paul, but what the hell had turned her on? She had needed to feel safe, perhaps she was made that way, yet she would have died had she betrayed her beloved Matthew.

Finally, she sat down and drew her knees up under her chin and placed her arms around them. She told Paul the whole story and saw the stark emotion choking him as he gulped, "We would have been happy, Debbie!"

Sensing his urgency to be reassured, she knew this was all better out than in. "We would have been happy, Paul, but I would never have known Matthew's love. You were the first man to awaken my love, teaching me how to love and I never stopped loving you, I still do, but I told Matthew all of that. I locked your love away deep into my heart.

He pulled her back into his arms, "I'm so glad you told me, Debbie. You were the first woman I ever loved and you will always be the last!"

Her husband was in hospital, yet she could feel Paul's need as his body shook uncontrollably. In spite of her disgust with herself, she let him kiss her again, remembering the sincerity of his love. This time, the kiss lingered and broke off. He held her gently to him and she knew, the danger point had been met and passed.

This should all have been discussed before and she knew it. Seeing her confusion, he ruffled her hair, "I have a secret love and a secret daughter, that'll do for me and thanks for telling me everything, Debbie!"

Debbie had to admit she did feel better for their talk. It had put a lot of things into perspective and had taken some of the strain from the never ending night. Somehow a strange calm had hovered over them, leaving them in companionable silence.

CHAPTER THIRTY NINE

Debbie felt her heart rush into her throat as the shrill ringing of the telephone broke into the silence. Her

Whole being shook as she lifted the receiver, Paul was beside her as the voice explained, "Mrs Ross, could you come along to the hospital? Your husband is floating in and out of consciousness and his condition is critical. The doctor will be waiting for you!"

Words formed on her lips and stayed there. Paul, having heard the voice, took the 'phone, "We'll be there immediately, thank you!"

He gripped her shoulders, "Debbie, go and rinse your face, I'll pour us a quick coffee and ask the chauffeur to pick us up. It would be unwise to waken your parents, we'll leave a note, after all, we could well have some more news later!"

She felt herself being propelled into the bathroom, noticing Paul swish water over his face. He forced the scalding coffee into her tight lips, the warmth hitting her stomach and bringing her back down to earth.

Fear clutched her heart, the night was dark and dreadfully eerie, with a quietness that terrified her. Paul's hand clung to hers as the car finally pulled up in front of the hospital. Vaguely, she felt herself walking down a never ending corridor and a kindly doctor taking her arm, "Ah, Mrs Ross, come into my office!"

The rasping voice couldn't have been hers, "I want to see my husband. Where is he? What have you done to him?"

Everything seemed to be swaying. Paul's voice drifted in from afar, "Doctor, I'm Paul Howarth, a close family friend. I would like to stay with Mrs Ross, perhaps you could tell us the state of Matthew's condition?"

Sitting in the huge leather chair, Debbie felt herself shrinking. Terror filled her as the doctor's voice came to her. "Mr Ross was trapped into the car, his legs were badly crushed. We think we have managed to save one leg, but the other one had to be amputated!"

A strange feeling of being outside and looking in had gripped her. The chair seemed to be growing bigger as she tried like a child to get down. Paul's hand squeezed hers as he asked earnestly, "Doctor, is he going to pull through?"

"Mr Howarth, he also had severe internal injuries. We have worked on him since he was admitted, but he is still haemorrhaging. He is literally drifting in and out of consciousness. I'm so sorry, we have done all we can for the moment. The next twenty four hours could be vital!"

"I want to see my husband," said Debbie flatly.

Apparently the doctor nodded to Paul and turned to Debbie, "Mrs Ross, we are deeply saddened by this. Your husband has been asking for you, but he needs you to be brave. He doesn't realise that he has lost his leg, not yet.

You're a very brave young lady, but tonight, you must play the role of a lifetime," he added kindly.

Balling her hands with a new determination, she managed to stand up. Her head had begun to clear as she turned to Paul, "I would like you to come with me, Paul. Thank you very much, Doctor, I'll tell Matthew nothing, apart from good news!"

Paul watched with alarm, she had not broken down, but had gone into an icy calmness that frightened him. Arriving outside of the sideward, her head was erect, her composure seemingly total. He felt violently sick at what they had to face, again she amazed him.

Debbie stood as though transfixed in the doorway. Her mind slowly absorbed the machinery that was plugged into the man on the bed. Bleeps were coming from the machines and drips filled his arms. In a flash, she was at his side and feeling a chair pushed behind her, she sat down. Paul could only gasp and walk over to the window.

Finding a space that didn't contain a drip, she squeezed his arm, "Matthew, darling, I'm here," she gulped as the heavily bandaged head moved slightly. His eyes flickered into awareness, his voice barely a whisper, "Debbie, darlin', I'm so sorry about this, so I am. Did Paul bring you, dearest?"

"Yes, darling, don't worry, just rest and recover!"

Paul could not check the tears that flowed from his eyes as again he heard Matthew, "Debs, you gave me the happiest four years of my life, so ye did ... If ever you want to marry again, it'll be with my blessing. You were born to be loved ...," he struggled.

"Sshhshh, rest, darling. You will get better, you have to. Darling, I had some very special news for you tonight!"

Her voice was suddenly strong, as though charged with a new found energy. Matthew ran the tip of his tongue over his gorgeous lips, "I know, darling. I think I guessed last night. You're pregnant, aren't you? ... Debs, I always know how much you need to be loved when you're p pregnant ... Dearest one, I've let you down, I won't be there!"

"Matthew Ross, don't you dare say that to me. You have never ducked anything in your life, the children need you, I need you. Anyway, I'm sure this is a boy. I did make you a promise that we would have a son, didn't I?"

For a brief moment, she saw an attempted smile around his sensual lips. A heavy sigh left him, as he gasped, "Debs, Debs, ... Debbie ....!"

The machines rose into a long pitched bleep. Staff rushed in to surround Matthew and moved her away. Paul had been asked to take her outside. She watched with horror, "Do something, he isn't ready to leave yet. He has so many people waiting for him, our children, ..., do something!"

Her impassioned pleas rung in the air as Paul led her into the annex type room, sat her down and lit her a cigarette. There was a police officer in there, he stood hastily to proffer change for the vending machine. He asked Paul about Vanessa, she heard his tormented reply, "Yes, I'm prepared to identify the body, she had no relatives!"

Suddenly the door burst open, gravity filled the face of the doctor. "I'm so very sorry, Mrs Ross, but Matthew has slipped away. One good thing to remember, he did know that you were with him at the end. Please accept out deepest sympathies!"

"Thank you, Doctor, I know you did all you could," came her stunned tone of acceptance.

Vaguely, she remembered signing some papers. Paul had broken down completely with the news. Once he had composed himself a little, the officer asked him to accompany him to the mortuary.

Paul was absolutely shattered as he went to the icy cold place. Gazing down on Vanessa's body, he almost screamed at the mess that lay before him. It was impossible to remember that such a short few hours earlier, her body had been filled with vibrant life as they had indulged in a heavy dose of sex, prior to her leaving for Preston.

By the time he returned to Debbie, he looked ill and haggard. His body shook with shock and sorrow. Taking his hand, she gasped, "I'm so sorry, Paul!"

The knock on the door heralded the arrival of a porter, "Excuse me, Sir, I thought you would wish to know that the press are outside!"

Turning to Paul, she explained that Matthew had died just after four and as it was nearing five, they should get home. Her voice still strong, "Mum and Dad should be told by us. If the media know, it won't take long to let the rest of the world know. Come on, Paul, the children will be up and somehow, …, somehow," her voice trailed away.

Reaching the huge exit doors, Paul opened them. Flashes from the many photographers as the first indication that the television crews had arrived. Debbie allowed herself to sink into Paul's strong chest, feeling his protective arm slide around her waist. Questions were hurled from every direction, "Debbie, will you carry on working? How bad was the crash?"

Paul's voice raised in anger and grief, "Leave her alone, for God's sake. Her husband has just passed away, she needs some rest. She is also two months pregnant, now please let us through!"

Instantly, he realised that he couldn't have said anything worse. Microphones were pushed into their faces, "Is it true that you are pregnant again? When did you first hear of the accident?"

The police then eased everyone back as she felt her legs carrying her to the car. Arriving home, they found much more of the same. Finally though, they were inside, closing the door and she leaned heavily onto it.

**

Turning to Paul, she inhaled deeply, "We'll wait down here till Mum brings Emma down. You put the coffee on and I'll ring Richard, I couldn't bear Jenny to hear the news via the media!"

Reaching for the receiver, her hand shook as she dialled the number. Hearing Richard's cheery voice nearly broke her, "Debbie, it must have been some party over there, are you just going to bed?"

"Richard, I'm sorry, but I have some tragic news for you both. The media already have the story, but I want you to tell Jenny quietly!"

Goosebumps spread over her, "Richard, I've just come back from the hospital with Paul. Matthew lost his fight for life at four fifteen!"

Hearing the choking gulp and the spluttered question, her heart went out to him, "What fight for life? Christ, Debbie, what the 'ell are ye talkin' about? Bloody 'ell, I thought you said, … , it sounded like Matthew was dead!"

She fought for control as she briefly told him the details, "I didn't want either of you to hear it on the news, especially Jenny. Please tell her gently, Richard!"

He sniffled as the tears broke from him, "Is there ought we can do, Debbie? I can't believe this, Jenny won't believe this. Christ, Debbie, I'm so very sorry!"

"I know, Richard, see you soon!"

Replacing the receiver, she noticed the white of her knuckles where she had gripped it so hard. She walked over to the table, Paul had brought in a tray of coffee, with several mugs and was quietly sobbing on the settee.

Hearing the familiar footsteps of her parents approaching, she braced herself. Jim carried Emma in one arm, his other arm around his wife. Debbie looked at them, they were both ashen, their eyes heavy with pain.

Ellen's eyes lifted, "Have you rung yet, dear?"

With a composure she had never know, she took Emma and began to feed her. Jim came over, "Debbie, haven't you rung yet? I mean, its gone five thirty, dear," he gulped and rested his hand onto her shoulder.

"Dad, there is some coffee on the table. We have just come back, I told Matthew about the baby, he was pleased, in fact, he had guessed. I begged him to stay, but he had to leave!"

A strangled yelp left Ellen, "Do you mean? .. Oh, Paul, tell us," she demanded. Paul finally summoned enough strength to stand, "Debbie has been like this since he died. The reporters were outside of the hospital, it will be on the news. We received a call around three!"

His voice had broken as he told them of the situation and added, "Ellen, they had so much, I felt I was an intruder in their own intimate little paradise!"

Jim took Ellen into his arms as the three of them broke down badly. Debbie watched Emma, her little face breaking into smiles as she suckled contentedly. Whatever was she going to say to Kelly and Verity? Lucy was a little young to understand, but old enough to know that something was radically wrong.

Irene and Alma arrived, both of them breaking down as the news continued to unfold. Debbie was the only one not to cry. She couldn't, her heart was frozen. Paul turned on the radio to catch the news. The announcer's voice was crystal clear,

"The happy reign of the perfect couple from Lancashire ended tragically just a few hours ago. Matthew Ross was involved in a serious road accident

last evening. Vanessa Fairclough, close friend and fellow worker was killed instantly, they were travelling home after the successful launch of the Miss Kelly magazine in Preston. Matthew died early this morning after surgeons had worked tirelessly to save his life.

His wife, Debbie Hudson, was at his bedside. He leaves a wife and four children. It is being widely reported that Miss Hudson is at present pregnant again. The couple shot to fame....!"

It seemed to go on and on, relating to their past history and success, until Paul reached out his hand and switched it off.

There was much discussion, but Debbie decided they would all stay together for the rest of the day. Irene and Alma would field the questions as best the could, Paul would shower and use one of Matthew's clean shirts, meanwhile she would have to tell her children.

Paul went into shower as her footsteps faltered. She remembered this was the morning she and Matthew were to have stayed in bed, made wild delicious love as they celebrated the child she now carried. Her body burned for his love, she should be in his arms right now, feeling his hands caress her body. How she wanted him, in her arms, in her bed, inside of her, her need so real, she felt tiny orgasms gathering in hr secret passage, the very passage that Matthew had made his own and craved for his manhood.

She heard Kelly and Verity, not only wide awake, but arguing. "Daddy is taking us to school, Mummy said he would," came Kelly's authoritative voice.

Seeing Debbie, they ran to her, "Isn't Daddy taking us to school?" They asked in unison as nausea swept her.

"Now, I want you both to sit down and listen carefully. You know all about Jesus and his pretty home in heaven, don't you?"

"Yes, Mummy," came the wide eyed response.

Looking at Verity was like looking at Matthew and momentarily, Debbie closed her eyes against her children as she inhaled deeply, "Jesus has a very special home in heaven and sometimes he allows someone very special .., to go and live with him. Daddy has gone to live with him and he asked me to hug you both!"

Weakness made her giddy as she sat down on the bed. Kelly screamed, "I don't want my Daddy to live with Jesus," and her blue eyes spilled over. "I want my Daddy," shouted Verity.

Debbie just sat there, exhaustion her companion, both children were sobbing as their eyes filled with accusations, "Why did you let Daddy go without us?"

Paul had come from the shower, pausing so as not to disturb her. Yet again, he felt tears spring to his eyes. He could feel Debbie's pain, feel the children's torment. There was no way in which they could really understand, they just wanted to see their father. Walking into the room, Kelly ran to him, "Uncle, Paul, you tell Mummy not to let Daddy go!"

His eyes met Debbie's grief stricken eyes. She had not taken the news in herself yet and was explaining it to her little ones, with a calm that amazed him. If only she would break down, kick the furniture, throw something, anything to relieve the bottled up pain.

They sobbed with Paul until Jim joined them. Again their impassioned pleas were hurled at him. He choked, "I'll take Lucy down for her breakfast, dear. If the children can manage school, they would be just as well off, the atmosphere is filled with deep sadness!"

Finally, with Paul's help, she managed to persuade them to go to school. Irene took them, explaining to the teacher the wretched circumstances that had befallen them. Jim looked up, "What are we going to do about funeral arrangements? Did Matthew leave a Will, dear? Hell, Debbie, I'm so infernally sorry!"

Her smile was sardonic, "Being a man of law, I'm sure he left one. In fact he made one for us both, simply stating that everything went to the partner, with even sums of money to add to the little ones' trust funds. He also wanted to be cremated, its upstairs somewhere!"

Realising what was soon to happen, she gulped, "Whatever happens, there is no way in which I will permit the children to attend. I want them to remember Matthew as he was, not in an unfamiliar, ugly box. Perhaps one of the cooks will stay with them!"

Paul shook from head to foot. "I'll make the arrangements with Jim's help. We'll also have to make some for Vanessa, I'm sure she preferred cremation. Hell, the soddin' price we pay for success, is it damned well worth it?"

Debbie rounded on him, "Paul, how dare you? We all wanted to be successful together. Matthew loved us all and would be desperately saddened if he thought we would let it all slip away. My reason for carrying on will be for him, his children and just about everyone who relies on us for a living!"

Ellen broke down again, "Debbie is right, Matthew would never want to see us like this. I'm also sure that he would want Vanessa's funeral alongside his!"

The telephones were now ringing non stop. Reporters had been round for various statements and Paul turned to Debbie, "What do you want me to tell them, Debbie?"

"I don't know, Paul. We must never forget it was the public that gave us our success. We owe them and the media, perhaps we can prepare a statement together, it will take the pressure off, at least for a while."

Her hand had gone us to massage her throbbing temple. Paul clung to her, "Debbie, please cry, this is going to make you ill, you have so much on your shoulders. I'm sure Brian will pop in shortly and give you something to ease your pain!"

"I can't afford to sleep, Paul. You saw the state of the kiddies earlier, I have no reason to think they will be any better when they return. In fact, I will probably have to go over it all again. You were a rock for them and I could use that strength, just for a few days, Paul!"

Eric Morgan sat stunned as he heard the tragic news. It was inconceivable to think of Vanessa being dead. She had given his late wife so much, made him realise he had married a diamond, albeit too damned late.

His eyes misted as he listened to the tragedy that had befallen the Hudson family. Since the death of Maralyn, he had drifted from bar to bar, drowning his guilt, finding someone to shag mercilessly and allowed himself to sink so low, it seemed impossible to climb up again.

He had placed the magnificent penthouse in Blackpool up for sale. Too many painful memories lurked and his ultimate idea was to move to London and make a hit of his last magazine base. Amanda had left and gone to New Zealand, promising never to contact him again and at the time that had suited him fine.

Several urgent messages had come from his last magazine, yet he had failed to act. That was until a certain black haired woman, in her late thirties, had appeared at his apartment door. Her manner was brusque, as she made her point, "If you don't come down to London and pull your weight, Eric, you might as well sell up and let someone else, who does care, take over. What's it to be, are you with us? Or are you going to continue to handicap our venture?"

She glared so hard, he wanted to chuckle at the defiance. He had only met her once before and had not taken in the charms of Rebecca North. Her black eyes pierced his as her sensual, full lips, had delivered the ultimatum. Her voluptuous breasts rose and fell with beauty, beneath the tight fitting, low cut, little black dress.

Eric felt himself harden with annoying rapidity as his eyes dropped to Rebecca's feet. They were dainty in the black court shoes, her slim ankles were the start of her shapely legs and without realising what he was doing, Eric found himself pouring them both a drink and watched the sophisticated way she sat herself onto the settee, folding her legs as a model.

She raised a heavy, black eyebrow and asked, "Well now, Eric, what are we going to do about this magazine? I'm prepared to work by your side day and night, but I'll not take kindly to being messed about. If you have nowhere to live in London, you're welcome to a room in my apartment, at least till you find somewhere. So, what's it to be then, cos I sure as hell want no more messing about?"

Even as she had spoken, Rebecca had seen the shapely bulge in Eric's trousers. She had heard about his reputation and being a sexually demanding person herself, somehow fancied making it with this man, whilst saving her job and security at the same time.

Mopping his brow with his handkerchief, he tried to cross his legs and without warning spluttered, "Fair enough, Rebecca, we'll mess about together!"

He never knew what to expect, but it was nothing compared to her next move. Rising slowly to her feet, she began to remove her clothing. He fell backwards in his chair and placed his hand over his throbbing cock. Her dress was folded over the settee, followed by the rest of the flimsy underwear.

Rebecca was no new comer to this game and noted his eyes roaming her body. Her skin was pearly cream, her breasts full and firm, with rich brown rigid nipples. She placed her hands onto her hips, gyrating them with tantalising seduction and eased her black nest of curls for him to view. "Don't you fancy what you see?"

Eric had become transfixed as he stared at the feast of delights before him and then she was riding him. Her head was thrown back and he could see all of her, the pulse that beat in her neck, the sumptuous nipples, the slim abdomen and the forest of curls that had taken his cock and secreted it.

They had been together since that night. He had moved to London, where they now lived together, neither of them wanting marriage. A few months later, he had heard from Amanda, via the magazine, she had written to tell him how sorry she was, informing him she had married a New Zealand rancher and was learning to shear sheep. Apparently her new husband had been widowed and left with two young sons, they had taken to Amanda and most surprisingly, she had fallen for them. Her letter had ended with an invitation for him to visit and bring a friend along.

Life had taken a great turn for the better and once again, Eric found his life to be full. He had earned respect amongst his peers and Rebecca had promised him, if he dared stray and behave as he had with Maralyn, he would be on his own.

After his brief reverie, he bowed his head with sorrow. He would attend the funeral services and offer his heartfelt, very sincere condolences to Debbie, Paul and everyone in the sad household.

**

Debbie had been right, the children did need further reassurances. It was almost farcical, but their little faces held real accusation. Somehow they believed that she had agreed to the departure of their Daddy. That fact alone tore at her heartstrings, yet she could understand as they were used to Matthew and herself always agreeing.

Paul had given the statement over to the press. He looked shocked and ill as he came back indoors. "I've arranged with Don Prescott to take over for a few days, Debbie, he knows what he's doing. Funny thing you know, only yesterday, Matthew had suggested we train him with a view to opening up again in New York!"

"Paul, if that's what Matthew suggested, we should try and do it. He knew what he was doing and had so many ideas. I don't know how I can .. cope!"

A grief stricken Brian called and left some medication for Debbie, his eyes filled as he tried to say at least something comforting, but there was nothing.

After popping into the office and noticing an offer from Australia, Debbie felt the need to be alone. Matthew had always spoken of visiting down under and the offer hurt, although she didn't go into any detail.

237

The children were having tea with her parents, Paul had gone to pick up some clothing and once more that dreadful fear hovered, the unease had been with her for months had actually gone yesterday. At least she thought it had gone, but no, it still lurked in her mind and she doubted she would ever be the same again.

CHAPTER FORTY

Hank Marcovitze walked into his office and poured himself a scalding hot coffee. He automatically turned on his television set, his job more or less demanding he keep his eye on the news. Suddenly, he became riveted as he heard the tragedy of Matthew's death.

Swapping his coffee for a stiff drink, he stared in horror as he watched Debbie emerge from the hospital. Paul looked dreadful as he tried to protect her from the press. She seemed so frail, his eyes filled as he heard the statement, telling the world of her last moments with Matthew.

His fingers ran through his hair as a desperate need to hold her entered him. He couldn't bear her pain, his body shuddered with shame, he had envied Matthew, been blindly jealous of him, "Dear, God, forgive me," he shouted to the empty room.

The news bulletin was flashing through some of their past successes. His eyes fixed on her lovely smile, her hair bobbing in the breeze, her body heavy with child, her body slim and sensual. Yet always her eyes beheld her husband with love and no one could have doubted his love for her. A lump landed in his throat as he could bear no more and knocking back the last of his drink, he kicked the television off, unable to listen.

He would fly over for the funeral and offer any help he could. Then sneered at himself, what did he think he could do to ease her pain? Lighting a cigarette, he walked over to the telephone. Was it his place to ring her? Had he the right to intrude into her private grief? Would she feel better to know she was dearly loved over here?

Questions tumbled about his mind, like acrobats in a circus. He had been offered a good network position in Britain and was due to leave to discuss it in a month or so. If he could get them to agree, he could possibly bring the talks forward.

Hank knew only too well that Debbie was surrounded by loved ones, but needed to see for himself that she was indeed alright. Somehow, he couldn't see her getting over this. Oh, damnation, he almost cried out, 'was she being punished for *his* mental infidelity? Would she ever forgive him for loving her? Would she turn to Paul?' Hell, she knew nothing of the workings of his mind and right now, they mystified *him*.

Without further thought, he dialled her private number. It would probably have an answer machine on, or someone else would reply, but he needed to speak with England, that would bring her just a little closer. His heart almost broke as he heard her voice.

The receiver seemed to be alight in his hand as he heard the authority in her voice. If only he could hold her, soothe her, dear oh, lor, his body had become aroused and burned with longing. Resisting the urge to hang up till he could compose himself, he gasped, "Debbie!"

"Hank, golly you must be a mind reader. I've been downstairs all day, this is the first time I've come up to our flat!"

He could sense the icy calm in her. His breathing became laboured, "Debbie, honey, gee, Debbie, I've just heard the news. Hell, honey, I sure am sorry. Is there anything I can do? I guess I just needed to let you know that we are all saddened over here!"

Her voice shook a little, "Thank you, Hank, I think this has shocked everyone. As you say, it's very comforting to know that you are thinking of us. How are you?"

"Debbie, I thought I would fly over for the funeral," he added lamely.

"If you do come over, you can stay with us. We'll all be pleased to see you," a sob caught in her throat.

"How have the children taken the news, Debbie?"

"Hell, Hank, they see me as Judas. Bless them, they can't understand why I agreed to let Matthew go without us.

Hank shuddered, realising she hadn't accepted this herself. "Debbie, I was due to come over in a month or so. I've been offered a network in Manchester. I was going to chat things over and if all went well, I would have moved to England later in the year, maybe early next year!"

Anger with himself smothered him. He was trying to move to avoid seeing her and Matthew, making sure he was out of the country for their next visit. What a selfish bastard he felt, yet here he was prattling on about his own future, while her heart was breaking. Her response nearly floored him, "Hank, that is wonderful news, it would be great to have you over here!"

"Debbie, the plan was for me to travel back with you all next year, shoot the series we had planned, covering both countries at once, but sadly, in the light of such sad news, that will all change," he was babbling, not knowing how to offer comfort, now knowing he would make sure he *was* around if she did come back.

Her voice strengthened, "Why, Hank? Matthew would never accept us not fulfilling our engagements, although I must admit, I'm very muddled at the moment!"

Everything suddenly began to overwhelm her. She felt her body begin to shake again. Nausea filled her again as she thought, 'how kind of Hank to take the trouble to ring and offer help'. Like a flash it hit her, "Hank, you know the plaque we were to unveil? I ... I don't want it to be the Debbie Hudson unit. .. I want it in memory of my husband, could you sort that out for me?"

Her pain reached him, "Debbie, that is the least I can do, honey. For what its worth, I think it would be a wonderful Idea. You sure sound calm, you haven't broken down yet, have you?"

"Hank, I must go now, see you soon, we'll let you know about the funeral," she gasped as the line went dead. Hank wrung his hands, why of why did she have to suffer?

**

240

For the next few days, Debbie found herself deluged with work. Her children were gradually accepting that Matthew had gone away. There had been so many people around them to give comfort and love, they were beginning to settle, albeit slowly.

Each night she had drunk some wretched medicine that had knocked her out as soon as she had fed Emma. Paul slept in the spare room, near to her, just in case she wakened or her children needed comfort.

His need to hold her became unbearable, but he hadn't dared to go near to her. He also threw himself back into work, his misery intensified by the loss of Vanessa. Messages of sympathy were arriving thick and fast and in spite of Debbie asking for donations to be made to the hospitals, instead of flowers, they were both pouring in.

The eve of the funeral arrived, Hank arrived and would stay in Ellen and Jim's spare room. It was a most peculiar span of time, moments when everything was normal as always and then the events of the last few days would flood around them, releasing every sensation under the sun.

During that evening, they had all spoken of Hank's subsequent move to England. He had managed to fit in his talks and they had gone much better than he had dared to hope.

Sipping her drink, Debbie asked, "Where do you live now, Hank?"

"I've got a penthouse in New York, but I'll sell it. We also have a gorgeous, rambling home in Nevada. My parents live there and I pop over to see them whenever possible!"

She realised how well she knew him, yet knew nothing of his personal life. She watched the easy way he settled into the lounge chair, almost as if he belonged there and she sighed, "I bet they'll miss you, if you do come to England, but then, they can always visit, especially when we have the flat over Mum's done up!"

"We must get that job done," interjected Paul.

Hank watched her parents, he could see they were deeply concerned for their daughter. It was almost as though nothing had happened. He had held the children prior to them going to bed and felt the warmth and trust from their little bodies, yet Debbie's lovely eyes were dead in her ashen face.

**

Paul wandered into the garden, the sadness suffocating him. Hank went over to him, "Hell, Paul, has she broken down at all? She must be wound up like a fuckin' clock inside. I dread the spring breaking, she sure will fall apart big time!"

Digging his hands deeply into his pocket, Paul responded, "Hank, we're all worried sick about her. In fact I've done everything possible to make her break down. She sobbed on the night it happened, whilst we were waiting to hear from the hospital, but then, this icy calm settled. Her parents are worried sick, so are Irene and Alma. My only hope is that she is holding herself in check till after the funeral!"

"I sure wish I was here to catch her, Paul!"

241

Paul smiled wryly, "I know Hank, fortunately, I will be here. You're in love with her too, aren't you, Hank?"

"Yup, there sure is no doubt about that, Paul. I think I fell in love with her when I first met her. Hell, Paul, the times I've tried to get her out of my system. I don't even fancy dames anymore, but I can't see Debbie ever wanting another man, not after Matthew!"

Paul knew only too well how Hank felt. He grimaced, "Funny, Matthew fell in love with her on sight, Hank. She's still very young, she may turn to me and I'll be there, but I don't fool myself. One day, she may be ready to fall in love again, but it won't be with me. I would have died myself to save her this, I'm a bloody idiot telling you, but I shouldn't write a romance with you and her off yet. If you do make it with her, I'll feel like killing you, but I love her too much to hold her back, at least you'd be good to her!"

He was almost breathless as he spoke truthfully. The two men eyed each other, both sick with helplessness. Hank proffered his hand, "Gee, Paul, let's hope the best man wins, let's hope she finds happiness again, even without either of us!"

**

Debbie had managed to take her children over to the staff quarters, it was just a little bit further away from the press and media. Every member of staff was devastated by the tragedy and the boardroom was now filled with glasses, drinks and food as many friends would return after the service.

She had refused to go to the chapel of rest, she had no desire whatsoever, to see her husband laid out in a box. Her memories were that of a vital and loving man. Even now, she could practically feel his strong arms holding her, his mouth seeking hers. How she wanted him, how she needed him. And then there was Paul, he had to face his own goodbyes to Vanessa and she shuddered violently.

Her long legs were now clad in black nylons, her dainty feet gelled into black, suede, court shoes. Stepping into her black jersey wool, two piece suit, she noticed the pallor of her face. Her mind flickered over the past, how she had first met Matthew, how he had asked her to marry him, how he had tried in vain to hide his arousal, to the point of ordering her to bed.

A tender warmth entered her heart momentarily as she swept her hair into a neat pleat. Her eyes took in the solitary figure of a young woman in black attire. The only relief was a gold cross and chair around her swanlike neck, an early gift from her beloved Matthew.

Inhaling deeply, she made her way slowly downstairs. Her parents waited with sombre expressions, they would share the first car with her and Paul. Alma, Irene, Hank and members of staff would follow.

Feeling the pressure of Paul's arm leading her, Debbie emerged to the flashlights of the press. She shuddered as her eyes caught sight of the ugly hearses, ugly in spite of the many flowers that adorned them and the rest of the cars.

242

Crowds were everywhere as she heard shouts of "Good luck, Debbie, chin up, Debbie!" Even the police officers stopped to salute as the sad cortege passed by. Her eyes became riveted onto the box, the words, 'Daddy' and 'Matthew' were florally displayed, now choking her.

Numbness seized her, she didn't remember her legs responding, but they obviously did. Many words were spoken in tribute, yet they seemed to drift in from another planet. At last the organ playing softly as the curtains drew across the coffins. She never knew how she resisted the urge to run and join her husband.

Her heels clicked amidst the gentle sobbing of the congregation. Paul was leading her, along with her parents to the massive wood door that had been opened. They were to stand and shake hands with the many mourners and waves of dreadful sickness now engulfed her.

Hank watched her slim body tremble. She looked lost, deeply in shock and driven by sheer will power. He leaned over to kiss her cheek as he walked by. His eyes were filled, yet hers remained blank and vacant. If only he didn't have to leave later in the day to return to New York.

Jim took his daughter's arm, "Come and see the beautiful banks of floral tributes, dear. You've been exceedingly brave, but a few tears would help to ease the pain!"

"I know, Dad," came the hollow response.

More and more photographers had joined them and covered their progress up to and almost inside of the castle. Debbie grabbed a glass of scotch and scurried away into a corner of the board room.

Glancing around, she noticed for the first time, who was there. Richard and Jenny came over to her, both with red, swollen eyes. Jenny's heavy body shook with grief, "Debbie, we can never tell you how dreadfully sad we are. You and Matthew ..," she gasped.

Again Debbie found herself comforting them as well as Mark and a very wobbly Sally. There was no doubt about it, everyone was in a state of sheer devastation.

Several drinks later, she felt slightly heady. Everyone had eaten and slowly began to drift home. Hank stood before her, "Gee, Debbie, you sure were great today. I know I'm a long way away, but, well you know. I will ring often, unless you would rather be left alone ..!"

He saw a brief flicker of light in her lovely, but so dead eyes, her body leaned into him, sending fire coursing through him, "Thank you, Hank, please thank Joanne for me, did you see the flowers she sent? I *will* reply to everyone personally. Hank, I would love to hear from you, anytime you are free," she sighed and brushed his cheek with her lips as he forced his feet to leave.

**

Kelly and Verity were very muddled seeing so much sadness, but with a lot of help from her parents and Paul, they were all finally in bed. Debbie kissed them all and Lucy clung to her as though she understood her mother's sorrow. After they settled, she knew she wanted to be back downstairs with her parents, with Paul, with anyone, rather than face the emptiness within her.

Everyone was toying with their food and as Debbie sat down, Paul announced, "I'll stay here tonight, just in case I'm needed. The whole day has been riddled with trauma!"

Jim seemed to wake up, "Talking of trauma, Irene was telling us that you have been asked to write a book on your own trauma, Debbie. I know it's a bit early to make such a big decision, but I think it could be a tremendous help to others!"

Ellen rounded sharply, "Jim, I hardly think this is the time, for goodness sake … its far too sharp in her mind at the moment. We're as bad as the damned media," she gulped.

Paul placed a comforting arm around Ellen's shoulder and pointed out, "Debbie has been working since this all began. Providing she can cope, I think it would also be therapeutic for her. I even think that I could probably help her through it. What d'you think, Debbie?"

"Yes, it could help other families, I would like you to help me, Paul!"

Suddenly, she remembered the little life inside of her and decided she must eat at least a sandwich. She smiled wistfully, "I must think of the babe, Matthew was really pleased about it!"

Tears began to prickle behind her eyes as she heard Emma's little whimper over the intercom. Jumping up, she felt heady and hastily kissed her parents 'goodnight'. Turning to Paul, she added, "I'm going up. I'll have a nice shower and feed Emma. I do thank you all from the bottom of my heart, your support has been tremendous!"

Debbie stripped the black attire from herself and stepped into the shower. She remembered the way Matthew had run the soap over her body, the water now cascading onto her was as a caress from him as she frantically yearned for his body.

Running to his wardrobe, she took out his checked, short sleeved shirt. It smelled of his muscular, manly body, no matter how often she washed his clothing, that delicious 'he man' aroma never left the room. She slipped it onto herself, her fingers running over the smooth cotton as it soothed her.

Luxuriating in the softness and nearness of him, she lifted her babe to change her. She had not buttoned the shirt, allowing her daughter to grip her breast. Watching the happy little smiles as Emma suckled, Debbie felt stifled with loneliness. Clenching her fists, she cried out, "Matthew, why did you leave me? I need you, we all need you. For God's sake, I promised you a son and I'm sure we're having one. How dare you leave me .. us?"

She had cried out to the empty room and swiftly placed Emma back into her cot. The tears then began and clutching a pillow, she allowed them to fall. Her insides were racked with stabbing pains of desperation. She couldn't cope like this and anger mingled with misery. Choking and sobbing, she sought solace in the lifeless pillow, "Matthew, I need you, come back to me!"

244

Paul watched her as the words choked from her shaking body. He stood transfixed in the doorway and listened to her breaking her heart. She needed this, she had been bottled up like this for over a week. As soon as he heard the sobbing die down, he would go to her, soothe her, comfort her.

He had just come from the shower when he heard her impassioned pleas. It choked him to see her wearing Matthew's shirt. She looked so fragile, the hem of the shirt barely covered her bottom. Her gorgeous legs stretched seductively as her body shook. How the hell could *he* help her?

Debbie felt her heart breaking within her. She was just realising with shock, that her beloved husband had gone. Anger returned, why had he left her like this? They had always talked things over, but this time he had gone alone. Somehow, the anger overpowered the grief. Her body shook all over as she felt strong arms lift her.

"Ssshhh ..,Debbie, I've got you," came Paul's soothing voice.

A deep safety entered her as she felt her head pulled onto the rug like chest. His hand was brushing her hair from her face, a sigh choked from her, "Paul, keep holding me, don't leave me alone. Make me safe again!"

His heart thumped into her ear, tears dripped from his cheeks, spilling into her hair. He had just wrapped a towel around himself when he had heard her. Now, her fragile body shook in his arms as he noticed, she was naked beneath the unbuttoned shirt. His blood burned like fire and he felt his manhood harden beyond his control.

Gently, he lifted her tear stained face to his. His mouth covered hers as he crushed her to him. This was just what she needed, arms to hold her, a mouth to bring her to life. Someone to make her feel warm inside.

Mindlessly, she found herself responding. His tongue invaded her with aggression, sending fire through her. Nothing coherent existed outside of this moment. Paul felt her body pressing into him, there was no doubt in him, her need was real.

Easing her back onto the pillow, his hand ran over her body, brushing the shirt aside. Once again, he gazed upon her gorgeous body. His mouth returned to hers as his hand continued to roam. Meeting her eyes, he saw the passion smouldering in them. She was beautiful alright, too beautiful for him to control himself.

Debbie felt her body floating, each touch from him left fire in its wake, bringing her back to vibrant life. Running her fingers through his rug like chest, she heard him whimper, "Debbie, darling, Debs, I love you!"

Her arms looped around his neck, her mouth sought his, her body writhed into his hardness. Inhaling to fill his lungs, he gasped, "Debbie, if I stay here, so help me, I will take you. Christ, I'm only human!"

"I know, Paul and I do want you!"

As she had spoken, her body eased naturally beneath him. A greed so great gripped her as she felt him hard above her. "Oh, Debbie, I love you," she heard him gasp as he raised his body. Her mind was in the past, her body arched eagerly towards him and seconds later he was within her, filling her.

Their eyes locked almost in shock. He had never forgotten her beautiful love, again he saw the jets of perspiration spring across her forehead. Her head was thrown back as he saw the pulse in her neck throb beneath her skin. His mouth moved down to torment her turgid nipples, extracting moans of delight from her.

Moving his mouth from breast to breast, he chewed on her hard buds and slowly moved his hands down to grip her buttocks. Her knees raised to allow him to thrust deeper into her, the pace he set was perfect for her. Her hands moved to grip his taut buttocks as he pounded helplessly.

She felt the scream leave her as with wonder, she felt the convulsive shudders begin. Her body continued to lift to him as her orgasm reached its heady peak. Gasping and panting and biting each other, he groaned loudly, "I'm coming," as his passion left him and his mouth bit into her, the unending dregs straining from him.

Shivering and shuddering, his body draped onto hers. She had never needed this more than she did tonight, his body still shook uncontrollably as his mouth now dropped kisses over her face. Blindly, they began to stumble from the quake that had shaken them.

His arms crushed her to him, "Debbie, I've longed for this moment, never thought it would happen. I s'pose I should say I'm sorry, I can't, it would be a total lie. I love you desperately!"

Allowing him to roll from her, she sat up. Reaching for her cigarettes, she lit two. Handing one to Paul, she waited for the flood of guilt to fill her. Nothing happened, her needs had been fulfilled and she should feel wretched, but she couldn't live without love and passion and yes, sex.

Paul's hand claimed her breast possessively, "Debbie, you're going to tell me that this must never happen again, aren't you?"

She sighed heavily, "If only I could be so bloody correct. No, Paul, I can't say that to you. I wanted you just as much as you wanted me. If anyone found out, hell, even I don't believe how shallow I must be!"

Sitting up beside her, he reached for the ashtray, "Debbie, don't feel guilt, darling, no one need ever know. We both found tremendous solace with each other, surely that can't be so wrong. It would have been shocking had we yielded the other night, but you know, I never stopped loving you!"

Confusion filled her, "Paul, this can't be right. My husband is barely cold and already I take another man. I can't believe my own behaviour!"

"Oh, come now, Debbie, you know full well that I'm not just another man. Matthew said you were born to be loved, he was right. We both lost our bed mates, Matthew knew you worshipped him, I feel he would be happy to know we can help each other!"

She knew, every word he uttered was true, yet somehow there should be some guilt. She was also playing around with Paul's emotions, he was in love with her. She loved him, but probably not in the same way. What a damned mess she had landed herself into, for she realised that she wanted him all over again.

Paul took her hand to his lips and kissed her palm. He must have read her mind as he said softly, "Debs, you think I'm going to try to heavy you into marriage one day, don't you? Dearest, I know you love me, but are not 'in love' with me. One day, you will probably meet that man, but for now, who are we hurting? Why shouldn't we make each other happy? We are both very sexual animals, both horny, fortunately we can more than satisfy each other. What do you say, Debs, come on now, cards on table!"

He gulped as he ran out of breath and tears stung her eyes, "Paul, you know me so darned well. You're right of course. I don't see me ever marrying again and I certainly wouldn't want the children to see us in bed together. Sex is obviously very important to me, but I don't want to play around with your feelings. You say I may meet someone else, I doubt that, but what would be left for you, if I did meet someone?"

Swallowing hard to refrain from suggesting she had already met someone, he simply said, "Precisely nothing, Debbie. But if and when that does happen, you must take your happiness, till then, share your love with me!"

Her arms went around him, "Paul, I can't tell you how much you've helped me. I can't see myself coping without you beside me. I .. I ... don't really want you to leave me alone and I know I'm being selfish!"

Tenderly he held her, "Darling, I agree with you about the little ones. I'll leave here before they waken and if I come round to you each night, about nine, we could put some time into the book. Together, we can transport each other away from grief, at least for a while. I would also like to feel, .. to feel that I can help with this baby!"

With a strangled gasp, her lips sought his. Crushing her to him, he gasped, "Hell, Debbie, I've just taken you and already I'm rising again!"

"I want you, Paul!"

Long after he had fallen asleep, she lay there completely fulfilled, satiated. Although her mind was a labyrinth, she felt that Matthew would approve of this arrangement. He had been there when Paul had left her, he would agree with Paul helping her now. Nevertheless, she knew she would have to explain to her parents. Would they be ashamed of her behaviour?

**

Over the next couple of months, Debbie found her mind to be on overdrive as inspired urges throbbed from her fingertips. Ideas poured from her as her pregnancy developed. Aran knitting was on its way back into fashion and she had been asked to come up with some 'quick' new designs.

Again, she had been asked to cover the finer points in a short series of programmes. 'Miss Kelly' was prospering beautifully, both in Preston as well as Morecambe. At least Matthew and Vanessa's work had not been in vain. Her heart never ceased to search for her dead husband. He had also been her best friend, although mercifully, the children seemed to accept his death.

Debbie began to feel much better in herself and was asked to design some exclusive crochet dressed for young bridesmaids. Apparently they would be

247

for a huge society wedding and after the big day, she would be permitted to release the patterns.

She had to admit, it was Paul who had helped her to face the future. Night after night he came to her, both of them working on the book. Sometimes she would break down as she relived certain parts in her mind.

Most mornings, after he left, she would lie there and thank God, for guiding him to her. His love was ardent as well as sincere. He transported her away from sadness, albeit for brief intervals, but she couldn't have coped without him, shame or no shame.

**

Hank had thrown himself body and soul into his work. He had left England with a little ray of hope and having fought to 'phone Debbie, now picked up the 'phone with confidence. Her voice always seemed to lift when she heard him and today he knew his own voice held an air of mystery.

He gave a carefree little chuckle, "Gee, Debbie, it sure is good to hear you sounding so much better. I'm praying that you can all come over, say, late January, early Feb., and hopefully stay till late November. My news is great, remember the T.V. station that asked me to anchor? They've agreed to all of my suggestions, providing of course, that you all agree, honey!"

"Agree to what, Hank? Stop teasing and tell me!"

She sounded happy to hear from him, if only she would agree to his new proposals, hell he had pulled every string to make if possible. Drawing in his breath heavily, "Debbie, honey, I take over the new station in England next year. Now, we want a couple of series from you, we also want to launch the book on 'trauma'. The beauty of the deal is, that whatever you do over here, can be done for Britain and all under my direction. That's why it must be a fairly long stay .. Oh, Debbie, please say yes, honey," he gabbled on like a child.

Would she ever know of the desperation that plagued him as he waited for her answer? Debbie was amazed by his quick perception at the idea of running two lots of series at the same time and giggled, "Hank, you're totally incorrigible. Of course I'll agree, but will have to check with my parents. I'm sure they'll agree though!"

"Debbie, you sound happy about it. You *are* happy about it," his voice rose with surprise and delight.

"Yes, Hank, I'm happy about it. I'm lucky to have Paul helping me with the book. He's been a real tower of strength for me and I don't deserve him!"

Stabs of bitter disappointment churned inside of him. Of course it was natural for her to turn to Paul, he wanted to comfort her himself. He was so apprehensive, he decided to take the bull by the horns, he had to know one way or another. Gripping the receiver tightly, he gulped, "Debbie, you sure sound close to Paul. Do you think you may end up marrying him one day? It's obvious how he feels about you."

Briefly, she thought she sensed and urgency in his voice. Guilt then flooded her, could Paul have told him about their present way of life? No, he wouldn't do that.

Hearing the hesitation, Hank interjected, "So you are thinking about it then?"

His blood ran cold, he didn't want to know anymore, yet he had to know. The chuckle was still in her voice, "No, Hank, I'm not going to marry Paul, not now, not ever. He knows the situation exactly, he's far too kind to deceive. We both needed comfort and that's where it ends. Anyway, what the hell am I answering to you for?"

Although she ended with a chuckle, he exhaled the breath he had held, "Debbie, I sure am sorry, honey. You're right, it isn't any of my business. Am I forgiven?"

"Yes, Hank, you're forgiven. You should find a young woman and get married, have lots of children and that will keep you busy!"

He guffawed, "I'm not the marrying kind, I told you that when I first met you. I would love the children side of life, but I can't have the woman I fell in love with," he added sardonically.

"Hank, I'm so sorry about that. She must be blind or stupid, not to want someone like you. Anyway, I'll speak to you soon!"

Holding the receiver in his hand, he punched the air. She would never know just how much her words had meant to him. There was no question of her marrying Paul and she thought *he* was worth a passing glance. At last he felt a euphoria of hope.

**

Richard rang in June, his voice soft as he tried to conceal his deep happiness. Somehow it felt wrong to be celebrating when Debbie had lost so much. "Debbie, Jenny and I have a baby daughter, we're calling her Debbie, do you mind?"

"Richard, that's wonderful news, heartiest congratulations. I'd be honoured for her to have my name. Give Jenny our love and see you soon," she smiled sincerely.

Sensing Richard's obvious discomfort, she waited for him to continue, "Debbie, are you coming to terms with … well you know? Bloody daft question, I felt almost guilty ringing you with …!"

"Don't be silly, Richard, we all love good news, especially when it comes from someone so close!"

Debbie ran down to tell her parents and after hugging her, wholeheartedly agreed with the name. As she left them, she paused and inadvertently overhead Ellen say to Jim, "I think Debbie is sleeping with Paul. Something's keeping her going apart from sheer will power, do you think she's wise, Jim?"

"I think she is, darling. I'm sure if we asked her, she wouldn't deny it. She knows what she's doing and it does explain the reason for her coping so well. I'm sure she would make sure that the children don't know about it!"

Stunned and shocked beyond words, Debbie just stood there. The summer was already proving to be hot again, yet anger filled her. This was how her parents saw her, was this how the rest of the world would see her? Was she simply riddled with guilt?

Balling her hands, she knocked on the door and went back into the room, her eyes becoming saucers as she saw the restlessness in Ellen, "Mum, I almost overheard what you said. Is there something you want to ask me?"

"Are you sleeping with Paul, Debbie?"

Jim gasped softly, "Ellen, its not our business, darling. You've been edgy over the last few days, what's the matter with you?"

"I don't want her hurt again, Jim!"

Debbie gave a wry smile, "Mum, Dad, excuse me, I *am* here, you know. Yes, I have been sleeping with Paul. I know you must think I'm shallow, but we were able to offer each other solace. He leaves before the children get up and we both know where we stand. Sorry if I've disappointed you!"

Ellen gathered her and suddenly their pain reached to the other. Debbie knew her parents would never sit in judgement and realised it was only concern that had brought about the question. Her eyes watered as she said, "Mum, I've told Paul that I don't want to marry again. Hell, I miss Matthew like crazy, but know he would understand.

She patted her tummy, feeling the fluttering of new life. Ellen held her, "Of course we understand, dear. You and Paul were always close. You haven't a shallow bone in your body, it's me being over protective!"

CHAPTER FORTY ONE

August arrived in a blaze of heat and Debbie worked outside with the little crochet dresses. She had chosen a soft peach cotton, making the bodice in various types of stitches. She was asked for short sleeves, but a full flowing skirt, filled with flowers, crocheted neatly into the work. They did now look truly exquisite as inspiration flowed through her deft fingers.

Irene locked them all into the safe, realising there would be a huge demand after the wedding. Turning to her, she said, "Debbie, they are absolutely beautiful and although the photographer has done well, it doesn't have Matthew's finesse. He was so brilliant, sorry, Debbie, it chokes me to see you without him!"

"Me too, Irene, but he left us so very much!"

Several times, Debbie made her way to the balcony, she foolishly thought she would be nearer to Matthew in their very secret place, but no matter how she willed her feet to mount the steps, she found they would not obey her.

Paul arrived later in the evening, his excitement almost irrepressible, "Debs, I know it'll be a board decision, but it seems that we could buy the New York offices and launch 'Miss Kelly' over there!"

"That's good news, Paul. I'm sure the board will agree. It was something Matthew would have wanted, how sad he never knew!"

"Sad indeed, babe, let's hope that Don Prescott agrees to working over there. If not, I'll have to go over for a while, just about the time you're ready to come back. Hell, Debbie, I'' be lost when you are over there," he groaned.

Offering her lips to him, she took his hand and placed it onto her kicking babe. His eyes always softened as he felt the ripple, "Darling, I missed all this with Kelly, thank you for allowing me to share with this one. Somehow, I feel Matthew would be relieved to know!"

Night after night, she lay in his arms realising just how much he had missed with Kelly. He was always eager to keep his hand on her, waiting for the kicks. There was no doubt in her mind that this was a boy. At least she felt that Matthew would know, she had kept her promise, the gift of a son and that soothed him.

**

Hank never missed calling her, she looked forward to his cheery calls and today was no exception. "Hi, Debbie, I've just heard from the hospital, they are only too pleased to dedicate the wing to Matthew. I was thinking, honey, if you're spending the bulk of next year with us, would you find the ranch, a little ... well, a little .. overpowering?" His words were clipped as he stammered helplessly.

"Oh, Hank, I'm truly thrilled about the hospital and thank you. Of course we'll stay at the ranch, the children love it there. Why would it be overpowering?"

"Gee, Debbie, I should mind my own business. I just thought there may be too many memories there!"

Her throat constricted, "Oh, Hank, how truly thoughtful of you. I have memories all around me, but each memory of Matthew is a happy one. Hank, it's a wonderful feeling to have you for a friend, a dear friend. In fact I'm already looking forward to seeing you again!"

Closing his eyes momentarily, he savoured her words. Inhaling deeply, "Debbie, honey, I sure could use a huge favour from you!"

"Anything within reason, Hank," she chuckled.

"Debbie, would you be my partner for a huge charity bash? You see, we are apparently requested to fly into Washington and stay in a luxury suite. Hell, honey, I'm making such a mess of this .. we've been elected to be joint guests of honour!"

Her mind raced as she thought of such a super idea. Mindless of her tongue, she chuckled further, "Hank, that'd be wonderful, I would be proud to be a guest of honour with you by my side!"

He began to relax a little as he continued, "Thank you so much, honey. By the way, I'll be placing my penthouse onto the market, directly after Christmas. There'll be a lot of filming done from the ranch and I'll need two crews. Do you think you can put up with me at such close quarters?"

Funny, she had never noticed the deep American drawl to be so rich. A strange excitement entered her, "Hank, I think it would be lovely to have you around. The kiddies are looking forward to seeing you again!"

Hank thought he detected a seductive note in her voice. Had it been there? Was he kidding himself? Either way, he had plenty of time to be with her, although their schedules would be extremely heavy, he knew he would work well, especially with her for a subject.

Not wishing to outstay his welcome, he sighed, "Debbie, I'll sort it all out. Incidentally, several dresses will be sent to the hotel suite, you can choose exactly what you want. Take care, honey, speak to your soon, kiss the kids for me!"

**

Paul arrived home, his gorgeous blue eyes lighting up. "Hell, what a day I've had. The only thing keeping me sane today was thinking of you!"

His arms went around her from behind, his hands coming to rest on the restless kicking of the babe. Turning to offer her responses to him, she explained the 'phone call from Hank. His smile was almost one of resignation, "Debbie, darling, I think it's a wonderful tribute to you and Hank, I bet he's very excited!"

Debbie felt an urgency about his kisses, they were hungry and frenzied. Standing away slightly, her eyes lifted to him, "What's wrong, Paul?"

"Nothing's wrong, darling. I'm just happy we have this time together!"

His love that night seemed to go on forever. Time and again, he took her out of the sadness that lingered horribly and satisfied her eager body. Over and over he shook and shuddered, his lips burning hers and setting her body alight.

Amazed by his constant need and knowing that he was all she needed to cope, she gripped his head. "Paul, what *is* the matter? This feels like it did that night on the hill, almost as though you're going to say goodbye to me again!"

Gathering her to him, he gasped, "No, dearest, I'm not going anywhere. I just dread you going away from me. I know one day you will leave me and I know I will pull myself together, but I don't relish it!"

Pushing his head into the pillow, her hand traced the contours of his face, her mouth brushed his. "Paul, don't, I'm not leaving you for good and anyway, why worry now? I won't be leaving till well after Christmas. Right now, my love is yours for the taking, you know that, darling!"

Feeling her heavy body moving restlessly beside him, he felt tears sting his eyes. He knew full well how Hank felt and the way she had spoken earlier, had seemed to indicate that she was beginning to see him in a different light. He could feel her warming, quite subconsciously to Hank. He shuddered, she had given him so much just recently, how he wished will all of his heart that he had never left her.

**

Debbie had finished her winter collection of knitwear for Haywood and they had now moved to the larger site. Alma had never been happier, she had prayed for Debbie and marvelled at the way she had coped. Irene held the same admiration, after all, they had both expected some kind of breakdown, but instead, she had continued at the helm.

Paul had popped her to see Mark and Sally who were so happy and on their way back, they had popped in to see Richard and Jenny as the shop receipts now grew to gigantic proportions.

Kelly and Verity continued to love their nursery and facilities for a similar project also existed in the States. They had confirmed that Lucy could also accompany them as Debbie felt it vital for them all to attend, not just to learn, but to mix well with other children.

Verity grew more like Matthew by the day. She was a real Irish Colleen and just like her father, very easy going. Kelly was stunningly beautiful, yet so like Paul. Lucy seemed to be a mixture of herself and Matthew, she was a happy, yet slightly shy little girl. Emma, who now had her own room was a typical tomboy, filled with curiosity and never happier than when playing with sand or soil.

Watching them play, her heart would swell with pride, they loved being with their grandparents and although they were also busy, always made time for them. Lucy often helped Ellen in the kitchen and loved rolling pastry, as Ellen gave her her own little rolling pin and board.

**

September arrived with a continued blaze of heat and Debbie only had two months to go. Brian had insisted on being called when her labour commenced, he was a little concerned, she could well go into shock and he was taking no chances whatsoever.

She began to feel very tired and suffered immense back ache. At times she would pine for Matthew, longing to go up to the balcony, but her footsteps would always falter as she became transfixed.

At times she would watch Paul and wonder how she would have coped without his selfless love. Had they not been young lovers, there would have been no one else she could have turned to. Some days though, she found she didn't like the person she had become, but shrugged it away from her mind.

Waking from a restless sleep around three in the morning, her body was racked with searing pains. Turning to Paul, she watched the rise and fall of his chest. Terror struck her, the pain was suffocating, not like any pain she had ever known. Trying to ease herself into a comfortable position, an agonised squeal left her.

Paul jack knifed upright, his brain instantly alert as his arms flew around her. "It can't be the babe, not yet!"

"I think it must be, Paul, ring Megan," she choked as her face contorted with further pain.

Megan and Brian arrived breathlessly. Brian swiftly checked her over, "It is the baby, Debbie, I think we're going to have to deliver immediately, can you push for me, dear?"

Paul sponged her burning face as the pain grew worse by the minute. Brian soothed, "We will have to use forceps, Debbie. Keep still, I don't want to hurt you!"

She felt Paul grip her as Brian pulled the baby from her, "Its all over now, Debbie," exclaimed Brian as he walked away.

"Give my baby to me, I want him," she screamed.

There was a strange silence in the room. A curtain of gloom seemed to descend over her. Paul's arms held her tightly as Brian came forward, "I'm sorry, Debbie, there was nothing we could do, he just wasn't strong enough. In fact, I think he died quite a few hours ago, that would explain the dreadful pain!"

He breathed deeply to keep his own sadness under control. "Debbie, when you had the dreadful shock of Matthew's death, baby was still forming, he would have been dreadfully handicapped, one day we may be able to tell in advance and of course the likelihood of this happening again are minimal .. I'm so sorry!"

Stunned beyond words, she watched the tears pour from Paul's eyes. Megan broke down and tears ran down Brian's cheeks. "Debbie, what name would you have given him? We will take him with us, but he can still be christened!"

"His name is Matthew. I promised Matthew a son, he would have been heartbroken, I couldn't even get that right, could I?"

Gingerly, she sat up, hell, her whole body hurt. "I want to hold him. Brian, give him to me, I need to kiss him goodbye before he goes to live with his father," she choked.

Paul gripped her as the green wrapped little bundle was placed into her arms. She looked down at the tiny face, he was blue, he had not even gasped for air. Gently she raised him to her lips as she tenderly brushed the tiny head, "Darling, I wanted you so much, but your daddy wanted you more!"

Megan turned to Paul, "Could you pop down and bring her parents? She has been through a dreadful ordeal, she'll need to get this lot out of her system!"

"Yeh, but I don't think she should be holding him, he's dead, for God's sake!"

His voice throbbed with his own pain. Never had he seen so much suffering as he had witnessed over the last couple of hours. Taking his shoulder, Brian said, "She does need to hold him, old chap. I know it seems bizarre, but it does help the parents to come to terms with the loss, I mean if they get a chance to say goodbye!"

Ellen and Jim held each other, pain hung from their eyes. Debbie watched them, her heart crumbling, "Mum, Daddy, I even got this wrong. Do you think this is a punishment for my seeming betrayal of Matthew?"

"You didn't betray Matthew," sobbed Ellen as she took the little bundle from her daughter's arms. A tearful Megan left with the baby as Brian prepared to give Debbie and injection. Everyone had tears rolling down their cheeks as Brian sunk a needle into her clammy skin. "Paul, she should sleep shortly, can you sit with her? I'll be in later!"

"Of course I'll sit with her," came Paul's shocked voice.

His arms rocked her as though she was crying, but again, she couldn't cry. Jim said, "I s'pose you had better issue a press release, Paul, hell fire, this reminds me of Tony all over again!"

Like a flash it hit her, that as exactly what she remembered. She recognised that eerie silence, yes, it was like a re run of Tony's death, only this time, she couldn't run. "I think we should tell the kiddies ourselves, they'll probably feel better if they think he has gone to live with Matthew," she sighed.

The children seemed to accept the news with resignation. As though they expected the worst and she made a mental note to work on their little natures. Granted they hadn't seen the little chap, but she didn't like such cynicism in her children. As she hugged them before they left, she felt the injection taking effect.

Her arms went around Paul, "Thank you for being here for me, darling, Paul. I can't believe that my body will never carry another child. I did so want a son!"

His arms held her with tenderness, "Brian said there was no reason why this should happen again. I think you will have another chance one day. Now go to sleep, darling, I'll be here when you waken!"

They were the last words she remembered as she slipped into the gaping chasm that waited eagerly to claim her. Her body felt bruised again, battered again, empty again.

Hank turned on his television set. The sad news had been released and all of New York had wakened to hear the latest news. His mouth hung open as he listened to the newscast.

"The Lancashire Lassie's life has once again been hit by tragedy. Debbie Hudson, having lost husband, photographer, Matthew Ross in a tragic accident, has now lost the child she was carrying.

Debbie went into premature labour in the early hours of this morning. After an extremely painful and difficult time, the baby boy was still born. Doctors' reports indicate that Miss Hudson is in a stable condition, although she has been sedated.

Ironically, the couple had worked hard in the area of premature and low birth weight babies. A special wing in the neo natal unit has been dedicated in memory of Matthew Ross. Debbie Hudson is due to unveil the plaque early next year. Messages of sympathy are said to be pouring in, to the once, perfect couple from Lancashire!"

Hank slumped into his large swivel chair. His hands clutched the sides for support. Tears stung his eyes, he couldn't bear to think of how she was feeling. "How much more is she expected to take?"

He shouted out to his empty office, once more the need to hear her voice was uppermost in his mind. Lighting a cigarette, he paced the floor, he would wait till later on, she was probably still under sedation. His heart ached for her pain, his arms wanted to comfort her. She was so young, yet had lived a lifetime, endured every emotion that life could throw her way. His shoulders slumped as he prepared to sort out his day, but his heart had already flown to England.

Paul comforted Debbie's parents, who now feared a breakdown in their daughter. Once more Irene and Alma united to keep the press at bay, neither of them unable to believe the latest shock. Brian had been in to check her vital signs, "I will leave some tablets for her. She must take these Paul, to stop the milk from flowing in and I would like her to sleep well over the next couple of nights!"

Debbie wakened to find Paul sitting on the bed beside her. The dreadful truth seeped into the haze of her mind and her hand went to touch her empty stomach. Her eyes lifted to Paul, he took her free hand and brushed his lips over it, "I'm not very good at all at this, am I , darling?"

Although her own sadness swamped her, seeing the state Paul was in made her feel worse. Gripping his hand, she whispered, "Paul, it was perhaps the worst experience I've had to endure. I could never have born so much pain, not without you. Just knowing you were with me, was a great comfort …!"

"Brian has left some medication for you, Debbie. I've promised him you'll take it. Come on, try and sit up, take these," he choked.

Obediently, she eased herself up onto the pillows, she felt sore and riddled with discomfort. Taking the proffered tablets, she gulped them down with the water.

Paul then popped down to play with the children, more or less to give Ellen a break. Debbie sat in bed, once more her world crumbled about her. How she had yearned for a son, how happy Matthew would have been, but she now had to convince herself that his son had been destined to join him.

Her eyes filled as she remembered the pain and subsequent loss. Great gasping sobs tore from her, it was unbearable not having her child. Lost in the loneliness and emptiness, she knew, she could either wallow in grief, or be responsible and think of her other little ones, the latter would definitely apply.

The sobs still left her body as the 'phone rang. Her first reaction was to ignore it, but reason prevailed, someone had taken the trouble to ring her and she snatched up the receiver, "Hello!"

Her hands had gripped the receiver tightly, almost as a way to relieve the pain. "Hi, Debbie, honey," came Hank's flat toned voice and hearing his obvious sadness, made her tears overflow, "Oh, Hank," she gasped.

He didn't know what to say, he felt stupid, powerless, totally inadequate. Drawing his breath through his clenched teeth, he gulped, "Gee, Debbie, I don't have to tell you just how desperately sorry ... I was ... to hear the news. Hell, honey!"

"Hank, I do know, but thank you so much for taking the trouble to ring. Somehow, I'm going to have to pull myself out of this. I'd better arrange to write about my baby. At the moment, I'm not a very good advert for the baby wing!"

"Debbie, honey, don't say that. The disappointment would be felt dreadfully over here, should you decide against the wing. You're a brave little cookie and from what I can glean, the shock of Matthew's death had come at a time before the babe was fully developed!"

In spite of her misery, she had to smile, "Hank, there is no question of me not wanting the wing to work. There is so much that can be done and if losing my son highlights the research in to this field .. well .. it will not have been in vain. I desperately wanted a son, but once again, Paul has been a tower of strength," she jerked.

Golly her words stung him, yet he knew that Paul must have been the only person keeping her sane. Again he admonished himself, he realised that she didn't have a clue as to the way he felt about her. Why should she consider turning to him? With a little grimace, he said, "Get some rest, honey, I'll ring next week!"

**

Over the next few weeks, Debbie's strength returned, her body had swiftly returned to normal and she had indeed been asked to write about the loss of her child. Her book on trauma was racing high on the list and many offers had come from the media, offers to discuss the matter and her desk was now cluttered with letters, many from abroad.

Hank had read the story, finding his eyes filling. It was beautifully written, with care being taken to cover the various points. Yet, typical of Debbie, she had found a way of lifting the depth of gloom, to a rung higher, to the point of some kind of acceptance. He had tried so hard to fly to England, but the work between the two companies was keeping him bogged down. He vowed that the two days they would spend in Washington, would be filled with excitement for her.

Debbie had begun to work on her summer collection, she knew she was well in advance, but the way she had been knocked still shook her, making her romp ahead of herself. Irene answered the bulk of the letters for her to sign. Ellen was busy preparing her cookery translations, ready for the series in the States.

The big society wedding was due to take place and an element of excitement buzzed around the castle. There would be a huge demand for the outfits, but they were all ready and waiting.

Paul came home rather late that night. He looked tired and worn around the edges. His restlessness was even more pronounced, worrying her. She went over to place her arms round his neck, seeming to realise the torment his body was enduring, laying beside her night after night, her own body was also in torment.

Basic instinct warned her he would not move on her, it was down to her. Allowing herself to gel into his handsome, rigid body, she became shocked, "Don't, Debbie, I can't control myself. It's becoming increasingly difficult to lay beside you at night!"

"Paul, do you mean you're fed up with me? If you want to leave, it will be with my blessing. You helped me through the two toughest times of my life. I wouldn't try to hold you back, but I would miss you like hell," she gasped.

Rounding sharply, he gulped, "That's what you think, is it? Hell, Debbie, you know I love you. Its just torture to lay beside you and not be able to touch you!"

Stretching almost cat like, she noticed the healthy bulge in his trousers and whispered, "I'm going to bed are you coming? With a resigned shrug, he loosed his tie and slipped it off, "Yes, alright, I'm tired, sorry I was so snappy!"

Watching him divest his clothing, noticing the neat way in which he hung his suit, she moved over to him. Scarcely able to breathe, so great as her need, she asked, "Can you pull down my dress zipper, Paul?"

She felt his hands as he swished it down and pulled away, allowing it to fall to the floor. Standing before him, she was clad only in scanty panties and bra. Her hands went to open his shirt, as he grunted, "Hell, Debbie, I'm not make of granite!"

"Thank goodness for that," she panted as she continued her quest. Momentarily, they rocked on unsteady feet, until she felt herself falling onto the bed, Paul fell with her, landing on top of her and their union was instant.

His hands now roamed her body as they remained united. His mouth ran along her shoulder, biting her. "Debbie, darling, you are all I could ever want. You know me so well, don't you?"

"Mmmm, Paul, that's only natural. You taught me to love, taught me to enjoy sexual delights. Mind you, knowing what I know today, I don't know how you went for so long, before the first time we made love!"

"Neither do I, darling, neither do I," he smiled sardonically. "Dearest, if only you wanted to marry me, my life would be complete, but you don't want to marry me, do you?"

Pangs of guilt joined the eruptions that still blasted within her. A frown furrowed her brow, instantly his thumb brushed it away. "Debs, I know you're not for me, not on a long term basis anyway. Sadly for me, you'll meet someone that can make you feel as you did with Matthew. Meanwhile, I'm more than content to share your love!"

"Paul, what do you mean? You've said that before, I don't know anyone else that I could love like this," she choked.

"I know you don't, little one, but we don't know what's around the corner. Something in you is warning you against marrying me and if you were to re-marry, you know I wouldn't ever make a pass, I never did!"

As he rolled from her, she broke down completely. "Paul, you make me feel so cheap and shallow, I love your love, I couldn't respond like I do, not without a rich depth of feeling. Matthew was right, I do need to be loved, but not at the risk of hurting you. I feel so bloody guilty as though I'm taking everything you can offer, when you could find someone that does want to marry you," she sobbed.

Jumping from the bed, he went and poured them a drink. She was hurting this man and couldn't understand why. At one time she had desperately wanted to marry him, but not any more, in spite of the fact that he didn't mean immediately.

Totally convinced she didn't even like herself anymore, she gulped down the drink Paul had poured for her and refilled the glass, "Paul, whatever I'm doing wrong, please forgive me!"

Swirling his drink around the glass, his eyes locked hers, "Debbie, when we fell in love, I *knew* it was the real thing. After all, I did have many flings, but, as you say, I was your first love and nothing can take that away from me and had we been married then, we would have been bloody happy. Then you discovered that added something, the added something that makes love pale into insignificance!"

He watched the questions form on her face. Gulping his drink, he continued, "You see darling, there is a difference between loving and being 'in love'. You love me, but were 'in love' with Matthew. I know you understand the difference, Debbie. If you don't find that special something say, in about five years, I'll insist that you marry me, deal?"

Part of him couldn't believe what he was doing. He was digging his own grave, jumping in and literally puling the soil back over himself. He knew only too well how Hank felt about her, given time, he was sure she would realise that she could love him.

There was no way in which he was being noble, he knew that if he could have persuaded her to marry him, he could have made her happy, he also knew that he would be forcing her to miss the very thing, she not only needed, but richly deserved. And if she didn't waken to Hank's feelings, then ... well ...

Her tear filled eyes met his, the trust in them was the same trust he received from her children. Her beautiful, sensual mouth moved, "Paul, I think I know what you mean. We are so happy together, if I .. if I married you, would you stay with me?"

The words stammered from her as he brushed her perfect breast, his voice became hoarse with desire. "Darling, that wouldn't be the answer. I'll always be free for you. Mind you, if you did find Mr Right, I would need a companion. As you know, Debs, I'll always need to shag," his lips tightened as though in disgust.

For the first time, she saw the bitterness in him, he was ashamed of his needs and something told her, apart from herself, Vanessa must have been the only woman to even touch his heart, let alone enter it. He looked humble and the need to reassure raced through her. With a hesitant gulp, "I'm the same then, 'cos I need to shag!"

Suddenly, he guffawed with laughter. Her eyes widened as she wondered what was so hilarious. "Oh, Debs, that sounded funny coming from you. Many women, and men for that matter, use that language to turn each other on. You turn men on by your innocent simplicity!"

"I'm anything but innocent, Paul. I can't live without sex anymore than you can. So, I must be game for a shag," she reasoned.

Fire surged through his veins as he chuckled softly, "You wouldn't know how to shag anyone, Debs. With you, little one, its called making love, there's a vast difference!"

"I don't care what its called, Paul, it's a need to indulge and I love it!"

Crushed in his arms, her mind swirled around like light snow in a heavy wind. She felt loved, bewildered and frightened. Part of her understood Paul, but for the life of her, she couldn't envisage herself like this with another man. 'But you thought that before you loved Matthew, didn't you?'

The voice came from within, the question posed was close to home. Her brain felt tired, there were many things to be sorted out. Perhaps, if she concentrated on the forthcoming trip, she would have found answers by the time she returned.

Confusion filled her as she turned her body to Paul. His caresses became urgent again and whatever she didn't know, she *did* know, this was what she loved.

**

Christmas was a very sad time for them all. Matthew had gone, her baby had gone, yet looking at her daughters, she knew she was still a lucky lady.

Her parents had grieved so much, it was almost a relief to know they would soon leave for the States.

Irene and Alma joined them all for Christmas, both sharing her parents' spare room. Debbie knew, beyond doubt, that her not so little empire was made up of people she loved and who loved her in return.

Jenny and Richard came for tea on Boxing Day, their eyes radiating the joy of their own little family. Mark and Sally also joined them and the castle became alive again, with all the children, playing, cooing or crying. Nostalgia nevertheless ran rampant, all of them feeling the bitter loss of Matthew.

Time after time, she stood by the door to the balcony, but her feet would not take her up to the top. Perhaps there was a right time for everything and obviously, it wasn't now.

Fighting the losing battle to climb those steps, an idea suddenly hit her. While they were away, she would have the children's bedrooms decorated, it was just a matter of leaving the details for Irene to arrange. She would also have her own room changed, including the bed. Flicking through the pages of a well know magazine, she found just what she was looking for. A huge inviting, four poster bed. It would be perfect for her room, especially when Paul finally returned.

Hank 'phoned a couple of days before they were due to leave, "Hi there, honey. Thought I'd better confirm that the hotel suite is booked for us. The ball is a Valentine Ball and I can't wait for you to be my partner. Are you scared of sharing with me?"

Never did he cease to amaze her. He always made her want to chuckle, perhaps it was his rich American drawl. She returned the teasing banter, "Should I be scared? I can always cry for help!"

"Sure you can, babe. I'm looking forward to it!"

"So am I, Hank, after all, it is to raise money for Charity!"

"Great, babe, I'll meet the 'plane and join you at the ranch!"

**

Paul's love the night before they departed, left her stunned by its ferocity. His kisses were filled with a longing hunger, his body shuddered as time and again he raced them into fulfilment. She was going to miss this, probably more than she would miss her beloved Morecambe.

He had finally fallen asleep with her locked safely into his arms. Somehow she noticed, that even in sleep his muscles were twitching. Like her, he knew it would be almost a year till they could enjoy each other again. Her mind was in turmoil as she fell into a restless sleep.

Debbie felt somewhat melancholy as they arrived at the airport. Her eyes watched her daughters and knew that mercifully, the younger kiddies didn't remember their daddy. Walking up to the jumbo aircraft, her breath caught, Matthew had been with them last time. Would she ever be able to forget him? Of course not, she didn't want to, they had been so blissfully happy.

Paul kissed them all and her body had shaken with the many mixed emotions as she made her way to her seat. Joy to be taking her children for a holiday, sadness that Matthew was no longer with them and looking at her parents, she knew they felt the same, yes, a change would do them all a world of good.

**

Paul Howarth watched the aircraft circle before take off. His eyes filled, 'There goes my reason for living, there goes my everything'. The words of the song had darted, totally uninvited into his addled brain. Nothing short of a miracle, or a tragedy would bring her back to him. A miracle he would pray for, a tragedy, not at any price.

CHAPTER FORTY TWO

Debbie rose to belt her children as the pilot issued the instructions. They had all been fairy quiet on the journey, obviously each lost in their individual thoughts. The press had seen them off and were already visible as the 'plane eased its way along the runway.

Having hugged everyone, Hank placed his free arm around Debbie, "It sure is great to have you here, honey!"

There was something different about him, but she couldn't quite put her finger on it. Shrugging her shoulders with a happy resignation, she just allowed herself to be led to the press. Nerves had long since become part of her past, but today, she felt a slight annoyance at some of the questions, "How does it feel, arriving here without Matthew?"

Catching Hank's serious expression, she resisted the almost obvious sarcastic retort. Instead she replied coolly, "It's a very strange and sad feeling. However, we're doing just what he would have wanted, keeping our engagements and making sure that the company is safe for us all. Incidentally, it hurt when the baby was still born," she added caustically.

Hank watched the defiance in her, how cool she appeared, yet he now realised that she kept the hurt to herself. The lines of shock still etched her beautiful face, but as always, her enthusiasm for the job in hand shone through.

Hastily he shrugged the press off and escorted them to the waiting cars. Kelly held his hand, "Can I sit in your car with you and Mummy?" "And me," chirped up Verity. Chuckling happily, Debbie held Lucy in her arms as Hank helped them all into the chauffeur driven car, sliding himself in with them.

Jim, Ellen and Emma went with the luggage into the second car. Hank had never felt so much pleasure as he did now. Surrounded by the children and the woman he could never forget, he wondered if he could ever interest her in himself. "Debbie, I sure hope you won't find me underfoot at the ranch, if I am, promise to tell me, honey!"

"I promise, *honey*," she quipped.

Arriving at the ranch, the trees were decidedly bare, the flowers were waiting to bloom, yet there was tranquillity here, her eyes misted as she could almost feel Matthew's presence. Somehow, if he were to be here, she got the distinct feeling of approval.

Typical of small children, hers settled down almost immediately. Debbie noticed the way they constantly sought Hank's company, he chatted to them, treating them like young adults. When she bumped into him, she said seriously, "Hank, if the kiddies get under your feet, you must tell them. They understand about being busy!"

"Debbie, honey, they don't worry me at all. I love their company, they're so unpretentious, don't worry, I'm also used to interruptions!"

He was such a dear person and her heart warmed. She knew he was used to a hectic schedule, after all, his 'in depth' documentary programmes had won him the award for top journalist, hence the reason for him being invited to host the bash for charity, with herself as top personality and designer.

Ellen happily prepared for her cookery series and Debbie managed to sort out the advanced crochet series. Hank also wanted her to attend several chat shows, Joanne being included. In fact, he had arranged for them both to be interviewed, he was in as much demand as herself.

A couple of days prior to the Ball, Debbie wandered outside. Her feet took her to the large gate that led into fields. Leaning on the gate, her chin on her folded arms, she glanced over the horizon.

Her eyes rested on the almost bare tree. Matthew's tree, the one they made blistering love under. Subconsciously, she inhaled deeply, releasing her breath slowly in a sigh.

Involuntary shudders ran through her as Hank's voice boomed, "Memories, Debbie? Do you feel sad being here again? You're such a dear person, you never deserved the sadness you had to endure!"

Having nearly jumped from her skin, she sighed again, "Hi, Hank, I was just remembering, not sad. I don't know so much about being a wonderful person, at times, I find it hard to even like myself!"

Although she spoke without thought, she did feel that her behaviour left a lot to be desired. Turning to him. She saw the query in his face, "Debbie, honey, I sure can't believe you've done anything to reproach yourself for. Hell, you lost so much!"

"I didn't have to hurt Paul. I know I've hurt him, yet he is so understanding," she added sadly.

"However have you hurt Paul? Debbie, tell me about how you both came to split up in the first place? Honey, I shouldn't ask, should I? I guess it's the journalist in me!"

Flashing a wry smile in his direction, she explained about Amanda and her own hasty marriage to Matthew. Even admitted that Paul knew of Kelly and had done prior to the accident.

Hank gasped, "Gee, Debbie, you must have been shocked out of your mind. I'm sure that Paul more than understands, he was the one that left, wasn't he?"

In spite of asking, he knew from Paul that it had been all his fault, but Paul would tell him no details, saying, "If Debs wishes you to know, Hank, she'll tell you!"

Rubbing her forearms as if soothing herself, her tone was flat, "I feel nothing short of a bed hopper, Hank. First of all I hopped into bed with Matthew. And then directly back to Paul. How can you admire a shameless person like myself? One who seems to exist on sex, one who seeks her own fulfilment, without care?"

"How many men have you had, Debbie?"

She gulped heavily, "Hell, Hank, do you mind?"

264

"Sorry, honey," he added.

Suddenly she smiled, "I'm touchy, Hank, probably because the truth hurts. I've only ever loved two men. Matthew had loved me for quite a while and it did make sense to marry him. We were perfect together and I never regretted that decision. When he died though, I didn't break down until after the funeral. It was Paul that I turned to. Hank, I wanted his love, I needed his love and now I've hurt him!"

Hank watched the shame spread over her face, yet she had done nothing to condemn herself for. He knew she had turned to Paul, yet Paul had assured him she would not marry him.

His arms ached to hold her, but it was too soon. He had already taken the biggest gamble of his life. "Stop worrying, Debbie. Your children are well balanced and happy. Come on now, we have a Ball to attend, I also have a proposition to make to you afterwards!"

He cursed under his breath, he hadn't meant to say that, she was just so easy to talk to. That was what had made her into the celebrity she now was. Mercifully, she had not taken him too seriously, but added, "Hank Marcowvitze, if you want to propose a further schedule, you can forget it. We're all snowed under and that includes you!"

Her voice was lighter now, perhaps she felt better for talking to him. Gripping her hand, he teased, "No more work, Madam, just relax and enjoy with weekend!"

As she left him, her heart felt lighter. She would never know what had prompted her to confide her innermost feelings to Hank. Almost as though it had been a duty, the words had just slipped from her. Tripping upstairs to bed, she realised that Hank had said more or less the same as Paul, putting everything into a proper perspective for her. For the first time in ages, she fell into a guiltless sleep.

**

Saturday morning arrived, it was frosty, yet deliciously crisp. Hank had asked the chauffeur to take them to the airport and having loaded the luggage, he rushed back to say goodbye. Ellen and Jim hugged him, they all seemed to have some sort of secret, but undoubtedly Debbie would soon be put into the picture. Locked into her parents' arms, they said, "Now relax and enjoy yourself, dear, the children will be fine. You're in safe hands, so enjoy every moment!"

Hank kissed the children one by one. Her heart went out to him, he did really love her little ones. Kelly's arms went around his neck, "Will you kiss Mummy for us?"

Debbie felt the flush creep from the belly of her and land squarely into her cheeks. Catching her eye, Hank whispered to Kelly, "I think I can arrange that for you all, but it will be four kisses, won't it?"

She noticed the look that passed between her parents and Hank, but before she had time to analyse it, they were in the car and speeding towards the airport.

Arriving in Washington, a courtesy car awaited them. Stirs of excitement accompanied the nerves that were beginning to gather. She watched Hank, his total composure seemed to rub off a little. His eyes were dancing as he helped her out of the car which was now parked outside a very majestic looking hotel.

Her happy excitement thrilled him. Many women would have accepted this with an everyday matter of fact attitude, but Debbie never hid her delight. Her gorgeous eyes shone as a swish looking doorman stepped forward,

"Good afternoon, Madam," he said as he touched his gold braided cap.

Walking across the heavy piled, burgundy carpet, she felt her feet sinking. Highly polished tables and chairs were dotted about at tasteful intervals, obviously for many private conversations. Heads turned to acknowledge their arrival, leaving a heady atmosphere around them.

The elevator was just as ritzy as the vestibule and the bell hop pressed the button for the penthouse suite. Watching the porter carry their luggage in, she felt nervous at the total grandeur. Hank handed over the tip, which was received with pleasure and dignity.

Sheer unadulterated luxury surrounded them. The carpets were mixtures of creams and beiges, gripping their feet into the rich depth. Three very large settees were scattered with pretty cushions and although the central heating was working to perfection, there was an imitation log fire to sit around and probably watch the massive television screen.

Lost in wonder, she kicked her shoes off. Hank chuckled and taking her hand, he led her round to explore, "Let's sort out our rooms!"

There were two sumptuous bathrooms, with sunken baths and separate shower cubicles. One was in deep, almost navy blue, with gold fixtures and fittings. The other one was a deep rose pink. She gasped, "Hank, they're gorgeous, which colour do you want?"

Loving her deep sense of humour, they quickly realised that the decisions of who would sleep where, had been made for them. Hank's belongings had been placed into a lavish double bedroom, complete with television and tea making facilities. He hung his dinner jacket carefully and she shuddered, remembering how handsome he looked when dressed in evening attire.

Wandering into another large room, Debbie thought she had never seen anything so positively feminine. A huge four poster bed was draped with pretty pink satin folds, clipped back into small gold fitments. The wardrobes were fitted with a selection of dresses and flimsy shoes. The dressing table took over the whole of one wall and boxes of make up were laid out, together with every bath oil under the sun.

Turning to Hank, she gasped, "Look at these beautiful dresses. Which one would you like me to wear? I suddenly feel very nervous!"

"Gee, honey, you'll look great in any of them. I think I'd like to see you all in white. Somehow that seems to sum you up, pure as the driven snow!"

"After my evening of true confessions? Hank, I feel foolish to have exposed my heart to you, but I must admit you did help me. At least things are more in perspective for me!"

"Honey, you can open up to me anytime," he added with sincerity.

They ordered a small meal to be served in their suite and both ate with hunger. As they sipped their coffee, Hank asked, "Is there anything you need? There's a mall of shops below the hotel and I need to pop out for about half an hour. We'll then have to get ourselves ready for a seven o'clock reception and ring the children, of course!"

As he left, a strange insecurity filled her. Balling her hands, she decided to sort out her attire for the evening. She would definitely wear the gorgeous white chiffon dress. It felt cobweb soft as she ran her deft fingers over it. Folds of chiffon made up the bodice, which was reinforced to hold up a good firm bust. A single red rose, surrounded by tiny silver leaves, rested daintily into the cleavage.

Many layers of material made up the full, flowing skirt, which began from her tiny waist and draped seductively over her slender hips, before swishing around her ankles. She would stocking her legs in the sheerest, skin coloured nylons, before slipping her feet into the exotic, silver strap, high heeled shoes.

She could frame her face with small curls, drawing back the sides of her hair into tiny imitation diamond combs, to hang loosely down her back. Tiny white satin panties and suspender belt were the only form of undies she would need.

Having sorted all of that out, her hands began to shake as she laid out her night attire. She had purchased a pretty white satin nightgown, it fitted her body to perfection and tiny straps slipped over her shoulders. She had a matching negligee to wear over it. Probably she could wear this for breakfast, or even tonight if she and Hank decided to take a nightcap together and discuss the events of the evening.

"I'm back, honey," came Hank's voice as the door slammed. Her body shook with relief, she really was, very, very nervous. "O.K. Hank, I've just been sorting myself out for later. Golly, I feel ever so nervous, do you?"

"No, not one bit, but then I have you for a partner!"

"Where've you been, Hank?"

Who the hell did she think she was? She had sounded almost domineering, but Hank chuckled, "Just attending to a bit of business, why, did you miss me?"

"Yes, Hank, I think I did. It felt strange being here alone, anyway, you shouldn't have to attend to business today. The whole weekend is being taken up with the Ball!"

His heart pounded, she had no idea just how magnetic she was. The very simplicity of her astounded him, most women would die rather than admit to being lonely. With a mischievous grin, he added, "You mean you missed me, an old man like me?"

"Ahh, poor *old*, Hank," came her jocular retort.

"But I am old compared to you, honey. I'm thirty nine already and have nothing to show but my work!"

Her eyes lifted to him, "I think a person is as old as he feels. You have a splendid work record to show for it. Anyway, I thought you had a secret love, why don't you marry her?"

Before her eyes, his face closed. She had obviously hit a raw nerve. Now she felt the need to get him to talk to her, it may well help him. Her talk with him had certainly helped her, yet something seemed to be holding her back. The time to talk, if there was such a time, was later this evening, probably over a drink.

Hank picked up the 'phone and asked for a tray of coffee to be sent up, at the same time, he requested an outside line. His eyes danced as he dialled the number, "I want to talk to the girls first, they'll be thrilled to hear from us!"

Feeling her heart lurch with pride, she heard her little ones almost shouting to Hank. His eyes lit up further as he listened to them and for the very first time, Debbie noticed the gold flecks in them. Having reassured her children that she was well, she replaced the receiver with a contented smile.

"They sure seem happy enough, mind you, Debbie, I'm missing them already. C'mon, I think we'd better get ourselves ready. I suppose you want the pink bathroom," he teased.

"You could look a little out of place in pink, HONEY!"

As they drifted over to their respective bathrooms, he called, "Hey, Debbie, I almost forgot, I've been asked about you running through another pregnancy series, using Emma's birth. Would it be too painful for you? We've had a hefty post about the subject, think about it, honey?"

"I certainly will have to think about it, Hank. But I suppose you're right, after all you understand the market pressure!"

**

Debbie stepped into the sunken, foam filled bath. This was sheer luxury, in fact she would bear this in mind for the castle. Mentally, she could see her little ones loving this. Soaping herself, she felt the tension being given up to the depth of the foam. Her heart was dreadfully unsteady, yet why? She couldn't begin to understand.

Sitting down in front of the dressing table mirror, she brushed her hair till it shone. Gently, she eased the combs into position and felt more than happy with the result. Her hands began to shake as she applied her make up and she noticed her eyes smouldered as a sparkle seemed to have appeared from nowhere.

Finally, lifting the dress from the bed, she almost dropped it again. There was a very expensive velvet box laying beneath it. Her shaking hands opened it as a gasp escaped her lips. The note read, "I hoped you would choose this dress, honey. Please wear this for me, my first gift to you!"

The drop earrings matched the gorgeous neck piece and sheer shock accompanied the gratitude she felt. He had not only guessed correctly, but had also reasoned that gold wouldn't offset the dress as beautifully as his gift would. Her heart pounded so much, she thought everyone would see it through the bodice of her dress.

Stepping back from the mirror, she knew she looked good. It had taken her all her time to fasten the choker and earrings, so great had been her surprise. Confusion swamped her as she heard Hank, "C'mon, honey, we must be underway!"

Opening her door, she saw him standing there and somehow had never realised just how strikingly handsome he was. His eyes turned to her, a gasp left him, "Stay right where you are, honey!"

He needn't have bothered telling her to stay put, she had become transfixed. His eyes drank in her beauty, she looked as a portrait freshly hung, standing framed in the doorway. His eyes took in the rose, his body envied it its resting place. With a strange hoarseness, he murmured, "You look absolutely beautiful, Debbie. I sure am a lucky guy to be your partner!"

Her voice faltered, "Hank, I ... I don't know what to say, this is so .. so lovely," her hands went to her throat as she spoke.

"Then don't say anything," he gulped.

"Golly, Hank, if we weren't ready to leave, I think I would've given you a kiss. I'm overwhelmed, but thank you!"

Wondering why she allowed her tongue to run on without thought, her mouth dried. His smile devastated her, "Well, I'll hold you to that, when we return. Incidentally, I have to give you four kisses, or had you forgotten?"

"No, Hank, I hadn't, but wondered if you had!"

Right now Hank would have given anything to stay at home this evening. He even felt a stir of hope, her beauty bewitched him, there was an ethereal aura about her. Turning to hide his giant sized arousal, he coaxed, "Come on Debbie, we definitely can't be late!"

Everything that went on that evening, she felt had been done automatically. The handshaking, the eating, the toasts and proposals. Many people rose to speak as she became more and more aware, of the man sitting beside her. Whatever was wrong with her? Could her confusion be seen?

Background music had come from the band as they had eaten, but now a voice spoke, "Will you take your partners for a waltz? Perhaps our guest of honour would like to start the evening off?"

Applause blasted with the music. Her feet had suddenly sunk into granite, her body felt rigid as she felt Hank's arm slide around her, "Come on, honey, I feel the pressure too, but we can do this, together we *can* do this!"

Miraculously her feet moved as her body sunk against him. He was very light on his feet, she had learned that many moons ago. His breath on her forehead was hot, unbalancing her. Her stupid heart lurched into her throat, she was becoming besotted about this man, wanting to learn how he kissed, how he caressed, how he ... Yet he had already lost his heart to another.

Many men danced with her that evening, just as many women danced with him. She had all but forced herself to make polite conversation, but her eyes were constantly drawn to the man with the gold flecks in his eyes.

Every ounce of her wanted to leave, sit down, think about her strange feelings. She would have to wait till the end as she and Hank would have to leave officially first. Several times she gulped down the champagne that seemed to come around with startling speed.

Strains of music led the rich tenor voice that sung 'The last waltz' She felt his lips brush her forehead as suffocation overcame her. She had never thought of Hank in this light and told herself she was making a mountain out of a molehill.

His eyes locked hers, "Have you enjoyed yourself, honey? You look like a bride in that dress, a gorgeous bride at that!"

As the music ended, the lights came back up and she felt him take her arm. He would lead her towards the exit as the other guests lined up to applaud them. Never had she felt so pleased to leave anywhere, her mind, once again in a dreadful turmoil.

CHAPTER FORTY THREE

Debbie's heart thumped painfully as Hank led her to the swish elevator. She had noticed many women's heads turning in his direction, he was a tantalisingly handsome man. His very restlessness had added an extra charisma, right now though, she felt extremely shy and unsettled. Again she asked herself, 'what the hell is the matter with you?'

Hank looked down at her, "Have you *really* enjoyed yourself, Debbie? I must admit it went perfectly and a lot of money was raised. Are you tired, honey? Can we have a drink together?"

"Strangely, Hank, I'm not tired, a little tipsy perhaps, but I feel wide awake and would love a nightcap together. I do want to get out of this dress though!"

"Yep, I need to climb out of this monkey suit!"

Arriving into the suite, she noticed that a bottle of champagne, complete with ice bucket and glasses, had been placed onto the table. Her legs trembled so much, she could scarcely walk into her room.

Hanging her dress neatly into the wardrobe, she removed her shoes and stockings, leaving her panties to sit under her pretty satin nightgown. Taking her negligee and slipping it on, she walked gingerly back into the large room.

Relief surged through her as she noticed that Hank had not yet emerged. Walking over to the settee, she sat down and tucked her back against the arm, leaving her legs to stretch parallel with the back. Once she snuggled into the corner, she drew her knees up and wrapped her arms around them, giving her a feeling of safely.

Almost immediately, Hank entered the room, wearing a tasteful bathrobe. Debbie gasped her surprise as his eyes rested on her, a worried frown appeared as he asked, "Am I not dressed decently, Debbie? What made you gasp?"

"Its just .. just that you reminded me of Matthew for a moment!"

His eyebrows raised, "What did I do to remind you, honey? I didn't mean to upset you. Let's open the champagne, shall we?"

"That's a good idea. You haven't upset me. The night after we married, well, he came out of the bathroom dressed just like you are now!"

His eyes never left her, she looked even more delicious if that were possible. Popping the cork, he filled her glass and leaned over to hand it to her. "When did you realise you were in love with Matthew?"

Gulping her drink, she flushed, "The first time he made love with me. It was funny really, we both walked along the beach for nearly three hours, as though putting off the ultimate moment!"

Her face took on a wistful look as her glass went back to her lips. He lit them both a cigarette, "Where you dreading it? Hadn't he tried before? There I go again, asking impertinent questions!"

"Don't worry, Hank, they aren't offensive when you ask. I only found out that he loved me two days prior to the wedding!"

The little chuckle she gave, choked him and he leaned over to fill her glass. "I love your honest simplicity, honey, sounds to me, you both had the right ideas on marriage!"

"We did, Hank. He used to tease me unmercifully, yet we never had a cross word," she sighed happily.

How wonderful it was to hear her able to laugh, able to remember her happiness, even to share it. Her hair fell tantalisingly down her back and he gulped, "You are a beautiful woman, Debbie. I know that you and Matthew were truly happy!"

"We certainly were, Hank. Anyway, enough about me, tell me about the woman who has stolen your heart?"

Her mouth dried, she realised she didn't really want to know. Licking her lips, she straightened her legs and turned to look at him. He smiled, "Gee, Debbie, haven't you guessed?"

He was on his feet and walking towards her. Taking her glass from her, he placed it onto the table and sat down beside her. She could see his breathing was uneven, his hand gently tilted her chin. The gold flecks met hers as his lips moved softly over hers.

His kiss was like the gentle brush of a butterfly. A symphony began in her mind as is lips moved over her face like the soft glide of a bow over a violin. His other hand gently touched her hair, his fingers running through it, until he steadied her head.

Feeling his hand still under her chin, the gentle pressure lifting her mouth to him. The music still very soft, very slow, very sweet. His body shook with hers, his mouth moved over her eyes in a rhapsody of delight. Returning to her lips, the drums began to rumble as the pressure increased slightly.

Her head was bursting, she had never felt like this before. His arm closed around her shoulder, pulling her tenderly to him. The cymbals now crashed as his other arm closed around her. She couldn't breathe, his tongue ran along her lips as if waiting for an invitation from her. Headily, she allowed her tongue to meet his, longing for his invasion.

Hank felt the deep response in her as he eased his tongue into the silken sheath of her mouth. He wanted to grip and pull her, but she was clearly enjoying the tender manner he was offering.

Many words sprung into his mind, but he didn't dare break the magic of the moment, he must not frighten her. Hearing her soft groans was like a beautiful symphony to his ears and he couldn't contain the moans of ecstasy that escaped him.

Seeing the passion smoulder in her ebony eyes, he felt like crushing her to him. His arms still added light pressure to her back and his hand ventured to touch her breast. He knew she was deeply aroused, he could feel the turgid nipple grinding into him, sending fired of hope through him. Hell, he was so hard, it hurt and even trying to cross his legs didn't help much.

Needing to tell the world of his love, he knew better. His hand covered her breast through the satin, he had longed to touch her, feel her. He didn't know where the next breath was coming from as his heart thumped without mercy.

Inhaling to fill his lungs his mouth returned to hers. Applying gentle pressure, his hand removed her gown and strap from her shoulder. Little yelps let her as his mouth sought to locate the pulse that throbbed without pretension. Resisting the urge to bite her, he allowed his hand to bare her breast.

Debbie had never felt anything so tastefully beautiful as the strains of the rhapsody continued. Fire coursed through her as he kept one hand on her back, his other hand caressed her silky breast, his mouth following each caress, until his tongue swirled around the throbbing, pink, hardened peak.

Mindlessly, she ran her mouth over his face, pausing only to grip his lips with hers. Tenderly he eased her arms from its trappings, at the same time slipping the other shoulder clear. His sharp intake of breath as her breasts were revealed sent her spiralling with desire.

Debbie felt herself squirm as he lifted them to his lips. He was a consummate master of his art and she an obviously willing pupil. She now knew exactly what Paul had meant. Her mind couldn't concentrate, didn't even want to, on anything outside of this moment.

Watching Hank's head move from one breast to the other, was a wonderful form of delightful torture, yet not once had he made a rough movement. She felt like a priceless work of art, being handled and treasured as such.

Sighs escaped her as her mouth roamed his neck, her tongue traced the whorl of his ear. She longed for him to say that he loved her, she longed to tell him, but like him, she daren't risk spoiling the magic.

Her hands opened his robe and ran through the hair of his chest. Her finger tip ran down through the tangle of hair, to the hard ridge of muscle about his waistband, her ears sharply tuned for the roughened intake of his breath.

Groans left him as again, his arms went around her, the pressure gentle on her back as she felt her breast pressing into the hard wall of his chest. She could hear his heart beating wildly as she now sought for air to fill her lungs.

His hands moved to take hers, his fingers entwining with hers, lovingly he took first one and then the other to his lips. Once more his hand lifted her chin, his lips brushing hers and parting them for his tongue to gently invade her. Never had she felt such wild passion, yet so much tenderness.

Wordlessly, they continued searching each other, her arms slipping his robe from his shoulders. His shorts revealed the depth of his arousal as groans of longing left him. Her body so far was absolutely gorgeous, how desperately he had yearned to have her like this. Accepting her delicious responses was like sipping nectar.

So many words longed to leap from his lips, whisper into her ear, but nothing could destroy the magic of these precious moments. Heaving heavily, his hand slid gently over her abdomen and round to caress her slender hips.

She longed to scream out her desire for him, her whole body was sensitised and eager.

Over and over his hands returned to hold the side of her head, his mouth roaming over hers. Her gasps of obvious delight just fuelling his fire. He could feel the beautiful heat from her aroused body.

Helping her to kneel slightly, he eased her gown downwards, his breath catching in his throat as the tiny white panties were the only covering on her body. Momentarily, his eyes lingered seeing the dark swelling beneath the satin.

She felt the delicate pressure of his arms closing around her. His eyes found hers, the rich ebony choking him, the misty damp tear was beauty incarnate. Never had he probed so deeply, so lovingly, so desperately for the squeals of delight she somehow found so easy to impart.

Feeling his hand turn to fire, he eased it into her panties and gasps of wonder shot from him as his fingers touched the crisp curls. His other hand pulled them from her and with a frenzied sigh, he touched the moist juncture that joined her hips to perfection.

In his wildest dreams he had never imagined anything like she really was. Her body shook helplessly in his arms, her eager mouth turning to him and dropping kisses onto his chest. It was all he could do to hold himself back as his penis became so engorged, he thought it would burst.

Holding her softly to him, she felt him easing her back. His flecks of gold seemed to have turned molten as fire smouldered from his eyes. Eyes that spoke of love, eyes that sought hers for answers.

Moaning softly, she longed to give him the answers. No one had ever held her like this, tantalising her, tormenting her to dizzy heights. His arm still around her shoulders as his free hand brushed the hair from her face and holding her mouth still, his finger parted her lips. Exquisite sensations of joy filled her as she realised, he was now stealing her heart right from under her nose.

His hand moved over her breast, pausing to rub his thumb and forefinger over her peaks of sensitivity, bringing her swollen tips to bursting point until his mouth appeased them. Guttural groans left his lips as his hand continued over her flat abdomen.

Momentarily, he lifted his head, he needed to gaze upon the whole of her body. He could not hold back the gasp of delight as the pink flush of expectancy covered her. His lips moved back to hers as he grunted his way through the kiss.

Her inner thighs quivered as he gently ran his hand along them. She squirmed delightfully as his arm continued to hold her shoulder, a finger freeing itself to caress her chin. Instantly, a crazy, confused delirium filled her.

Headily she slipped his shorts over his taut buttocks and felt his body tense. Her gratitude to the Almighty for the gift of sight, suffocated her. Hell, he was gorgeous, standing proudly before her and throbbing with desire. A tormented cry left him as he felt her soft caress, inciting him to fever pitch.

Choking with desire and praying for control, he gently covered her body with his. His finger slipped into her, feeling her pelvis rock. His mouth again claimed hers, so gentle, so tender, so filled with a passion that was rapidly becoming urgent.

Hank never wanted these moments to end. All he could hope for, was that he didn't ruin the magic. The tiny curls that framed her beautiful face had turned into damp tendrils as jets of perspiration sprung across her forehead.

Debbie felt the pressure from his mouth deepen on hers, her heart pumped as he removed his hand and lifted himself. Their eyes met and travelled over her swollen peaks and beyond, stifled with desire she drew her knees upwards, eager to welcome his majestic hardness.

Deep, uncontrolled jerks ripped from him as he felt himself drawn into the soft coven of desire. Their eyes locked with a bewildered wonder. His hands climbed up her back, the palms flat against the back of her shoulders. His fingers softly gripping her shoulders, she felt the heat burning from his body.

As if by mutual agreement, neither moved. His mouth went over hers and then her legs folded around him, locking him tightly into her. He would never know how he hadn't let himself go completely, the need to fulfil her now the most important item in *his* love of *her* havoc.

Words sprung to Debbie's lips and stayed there. Feeling his mouth move down to claim her breast, she was ready to scream out so great was her need. He began to move, cautiously, tenderly, the soft pressure on her shoulders was driving her into delicious frenzy.

Hank was gripped into her silken sheath and could feel her expand and contract around him, making him groan in agonised delight. She would never know of the extraordinary pleasure she was serving up to him. The demands of her wonderful honey comb left him in no doubt whatsoever, she could love him, her every move, her every response screamed love with a capital L.

Groaning helplessly, he realised there were two ways of declaring love, one was with words, the other was Debbie's way, with her eyes, her body, her eager desire to please and enjoy. She was matching him thrust for thrust as he moved rapidly, unable to control his strokes and then he felt her body tense and knew she felt the earth shattering convulsions racking the whole of her body.

Hungrily, her mouth turned to him as he felt himself burst, not in comfortable spates, but a long heady burst, till he had nothing left to give. Deep groans had accompanied his perfect thrust as her helpless moans left her. Her legs had held him beautifully locked into her.

Gasping, panting and kissing each other, their bodies still moved as one. Her arms looped his neck as he slumped gloriously onto her. Although fighting for breath, neither could let go. His body shook unmercifully as his arms gathered her, once again with sheer tenderness. Gripped into an emotion so deep, it had no name, they both waited for the sweet ebb of passion that would surely follow.

Hank shuddered with love, he had longed to have her like this, longed to feel her caresses. Never had he envisaged the beauty with which she gave. Never had a woman made him feel loved like this. Never had he been shattered and shocked right down to his primal roots.

Debbie felt riveted, her whole body had sought such fulfilment. Hank had left her without words, without thoughts, just lost deeply in a place leaving her without desire to return. Her head moved to kiss him. Finally lifting his head, his eyes held hers, "Babe, you'll never know how much I love you," came his hoarse whisper.

Stunned beyond words, Debbie found there was no sign of the ebb of passion. A divine lethargy spread through her, Hank's head was embedded into her neck, his mouth still savouring her as his lips roamed gently along her shoulder. Making love with this man was a total experience, a sensual feast of vibrant life.

She never knew how long they laid locked as one. Her head began to pound as her mind swirled in confusion. There was no doubt in her mind, she was in love with this man. Crazily, she recalled how eager she had been to hear his voice on the 'phone, how totally comfortable she now felt with him, after all she had emptied the secrets of her heart to him.

Sadness also struck her, she knew that Paul must have known. She could however, only feel a deep gratitude to him. Sighing with sheer unadulterated pleasure, she felt him begin to move. Her arms now instinctively needing to hold on to him.

Reluctantly, he lifted himself from her. Easing her into a sitting position, he kissed her with a warmth she couldn't believe. Leaning over, he poured the almost flat champagne and after lighting them both a cigarette, his eyes met hers, "Debbie, dearest, Debbie, you know I'm hopelessly in love with you, don't you?"

Her head nodded stupidly, yet still words would not leave her. She was shocked to the core at what had happened to them and realised that she wanted it to happen all over again.

Watching her drink her drink straight down, he again turned to her, "Debbie, gee, honey, say something to me. I felt your love, babe. Honey, did I hurt you? Please, speak to me!"

His eyes roamed that gorgeous body and he couldn't believe she had given it to him. His hand took hers to his lips and his mouth kissed each pad of her fingers and her eyes widened, "Hank, you … you didn't ..hurt me. I feel full of shock. Somehow, I can't .. can't believe tonight," she stammered.

Lovingly his arms gathered her to him, his hand brushed away the curtain of hair that had fallen over her face. Possessively, his hand fondled her breast as he felt her body still shaking. "Honey, tell me how you feel at this precise moment? Remember, I'm the guy that loves you!"

Lifting her eyes to meet the gold flecks, her look never wavered, "Hank, you made me feel like a precious piece of porcelain, to be handled with care. To be treasured and cosseted, in fact truly cherished. I know beyond doubt, that I am hopelessly in love with you. And, I never *ever* thought I'd utter those words again!"

Drenched with joy, he inhaled deeply, "Gee, honey, I see you as a precious object. I never dreamed I'd be lucky enough to hear those words from you, yet somehow, I sensed we'd be great together. You've made me the happiest man in the world. Hell, Debbie, I know I'm rushing you, but would you do me the honour of becoming my wife ... or do you need time?"

The room seemed to be swaying and her arms gripped him, "Hank, I don't know what to say. It's funny, because every single decision I've ever made, has been one mad rush," she gasped.

"Were any of those decisions wrong, darling?"

"No, Hank, in fact they were very right. I know I want to marry you, but I just don't know what to say!"

"How about ... yes?"

Her lips met his in a kiss of celebration. She couldn't come to terms with such a violent passion being administered so tenderly. Urging the kiss to continue, she felt salt in her mouth. Gently, she eased away to find him turning his head from her.

Startled to her roots, she gasped, "Hank, I've upset you, darling, what have I done? Don't turn from me, my love. I have never felt so whole and complete!"

Sobs fell softly from him. He gasped painfully, "Hell, Debbie, what a bloody fool I am. I've loved you almost since our first meeting and now I know you love me, hell, honey, I can't believe it. I backed my entire future on your love!"

Bewilderment rushed through her, tears sprung to her own eyes. How dreadfully humble he appeared, how he must have worried about tonight. However had he managed to conceal these feelings? Her voice shook, "You'd better believe it, Hank. I do love you and that's a fact!"

Tears now poured from them both. An obvious reaction to the searcher having found his treasure and to a heart that had been filled with untold misery, a release from pain to splendour. They clung together, solace rapidly turning to passion. His hands again roamed her body, his voice hoarse from the sobs, "Debbie, honey, all the time we were making love, I wanted to tell you how much I loved you!"

"Why didn't you?"

"I was petrified of frightening you. Petrified of breaking the magic we were sharing. I have never had to fight so hard in my life, the words were just waiting to fall from my mouth," came his choking admission.

"Hank, darling, I think it was all the sweeter without words. Your actions spoke for you. No one has ever loved me with such a deep tenderness. I feel so much in love and so very happy. In fact, I want you all over again," she added with her usual simplicity.

Once more she felt the hardness of his body as he transported her to heaven. This time though, as they waited for their passions to ebb, they both felt the need to offer tender caresses, to offer and receive words of love. Their after play now a captivating finesse of pure delight.

Her eyes rounded as they lifted to his, "Hank, we should've gone to bed, or didn't you fancy being engulfed in pink satin drapes?"

The little chuckle had once again sprung from her, filling him with a mixture of deep love and relief. Holding hr face, he croaked, "I know we should go to bed, honey, but unless you prefer not to, we really must talk!"

She frowned, he brushed it away. They must talk, but for a while they could stay as one. Leaning to drag his bathrobe over them she felt herself enveloped in his arms and the sweet kiss of sleep, to take them into oblivion.

**

Debbie awakened a short while later and for a moment she was disorientated. Only when her hand touched the hard male thigh thrown across her, did her memory supply the detail. Hank stirred, but the leg and arm were not withdrawn. Her heart thudded uncomfortably as her arm went out to touch him.

Instantly he opened his eyes and moaned contentedly, "Hi, honey," as his arms drew her to him. Smiling with a new found wonder, she leaned over to kiss him. "Debbie, I always want to wake up like this. Any regrets, little one?"

His lips moved along her cheek as he continued, "First of all I'm going to ring for a tray of coffee, we just *have* to talk!"

The urgency in his voice worried her, she watched the way he ordered the coffee, his total ease as he dealt with others, yet somehow he was restless with her. Little pangs of fear entered her. Slipping her negligee onto herself, he popped his robe back on and she asked, "Hank, there's something wrong, I can feel it. You're not relaxed with me, are you?"

His fair hair was gloriously tussled as he took the tray from the smiling waiter. Glancing at her watch, she was startled to see it was only six o'clock, yet she felt as though she had slept for hours.

Hank poured the coffee and handed a cup to her and gulped, "How dare you look so beautiful at this time in the morning? Hell, Debbie, tell me I'm not dreaming?"

Her hair was shimmering, but ruffled, her eyes held real concern, yet he loved her more than ever, her gorgeous lips moved, "Hank, you're not dreaming. But there is something bothering you, I mean I love your compliments, what woman wouldn't? I do however, want to share any problems!"

"Such wisdom from one so young," he stated with sincerity.

"Come on, Hank, stop messing about, you said we must talk. I'm waiting," she choked as fear began to overwhelm her.

278

He dragged his fingers through his hair, his face was serious, "Debbie, I've more than jumped the gun. Last night, I don't know if you remember, but I told you I'd gambled. .. I felt that if you did feel anything for me, we'd discover it here, on our own!"

Her eyes never wavered as she watched him continue, "I knew I couldn't work beside you for almost a year, unless I knew there was at least some hope. When I went out yesterday, it was to collect a ring. .. Oh, Debbie, after discussing my ideas with your parents, they more or less agreed with me!"

"You mean they already know? Hank, you had no right to discuss me .. without me," she retorted somewhat childishly.

"I know that, honey, but I'm just a helpless guy. They know how I feel about you, so does Paul. No darling, let me finish!"

He raised his arm defensively as she almost spluttered, "Hank, you'd no right to do this," and she burst into laughter. He looked so sheepish and her heart filled with love. "Hank Marcowvitze, I should be angry with you. It wouldn't surprise me to learn that the preacher was calling in later!"

His eyes held hers as she took the cup to her lips. Suddenly, she remembered the looks that had passed between him and her parents and she knew. "You've done just that, haven't you, Hank? You must have been damned cock sure of me. I almost feel angry with you," she gasped in disbelief.

"Only almost angry, honey?"

Something warned her not to be too angry. As he said, he had virtually gambled on what others had told him. "How did you know that I'd say yes? What happens if he turns up and I'd said no?"

Almost as a child, he confessed, "Well, I have to call him before eleven. He has all of our particulars, if we do need him, he'll come around one and bring a couple of witnesses and photographer. Debbie, I'm certain that you parents agree to a quiet wedding, to avoid press speculation. We'll just announce that we are married. You know I love the children dearly, please, please tell me you're not cross with me?"

Gulping the hot coffee down, it hit her stomach with a thud. "Hank, what if I hadn't agreed? I shudder to think what would have happened to our working relationship. I don't know how my parents could speak on my behalf, even Paul. I now feel guilty about him!"

"Honey, hell, if it had gone wrong," he grimaced and lit a cigarette. "If it had gone wrong, I had arranged for my deputy to take over here and I was going to England. When you returned, well, I'd come back to New York. I shouldn't have placed so much on this weekend, but for me, it was make or break time!"

Debbie watched the familiar restlessness in him. There was nothing cock sure about him, in fact she had never seen him looking more insecure. Yet, everything he said was true, had they announced their intentions they would have been hounded. There was probably some speculation going on about last night. They had, after all, arrived as a couple, albeit as co hosts. She also realised that her parents would agree with her, a natural truth to her children would be far more acceptable.

Having tried desperately to be angry with him, she knew he had acted in all of their best interest. If she hadn't declared her love, he would have walked away without telling her, of that she was sure. He had kept his secret while she had been out of reach, yet now, he needed an anchor.

She also knew that his nerves must have been near to breaking point, no wonder he had broken down. Pouring some more coffee, her eyes lifted to him. His eyes were filled with concern, uncertainty, love and yes, a real element of fear.

Standing up a little unsteadily, she walked over to him and sat herself firmly onto his lap. Her mouth found his as his kiss explained the true longing in him, breaking slightly away, she asked, "What if we had made love and found we didn't even like it?"

"Honey, even if it hadn't worked out, I would always have had last night to remember. Many times I imagined our love, it sure was never as beautiful as it was last night. Mind you, I had intended to propose first!"

Succumbing to his lips, she melted as his tongue began to learn the inside of her mouth. Suddenly, her eyes flew open in panic, "Hank, what am I going to wear? My hair needs washing, oh, I'll never be ready!"

A hearty guffaw left him, "Darling, I want to marry you in that dress, I told you last night that you looked like a bride and there's a tasteful bolero to match. I'll jump back into my monkey suit!"

"What about your parents?"

"They'll be longing for the 'phone call from us. I think they'll join us in England at Christmas. We must also ring Paul, but let's not tell the children till we get home!"

She smiled to herself, he certainly had been a busy little bee and she loved him for each little thought he had placed into this weekend.

Pinching her nose tenderly, he gulped "I love you so much, Debbie Hudson. We'd better get ready and after we have made our 'phone calls, I'll make mad passionate love to my wife, I want to examine every part of your body, slowly!"

"Hank, this is why we didn't fly back today. I never knew you were so crafty," she smiled.

"Not crafty, my darling, just desperate!"

CHAPTER FORTY FOUR

Debbie watched the foam swirl into the bath and slipped her negligee from herself. Could this be the same person that stood here last night? No, it couldn't be, this lady was happy, revitalised, treasured and cherished.

Hank called out with concern, "Debbie, darling, will it hurt you too much to remove Matthew's ring?"

Pain hovered momentarily, she sighed, "Hank, Matthew would give us his blessing. Funny enough, I'm sure he guides me, I know this is right, it feels right. I will keep his ring though and I will always thank God for sending him for that interview. We truly were idyllically happy, you know that, Hank. Yet I do feel there will probably be some nasty jibes about us, especially about the lack of time since he died!"

"Will it hurt you too much, honey?"

"Not really, you see I know Matthew would approve. We both believed in the saying, 'to thine own self be true'. No matter how long we waited, it would not alter a thing, would it?"

Nervously, she prepared herself. The lady in the mirror had just one subtle difference to the lady last night. This woman glowed with love, her eyes danced, her heart almost thumped from her breast. Slipping the bolero on, she smiled, Hank must had hidden it and replaced it again, yet she had noticed nothing.

Lifting her left hand, she held her ringed finger for a moment. Sliding the ring from her finger, she held it to her mouth and kissed it softly. Raising her eyes heavenwards, she choked her words, "Matthew, thank you for our wonderful life together. I wore this ring with so much pride. I know you understand and although your children will never know you, they will always remember the love you gave to them. Hank and I will make sure of that … they may even come to know him as 'daddy', that would be wonderful for them, but when they grow up, we'll tell them of you. Our public will never forget you either, Matthew!"

A tear glistened as the door buzzer sounded, Hank called out, "Are you ready, honey?"

Almost shyly, she walked into the room, her heart lurching when she saw Hank, he looked as he had the night before, but there was an added self assurance about him. Moments later, they were pronounced man and wife. She felt his kiss, deep and tender, "I love you, Mrs Marcowvitze, I love your children!"

After several photographs had been taken and a promise that they could collect them later, they were alone. A very large bottle of champagne arrived and Hank walked over to pop the cork, both of them giggling as it spilled over into the glasses, he raised his glass, "To my beautiful wife. May you always be as happy as you are this moment, darling, Debbie!"

"And you, Hank, may you never regret this day!"

He had chosen her ring similar to the one Matthew had given her. It felt strangely new as his hand took hers and placed a single, rather large, solitaire diamond beside it. His eyes burned into hers, the gold flecks shone, his voice husky with desire, "This ring is for and about you. A bright light that shines with love. A light that has shone at the end of my tunnel for so long now. Debbie, I love you body and soul!"

Tears stung her eyes, "Hank, darling, its absolutely beautiful, it reminds me of the sheer, flawless love you have given to me. Let's ring our families, oh, Hank, you've made me feel whole again!"

**

Jim and Ellen Hudson had spent an almost sleepless night. The kiddies had been as good as gold, yet Ellen had constantly looked at the clock, her voice cracked with emotion, "Jim, do you think we should have agreed with Hank? I do hope they don't hurt each other. I want to see Debbie completely happy again!"

Holding her auburn head, Jim soothed, "Everything will be alright, darling. Even if Debbie doesn't discover that she's in love with Hank, she wouldn't be unkind!"

They were just about beside themselves as the 'phone finally rung. Having both jumped up to answer it, they both stopped. Jim smiled and held his breath, "Don't worry, Ellie, I think its good news," he gasped.

Hearing his daughter's voice, he could feel the emotion in her, for she had barely gulped, "Dad!"

Fighting to keep his own voice under control, he jerked, "Tell us, dear, do we have to congratulate you?" His heart burst as Ellen snuggled into him, they both heard Hank, "Tell them, dearest. Hi, Jim, Ellen, my new wife is beside me and I can never thank you enough!"

Kissing the top of Ellen's head, he gulped, "They are married. Oh, Ellie, they sound so happy, at least Hank does, Debbie has only managed, 'dad' so far!"

Jim knew his daughter could feel their tension and finally she managed, "I ought to tell you both off, but as usual, you were both right. Please don't tell the children till we return!"

Ellen's choked voice whizzed down the line, "Debs, we're so pleased. The children are longing to speak to you, but of course we won't tell them. Daddy and I wish you both every happiness under the sun. Have a wonderful special day!"

"Thanks, Mum and bless you both!"

The children chirped happily as Hank told them, "Yep, Mommy is having a lovely time We have some photographs for you when we see you tomorrow. Yes, I sure did remember to kiss her for you. See you soon, Pumpkins!"

Ellen's eyes brimmed with tears as her husband took the 'phone from the children and hung up. Her heart went out to her precious daughter, was she destined to have a lasting happiness this time?

**

Debbie watched the tenderness in Hank as he had spoken to the excited children. Overjoyed beyond words, she went into his arms and kissed the man she had just married. Apprehension then filled her as she saw him dial his parents. Swiftly she downed her drink and refilled her glass. His eyes lit up, "Hi there, Mom, Pop, I'd like to introduce you to the new Mrs Marcowvitze, hold on a sec.!"

Never expecting to be stuck straight onto the 'phone, her mouth dried. Within seconds, she knew where Hank had inherited his charm. His mother spoke with a natural ease, "Hi there, Debbie, we feel we already know you and your beautiful children. Our boy has spoken of nothing but you since he met you. We look forward to our hopeful visit with you at Christmas and a sincere welcome to our family, my dear!"

Hearing Hank's father echoing everything in the background, she felt suffocation grip her, but gasped, "Thank you Mom and Pop!"

Hank's hand entered the top of her dress and as she handed the 'phone back to him, she stood still, she rather liked what he was doing and she also knew he knew it. His voice boomed with his new found confidence, "Everything went swell, Mom, we'll release a photograph with a brief announcement later on. My bride looked adorable, see you both soon!"

Debbie knew the next call was going to more than hurt. Hank kissed her long and hard, "Honey, I think the sooner you do this the better you will feel," he murmured softly.

Hearing Paul's voice, she just gasped. She didn't quite know how to begin. Fortunately, he spoke, "Debs, you did go through with it, didn't you? I prayed you would. In fact, in spite of the early hour over here, I drunk a toast to you both!"

She was startled by his complete composure. Never would he allow her to know, he had wept as the appointed hour had approached. He knew if she did recognise her feelings for Hank, she would never look back. He loved her far too much to gamble with her happiness. He heard her gasp, "Paul, thank you for being there for me ... I am ... so ... sorry!"

Her voice trailed off and he knew this was just as painful for her, albeit a very different pain and today must be a day to remember. Inhaling deeply, he steadied his voice, "Debbie, tell me, are you happy, love?"

"Yes, Paul, very," she mumbled as guilt filled her.

"Good, now take are my love, both of you be happy!"

Turning into Hank's arms she felt sad and happy all in one go. His hand brushed her hair, "C'mon now, honey, Paul is very happy for you. If I don't order some food, I will ..," her mouth cut off the rest of the sentence.

If she lived to be a hundred, she would never be able to explain the rest of that day and night. Their eager bodies drifted into and out of heaven, barely had they slept for more than the odd hour. They had certainly found that special something that only people 'in love' can share. She was indeed a lucky lady and as far as Hank was concerned, he sure as hell was a lucky chap.

**

The next morning, Debbie couldn't wait to go to the airport. Her heart pounded with excitement. Many times she had rehearsed how to tell her children, but knew, it would be spontaneous and definitely off the cuff.

Hank dressed with the same sense of urgency. The papers already carried the news, 'Debbie marries Hank, her Yank', followed by 'Debbie Hudson finds happiness after tragedy' and many more headlines had hit the news stands.

Many members of the press had gathered outside of the hotel, Hank brushed them away, "Debbie and I will hold a full press interview at the ranch tomorrow. Right now, we just want to get home!"

Feeling the 'plane bank and land in New York, Debbie felt sick with excitement. Hank was just as bad as she was. They swiftly cleared the airport as the chauffeur collected them. The weather was freezing as they arrived outside of the ranch and the children had obviously been kept in the warm.

Gripping each others' hands they entered the living room. Jim and Ellen rushed to hug them and the children all but knocked them over, "Mummy, you look pretty, did Uncle Hank kiss you goodnight?"

Kelly and Verity had almost sung the question as Lucy ran to Hank, who swept her into his arms. Emma ran to Debbie, who led them all to the settee and sat down. Her voice shook, "Now, you want to know if Uncle Hank kissed me goodnight, is that right?"

"Yes, Mummy," they giggled.

Watching their wide eyed innocence nearly broke her. They were so very trusting and she almost spluttered, "Well, he did kiss me, in fact he married me yesterday!"

Having dropped the bomb, she held her breath as she waited for the reactions. Kelly and Verity jumped onto her, "Oh, Mummy, did you really get married?"

"Yes I did. We both love you very much and want us all to be together forever!"

Hank watched them, realising that he too had held his breath. Kelly turned to hug him and then went back into Debbie's arms. "Mummy, were you really a bride? Have you got some pictures?"

Exhaling the breath he had held, Hank took the photograph from his pocket. "Yes, Kelly, Mummy was a real bride, a very beautiful bride, just like in a fairytale. I love her very much indeed and I love you, Pumpkin!"

Having handed over the picture, tears threatened Debbie as she watched her children search the photograph, their eyes rounded with wonder. "Oh, Mummy, you were pretty," they chorused.

Lucy still clung to Hank as excitement seemed to spread through the room. Verity's face was pensive, suddenly her eyes lit up, "Mummy, if you married Uncle Hank, why can't he be our new Daddy?"

Scarcely able to breathe, so great was her delight, she gulped, "Perhaps he will be. I think you should ask him, don't you?"

They turned to Hank as if imploring him and her parents eyes filled. The moment was so poignant, it choked them all. Hank cleared his throat, "Kelly, Verity, Lucy and Emma, I would be proud to be your new Daddy. I love you all very much indeed!"

Hastily, Debbie wiped the tears that were about to fall. Her parents were in each other's arms. She felt Hank's arm slide around her, as between them, they cuddled the children. Her eyes met his, "Thank you, darling, thank you for making them as happy as you've made me!"

"Hey, Jim, grab a camera, take a shot of us. Tomorrow, I will arrange for a shoot of us all!"

Poor Hank, for the rest of the day, he could do nothing, not without the children hanging around him. Feeling guilty, she smiled, "Darling, you must tell them to leave you alone. Just because you've agreed to be their new father, doesn't mean they can dictate your life!"

"I know, honey, but let them get used to everything slowly. Right now, I'm thanking God that they don't resent me. We sure are lucky, Debbie, it'll be your turn tonight," he chuckled.

Somehow, he always made her laugh, turning to her parents, she hugged them, "Are you sure you both approve? After all, you both conspired with him," she smiled and continued, "When I think of all the beautiful women he has taken out, I can't believe he loves me. The fact that he loves the children, is almost a dream come true. I think our marriage will be so special, almost like Matthew and me. You both share that magic, and I know I'm lucky to have a second chance!"

Jim still had his arm around Ellen, "Debbie, we couldn't be happier for you and Hank. He may have been out with many beautiful women, but to him, you're beautiful. Look at the way he has taken the kiddies with him. Mum and I both knew how he felt, it seemed right for you to be alone and give you a chance to sort out your own feelings. We haven't seen you so happy, for a long time!"

Hank returned with the little ones, "Hell, Debbie, there is a stack of work to get through, I feel guilty that we didn't have a honeymoon, but we will make time later in the year. C'mon now, let's get our little tearaways to bed, have a meal and an early night!"

Although it took a little longer than usual, the kiddies had finally gone to sleep. Hank headed towards her room, "Honey, would you rather use another room? After all, this was the room you shared with Matthew!"

"I understand what you mean, Hank, but we must gently lay his ghost to rest. He was a very philosophical person, and I know he would advise this method. Also, once the weather gets warmer, we must make love under that old oak tree. We both felt so much happiness there!"

After another night of sheer bliss, the morning arrived as the eager children burst in and hugged them both. Looking around him, Hank had never felt so happy, holding the children tightly, he grinned, "I sure think I'm gong to enjoy my new role in life. Being a husband is wonderful, being a father is great!"

**

All too soon, the press arrived in droves. Hank was to conduct the television crew and under his direction, it went without a hitch. The children posed with him, Debbie and her parents posed with him and it was more than obvious that the family were filled with serenity and warmth.

Grace and staff had all offered sincere congratulations and Debbie thanked them all, apologising as the 'phones never stopped. "Grace, perhaps you could contact Irene for me, explain that I'll talk with her later and Hank will release further news!"

Debbie then faced the hostile press. The very reporters that had broken the story about Amanda and Paul, were now gnashing their teeth with a sick kind of relish. Quite prepared for them, she still ricocheted at the questions.

A determined, middle aged man thrust his microphone into her, "Don't you think you married rather hastily? After all, Matthew hasn't been dead for a year yet. Did you and Hank carry on *before* your husband's death?"

Anger and hurt filled her, "I don't think I'll dignify such a tasteless question with an answer!"

"You must feel some guilt, Miss Hudson. You can't 've been as much in love as you'd have us believe," he persisted.

Jim placed his arm around his shoulder. She felt, rather than saw Hank's fury. He could control his programme, but not one could control the tabloids. Turning to him, she saw his face was ashen, apart from the day he had dashed out to the ranch, when the other story had broken, she had never seen such anger in him.

His knuckles had turned white as he clenched his fist with venom. With a calm that surprised her, she added, "Matthew and I were exceedingly happy and you all know that. It broke my heart when he died, however, he would be the first to approve of my actions. Our children are happy, my parents are happy and Hank's parents are happy!"

"You're bound to say that, after all you want to keep your so called good reputation in tact," came the caustic reply.

Suppressing her own anger, she took a sip of water, "If you knew Hank Marcovitze, you wouldn't be so crude. He may have had deep feelings for me, but he's not the sort of person to make passes at married women. As far as I'm concerned, we have our priorities in the right order. Perhaps you feel professional jealousy. He's a brilliant journalist, his work is revered worldwide, while you have to gather rubbish for the tabloids to print. That will be all for now!"

Applause from the dignified press startled her, "You tell 'em, Debbie. We all wish you happiness and as you say, Hank is a real swell guy!"

Hank sat there dumbfounded, never had he felt so much anger, but marvelled at the way she had conducted herself. His eyes met hers, "Come

286

now, honey, we've answered enough questions. We'll be interviewed together on the Joanne Day Show in a couple of months or so!"

His voice had been aimed as much at the gutter press as it was for her. He had naturally swung Emma into his arms as they walked into the ranch. They had all turned prior to entry, all of them giving a happy, if not defiant wave.

Once inside, she felt he was about to explode, "Hank, darling, its no good feeling anger. We have to expect criticism as well as praise. To be truthful, I can scarcely believe the story myself. As long as our own consciences are clear, let them get on with it. I love you, Hank and no one can take that from me!"

**

Debbie found herself surrounded with sacks full of letters. Her book on trauma had touched the hearts of many. People had found it helped them to cope, some found it difficult to come to terms with, but they all poured their hearts out and Debbie tried to answer them personally.

She had the same reaction from her story of coping with still birth, yet it never ceased to amaze her how much strength people could gain from her. Her popularity seemed to soar rather than plummet from the tabloid reports. She had now been asked to consider writing about marriage the second time around.

Life was hectic, but seemed to go on in a blur of bliss. She knew she would look forward to writing about Hank and felt certain, there would be a huge input from him. Watching him work, his face a study of concentration, she found it hard to believe the deep passion that rested just below the surface, yet with a shudder, realised that she knew how to bring it to the fore.

Hank had juggled his time well, he was determined to accompany her to unveil the plaque and open the Matthew Ross Wing. Doctor Jarvis had welcomed them warmly. Many young parents had stopped her to ask how she felt about the loss of her babe. Her eyes filled, but her voice was crystal clear, "Its horrific to lose a child, but somehow, seeing this Wing open eases the pain. Many babies can now be saved and many parents can hope again!"

**

Mid April arrived and Hank was still pestering her to do a further programme on pregnancy. The opening of the new wing had sparked off a further need for knowledge. His mail was almost as heavy as hers and his gold flecked eyes melted her into submission. Kissing her with untold gratitude, he asked, "Honey, what title should we use this time?"

"Wait till its scheduled, Hank, you never know, I might well have an inspired urge by then," she chuckled.

Debbie knew she would find inspiration, she knew she was pregnant again. She had made an appointment with Doctor Jarvis, without Hank noticing, she need to know all was well, before she broke the news.

Stifled with joy, she had undergone a pretty thorough check up. It was now confirmed, her baby would be due in November.

Arriving home in somewhat of a trance, she went upstairs to their bedroom. Closing the door behind her, she leaned heavily against it. Tears of joy overwhelmed her. Kelly would be five, Verity four, Lucy three and Emma two. They would be delighted and again, she felt sure it would be a boy.

Seeing her beloved Hank, she knew exactly how she would tell him. That night, having reached a perfect plateau, he gasped breathlessly, "Honey, that was absolutely wonderful, but whatever brought it on, hell, it felt as though you never wanted me to stop!"

"Was if really different, Hank? Did you feel an added need?"

"Gee, Debbie, that is the understatement of the year. I didn't think our love could gain in perfection, but tonight you sure showed me I was wrong!"

Debbie felt the divine lethargy spread through her. Her heart thumped mercilessly as her hand lifted to caress his cheek. "Hank, you know that series you want to run?"

"Yeh, honey, what about it?"

His head raised and his eyes met hers. Running her tongue along her lips, her arms went around him, "How would you like to run it with a really pregnant woman?"

"That would be ideal, babe, but I don't want to discuss work. I want you to seduce me again!"

Mischief filled her, he was still lost in desire. Normally he would have realised what she had said. The man that was once married to his work, didn't wish to discuss it, but then, neither did she. Taking his head into her hands, she added, "I do have an extra need for you, Hank, maybe its for both of us!"

Even his breathing seemed to have stopped as though he had become frozen. His mind pounded, pregnant woman, love us both. Rolling his eyes heavenwards, it hit him, "Gee, honey, what are you saying, are you telling me …?"

Her mouth swallowed the sentence, "Yes, darling, the first week in November, I hope you'll want to attend the birth of your own flesh and blood!"

His eyes glistened as he gathered her to him. "Honey, I just can't believe this. I sure never expected this, you are happy, aren't you?"

Debbie could feel his elation and her eyes filled, "Yes, I'm truly happy and we did nothing to prevent it, did we?"

He was now holding her with the same tenderness as he had used on their first night. His lips brushed hers, "Honey, good job I've arranged for some time off. I'm still shocked out of my brain, I never dreamed of this, not yet anyway!"

"You mean, you didn't have to try, but I think I would like to be in England when it is born. Can you fix that, darling?"

"Anything you want, my dearest, Debbie, anything you want," he mumbled and crushed her to him.

CHAPTER FORTY FIVE

Hank and Debbie both decided to allow Joanne to break their precious news. She had been totally delighted herself and obviously couldn't wait to be the first with the update.

Apprehension gripped Debbie as the moment for the show arrived, together with strains of 'She's a Lassie from Lancashire'. Memories of Matthew drifted through her, till she reasoned, he had come along to add his blessing.

After the applause died down, the questions began, "Debbie, we know it was a tragic loss when Matthew died, how do you think of him now? How do you respond to the accusations that you married too quickly after his death?"

Inhaling deeply, she replied, "We all think of Matthew with very much love indeed. He may be gone from us, but he will never be forgotten. I don't think it would have made any difference as to how long we waited, it would not have brought him back!"

She paused to sip her water, "I think perhaps the secret lays with confronting the ghosts, not hiding from them. Hank and I realised that the children may have been difficult, but they were happy. We are delighted to know they are filled with security. Matthew would have approved fully!"

Her eyes met Hank, it was his turn, "Hank, you sure seem to be happy after all this time. How did you feel about taking on four children?"

Clearing his throat, "I am happy. I love the children, they are as easy to love as Debbie is. I think she has a wise attitude, she didn't ask the children to call me Daddy, they asked her after our marriage. They are delightful and I adore them!"

Debbie smiled wryly, all of a sudden he seemed to be an expert. She luxuriated in the sensual curve of his body, only she knew every single intimate inch of him. Only she knew of his intense passion, his long legs stretched in front of him, his ankles crossed with seductive ease. He was gorgeous, he was hers and there was no doubting the sincerity in the audience.

Joanne's eyes filled when the last part of the programme arrived, "Debbie has been through so much pain since she was over here. I'm not alone in wishing her and Hank everlasting happiness, but they would like their friends to know, they look forward to a further birth in November!"

Poignancy hung around the studio. The applause was almost thunderous, but Debbie doubted there was a real dry eye amongst them. Hank was asked the obvious question, "Hank, aren't you worried about wanting to spoil your own child? After all it could be forgiven!"

"Not in my book it couldn't I'm absolutely delighted to know that my wife carries my child, but I'm father to them all. Those little ones trust me and I would never betray that trust. They had a choice about me being their father and it was *them* that welcomed *me*!"

**

Although they were tired upon arriving home, it had been a wonderful afternoon. The trees had turned green again, the flowers had begun to blossom and life was vibrant again. As she went into her husband's arms that night, she gasped, "Hank, walk me over to the oak tree and make love with me!"

The moon shone from a midnight blue, star spangled sky. The breeze blew gently, lifting her hair as they walked. The air was heady with scented aromas, heralding the onset of summer.

His hands slipped her shift from her, allowing it to form a pond around her feet. Moving as one, they sank to lay on the grass. Moulded as one by the heat of their passion, moonbeams slanted through the fringed fronds of dark mystique, dancing on their bare bodies.

Sobbing with relief, tears scalded her cheeks as she lay curled against him. Slowly a sweet aftermath flowed through her body, a release from a tension she hadn't been conscious of before tonight. His hands stroked her face softly, "Honey, have I hurt you? Did I make you cry, Debbie?"

His voice was soothing as she lifted her mouth to his and gulped, "Hank, dearest, with your love and help, I have passed another milestone. Darling, Hank, never let me go!"

"Honey, there sure is no fear of that. Tonight hurt you and I wonder if it is wise?"

"It is wise, Hank, I never realised how much I needed to share these moments. A less understanding man would feel jealous, maybe even anger, but you allow me to rid my grief in my own way. Let's go back!"

Locked together they walked slowly. Hank knew she had been deeply cut up. She was right though, if he didn't allow her to share her grief with him, she would bottle in inside of her. Suddenly, he felt proud that it was he she had turned to.

Stopping with a jolt, his hands cupped her face, "You sure were great today, honey. I felt so wonderful with my wife, our news, hell, Debbie, are you sure you want to do the series? I'm still playing around with the idea for a title!"

"It will come to us, darling. I can and will do the series, you've no idea how I feel about this baby. And I long for England again!"

**

June arrived with a blaze of heat. Debbie had never felt so well and happy. Her series on crochet had been a resounding success and the mail had come in heavier than before. She had persuaded Hank to co author the book on 'Marriage for the second time around'.

There were so many things he could add. How he felt about it himself, his reactions to the children. Although Debbie knew only too well of his feelings, there was so much detail he alone could find words for. She knew, it is the small things in life that can make or break.

As she prepared herself for the hospital check up, she noticed that her waist had thickened more than usual and her bump was quite pronounced. She would just have to slim down after the birth, she consoled herself.

Hank had tried desperately hard to be free to accompany her, but work was hectic. "Honey, I know I've learned all of the drill, but I still feel a need to be with you, especially during the examination!"

"I'll be fine, Hank. Darling, just as long as you're free for the birth, I'm entirely happy," she practically purred with contentment.

She knew he was worried in spite of his happiness. Ironically though, she felt no fear, never a woman to believe that lightning would strike twice, she believed her baby would be safe. Yet lightning had struck her twice, in the love department.

Holding her tenderly before she left, he whispered, "You're having a scan today, aren't you? I believe they give you a photograph, bring it home, honey. Are you going to ask what we're having?"

"They'll probably tell me, but between you and me, I'm sure it's a boy," she chuckled.

Debbie had heard much about the scan technique and found herself full of interest. She was asked to slip into a cotton gown and then hop onto a bed, beside a small, television type of machine. After being smothered with a sticky kind of jelly substance, the doctor began his examination. Turning to the screen, tremors of excitement shot through her. Amidst the blur, she could just about detect the baby's head.

With the help of the doctor using the tip of his pencil, he explained, "There's baby's spine and limbs," and then moving the pencil further down, he added, "And there's the other baby. As we suspected, Miss Hudson, you are carrying twins!"

Stunned, she tried to sit up. Doctor Jarvis came in, his reassuring hand keeping her still, He smiled, "Debbie, they are both fine healthy babies, but they could arrive up to a month or so early!"

"Will I have a son?"

Stupidly that was the first thing that came into her head as Doctor Jarvis re-examined the screen. "I think we can be sure, they are both boys, but you must look after yourself!"

"I will, but I do think I want to go back to England!"

Arriving home, she floated upstairs in a trance. Sitting on the bed, she gripped the tiny Polaroid and gazed at the two tiny shapes. Whatever would Hank think? Would he be as happy as she? When would she tell him and how?

Suddenly, her body began to burn with desire. Popping the Polaroid into the bedside table drawer, she got up and walked to the window. Stepping onto the small balcony, she watched the children playing happily by the pool. Her parents were watching them as Hank walked out to see if she was back.

His eyes were drawn to her, she looked tantalising, her hair fell about her shoulders. The pretty blue sundress fastened over her slender shoulders, and he knew, her only other garment was her panties. She was one very seductive lady, yet she looked no more than a teenager.

How dare she look so darned provocative? His tight jeans held his arousal in check and catching her eye, he gasped, "How long have you been back? Hang on, I'm coming up, is everything alright?"

Arriving breathlessly by her side, his eyes searched her face, "You look pregnant, you feel deliciously pregnant and you'll never know how happy you've made me feel!"

They were in each others' arms and oh, so swiftly they entered their own little paradise. Gasping and panting, he asked, "What are we having?"

Shudders of delight ran through her, "Hank, you know your Mom said you never do anything by halves? She's right, you've doubled up on this venture as well!"

Lifting her gently, he laid her beside him, his body almost covering hers. Tracing her contours, his hand came to rest on the movements inside of her. "Debbie, are you telling me?"

"Yes, Hank, I'm telling you, my darling!"

Seeing the thunder struck look on his face, she leaned over to open the drawer, taking the photograph into her hand. "Mr Marcowvitze, there are your children. I don't know how you did it, but we have to prepare for two!"

Suddenly it hit her, "Hank, darling, I think that would be a wonderful heading for the series!"

"What would, honey?"

"Preparing for two!"

His arms gathered her, "Honey, right at this moment, the series is the last thing on my mind. Let's go and tell the children and most importantly your parents!"

Hand in hand, she watched as Hank proudly announced their news. "I brought the photograph down for you to look at. Debbie assures me all is well. I must ring my Mom and Pop!"

The lump in Debbie's throat seemed to grow as she watched her parents and Hank pouring over the negative type film. Ellen had her usual little cry and Jim shook hands with Hank as he congratulated him.

Hank's eyes rested on his wife, how he loved her. Right now he longed for her to break the news all over again. The simplistic, yet highly charge manner in which she turned to him, never ceased to amaze and delight him, but he knew, arrangements must be made to get her home and the sooner the better.

**

Instinctively, Debbie began to design for two. Somehow she knew that the moment her news was released, Alma would want to be the first with the designs and as far as Debbie was concerned, Alma had earned that right. After all, it had been Alma who had first introduced her to Hank and her mind raced with sheer gratitude.

Irene was so happy as the two of them chatted one evening and Debbie instinctively knew, that Paul and Irene had managed to pair up, albeit as dear friends and bed mates, neither interested in marriage, but both needing sex.

She walked down to the gate to join Hank. They both leaned on it as they had the night of true confessions. Hank turned to her, "Honey, is there anything to compare to childbirth?"

"Hank, the questions you come up with, I don't know where they spring from," she chuckled.

"A desperate desire to know, I s'pose," he replied.

She thought for a few moments and added, "Ironically, its somewhat akin to making love. The pain is probably the pain of need to possess. The perspiration must be the passion. The heavy breathing, well that suggests the expectancy of what's to come. The climax is the birth and the panting, the sweet aftermath as the kisses rain on each other and the little life that suckles with contentment!"

Somehow the words had fallen from her lips. She realised it was almost as simple as that. His body tensed, his hand lifted her face, his eyes smouldered as the flecks of gold became molten, "Honey, that sounds so beautiful. The way you describe it makes it sound exciting as well as emotional," he gulped.

"Hank, it does feel like that. When you think of the effort we put into our love making, the joy we feel during and after the climax, it's a very similar experience," she sighed happily.

Hank felt fire coursing through him, hell how he loved her. Again he marvelled at her simplicity, no wonder her programmes gave so much reassurance to others. Even via the small screen, her sincerity radiated, she did make everything sound happy, exciting, something to look forward to.

Every little detail she imparted had been tried and tested by her. To her, there was no excuse for not researching her words thoroughly. She was a real personality and he was perhaps her biggest fan.

CHAPTER FORTY SIX

After so much rushing, they finally arrived back in England. The press were out in force and Debbie felt at complete ease with them. And, at long last, they were entering Morecambe. The children were excited as they drove along the busy promenade and Debbie wound her window down, to allow the beautiful sea air to embrace her. She had longed for this moment and loved Hank all the more for making sure it happened.

Irene and Paul were standing outside of the castle door when the cars pulled up. Debbie felt the warmth of their greeting as they both pulled the children to them, "Haven't they grown? They're gorgeous and look at the size of Debbie," came Irene's happy squeal.

There was no denying Irene's sincerity, her eyes conveying her secrets to Debbie. Paul hugged her and Hank, "You both look lost with happiness," he smiled fondly.

"We have you to thank for most of it," came Hank's booming gratitude.

Paul stood back and watched them. It had hurt so much to let her go again, but he knew he had been right. She was totally happy with Hank and she knew, he would always be here for her. He had found deep joy in sharing his bed with Irene, both of them loved Debbie, both of them were able to express their feelings in a satisfying passion.

He was only too happy to see that they could all work together again. Yes, the board meetings would hold the fun they always had. Irene had become a vital ingredient to the company's continued success. All in all, life was great.

Turning to them, he announced, "Mark and Sally had a little girl last week. They are longing to see you all again, so are Richard and Jenny, in fact, I don't think there is anyone not eager to meet Hank. We have a full meeting tomorrow, to discuss the opening of 'Miss Kelly' in New York. Apparently, Eric is doing a sterling job on his magazine in London, so everyone is happy!"

Jim placed his arm around his wife, "I think we'll all look forward to that, Paul. Hell, its great to be home and I can't wait to have an early night.
**

Ellen wanted nothing more than to return to her flat with her husband. To feel his tender arms envelop her, to embrace his caresses, to sleep with sheer contentment. Her daughter had found happiness, Hank loved her and her children dearly. His family were coming over for Christmas and gratitude sprung eternally. Never had she expected to see Debbie come out of so much torment and arrive home a new woman.

Turning into her husband's arms, her eyes lifted, "Jim, darling, when we left here, we hadn't a clue of what lay ahead. If someone had told me then, that our daughter would find so much happiness, I wouldn't have believed them. I long for the babes to be born, yet somehow think it won't won't end there!"

Stroking her beloved auburn head, he smiled, "I think you could be right, darling. Its so comforting to see the love shine from her eyes again. She's a lovely woman, remember how she helped us with Tony? Paul must have been the only one to guess her future. He's a dear person. Yes, my darling, Ellie, we have so much to be thankful for, not to mention our own completely love filled life!"

**

Debbie leaned over the brand new cots, her heart filled with love as she thought of her sons soon to be born. Hank came over to her and placed his arm around her shoulder, "Happy, honey? You must be worn out, I know I am!"

Her whole body began to shake uncontrollably, "Hank, I have one more ghost to face. Somehow I think I'm ready to face it, but I need you to understand!"

"Sure, honey, we've faced everything else together, now what is it?"

Looping her arms around his neck, her eyes met the tender gold flecks. "Darling … Matthew and I had a very special place. We went there every evening, I don't think anyone knows its there. Since he went .. I've never been able to take myself there!"

Wordlessly, she gripped Hank's hand. She opened the door and without a qualm, her feet walked unfalteringly, this was definitely right. Arriving at the top of the steps, Hank gasped, "You can see all around your little empire up here. And you've never been able to face it, I mean, before now, honey?"

"Never, but I know this is right. We would come up here, watch the lights flashing 'Miss Kelly', watch the friendly lighthouse flashing its own welcome, watch the sea. Matthew always called me Duchess up here!"

Her voice shook slightly as she had managed to tell Hank everything. He hugged her to him, "What a wise man Matthew was. I can understand his reasoning only too well, do you think he would mind me using his endearment?"

Sinking into his closeness, she felt her inner soul being given to the beauty of Morecambe. She could almost feel Matthew's presence, almost hear him telling her that he was proud of her and the way she had coped. He would also be proud of her choice in husband and divinely happy that her children had found someone to love and cherish them. A living father that they found contentment with.

Feeling a deep peace enter her, she turned to Hank, "Darling, I think he would love you to use his endearment. Just before he died, he told me that I had given him the happiest four years in his life. He also advised me to marry again, I suppose because we were so desperately in love!"

Hank could feel the emotion seep from her as she gradually began to relax. Her voice was a little hoarse, "Hank, when we first left the proverbial poverty trap, I vowed that I would never change. Money would never obsess me, it can't buy love, health or happiness. I think I can truthfully say that I haven't altered my outlook. Yet, in spite of the money, I still suffered loss, in fact, I've just about covered every emotion known to man!"

A heavy sigh escaped her as she found so much ease in unburdening the nightmares. "First, I loved Tony and he died. Then I loved Paul and lost him, then I found Matthew and loved him. We brought life into the world and again I lost him and our baby. Then, Hank, I found your love and we are going to give life. Hell, darling, I never expected to find a love like yours. I love you so much it frightens me!"

Tears stung Hank's eyes as he listened to her and thanked God she was able to get this out of her system. She was right, she had been through all of those emotions. Many people were never called upon to love so much, yet she was wise way beyond her twenty five years.

Gazing out at the huge empire, he could understand why Matthew had felt so proud of her up here. She handled herself and everything she touched, with a simplistic dignity and he too, could feel this lovely old seaside town reaching out to him.

Kissing her lips, he whispered, "I sure owe Paul a lot, he knew I was in love with you and allowed you to go a second time. Your men sure have been great!"

"I know, Hank, present company accepted," she smiled, "I can't wait to take you down to the shop, Richard and Jenny will fall into instant love with you. Suddenly, the world has come to life again, I feel happier than I deserve. Hank, take me down now and make love with me!"

"That's for sure, babe!"

His lips found hers as he crushed her to him, her head was spinning with love. At long, long last, she had fully come to terms with herself. The dreadful guilt had left her, a deep abiding loved filled her.

Glancing around the bay for the last time tonight, she knew she could come here again and again. Matthew had been so right, she did feel just like a Duchess.

THE END

Printed in the United Kingdom
by Lightning Source UK Ltd.
104249UKS00001B/43